"A clever and entertaining novel about the nagging ambivalence of love, missed connections, and the transcendent power of a great two-minute pop song...Hoffs spins the gears of her antic narrative with sharp, sardonic wit and an insider's feel for the mixed blessings of pop fame and a fickle public. But just as the wheels start to fall off, grace arrives...Such is the power of music; it can give us the key to ourselves at those times when we need it the most. Hoffs understands this acutely, which is why *This Bird Has Flown* rings so true. Read it with the radio on."

—Marc Weingarten, *Los Angeles Times*

"*This Bird Has Flown* is a blast of pure pleasure, an addictive medley of music, romance, secrets, and sex. Susanna Hoffs's captivating first novel is part British rom-com, part *Jane Eyre,* and one hundred percent enjoyable." —Tom Perrotta, author of *Mrs. Fletcher* and *Tracy Flick Can't Win*

"A total knockout...Bangles frontwoman Susanna Hoffs demonstrates her range...She hits the familiar beats of romantic comedy with such panache and gusto, every note feels fresh. Clutch your pearls as Jane swears, boozes, masturbates, and indulges, but just try to measure the size of her heart with any ordinary ruler...Ditto the writing. There is not a spare, bare sentence to be found. Instead, the pages are packed with wit and sly allusion and dialogue that strikes the ear just so...*This Bird Has Flown* is the smart, ferocious rock-star redemption romance you didn't know you needed."

—Beatriz Williams, *New York Times Book Review*

"Hoffs's immense writing talent isn't just confined to songs...*This Bird Has Flown* is a love story, a sweet and tender romance, but not just one between Jane and Tom—it's Hoffs's valentine to music."   —Michael Schaub, National Public Radio

"This bird has flown! High! #bestbooksofthesummer."
                                        —Jamie Lee Curtis

"A charming rom-com."   — Barbara VanDenburgh, *USA Today*

"Charming, beautiful, and deeply authentic...What an incredible gift for us all!"   —Laura Dern

"Irresistible."   —*E! News*

"*This Bird Has Flown* is SO GOOD. I cannot wait for people to dig in and read what a fun story Susanna's told here, with rock singer Jane Start. If you liked *Daisy Jones & The Six* or *Juliet, Naked,* I feel like you will love this one."   —Taylor Jenkins Reid

"This book is a blast. It satisfied the part of me that loves a hot rock-and-roll romance, with Vegas adventures and sold-out concerts and lots of champagne, as well as the part of me that loves a tender love story with an Oxford professor, with slow airplane kisses, drives in the British countryside, and long talks over tea. It's about art and new beginnings and love and friendship and regrets and fear and taking risks, and it's such a fun read."
                      —Jasmine Guillory, author of *Drunk on Love*

"Centered on a heartbroken one-hit wonder hoping for a comeback, this romantic comedy from Bangles frontwoman Susanna Hoffs is the literary equivalent of power pop with soul."
                                    —Nell Beram, *Shelf Awareness*

"Hoffs nails the life and heartbreak of rock and roll, academia, and our soul-nourishing connection to our very own soulmate so expertly she must have carved it in Norwegian wood! And isn't it good!"
                                                                —Tom Hanks

"A little bit romance, a little bit rock-and-roll—this isn't just a book, it's a love song, and it should come as no surprise that Susanna Hoffs has crafted the perfect one to put on your playlist."
                    —Christina Lauren, author of *The Unhoneymooners*

"Elegant, thoughtful, and ever so sexy, *This Bird Has Flown* will stay in your mind—in your heart—like a favorite song."
                      —Rachel Hawkins, author of *The Wife Upstairs*

"Hoffs write with a snappy wit that recalls rom-com favorites like *Bridget Jones's Diary*...A fun read that's perfect for lovers of pop music, classic books, and romantic comedies."   —*Kirkus Reviews*

"What a treat, and a pleasure, to find out that Susanna Hoffs can tell a story filled with characters as engaging as her song lyrics, who come alive to crack you up and break your heart, and tell it with all the confidence you would expect from a seasoned explorer of the depths of love, music, and life."
                    —Ayelet Waldman, author of *A Really Good Day*

"Hoffs crafts a convincing portrayal of a musician, whether on the big stage in a climactic scene or spontaneously harmonizing with a pub singer...and she enlivens the proceedings with playful irreverence."   —*Publishers Weekly*

"With *This Bird Has Flown,* Hoffs explodes onto a brand-new stage with a romantic roller-coaster ride through the rock-and-roll world she knows so well. In this sexy, page-turning treat of a debut novel, Hoffs writes as engagingly as she sings." —Helen Fielding, author of *Bridget Jones's Diary*

"Hoffs brings her knowledge of the music scene to this lively, spicy love story. Jane is an appealing character whose creative and emotional journeys are relatable and entertaining, and readers will enjoy watching her come into her own after years of struggle and self-doubt. Fans of Emma Brodie's *Songs in Ursa Major* will want to take a look." —*Booklist*

"This book will hook you like the best pop song that you can't stop playing—something that Susanna knows a little bit about!" —Molly Ringwald

"A tender, funny love story wrapped in a guitar-jamming rock-and-roll cloak. I haven't had this much fun reading a book in a long, long time." —Jessica Anya Blau, author of *Mary Jane*

THIS BIRD HAS FLOWN

A NOVEL

SUSANNA HOFFS

BACK BAY BOOKS
Little, Brown and Company
New York Boston London

For music lovers, and lovers, everywhere

———————

Back Bay Books / Little, Brown and Company
Hachette Book Group
1290 Avenue of the Americas, New York, NY 10104
littlebrown.com

Originally published in hardcover by Little, Brown and Company, April 2023
First Back Bay paperback edition, March 2024

Back Bay Books is an imprint of Little, Brown and Company, a division of Hachette Book Group, Inc. The Back Bay Books name and logo are trademarks of Hachette Book Group, Inc.

ISBN 9780316409315 (hardcover) / 9780316561129 (Canadian) / 9780316409414 (paperback)
LCCN 2022938859

10 9 8 7 6 5 4 3 2 1

CW

Book interior design by Marie Mundaca

Printed in the United States of America

PART ONE

Friday I'm in Love

There you stood on the edge of your feather,
expecting to fly.

—*Neil Young*

Chapter 1.

TEARS OF A CLOWN

Elevators are like life, when you think about it: You're either going up or going down. I was dressed like a whore and descending fast, alone, for a "private" in Las Vegas I should never have agreed to. There's always something a bit creepy about privates. But I was desperate. For so many reasons. If only my luck would change, and this would be the last dodgy gig I'd have to face for a while.

I was wearing a tiny scrap of fabric posing as a dress, half-hidden beneath my ex-boyfriend's vintage cardigan, the one possession I'd pinched, for sentimental reasons, when he'd left me for a twenty-three-year-old lingerie model. Two months ago.

Don't you dare cry. Not about him, not about this, not *now*.

I caught sight of myself reflected in the mirrored doors and flinched. Who the hell is that? Oh right. It's *her*. She dances, she sings, she *entertains*.

"Hang in there," I murmured, rallying. "You can do this. A gig is a gig is a gig. The show must go on!"

The doors slid open on Mezzanine, and Pippa appeared in silhouette, late-afternoon sun flooding in from an outlandish wall of glass, creating the impression of a shimmering halo above her tousled blond hair. Pippa, my angel, best friend, and manager, who'd winged all the way from London to rescue me from despair.

Our reunion was cut short by a commotion in the corridor. Pippa seemed to vaporize in a blast of white light, and I was knocked back by a warm body barreling blindly, and rather rudely, into the elevator, and *me.*

"Sorry! God, so sorry," said a richly resonant, Australian-accented voice. Two clumsy hands on my shoulders steadied me, and the warmth of them, the weight, sent an unexpected ripple through me. I peered up, caught the flash of a smile (apologetic) and the sweep of long hair (dark and glossy), and was locking eyes with a pair of big blue sparkly ones when Pippa reached in and plucked me from the elevator.

Hello, goodbye, I thought, as the elevator doors slid shut and he vanished in some terrible sleight-of-hand trick. His eyes had been so encouraging, his smile so profoundly sunny, that I experienced something I hadn't since Alex, my partner of four years, had confessed to cheating with Jessica: a faint stirring, something resembling optimism.

Pippa came back into focus. "*That* was All Love." She grinned, grabbing the handle of my roller bag, click-clacking ahead down the long corridor in her strappy heels.

I raced to catch up, glimpsing a preposterous imitation Eiffel Tower rippling in the heat mirage beyond the windows.

"What do you mean, that was all love?"

"Pop duo, from Australia, in the elevator," she said.

"Duo?" I'd only noticed the one.

"Brothers. Aren't they gorgeous? Playing tomorrow night at the arena next door. You *have* been living under a rock." Pippa shot me a look, brushing back perfect bangs. Her doll-like features lent her a striking resemblance to a young Marianne Faithfull.

Honestly, Pippa had pulled off a miracle getting me this gig. It'd been years since I'd done a show. She knew I needed the money.

I was living with my parents again, which at thirty-three was a demoralizing last resort.

And I was there… the sagging twin bed… dust motes dancing over four garbage bags I hadn't the will to sift through… all that remained of my life with…

"How have you not heard of All Love?" Pippa quipped, amused, incredulous. "They're *massive.*"

I had been living under a rock. She was right. That's how I'd missed Alex philandering, for *months.* My stomach plunged. How could I have been so clueless? And *he,* so heartless.

"This is us, darling, just in time for a quick sound check." We screeched to a halt before a pair of mysterious red leather doors. "God, I've missed you," she said. "This will take your mind off Alex, *surely.* Doing what you do best, in front of an adoring audience."

"Exactly." I forced a smile. *Lie.* I had zero confidence that I'd be good, that the audience would even remember who I was, or that it could possibly take my mind off *him.*

Pippa beamed and hugged me again. *Fake it till you make it.* Over her shoulder, off in the sunlit distance, I glimpsed hotel security rounding up a gaggle of fluttery All Love fangirls still loitering by the elevator.

The deserted events room where I was to perform for the bachelor party was a womb of crushed red velvet throbbing in faux candlelight. The decor reached for old-fashioned speakeasy: tufted banquettes, laminate dance floor, quaint cabaret stage—strangely bereft of instruments or musicians.

"Bloody hell," Pippa exhaled, joining me at the bar, back from a quick managerial tête-à-tête with one of the party planners. She pushed a Red Bull into my hand. "Turns out they didn't secure the pickup band. I'm *livid,* had it out with them."

I had to admit, this was a relief; no slight on pickup bands, it's just that I'd never played with one. When I was riding the momentum of my hit ten years ago, I'd toured properly. Back then, I could afford to pay musicians, and they were the *best*, my dear friends Alastair and James, who played bass and drums, respectively. If only I could beam them here from London. The thought of playing with complete strangers was unsettling. The equivalent of being set up on a blind date. And how often do those go well?

I glanced back at the empty stage. "Honestly, I'd prefer to play the set acoustic. But wait, there's not even a guitar—"

"No," she burst out, then plastered on a tense, conciliatory smile. "How do I put this? They suddenly prefer you 'sing to track.'" She released the air quotes and let her arms fall slack to her sides.

"Wait—*what?* But I've never ever done that."

"Because it's rubbish and pathetic, yes I know," she groaned.

I took a moment to process, tasting bile. Was it left over from the white-knuckle flight here, or some chemical response to relationship apocalypse? Or was it merely the thought of singing to track? I probably shouldn't risk the Red Bull, given my nerves. Unless I could get some vodka to go with it, which I probably shouldn't risk either. Fuck. How long *had* it been since I'd played a show? The fact that I couldn't *quite* remember—my stomach lurched again. Two years? The (sparsely attended) little club run. Could it have been that long? Had I disappeared so entirely into Alex's world since then?

"And there's more," Pippa said bleakly. "Per the party planner they really only *need* the one song, which of course translates to, they only *want* the one song…and after you prepared a proper set." She grimaced.

"Okay," I said, slowly, processing. "Sooo I rehearsed, slapped on a perverse amount of the old greasepaint, squeezed myself into this slutty dress, and nearly died on what I suspect was a decommissioned Aeroflot jet, to sing 'the one song.' To *track*. In Vegas."

Pippa was well aware of my fear of flying. "In a word, yes. *Sorry*. Fuck." She slumped, arms crossed, into a chair.

"Okay, yeah, right. No, it's all *good*," I assured her, surfing a fresh wave of nausea. "*Really*. I was just—*confirming*. A gig! Finally, at long last! I'm super grateful. And also, I love you."

Pippa sighed. "I love you too. This is not how I wanted this to go. But I thought, it's a job! The pay's good, and honestly it was a chance to see you after so long. And after everything, with...that fuckwit whose name I refuse to utter going forward," she added gently. "But on the bright side, this way, you're in, you're out! And rest assured, *you* are the only musical act!"

The red leather doors burst open, and a gorgeous statuesque woman in platform heels, wearing only a skimpy silk robe and glowing in backlight, surveyed the room.

"Well, that's a consolation," I said, taking her in. Pippa grimaced, mortified. Managers have the worst job. Whatever can go wrong will. But Pippa had had her share of triumphs, too—take Ol' Leopard Pants. Over the past decade Pippa had rebuilt his career as a legendary guitarist and solo artist despite his 1970s band the Rebel Knaves calling it quits. I knew she'd gotten him back on his feet in more ways than one. This wasn't merely a paycheck for her, she was all in. A true lover of music, and those of us who made it.

A woman after my own heart. I was lucky she was still with me.

"I'm *joking*," I reassured her as the woman swept past us, her miles of bare leg oiled with bronzer. I pictured her hours from now, scrubbing it off—another white washcloth bites the dust. The lengths we go to look "alluring." I gave the hem of my skimpy dress a reflexive down-tug and darted the woman a clenched smile of solidarity; she winked gaily back and parked her roller bag beside mine as one of the party planners set gift bags labeled *What Happens in Vegas Stays in Vegas* across the gleaming bartop. My sentiments exactly. But I was beginning to have a *very* bad feeling about this gig.

"You do look a bit green about the gills," Pippa murmured, leaning close, her features distorted, like I was seeing her through a wide-angle lens. "Oh dear. Let me see if I can't rustle up a sandwich or some crisps for you." She snatched a menu off the bar, and the color drained from her face.

I plucked it from her. A "menu" for the evening's "Entertainments." Beneath "Appetizer" was my name, alongside a screen capture from my old video for *the hit song,* in which I'm wearing a burlesque outfit and pink wig, perched at the edge of a chair with my legs, regrettably, spread. *Not again. The embarrassing default photo.* But it was meant to be an homage to Bob Fosse's choreography in *Cabaret,* mashed up with Sharon Stone's controversial "moment" in *Basic Instinct*! And the wig had seemed the appropriate iconography for the video's quasi-feminist statement about sexuality in post-1960s American cinema. I'd written a paper about it at Columbia! It was intended to be empowering.

In retrospect, it was delusional of me to think the video would ever come off as anything other than a chance for another scantily clad musician to shake her ass. Not that there was anything wrong with that. I was body positive! I was for shaking one's ass where and when one chose to shake it! And, I supposed it was better to have been reduced to the .gif of that moment than to have had no moment at all.

"This has been an utter cock-up. My fault entirely. You ought to fire me," Pippa said, miserably, as we hovered in the wings backstage.

She was being facetious. The truth was, I was *her* charity case. The only reason I could fathom that Pippa had kept me on as a management client was that she actually believed in me as an artist. This thought made my throat tighten.

"But if you *do* fire me?" she said, her brow sweetly furrowed. "Promise me we'll go on as friends?"

My darling Pippa. Her face killed me. It did. I was somewhere between nervously laughing and crying. Closer to crying.

"Don't be silly," I said, waving her off.

"Okay, good," she exhaled, resetting.

And even bona fide rock stars do privates, I rationalized, it's just not spoken of publicly when a superstar plays a billionaire's birthday party on some exclusive island for an astronomical fee. This was definitely at the other end of the spectrum, but I desperately needed the dough. The pay tonight would mean a deposit on an apartment, and a couple months' rent, a chance to make another artsy record, even if no one bothered to listen to it. *It would matter to me.* If I could ever write another song again, that is.

How had I ended up here? I stole a glance through a break in the curtains. There was no turning back. The party had indeed started. Rowdy frat-bro types crowded onto the dance floor awaiting my performance. Hopefully they were already intoxicated and the memory of this would be one of the things that stayed in Vegas. Also, the slapdash sandwich and vodka Red Bull were starting to take effect nicely.

"This is so bleak it's actually *funny,* right?"

"Hilarious," Pippa said.

"Will make for a charming party anecdote someday," I said.

"Exactly," she said. "And once you're done, I whisk you away to Nobu, where we will fill up on delights and drink ourselves silly. On me."

We let a moment pass, absorbing the cacophony.

"So, I look like a whore, and also officially am one," I said wryly, rallying.

"Pretty much." Pippa's deadpan gave way to a familiar mischievous grin.

I thought, *Just hang in there. This will be over quick.* Like when you've got your legs spread in the gynecologist's stirrups and the doctor says, mere inches from your crotch: *Relax. Just a little pressure and we're done.*

A frenzied-looking stage manager rushed over. He gave me a re-proving look and ushered Pippa into the shadows. Almost instantly she was getting in his face. I could just make out "Outrageous. Jane Start is an artist. What do you take me for? A pimp?"

Pippa returned dangling a Party City bag between thumb and index fingers like it was toxic. She bit her lip and sheepishly withdrew—

No. Way. A hot pink wig.

"Requested most emphatically by the bachelor. Feel free to reject this final degradation." She was genuinely forlorn; I couldn't bear it.

"The perfect button for my party anecdote." I faked a smile and whisked it from her.

"Drinks. Nobu. Very soon," she said, scrambling to tuck my hair into the wig.

And with great solemnity, she placed a wireless microphone into my hand. I winced down at it. I wasn't a talk show host, for Christ's sake—or giving a Ted Talk, although then it would be one of those Silicon Valley headset things, *even worse.* If only I'd had my guitar, and a mic on a proper mic stand.

I locked eyes with Pippa and a shiver tore through me, along-side a thought I'd been suppressing all night. *This* is what happens when you cover a song by Jonesy. Nothing else you *ever* do will *ever* compare. It was patently true; my success was inextricably tied to *his* brilliant song. It began and ended there. Everything I'd written and recorded since had flopped. And there had been that moment, ten years ago, when Jonesy had wanted to sign me to his label, and produce my next record. I'd felt relieved when it had fallen through—a desire for autonomy, creatively, and a sneaking suspicion that nothing with Jonesy was *ever* simple—but now, here I was.

Had I been my own worst enemy? Had I chosen the wrong path? Why did I still believe that I could write songs? That I had something meaningful to say?

It was official: This was a moment of reckoning. At the ripe old age of thirty-three, I was an over-the-hill one-hit wonder—and now, it seemed, a "Vegas entertainer" who "did" bachelor parties.

Pippa was reading my mind—I *knew* she was, I saw it reflected in her eyes as clear as the glint of a murderer's knife in a Hitchcock film. A wave of panic rose up in me, steep and sharp, a funereal thud, drumming in my ears—and I clawed for a rescue song. Wayne Newton's "Danke Schoen" began to oompah calmingly, ironically, inside my head.

Danke schoen, darling, Danke schoen, thank you for...all the joy and pain...

And just then, the opening strains of my hit began to swell through the sound system. *Showtime!* I would earn my money and rally! Nothing in this world could destroy my love for Jonesy's song. But my heart leapt to my throat—it wasn't *my* track pealing from the speakers. It was a horrible, cheesy *karaoke* version...

Pippa gaped at me, mortified, but I had only enough time to gag back the rest of my vodka Red Bull before a hot white spotlight snapped on, center stage.

I tumbled out into blinding brightness, stark and unforgiving, catching blurred glimpses of the sweaty faces of the audience as they slam-danced, crashing into one another like football players in slow-motion playback. They'd come here to have fun and I would give them that, even singing to a shitty karaoke track, even without a guitar to clutch for dear life.

I closed my eyes. I thought only of singing. I would stay in the unfolding present tense, in the *meditation* of singing. I would leave no room for stage fright or humiliation, no room for imposter syndrome or for Alex's rejection—I would think only of this melody, which felt grand in my throat, slipping silkily from my lips. What a thrill it had been, to reinvent this song, to sing it all these years! *Thank you, Jonesy, for writing this song.* And how did a person *not* dance to this groove, *not* move their hips, *not* give 'em the old rock 'n' roll hair flip, even while holding a Party City wig in place?

The high note was coming—it was coming coming coming and I would not fear it. I would conjure the old driving analogy and prepare myself... I would keep my hands steady but relaxed on the wheel... I would travel the road map of the song's melody to its final steep ascent and liberate the note from its shelter deep within me. And when it sailed out, clear and bright and free, it was as if it didn't belong to me at all, but to everyone else, and I thought, *My work here is done.*

Fifteen minutes later, Pippa and I hovered in a dark corner of the bar. She slid a glass of champagne to me and tossed back an agitated gulp of her own.

"Jane, seriously, you sounded brilliant. Despite the circumstances." She gave an apologetic sigh and studied my face. I knew she meant beyond me having to karaoke the song. She meant Alex. Living with my parents again. My intractable writer's block.

"Honestly, I forget how good you are, but then you're singing, and your voice is clear, bright as a bell, and all at once, you sound husky and soulful—"

"Stop," I insisted, embarrassed.

"You did. Trust me. I told them they could sod off about the meet and greet," she said, giving her hair a defiant shake. "The bachelor requested photos with you, *in the wig.* What would he ask for next? A lap dance?"

I should never have done that video.

Pippa straightened, reading my thoughts. "I'll get the money now, shall I?" she said, batting her eyes.

Oh, how I'd missed her.

We clinked, knocked back our drinks, and she slipped off in

search of the party planner. I was left to watch the drunken musclemen horsing around, to convince myself this had all been an edifying anthropological study. They didn't notice me, sans wig, tarty dress concealed beneath my ex's frumpy cardigan—small and obscure, no longer elevated by a stage. So, I'd humiliated myself while they leered through their cell phones, filming. Definitely a first world problem, I thought, and I suppose everything is relative, even reaching one's personal nadir, *with video proof.* But Pippa was on her way back, waving the check triumphantly over her head, and I thought, *I* will *get creative again. I'll prove to Pippa, to myself, I have more in me—future songs waiting to be written, to be sung.*

After my sophomore record had been a commercial flop, seven years ago, the record label unceremoniously dropped me; it felt like a death, but more shameful. I'd hardly released new music since, apart from a couple of songs for Alex's early, low-budget films, during our first few years together. Rather than write my way out of my slump, I'd lost faith, and distracted myself with Alex, helping him restore his first home, a midcentury modern at the top of Mulholland, courtesy of his mother's trust fund. Soon, I'd disappeared into his close-knit coterie of friends, believing they were mine too. There were Scrabble nights, pub crawls, weekends in Joshua Tree. Double features at the New Beverly Cinema. But all that had vanished after Alex had cast Jessica in his upcoming production. The loss of the life we'd built together was bewildering. Crushing. The truth was, I missed him, desperately, and all the years I'd thought we were headed toward something more—

Deafening EDM music swelled through the sound system and Pippa sidled back up. The cabaret stage flooded with light as an enormous layer cake was wheeled out. The audience stilled for only a moment before a dancer burst forth. Something glittery sailed over the heads of the men and crash-landed onto the bar.

"I hope that wasn't her—" I was shouting into Pippa's ear when the next undergarment smacked me right in the face, and it was *warm*. We gaped down at the beer-sticky floor, where a sequined thong glimmered. Pippa grabbed my arm, in solidarity, but then her eyes widened at something behind me.

Not something. Some*body*. Sparkly Eyes, from the elevator, was inches away. Alongside him was the other half of the duo, his brother. They both resembled Disney princes, with oversized features, Bambi eyelashes, dark flowing hair. No wonder teenage girls stalked them in hotels.

"Let's get outta here," he said, his lips grazing my earlobe, his voice unpredictably deep and plush.

I flashed on Alex, how our legs had tangled, propped on his white Corian coffee table late into the night. The jeweled lights of the San Fernando Valley scintillating beyond seamless right angles of glass. *Home.*

Not anymore. My throat tightened.

"I'm Alfie," the Pop Star beamed.

Of course you are. And I thought: *Why not?* He sparkled. He asked. And his name was Alfie. *What's it all about, Alfie?* I kind of wanted to know.

Besides, I'd just been smacked in the face with a G-string, which, when I thought about it, only perfected my future party anecdote. One could argue, things were looking up.

I slugged back the rest of my drink, surveying his face. It was a very nice face indeed. When the younger Disney prince moseyed up to Pippa, she blushed and darted me a look.

"Sure. What's stopping us?" I said to Alfie, over the din.

He smiled, extended an elbow, and I slung my arm through.

Chapter 2.

PEOPLE WHO NEED PEOPLE

It began with a cozy dinner at Nobu, in which the Lloyd brothers, Nick (the younger) and Alfie (the senior by a year), proved to be compelling company. They were both warm conversationalists, cheeky and clever and worldly beyond their years, and surprisingly persuasive.

Now outside, at the curb, Nick Lloyd was taking backwards steps toward an open limo door, gently towing Pippa with him, the rainbow neon of the Strip softly throbbing, receding in the vanishing distance.

They were insisting we take a drive with them, out into the desert; the night, according to them, was "still young," and I thought, *What a hopeful statement.* Still young. And *hope*...was precisely what I needed. Not to mention, they'd organized champagne. I was beginning to feel *human* again. I could think of no reason why two young men and two women, *of a certain age,* shouldn't have an adventure. Viva Las Vegas.

Pippa wasn't exactly resisting. I cast a sideways glance at Alfie. He smiled, gorgeously.

I reminded myself I should be sensible. Head back to the room. Raid the minibar. Shove chocolate mindlessly into my mouth while doing normal, prosaic things like stalking my ex-partner's

Instagram and dissolving into tears at the sight of hot Jessica, my replacement. It was only a matter of time before Alex realized his mistake. I'd never been surer of anything.

Nick whistled from inside the limo, Pippa snuggled up close. She shot me a crazy-eyed, indecipherable grin through the door. She'd flown all the way to Sin City for me. I couldn't exactly ditch her now, could I?

Pippa, Nick, Alfie, me, in that order in the back seat of the limo. We were somewhere on the outskirts of Vegas, and some amount of time had passed. Empty champagne bottles clinked at our feet. Out the windows were lunar landscapes, jaundiced moonlight, and sand sweeping over the pavement like surf. Crazy gusts of wind made the car weave a little, or maybe that was just *me*.

"My brother was crushing on you big time—when he was like thir-deen or something," Nick was saying. Turns out Nick and Alfie had slipped into the bachelor party and witnessed my entire karaoke performance from the back of the room.

And what was with the incongruously deep voice? Both boys had it. Must be an Aussie thing.

Nick swung his arm smoothly around Pippa, and she didn't ruffle. *If she's thirty-nine and he's twenty-two...* Technically she was old enough to be his "mum." Ooh la la.

Now Alfie was wrapping *his* arm around *me*. Thirty-three minus twenty-three was not *as* bad, but still, the smart thing to do was to politely wiggle free. But he was so nice and toasty, so nice and firm, and so *nice* generally. He offered me a sip from a fresh bottle. *I shouldn't. Really.*

"Very kind of you." I took a swig, simply to be polite. He smiled sweetly back...*People who need people...are the luckiest people...* I stole a quick glance past him to Nick, resting his free hand on Pippa's thigh, her head lolling onto his shoulder. I wasn't used to seeing Pippa like this, sort of unfurled.

"You sound exactly the same, *brilliant*," Alfie murmured. "And you still wear the wig when you sing. Like in the video."

Not if I can help it. I wanted to explain but his face had suddenly found its way to my neck, and before I managed to extract myself, his lips parted into a smile on my skin and just stayed there—*ping,* a sizzle of sensation darted like an arrow down the length of my body. But not painful. Definitely not painful.

I snuck a manic glance in Pippa's direction. She was now somehow sloppily entwined with Nick, who appeared very much in lust with her and her voluptuous curves. Could you blame him?

"I'll have you know," she said over the top of his head, "I've been looking after Jane Start since the very beginning. You could even say I discovered her, fresh out of uni and singing in a wee coffeehouse. And I think, Jane, you'll back me up on this, but *I* was the one to insist you release the video, when you had your doubts—*mmm,*" she trailed off, distracted.

"And I'll never live it down," I said, but no one was really listening. Oh, never mind. I felt myself dissolving into the sensation of Alfie grazing my neck…which was so very wrong, for so very many reasons. *Exactly.* I would not entertain the notion of letting *this,* whatever *this was, mmm,* go on, *mmm,* one, second, longer.

Ding!

"Sorry," I said, disengaging to dig out my phone. *Saved by the bell.* I waved the screen in his face for clarity, but it only illuminated his adorableness in the dark. "Just need to quickly check."

Alex Altman: Hey Jane. I know I'm not supposed to be contacting you. Sorry, but I wanted to give you a heads-up. I don't know how else to say it. Jessica and I are getting married. Really sorry, Jane. I truly am.

*   *   *

Alfie's hotel room resembled mine, simple and modern, lots of white laminate surfaces, the odd pop of the old Eames color palette in a pillow here and a throw blanket there—but his was the size of an apartment, with a snazzy open floor plan and wraparound views. So this was where they put the high rollers—the *current* chart-topping pop stars. It was, frankly, extravagant beyond anything I'd experienced during my fifteen minutes.

I fixed my gaze on an acoustic guitar leaned quietly at the foot of the bed, mostly to distract myself from the other thoughts I was suddenly having. *What good is sitting alone in your room?*

"Teach me your song?" Alfie said.

I craned back, thrown. Our eyes met. *"O-kay,"* I conceded.

He smiled, adorably.

Shit. Now look what you've gotten yourself into. Alfie was a fellow musician, a world-famous pop star no less. The fact is, it's more nerve-racking to sing for one person you kind of know than a sea of people you don't.

Thus came the insistent time-step of my infuriating heart as I perched at the foot of his bed with his guitar, and with a reticent flip of an internal switch, I toggled from me, *human,* to me, *human who sings,* and started in playing "Can't You See I Want You," grateful the champagne had softened the edges.

"That's *so good.*" Alfie beamed, once the final chord had rung out. "I've *always* loved your song."

Here we go. "It's not actually *my* song. I mean, I didn't write it. It's a cover, of a Jonesy song."

"You're *joking.*" He cinched his brow, in earnest.

"Nope. It's from his first album. Before he had radio hits, so maybe that's why people don't ever seem to put it together."

We took a beat, smiling at one another. *"You,* my friend, should cover it," I suggested, extending the guitar to him. That's the thing about great songs: they never get old. If only I could write one.

We swapped places and he began to pluck out the chords for

himself. Turns out Alfie was a massive Jonesy fan, but I mean, *who wasn't*. There was only one tricky guitar chord he couldn't quite master, so I found myself positioning his fingers on the fretboard, to show him. It felt weirdly intimate, even after the back-seat-of-the-limo canoodling. There followed a pregnant pause in which he peered luminously up at me. My cheeks blazed.

Alfie rose, took a slug of Dom from the bottle on the nightstand, and extended it to me. I took what felt like a monumental step closer to him, swigged the last of it, and set it back down with an indelicate clunk. He smiled, amused.

"You know, you're not even my type. Too pretty." There. I'd said it. Right to his face, apropos of absolutely nothing besides *proximity* to a *bed*. There were two cute chocolates in monogrammed wrappers on a pair of crisp, plump king pillows, and a calligraphed card: *Dear Mr. Caine, if there is anything you should desire during your stay with us ...*

Alfie was leaning against the nightstand looking at me, his head cocked.

"I'm probably the only person on this entire planet who's *not* in love with you," I insisted, a tad slurrily. "I'm just, *not*."

He smiled, unfazed.

God, he was pretty. How did a person *not* smile at that face? At which point he placed his index finger, very gently, at the center of my forehead and applied the tiniest bit of pressure, *and what choice had I* but to tip backwards onto the bed like a felled tree in a forest. Mmm. I couldn't help running my hands over the snowy-cool, tightly tucked coverlet. I did love the feel of high-quality bedding.

"Well, for your information, *you* are not *my* type *either*," he said. "Sweet Jane, *sweeeet Jane*." Okay, *now* I was impressed. He knew the Velvet Underground.

But oh hello, Alfie from Australia had one knee nonchalantly perched on the edge of the bed. I scooted back a little, patted the mattress. "Nice bed," I said, and reclined on one of the pillows, my hands tucked beneath my head, shooing aside the chocolate.

"Not to mention," he said, crawling toward me, a young jaguar stalking, "you...are much...too old for me." He swung one leg over, straddling me, very respectfully I might add, and smiled softly down.

This was either a brilliant idea or a *not* brilliant idea. I flashed suddenly on Alex and Jessica, just like this on our old bed. Not nearly as nice as this one, and definitely not as crisp.

Really sorry, Jane. I truly am.

No, Alex, you're not.

And then I was gazing up at a Disney prince, and he was tucking a lock of dark silken hair behind his ear, blinking his doe eyelashes in dreamy half-time.

"So, we've determined we're not into each other," I said.

"Right," he said.

"Then what are we doing?" I asked.

"I don't know," he answered, flipping me over in a single, seamless balletic motion, so now *I* was straddling *him*. He proceeded to gaze up at me with those huge, lustrous blue eyes. "I guess we're just *being bad,*" he said, the corner of his pretty mouth curling up, punctuated by a single, perfect dimple.

Bad. Yes. Very. But there's this thing: the healing powers of dopamine. Confusing, because I happened to love dopamine, and my instincts, which probably shouldn't be relied upon at a time like this, told me *I was very close to getting my hands on some.*

And there's this other thing, I thought, allowing myself finally to sink into him—*an erection.* There's something undeniably reassuring, or at least *flattering* about an erection. But also, compelling, the way it presses, so irrepressibly, against the fabric, making its divinely sculptural outline known, and felt, and *understood.*

There's a healing power in that too, isn't there?

Chapter 3.

HEAVY PETTING

"*Jane!* I've been ringing you all morning. We're meant to have breakfast together. *Hello?!*" Pippa was shouting over the line. I wished she wouldn't.

"Mm-hmm."

"Excellent. You're alive, sooo," she was murmuring now, and vaguely conspiratorial. "What *happened?* And where *are you* exactly?"

I sat up way too fast. All at once last night came rushing back: *the bed—the face—the smile—the wraparound night sky...* ALFIE. I searched my memory banks like a dog frantically pawing for a buried bone—and the memory surfaced. We did *not* "sleep together." *Relief.* It would have been pathetic revenge sex and *that* would only have made me feel worse.

"Jane, you still there? And where *are you* exactly?"

"In my room?"

"You don't sound convinced," she said, muffling laughter.

I flopped back down, head throbbing, and clicked on the speakerphone. Ugh. I'd gone and done all the things I'd promised myself I wouldn't, post breakup. Drowned my sorrows in drink, for starters. At least I was in my own room.

"I was only joking, darling. You deserve a bit of fun. That prat Alex, for one, and I don't need to remind you. You sang at a bachelor party last night." There was a pause. "*And,* you had rather a lot of champagne," she said, delicately. I could almost hear her grinning. "So, listen closely and do exactly as I say. No thinking. Just doing."

"But what am I doing?"

"You're taking the coldest shower you can manage and you're meeting me downstairs. The Hawaiian-themed place with the fake beach. I've booked a table. And bring your bag. We'll leave for the airport from here."

"*No.* I mean, what am I doing, with my *life?*"

"Oh, that." She laughed. "We'll get it all sorted at breakfast."

Pippa was tapping furiously away at her phone, head lowered, when I sank into the chair across from her.

"Right, then," she said, with a final jab, parking her phone facedown and pouring me coffee. "*So?*" She slid the cup to me.

"So. Why did we get in that limo?"

"No self-flagellation. There will be plenty of time for it later. I'll even provide the whip," she said, dryly.

"Thanks." We both took sips. "How is it that you're so perky? And where did *you* disappear to last night?"

She raised her brows, which could be interpreted as either *You do the math,* or *No comment,* as in a police interrogation. "If you could please contain your schadenfreude," I said.

"With regard to your original question, what are you doing?" Pippa deflected, buttering toast. "You're having breakfast on a fake beach in Las Vegas after karaokeing your hit. Brilliantly, I might add. But in a more global sense, I'd say you're getting back on your feet."

Was I? It felt the opposite. I'd vowed not to make the same mistake I'd made with Alex—jumping into bed with the first person who smiled at me. "I'm a dyed-in-the-wool, unabashed, card-carrying, *serial—monogamist!*" I burst out, warding off looks from the neighboring diners, including a church group in matching outfits.

"*Yes.* Right. Exactly." Pippa frowned, confused, trying to be helpful.

"Casual sex just isn't... my *thing,*" I insisted, in a quieter voice. I had *myself* for that. "And it was technically"—I'd googled— " 'heavy petting.' "

"Very disciplined of you," she said, suppressing a smile.

"I am a grown woman. I can go as far, or *not* far, as I choose." And what transpired with Alfie had been wildly consensual. There might as well have been a lawyer perched on the bed having us sign and initial, here and here.

"Precisely," she agreed.

"And when he escorted me to the door"—lanky, smiling down, hanging into the doorframe, the one cute dimple on display—"he said, 'I bid you a very good night, madam.' "

Off in the distance there was the sound of splashing, of small children squealing innocently in the fake tide.

I continued: "The *madam* part threw me for half a second. Am I that old?"

"No!" Pippa cried, and refilled my coffee.

I flashed on nubile Jessica and felt positively prehistoric.

"Could have been worse," I said, over the rim of my cup. "He could have said *ma'am.*"

"So much worse," Pippa agreed, over the rim of hers. "You really did sound fab last night, darling. Ahh Jonesy, the song that keeps on—"

She'd hardly gotten the words out when the earth seemed to slide off its axis: the mere mention of his name, and adrenaline crackled through me. "Why did you stay with me? Ten years ago, when Jonesy wanted to sign me, produce me, and I dunno... make me part of his stable. His 'brand.' Whatever *that* even means anyway."

"Jane," Pippa cried, her eyes wide.

Two roads had diverged in a wood, and I took the road less traveled, and if last night's performance had taught me anything, it was that I'd taken the wrong one.

"No. *Really,*" I said, emphatic. "But you stayed with me anyway. And I appreciate you never giving up on me. Or my career if we can even call it that. But it's come down to *privates.* To 'the one song.' To an embarrassing parody of my twenty-three-year-old self."

"You know what I always say," Pippa trilled, encouragingly. "You're only ever—"

"One good song away. I *know.*" She was right. But I'd tried and failed. Repeatedly.

"Precisely." Pippa beamed. "And there's a bit of good *business* news to share, a licensing offer..."

I silently prayed. Sofia Coppola, or Wes Anderson, or Paul Thomas Anderson, wanted to use one of the dreamy, atmospheric songs from my second album in a film.

"...for a TV commercial in Holland," she said, smiling up.

Oh. "The one song, I take it?" If I were Leonard Nimoy, the one song would be my Spock ears.

"A commercial for Gentle Caress, the synopsis *adorable* if you ask me." She began rattling quickly, like an auctioneer. Not a good sign. "Attractive young gent spies attractive young lady in the supermarket, both pushing carts through the aisles, smiling, eyeing, flirting, until they wind up reaching *simultaneously* for a package of—wait for it!—Gentle Caress, and after an awkward moment the gent gallantly places *his* in the lass's cart, grabs another for himself, and off they go, flirting wildly into the sunset!"

"Okay," I said cautiously. "Is Gentle Caress like, a lube or something? Or is it shampoo? Body cream? Ribbed condoms?"

"The money's excellent I might add...and, so, it's toilet paper," she mumbled, avoiding eye contact, refilling her coffee. "And there's a ticking clock on this one. The offer expires tonight."

Ugh, *no*. But I had no money. Unless you're the Rolling Stones or Jonesy, world-touring, it comes down to song licensing. And it could be worse. It could be a commercial for tampons. *Was* that worse?

"Okay," I said. "But only if you tell me what happened with Nick Lloyd last night." I needed *something* in return. It wasn't fair, her being so tight-lipped.

She gave her hair a defiant toss, color rising. "It's not what you think. Besides, everyone has—"

"Secrets? They keep from their *best friend?*" She blushed. "You saucy wench."

"You're just trying to change the subject."

Okay, I was, partly. Arguments in favor of Yes to Gentle Caress: I'd be buying artistic freedom…freedom from my parents. And when you think about it, people actually *need* toilet paper. It's like this dirty little secret.

I sighed. "You know your career is officially in the toilet…"

"It's just, that, I feel *obliged,*" Pippa stammered, "to at least tell you, even when an offer is—" She broke off.

"A little shitty?" I even managed to deliver it with a straight face. She smiled, relieved. And I knew she had my best interest at heart.

"It's fine, you can say yes."

"It's Holland, for fuck's sake."

"And the money from prostituting myself in Vegas won't last forever. But wait—Jonesy would have had to sign off on it, he wrote the song."

She shrugged. "Apparently, he has."

Oh, I thought, perplexed.

But as she dashed off the email approving the license, I had a terrible sinking feeling. This was what it had come to. My voice helping sell what people use to wipe their…And I happened to adore Holland. The Van Gogh Museum, the Rijksmuseum with all the Rembrandts and Vermeers.

"Yoga. On the phony beach," Pippa mused, staring out at a gathering crowd.

"Jessica is amazing at yoga," I said, morosely. "She's probably doing it right now. Or doing *him…fucking* Alex. I can't believe I didn't show you this." That was when the goddamned tears decided to make the entrance they'd been threatening.

"Oh no." Pippa thrust out a napkin as I slid her my phone with his text. "Bastard."

I agreed and blew my nose, unladylike. In retrospect, there had always been red flags, but the one that haunted me most, the one I could never forgive myself for, was that I hadn't *run* the instant I put it together: Alex hadn't technically been single at the start of things for us, either. He'd denied, *emphatically,* being in a relationship, yet somewhere inside me I knew.

We'd just begun dating. A small dinner party. His best friend from high school, Inez, peering up from her ricotta and peach crostini. In her eyes there gleamed a warning, a *Sorry in advance, but he will hurt you,* and then a sorrowful *What a shame: You're so good for him.* It was a warning I didn't heed.

"*I've* rather given up men," Pippa sighed, and gave my hand a squeeze. She'd never endorsed Alex. She'd found him "in-substantial." Something Pippa had only confessed, a bit futilely, *post*-breakup.

"But, Jane," she insisted, her brow sweetly furrowed, "I don't see you alone. I'm quite sure you'll survive this. And I promise you, it's all going to be okay. All of it. It's just *life.* Bloody stupid life."

Pippa, my angel.

"And anyway," she exhaled, "I reckon most people have wound up in a hotel room in Vegas, after a night of— Oh no. Too soon?" She slid another napkin to me. "Jane. Listen. Today is *truly* a fresh start." She began digging, with great purpose, into the depths of her handbag and then thrust out a boarding pass, eyes gleaming.

Right. Ugh. Another flight.

"Thank you," I said, doing my best to mask my dread. Honestly, I'd have rather walked barefoot through a scorching desert of broken glass than gotten on another plane right then. I glanced down. "First class?!"

"And *I'm* going with you," she said, pointing, now beaming.

I clapped a hand over my mouth. "London. What? We're going to London? You didn't."

"I *did,*" she said brightly. "Cashed in all my mileage points. Truth is I've been hoarding them for years, holding out for some future fantasy shagging holiday in Fiji with Dominic West. Pathetic really. But I just thought, after me bungling last night and well...*I miss you.* I couldn't send you straight back to your parents, now could I? At least come stay with me in London first."

I sprang up, flung my arms around her. "Thank you. I don't deserve you. I'm just so grateful."

"Oh, darling," she said, pulling apart. "It's nothing. I've accrued a lot of mileage, babysitting—"

"Leopard Pants?"

"Stop calling him that. He only wore them *once.*"

Pippa would never stop defending his questionable fashion sensibility. He *was* a true icon. His guitar playing on par with Keith Richards's, or, dare I say, Jonesy's.

"Poor old dinosaur," she sighed.

"You'll never give up on him."

"No," she said proudly, her chin raised, "I never will."

"I can only hope the same will be true for me." My throat tightened again.

"Of course it will, darling, but *listen,* I want you to think of London as a kind of mental-health mini-break—a chance to do some writing."

"Loads of writing," I insisted. I would make good on this promise to her. I felt buoyed, ready to surf this swell of determination. I would dig deep. Work hard. Persevere in the face of my self-doubt, my failures. I would *never* give up.

"I'm so pleased! And I've managed to snag us the first row of first class," she said. "But now we must get moving. I'll check us out. Organize a car."

"Okay! And *thank you,* from the bottom of my heart."

But she was already clacking away on her phone as I experienced an unfamiliar sense of glee, despite knowing we'd soon be flying over a very large, very deep body of water, because my dearest Pippa would be right there beside me. *Except—*

"Where is Kurt Cobain?"

"In a better place," she murmured, still typing.

"I mean my cardigan. *Alex's* cardigan."

Technically, it still belonged to him, but I had no intention of ever giving it back. And anyway, his *fiancée,* Jessica, would only sneer at the ratty old thing, and not appreciate that it was practically a doppelgänger for the one Kurt had worn on *MTV Unplugged.*

"Oh. Right."

It hit me all at once. "I left Kurt in Alfie's room."

"Did you?" She stopped typing, cocked a brow at me. "Well, I'd call *that* a Freudian slip."

Chapter 4.

KURT COBAIN CARDIGAN

Alex had been wearing the cardigan the night we met. We'd
struck up a random conversation in line for a showing of *Klute*
at the Nuart. He'd had that seductive rescuable look, tall but a bit
undernourished, somehow pale, like he'd been holed up for days
watching cool reruns of *Columbo* and *Mannix*. We'd connected
over cinema—Hollywood noir, edgy seventies auteur classics, all
iterations of sixties New Wave. On the second date, he revealed he
was a fan of my music, but that I wasn't at all what he'd expected,
"as a person." It had been a relief, not to be reduced to my .gif.
Alex had also reminded me a bit of Will, my younger brother by
two years—same age, same lanky build and olive complexion—
which had made him seem familiar, accessible, intelligent. I'd felt
comfortable with Alex. Generally, but also in bed, and what if I
never found *that* again?

But Alex wasn't that person anymore. He no longer produced
provocative low-budget indie films. He *executive* produced commercial Hollywood dreck, starring Jessica. Perhaps it was merely
the Kurt Cobain Cardigan that had created the illusions of smoldering depth, an artistic soul, *integrity?* Because he ruthlessly traded
me in for a younger model. A literal *Sports Illustrated* one, and
Alex didn't even *like* sports.

But I wasn't about to part with that sweater.

The elevator doors slid open on Alfie's floor, but still I hesitated. I should simply forget all about Kurt Cobain. Let go of what I now realized was some sick transitional object shackling me to my ex, and avoid all of this discomfort. The elevator doors began to close. Good, let them. I was officially off the hook. The Kurt Cobain Cardigan would be one of the things that stayed in Vegas. Along with my pride.

Except, no. I jammed my hand between the doors and darted out, rolling my small suitcase with me down the long hallway. I simply wasn't ready to part with Kurt.

With my finger a hair's breadth from the buzzer to Alfie's suite, I thought, *Fuck's sake. I'm not honestly intimidated by a twenty-three-year-old? Who just happens to be a pop star?* I pressed the buzzer. Anyway, there *was* such a thing as a man being too pretty.

Amendment: There wasn't. In the light of day, Alfie was breathtaking. The silky disheveled hair, and those pants, like half of a 1960s suit but more casual, sitting perfectly askew on his angular Australian hips. A rumpled Patti Smith T-shirt peeked from beneath the cardigan, which was adorably shrunken on him, and really, it was adorable he was wearing a Patti Smith T-shirt at all.

I thought, I actually *like* him.

"Hey, you," he said, peeling off the sweater, extending it to me. "How're you going?"

"I'm...*good*. How are you...going." *Awkward.*

"I wanted to run your cardi to your room, but I couldn't remember your name." I felt the color drain from my face. "I know you're *Jane*," he added quickly. "I meant your *tour* name." He gave me a soft punch on the shoulder and ushered me in.

"Oh," I said, thrown. "I'm—Maggie May." And parked my rolly just inside the door. Honestly, why did I bother with tour names at this point. Pathetic.

"Perfect." He cocked a brow, insinuating.

I know *what the song is about. And that I'm ten years your senior. No need to rub it in.*

"Michael Caine," he said, with a tip of the head. *"My* tour name, for future reference." He'd pulled off actor Michael Caine's perfect Cockney, which he'd famously used to portray the womanizing character Alfie in the film by that name.

"Got it." I tapped the side of my noggin, stealing a glance at the mussed king bedsheets across the room. *Much to unpack,* I thought.

Alfie smiled and the dimple appeared like the first star on a velvet night sky. I could almost hear the gentle saw of crickets. He took a few backwards steps, grinning, then spun on his bare heel and padded insouciantly toward the minibar, about which there was nothing remotely mini.

"Something to drink?" He offered up the contents with a theatrical sweep.

"No. Thanks. Actually, I'm off to London, heading to the airport soon." I made a swooping airplane gesture with sound effect, which I instantly regretted.

"Right, right." He smiled. "We're playing here tonight. Start of the North American leg of our tour," he said with an endearing hint of self-mockery.

"Wow...cool. Awesome." I hated each and every one of those words.

"Yeah—let the craziness begin," he sighed. "I only ever knew the one song of yours, but I listened to your other record this morning after you left. Really, *really* good."

Pull it together. "Oh. Why, *thank you. So much,*" I stuttered feebly back. Perhaps he was merely being polite. The songs on my second album had been dreamy, ethereal, a delicious pleasure to write. And far from the commercial pop my record label apparently expected, hence my being dropped. Yet I felt a little fillip inside and was touched.

Oh man, I needed to listen to *his* music.

"*So.* You know *Jonesy,*" he ventured.

I wanted to say, *Nobody knows Jonesy.* Perhaps not even Jonesy. But it was too big of a thing to get into now.

"Is it true? No one's allowed to, like, look him in the eye?"

I was suddenly at a loss. An apocryphal story, no doubt, yet how strange, how disconcerting it honestly had been those many years ago, to be in Jonesy's orbit. Now, as something of an adult, I could see his antics clearly for what they were: *control.* The thought gave me a shudder. If only Alfie knew. Jonesy orchestrated every encounter. He wrote the scripts, blocked the scenes, choreographed his entrances onto the sets he'd designed: a brilliant and unapologetic visionary, even when far from a stage.

"No. Not true," I said, referring to the no-eye-contact rumor.

We left it at that, slipping into a silence we filled by smiling at one another.

"Well...this is me," I said, finally, retreating. "And thanks for looking after my sweater. It was swell meeting you, and your brother, and best of luck on the tour." *Oy vey.*

He ambled over and leaned in the doorframe, with all the charisma of a movie star yet somehow not pretentious, only charming.

"So long, Alfie. Maybe our paths will cross again sometime?" I said.

"Hey, give me your phone. I'll put my number in."

I tried not to appear stunned by this and passed it to him.

"I meant it about your songs," he murmured, his eyes lowered, typing. "We should, dunno—try and write something sometime."

Is it possible he sincerely likes the record that ended my so-called career?

He flashed a quick smile through a swath of silky hair before returning the phone, very gently, into my palm.

Surely he was only being polite.

"That sounds fun." *Fun?* That was the best I could do? I found enough composure to send him a quick text, so he'd have my number too.

His phone dinged across the room, from the bed, no less, and my cheeks pinked, frustratingly, but he kept his eyes trained on me and smiled.

"Safe travels, Maggie May."

He leaned in, planted a soft peck on my lips, a casual Aussie thing, I was almost certain.

"And *you,* too," I said, grabbing my roller bag and making my exit.

"Jane."

I turned back. He'd followed me into the hallway; he looked cute standing there, his hands on his hips, barefoot on the wildly patterned carpeting.

"Keep singing," he said.

"Okay. I will."

No question, he was utterly adorable. When my phone vibrated, it was Pippa, wondering what had become of me. Still smiling, I swiveled around, and as I drifted down the hall, wheeling my bag, I could hear him softly singing again, the Velvet Underground: "Sweet Jane…"

So, I sang back, over my shoulder: "Standing on the corner, suitcase in my hand."

I listened for the click of his door, but the elevator came first, and I didn't look back.

Chapter 5.

MAN THIGHS

We are all prisoners in one way or another. Prisoners of our minds, prisoners of our bodies, or prisoners of the state as I was now, having been delivered into the gloved hands of a cranky TSA lady who ran them o'er hill and dale, my limbs splayed out like a suspect's. It wasn't *my* fault she'd just encountered erect nipples. It was freezing in there. Also, I was ticklish, and anxious, and almost anything could set them off. And dare I admit, it kind of felt good?

And I was alone, Pippa having received an urgent call on the way to the airport necessitating she fly directly to New York, to deal with one of her artists who actually paid the bills. She'd left me with the keys to her flat, and a hurried download of instructions (the front door lock was pesky, the dahlias in the garden craved a little love), reassuring me we'd be reunited in a matter of days. As I'd watched her click-clacking away down a shimmering white concourse, in her white trench and her white strappy heels, I imagined at any moment she'd whirl around and come running back to me, her lips moving in slow motion to declare: *FUCK LEOPARD PANTS. I'M FLYING TO LONDON WITH YOU!* But she'd disappeared into a sea of strangers, and I'd already forgotten everything she'd instructed me to do.

Despite my apprehension, I was first to cross the threshold of the jumbo jet after pausing to make three very necessary "lucky taps" on its gleaming exterior. I experienced a surprising frisson entering the first-class cabin. A tingle as I sank into my ample, ergodynamic window seat and fingered its myriad seductive switches. Fondled the complimentary travel kit and sniffed its contents. Released the lofty pillow and duvet from their hygienic wrappers. I thought, how funny that a few amenities, and a little extra leg room, could *almost* distract a person from an intractable fear of flying. But also, how lucky I was to have Pippa in my life. If only she were here, because God help whoever landed the seat next to me—I'd be crawling over them continually to get to the bathroom.

The rest of first class filed in, the usual suspects: a bronzed socialite swathed in lemon pashmina and her silver-haired spouse in a lavender Lacoste polo and Gucci loafers. The gorgeous Italian family with many vivacious bambini and a beleaguered nanny in tow. Various business executives in enviable crisp and perfected travel attire, slinging the latest tech. As they glided past, I couldn't suppress a "Please no, not the seat next to me" expression, which was universally returned with a look of "How did the homeless woman wind up in first class?" Perhaps it was the outfit: Kurt Cobain, over a vintage thrift store slip, no bra, no socks, and a pair of dirty canvas flats. Basically, desperate aging woman attempts early Courtney Love. So, sue me. I deign to choose comfort over fashion.

A text from my brother.

Will Start: Shit Fuck
Jane Start: Paris France.

(Our sibling code for "hey.")

Will Start: Check YOU out. [Link to video]

Footage from the bachelor party last night. Ugh. Luckily, only nineteen views (including him, presumably) and a partial clip. I tolerated a few seconds and began scrolling the comments, past a few conditionally positive ones employing much use of the word *still*. Such as: "Still got the moves for a chick past her expiration date." *Expiration date?!* "Still sounds pretty great, too bad she has small tits, but why does she wear ugly shoes?" *Because they're comfortable!* But then I got to "That's just sad. I can't believe Jane Start would play a crap bachelor party. Pathetic." And the retort to this: "What she deserves for flashing her crotch in that video. A total zero plain jane. Never got what anyone saw in her, especially Jonesy!" But perhaps worst of all: "She can't even sing anymore. She was obviously lip singing."

> **Jane Start:** I wasn't lip syncing! Where's the hangover emoji...I'm too hungover to find it...I need a reminder not to drink any-time soon.
> **Will Start:** 🫠You're welcome. And btw you sounded great. That person's an ass. Who calls it lip SINGING?!
> **Will Start:** But switching gears, how bout you and me going in on an apt? Current roommate situation intolerable, as yours must be. 😂 No offense to our dear parentals.
> **Jane Start:** Sure—but Pippa offered to put me up in London for a week or so first. At airport now 💀
> **Will Start:** Relax. You'll be fine. Just do your lucky tapping thing. It's worked so far?
> **Jane Start:** I just did! But SO FAR?! 💀
> **Will Start:** Gotta run. Job interview. Genius Bar.

Finally. This sounded promising.

> **Will Start:** How's Pippa btw? Haven't seen her in eons. Still a babe, right?

Jane Start: Yup. Super babe.
Will Start: Thought so. Tell her hi for me.

"Champagne?"

A tray slid under my nose; how pretty the bubbles looked when they caught the light. Fuck it. Who said no to free champagne? When I thought about it, this was a time to celebrate. Goodbye private gigs in Vegas, hello creativity in London.

And yet there was no way to ignore a kind of feral panic burbling just below the surface.

"Yes. Please," I said.

I flopped my phone facedown so the emoji would stop glaring at me and steeled myself for takeoff, as an announcement came over the intercom. They were expecting a full flight. Passengers were encouraged to settle in for an on-time departure.

When it came time for flight attendants to arm and lock the cabin doors, I could hardly believe the seat beside me was still unoccupied; if not Pippa, then at least I'd have the row to myself! Chocolate bars, lip balms, Benadryl (the poor woman's Ambien), and a couple of tattered paperbacks I'd grabbed from my parents' house cascaded across the seat. Just then another *ding* sliced the air, and something I'd never witnessed occurred: a flight attendant *un*-battened the hatch and a visibly breathless and agitated man was escorted onto the plane. I observed him keenly, anxious that my coveted row was in jeopardy, as the airline personnel studied his crumpled boarding pass and debated where to put him. Tall and trim, he studied the floor, collecting himself.

No, please, I'm begging you, mister—go back from whence you came!

The man, as if hearing my thoughts, looked up, and our eyes met. His features seemed to reconfigure into something resembling a smile, an apologetic one. He quickly bowed his head and returned to looking stressed, running a hand absently along his jawline and through sleek, wavy hair the color of wet sand. I noticed he was around forty, and had handsome, chiseled features. A bit weathered, but in a pleasing way. And there was an elegance to him that intrigued me.

Then came the chime, signaling the closing once more of the cabin doors. The flight attendant grabbed his roller bag and offered to take his jacket before gesturing to the seat beside mine. *Fuck.*

I gulped back the last of my champagne, inhaling most of it in a spasm of denial as he glided toward me, and time slowed. As I set about gathering my things from his seat, I became hypnotized by his languid, long-legged, soft-focus strides, realizing too late I'd only sent them sailing to the floor.

"So sorry," I choked, spewing champagne, as he towered, magnificent, in the aisle, looming above me. Mortified, I attempted to wipe my face discreetly with the back of my hand.

"No trouble," he returned, in a gentle dignified British accent, darting me the same tensed smile as before.

I experienced a jab of guilt for beseeching him to get lost, if only in my head, for he was now crouched, magnanimously gathering up my airport booty, including a chubby crayon lipstick emblazoned with "Baked Sugar Delicious" which he briefly studied before glancing up. His face was arrestingly close, and in that instant, I took in the little lines at the corners of his eyes, which crinkled downward when he smiled. The sandy stubble of a couple days' beard. And his eyes, the irises a luminous gray-green, the color of slate and moonlight and sea glass... of Turner paintings...

"There you are," he said, rising, setting chocolate bars and the Baked Sugar Delicious with careful deliberation atop my copy of Erica Jong's *Fear of Flying,* the words "erotic," "horny," "uninhibited," "sexual," leaping brazenly from the cover blurbs. He set the stack on my armrest.

"Thank you so much," I said, as he dropped into his seat. "I'd never read it, *hitherto,* so I thought, second-wave feminist classic, it's about time *that I did."*

Hitherto? Jesus Christ what was happening to me?

He gave a little smile, and nodded diplomatically, but offered no rejoinder to whatever all *that* just was. We settled in silently. I accepted another refill on my sparkling wine. The man sipped sparkling water.

The jumbo jet aligned on the runway, and I cued up my trusted airplane takeoff theme song, pressing play just as the wheels began to roll, as was my superstitious tradition. The music worked its proven magic immediately, transporting me to another time and place, where there was no fear, no pain, just song and champagne, groove and lift-off. I closed my eyes as we took flight, finding it hard to sit still, jittery but emboldened by the song, suffused with a rosy flush of tipsiness. After a minute or so, I risked opening my eyes, only to find the man looking at me. His lips were moving, but I had the volume cranked.

"Sorry?" I loosened an earbud.

"Must be good." He nodded at my iPhone. "What you're listening to."

"Ohhh *yeah.* I love this song."

The silver-haired socialites in the row across the aisle came into view, craning up from their seats and scowling. Whoops. I must be shouting. I hit pause, removed the earbuds.

"But I wouldn't call it, *good,* exactly. It's not…Beethoven," I said, making a quick assessment of the man: grownup button-down shirt. Simple, nice-fitting trousers. A classical guy. "Or, the Beatles," I added, so he didn't think I thought *he* was a boring square. "I mean, I don't reckon most people would say it's *good* exactly." I immediately regretted the air quotes around "good." At least the "I don't reckon" seemed appropriately British. "*I* think it's honestly brilliant. Although most people qualify it as 'brilliant' in an *ironic* way. *Not me."*

"Now I'm extremely curious," he said.

"I listen to it as a kind of music therapy. This song really helps with fear of flying. But, you're probably not afraid of flying."

"No." His gaze was arrestingly steady, yet *inside* there was unbridled energy flickering, moonlight glancing the crest of a wave—*oh god.* And he was so serious. Plus, so seriously nice to look at. "I'm not afraid to fly," he said.

And *fuuck, the accent.* "Well. If you *were* afraid to fly, I would highly recommend listening to this."

Our fingers grazed as I went to hand him the phone, and, thrown, I pressed it a bit aggressively into his palm.

He studied the screen, surprised. "The theme from *Shaft?*"

"You'd be amazed, but a little Shaft goes a long way."

"I *see,*" he said, widening his eyes, passing me back the phone, amused.

That didn't come out *quite* as I'd intended, but I needed to wrap this puppy up.

"The song makes me feel like I'm somebody else." *Boom.* I set my phone on the armrest between us. He glanced down at the album cover art—Richard Roundtree, in a leather suit, exuding extreme seventies-style badassery—then up at me.

"Like I'm someone who's *not* afraid of danger, but someone whose whole existence is about *facing* danger. Shaft's the private dick, the cat that won't cop out when there's danger all about."

He looked lost. *I know. I'm a small Jewish woman.*

"I didn't get much sleep last night. And I'm a little hungover, truthfully." I took another desperate slug of champagne and raised my glass to him. "Hair of the dog."

"Right," he said, and raised his. "To Shaft."

How could a person not smile? "I think you should just listen to the song, and you'll see what I mean."

"No," he sighed, shaking his head. "I can't imagine it could ever live up to the description you just gave."

His features unfolded into a warm open smile, and I felt a fluttery throb in my chest that seemed to dart around inside me like a tiny hummingbird until it found a little nest to cozy into, *zing,* right between my thighs.

The plane suddenly dropped as if through a trapdoor—slipping through space too easily before lurching back up again. I simply had *no choice* but to grab his hand, imagining somehow this would steady the plane. He didn't seem to mind.

"Are we crashing?"

"No. Not at all. The air is actually pushing the plane up."

I ventured a peek out the window, then back to my hand clutching his. "I'm so sorry. I do this sometimes on flights and I really don't mean to. Sorry." I clasped his hand even tighter.

"It's no problem," he said with unfathomable calm. "You can grip my hand as long as you need." He glanced past me to the darkening sky. Visible in the distance, a band of silver-lined thunderheads. "It's science really," he said, fixing his gentle gaze upon me once more.

The man proceeded to explain the physics of aerodynamics, in silky murmuring tones, but I was unable to absorb it, catching only the lilt and cadence of random words: *lift, drag, thrust, flow, velocity, viscosity.* I was utterly hypnotized by the movement of his lips, the way the hollows beneath his well-defined cheekbones seemed to beckon my fingertips to sweep over their sandy surfaces. At some point I realized he'd gently eased the angle of his hand, so that I was properly holding it, and that his lips had stopped moving.

"Are you a pilot?" Anything to keep him talking.

The plane jerked up again, then seemed to thud like a ball down a set of stairs. I clutched tighter, and he placed his other hand atop mine. Warmth radiated in all directions; big smooth palms, dwarfing my clenched little paw—*oh happy prisoner.*

"No," he said, serenely. "But I've always enjoyed flying."

"A lawyer?"

He laughed. "Definitely not."

"A member of Parliament?"

"I'm not that either."

He smiled, more broadly this time. He really didn't seem to mind holding my hand.

"Banker? No, scratch that. Fashion designer."

He shot me a *You can't be serious* look and glanced down at his clothes. Hopefully he hadn't noticed *my* outfit. Maintaining eye contact, I slyly drew Kurt a little tighter with my free hand.

"Hmmm." I had run out of things to say. Perhaps it was the way he was looking at me. In fact, I think we were having a staring contest, or rather a *smiling* one.

"I'm a professor, actually," he said, finally.

This exceeded my expectations. *Ding!* sounded a call button somewhere, as if in agreement. "What do you teach?"

"Warm nuts?" A cherubic-faced male flight attendant had galumphed into view.

We declined. But the attendant darted me a knowing wink. *Was I that obvious?*

"I teach English lit'rature," the professor said, drawing me back.

It got better and better.

"Might I tempt you then with refreshments?" The flight attendant again, this time with a festive gesture to indicate all manner of booze loaded onto a cart.

To drink or not to drink, that was the question.

"Yes, please, *won-der-ful,*" I said, extending my glass, at which point my seatmate finally uncoupled his palm. *I'm sorry for releasing your hand,* his tortured smile seemed to say. Or perhaps, *I'm sorry for you, because you clearly have a drinking problem.*

If only he knew how much champagne I'd had these past twenty-four hours. I flashed on Alfie: one bare thigh, mine. One bare chest, his. Blurred freeze-frame of olive-green cardigan a-sail over a sea of mussed bedsheets. Kurt Cobain! No wonder I'd left him behind. Instead of shame, I felt a surge of sudden freedom. What had transpired with Alfie was confidence-bolstering. Alex's cheating hands were no longer the last to touch me.

And why shouldn't I enjoy that freedom now? With my face discreetly tipped into my glass, I had license to peer at the professor's newly liberated hands, his lovely smooth nails like pretty seashells. And a-ha—*no* wedding band. He rolled up his sleeves a few ticks as he ordered, and there they were, the forearms, in all their glory. Men never seem to grasp the exquisite power of this part of their anatomy; they seem to fixate entirely on another. What dummies.

I was surprised and relieved when the man requested a glass of pinot noir. I was convinced he'd do the intelligent thing: sip water for the duration of the long flight and arrive at Heathrow hydrated and refreshed. Whereas I'd be pickled, little sugar crystals forming on my nose and eyelashes.

He raised his new glass to me, his eyes gleaming, all rippling currents and oceanic tints—

"We haven't formally introduced ourselves," he said. "And it doesn't feel quite right to go on thinking of you as your alter ego."

He'd been thinking of me. Huzzah!

My alter ego?

"Shaft," he said, inclining his head.

Oh! "I'm Jane." I composed myself and touched my glass, very daintily, I thought, *to his.*

"Very pleased to meet you, Jane. Tom."

Chapter 6.

HOT FOR TEACHER

Things I learned before the meal service. Tom taught at Oxford. He had spent a week at Stanford meeting with deans about their study abroad program. And just this morning, he'd given a guest lecture there on W. H. Auden.

I chimed in, "Stop all the clocks?" which seemed to impress him, though it was actually in the film *Four Weddings and a Funeral* that I first discovered it. I told him I adored the poem but was incapable of reading it without tearing up.

"Pack up the moon and dismantle the sun," he said, gently.

The most poignant line in all. Like clockwork my eyes pricked. There followed a funny, protracted silence in which he simply looked at me. It felt as if all the clocks *had* stopped, and I experienced an irrational, almost desperate tug toward him, this stranger, seated beside me. His quiet demeanor, the reassuring geometry of his face.

Alex's house on the hill. Tiny birds darting through slashes of morning sun. Our unmade bed still warm with him as he sped to the set.

Straight into the arms of another girl.

"See." I laughed, dashing away the embarrassing tears. "I wasn't kidding." *The poem. Alex.* "But honestly, how miraculous it is that a seemingly innocent collection of words, when strung together just so, becomes—moving, sublime. And apparently *dangerous* for someone like me."

"Yes," he agreed, and for an instant, I thought he might tenderly touch my tearstained cheek. How many hours were left on this flight? I wondered. And for the first time in my thirty-three years: *Please* let there be *many*.

"I have this theory," I offered, considering, "that for some reason, we feel things more deeply, or, profoundly, on a plane. Something to do with the altitude. Or being captive, thirty thousand feet above the earth, untethered. I only know that I'll be listening to a song, or watching some in-flight movie"—*or gazing at you*— "and suddenly, I'm, well, *this*." Gesturing to my face. "But, sorry, *sorry,* you were saying—about giving a talk at Stanford."

"Right," he said, rearranging himself.

He went on to explain that he'd missed his flight from San Jose to London, but hopped the next connection through Vegas, having lost track of time chatting with students, wandering the campus, stumbling onto the Rodin garden and finding himself loath to ever leave, return to— He broke off, as if censoring himself of some confession, and my curiosity was piqued. Return where? To England? Some special someone? But then he went on to say that by the time he'd made it to the gate in Las Vegas, the airline had sold his seat, and had to make good by giving him the only remaining one on this flight, next to mine, in first class.

"Lucky me," he murmured, looking so far into my eyes, the little hummingbird inside me roused again. "Professors aren't generally flown first class."

Oh.

Tom told me he taught the Romantics, but also the Victorians and even the Moderns from time to time, and I sensed he was about to ask me what I did when a statuesque flight attendant with a platinum chignon and a clipboard appeared.

"Miss Start," she mumbled, scanning a roster, "I see you've requested a special meal. Vegetarian, is it?"

"Yes, thank you." My dear Pippa thought of everything. The flight attendant scratched me off the list without looking up and proceeded to fawn over handsome Tom, who seemed not to notice.

After she'd sashayed away, I couldn't resist. "She called you Mr. Hardy. Your name is *Tom Hardy?*"

"My parents had no idea the trouble it would be. They are very kind people actually, my parents."

"But—you're not related to Thomas Hardy?"

"I'm afraid not. My mother is a great fan of the author, though." *Ah.* He smiled. A pause. We both took sips of our drinks.

"But—hold on. There's also an actor with that—"

"Yes," he said, wearily. Suddenly remote, suddenly less shiny.

Had I annoyed this Tom Hardy? Perhaps he was simply exhausted from running through airports. Or the wine had kicked in and was having a reverse effect to mine. Or it was simply a drag to share a name with *multiple* famous people.

He kicked back a big swig and turned to me. "You haven't told me what you do, Jane Start?"

I froze. *Did I have to?* It was all so painful. And complicated. "I'm a musician."

"Oh, really?" he said, surprised.

Exactly. *I know.* I must have looked like some spoiled divorcée from Malibu, trying to look hip in my street urchin rags. Sad, really. A real musician would wear...I didn't actually know. Something iconic. Jonesy in the blue sharkskin suit. Prince in purple. Stevie swathed in floaty scarves.

Flirty Stew returned with appetizers and loitered annoyingly, tempting Tom with fancy bottles of wine. He responded to her with polite indifference and I was suffused with the most glorious sense of triumph.

"What sort of music do you play?" he asked, when at last we were alone.

"It's kind of a long story."

"It's a long flight." He gave me a soft smile.

Look at me that way, and I will tell you anything. "Shall I start at the beginning?"

"Please do."

"I was born, bred, and buttered in sunny Los Angeles." Buttering my roll and taking the tiniest bite imaginable. "To Louise Silverman Start and Arthur Start, known to all as Lulu and, yes, we do in fact call him Art Start." I went on to tell him about my parents, minimizing the stoner hippie aspect and emphasizing the Ivy League intellectual part, and their cool collaboration as an architecture and design team. And I told him about my younger brother, Will, the genius of the family who hadn't done the genius thing yet; I left out the bit about his struggle to hold down a job, or have romantic relationships. Tom was quiet, his face steady, attentive. I liked his face, *very much.* "Getting around to *music.* When we were teenagers, my brother and I had this dream of starting a punk-rock Simon and Garfunkel cover band. *I know.*"

Tom looked as if he *didn't* know.

I sang a few bars of "The Only Living Boy in New York" and broke off, embarrassed. I'd forgotten that first line involved me singing *his name,* directly *to* him, and at such an intimate distance. "So picture that with fuzz guitars and a driving throbbing beat, played really hard and fast."

Tom set down his fork. "I think it sounds lovely. The way you just sang it. Soft and slow," he said, softly and slowly.

Fuuck.

I was granted a brief reprieve with the arrival of entrees. I regained composure by pushing the mysterious mud-colored vegetarian patty around my plate and attempting to gnaw quietly on carrot sticks. But, fearing I was boring him, I began speaking rapidly—like I was reciting horrible side effects at the end of one of those drug commercials—about going to Columbia University and majoring in art and dance. "For the fairly innocent little person I was then, New York City was pretty eye-opening."

"Mmmm, I can imagine," he murmured. I was hit with a sudden light-headedness, imagining Tom imagining me as first innocent, and then not.

"So, it was there, at Columbia, you could say I found my voice. Musically. And artistically. But also, where I founded a performance art group. Naturally, we made the odd absurdist film, all a bit self-indulgent really. Lots of gratuitous nudity and drugs—you know, the usual pretentious art school fare." STOP. NOW.

But Tom tossed back the last of his pinot noir and appeared ready to say something, only for Flirty Stew to descend, refilling his glass and completely overlooking mine. She slunk away but struck a pose at the edge of the galley.

"She *fancies* you."

He followed my gaze, dismissing my proclamation with a simple, sighed, "No."

Yet we watched as she made a show of undoing her bun, releasing a mane of bleached blond, which she tossed before casting a *Whoops, you caught me* look back at Tom.

But he turned to me instead and said: "Please continue. You were up to starring in art films with gratuitous nudity and drugs-taking."

Cheeky, and his dry delivery was exquisite. Yet it sounded so much worse when *he* said it. I wondered what had happened to those films. They were probably on a hard drive somewhere, or worse, now floating in the cloud. Disconcerting. "So, I had intended to go to grad school but then Pippa, my manager, caught me performing in a little coffeehouse in Brooklyn. She introduced herself and we had the most *terrifying* chemistry, like we both might implode from it. I could tell she liked my voice, my songs, in a way that really mattered to me. If she hadn't shown up precisely then, who knows?" I shrugged, beaming at him. But Tom's expression darkened before my eyes; for a second, he seemed to disappear to some faraway place.

"Go on, Jane."

He was back. I smiled at him, relieved, and he smiled back, and I wanted to stay like this forever. I wanted to rip his wine from him and drink from the very same glass.

"Oh, and she's *British*—" I stopped short of blurting *like you* and sounding like a complete numbskull. "So, don't freak out if I say 'whilst' continuously. Something I'm in the habit of doing, from hanging out with her for so long."

He took another slow sip. "You haven't," he murmured, "said 'whilst.' But I promise I won't *freak out,* if you do." And the little lines at the corners of his eyes reappeared like lovely lacework fans.

"Oh god—I still haven't answered your question about the kind of music I play."

"Don't worry, I'm enjoying listening."

I steadied myself. "Then *you,* my friend," I returned, with stunning composure, "must be drunk."

"No," he protested. "Well...perhaps a wee bit."

"What kind of music do I play." I let out a long exhale. "Melodic alternative sixties-influenced pop. With folk, folk *rock,* and country influences sprinkled in for good measure."

His soft smile was a beautiful thing to behold.

"It's sort of moot anyway," I said, shrugging. "Most people only associate me with this one song I released a decade ago, which was a departure from what I do normally...it was a cover of a Jonesy song."

"Oh. I know him, he's *brilliant.*" Tom straightened, his whole countenance brightening.

A jolt of anxiety coursed through me. I should be used to this reaction. *Jonesy*. Rock star, musical genius, provocateur, enigma—ladies' man. I was sucked back—a small club on the Lower East Side of Manhattan. My ballet flats sticking to the gummed-up stage, a mic reeking of beer. "The one song" had just been released, so we hadn't drawn much of a crowd, when Jonesy appeared from out of nowhere like he'd dropped in from outer space. Tall and gaunt and ghostly pale: the chiseled face, the slicked platinum hair, the not-of-this-world quality as he swaggered toward me playing electric guitar, in his shimmering sharkskin suit. The audience, realizing it was *him,* surging toward the stage—

Tom's face materialized, his head in an inquiring slant.

"'Can't You See I Want You,'" I declared. He appeared thrown. "The name of the song. That I covered. Of Jonesy's? It was a pretty obscure one, and some people aren't even aware that he wrote it." From the look on Tom's face, he was one of them. "And, umm, the video for it became quite popular."

"How marvelous," he said, brow knitted. "I'm sorry, I'm not remembering—afraid I don't recall seeing the video either. But I certainly will find them."

He sounded apologetic, he looked so earnest; I wanted to tell him, *Don't.*

The cabin lights dimmed. The flight crew whisked through, removing dinner trays and assisting passengers with their flat-beds, and a terrible, awkward silence descended between us. Why had I let myself drone on? When I could have been hearing *his* life story? He withdrew a book from his bag and reclined his seat. Right. He'd politely passed the time with me through dinner. The moment of connection had passed.

But his eyes drifted back to me. He seemed poised to speak. I felt my lips part. Two birds on a wire, a hair's breadth before flight—and then his gaze slid gently away, back to the pages of his book.

*   *   *

I, in turn, watched the film *Locke* (starring none other than actor Tom Hardy), which played out like a great short story, brutally naturalistic, poignant in its lack of resolution. *My* Tom Hardy had drifted off to sleep, along with the rest of our cabin, which was now shrouded in darkness. He looked peaceful, his book, *The Paying Guests* by Sarah Waters, splayed across his chest, his footrest extended, his seat reclined.

That's when I realized I had to pee, *desperately*. It had been easy to scooch past before his seat was adjusted, but now I was trapped.

I rose and faced him. There was only one way. Thus, I found myself on tiptoes, dress hiked just shy of my crotch, straddling an expanse of man thighs so lean and solid and sturdy, I could only describe them as architectural, like the oak beams of a manor house in the English countryside, or maybe Provence. I was lured closer to him by faint notes of lavender and lime, like their gardens might hold in summertime, and from here absorbed his finer details. The way unshaven skin shaded an elegant edge of jawline. The smooth open plane of forehead, save for tender lateral etchings. The straight proud line of his nose, which made me want to run my index finger delicately along it—

A stab of light arrested me. I flinched, craned back. None other than Flirty Stew at the galley curtain, a sour look on her face.

She yanked closed the curtain and swooped brusquely past. Tom stirred, warm tectonic plates shifting beneath me, yet I managed to propel myself into the aisle without waking him, then scurried in the dark to the bathroom.

Who was the strange woman in the mirror? Okay. So maybe I had expected the me of approximately six to eight years ago. *That's* how I pictured myself madly flirting with Tom. Here in the cruel light of the airplane toilet, I saw only dark circles, a pathetic remnant of cat eyeliner, a bad case of bedhead.

That was it. No more drinking for the rest of the flight, maybe for the rest of my life.

As I again approached my seat, I found Tom awake, faintly illuminated by a reading light. He glanced up and broke into a muted, sleepy smile. I returned it, lingering until he realized I couldn't move past his outstretched legs, and he fumbled with switches to lower his footrest.

Once nestled back in my seat, I twisted to face him in the near darkness. He was already looking at me, leaning close on the shared armrest. The moment felt charged, intimate, *almost* like we were alone. I searched for something to say.

"So, you're sure you're not Tom Hardy, the *ac-tor*." I did my best BBC accent.

"Quite sure."

"You don't actually look like him at all."

"No. And he's got tattoos, loads of them, so I couldn't possibly be that Tom," he said, in a dry way that utterly charmed me.

"Hmmm," I said, setting my chin in my palm. I was grateful for the soft light, especially after what I'd witnessed in the bathroom mirror. In the silence, there was only the sound of engines purring, of white noise, and my beating heart.

"How can I be sure you don't have a little cupid on your chest?" I imagined his bare skin, his warmth beneath the frail impediment of his shirt, and when our eyes met again, he had that same soft expression, that same stillness, and I was aware of the gentle ebb and flow of his breaths. All at once, as if by a will of their own, my fingertips drifted to the top button of his shirt, when he placed his hand very gently over mine. "You don't, do you," I said.

He shook his head—the faintest suggestion of a smile about to dawn, and without thinking, with only wanting, I leaned in and kissed him very softly on the mouth.

Chapter 7.

COFFEE, TEA, OR ME

I don't know how long it went on. I had only the sense of time compressing and expanding, each melting contact strung together with soft suspended silences, parted lips, before we drifted gently back together. My entire life before this moment seemed to disengage, like the stage of a rocket that had served its purpose and was now abandoned on the ocean floor amid the shipwrecks.

"Good morning and how are we?"

I roused and sensed Tom straightening. The cabin was suddenly suffused with sun. We must have dozed off.

It was the cherubic flight attendant of the warmed nuts. "Coffee, Tea? Me?" His accent: adorable, maybe South London.

"Coffee."

"Tea." Tom spoke at the same time, and we exchanged smiles.

We had breakfast, chatting, neither of us acknowledging what had transpired in the night. In fact, we conspicuously behaved as if nothing had happened. Part of me wondered why I *wasn't* fretting, relitigating my actions, my "forward" behavior with this virtual stranger. But the fact that Tom hadn't heard my song, nor seen my video, was liberating. It meant my failure to make a comeback in a decade, not to mention my failure with Alex—felt suddenly less humiliating. We were simply two people who'd made out on a plane, in some mutual moment of fancy. I resisted, as the previous wild night in Vegas threatened to flood back, and with it a sense of myself, unhinged, drowning. And now this. *Whatever* it was, with *him*. As if to underscore that feeling, the plane hit a pocket of air and a wing dipped; I clutched the armrests. Out the window, there were starched-white clouds drifting innocently over the verdant English countryside.

"It's always a bit bumpy going through the clouds," Tom cautioned, gently.

He leaned closer for a look and I felt the heat and pressure of his forearm pressed to mine.

"Typical English weather I'm afraid, even in summer. But not to worry." As the plane continued to shudder and bounce, Tom hesitated, then placed his warm palm over mine. A beat later, he clasped my hand. I stole a glance at him.

"Thank you," I murmured.

He flicked his face to me. "It's okay, I assure you. *Everything will be okay.*" He had a muted, beatific expression, *and I believed him.*

The metallic judder of the landing gear signaled we were close, and the jolly flight attendant returned with Tom's jacket. Then he crouched in the aisle with gleaming saucer eyes.

"Miss Start, would you mind terribly if I got my picture with you? The captain is about to make us all sit, and I'd never forgive myself if I didn't ask. I'm such a *big fan!*"

"Oh...yes...of course," I said, flattered. Plus, I'd taken a shine to him.

He stared down at Tom, who appeared a bit thrown. At least now he knew I wasn't a psycho who'd fabricated her entire life story.

"Would you mind, sir?" The flight attendant extended his phone.

"Not at all," Tom said, popping up.

I found myself gripped with self-consciousness knowing Tom

was behind the camera, and wondered what expression I should make. I decided to smile for him. Only him.

"Brilliant! My mates will be so jealous!" The flight attendant bounded up, and Tom edged around him so he could return to his seat. "Thank you ever so much, sir. And you, Miss Start. I dressed as *you,* last Halloween. Pink wig and all! It's somewhere on my Instagram." He began furiously scrolling but the call came for him to be seated, and so he promptly foisted the photos of us on sour-faced Flirty Stew instead.

As we taxied to the gate, I was desperate to say something, *anything* to Tom, yet stringing words together was nearly impossible against a sudden tide of new concerns: *Heathrow. Passport Control. Baggage. Customs. Forgotten instructions from Pippa.* And my phone hadn't been charged since yesterday, nor would my charger work in the UK. *Yet in a few moments he'd be gone.* Now would be the precise moment for one or the other of us to say: "Shall we meet for a drink sometime?"

We turned to face one another, and the air seemed to vibrate with promise. My thoughts began to unspool, uncensored, and I *imagined myself saying,* "Whisk me away—somewhere, any-where, would you? And just—ravish me—fuck me, gently and expertly—"

"Jane," Tom said, unsuspecting.

Thank god the words were only in my head. This had to be some kind of delirium. Dehydration, maybe.

"It's been—I've very much enjoyed—" he said, gazing gorgeously at me. But his expression clouded, and he wriggled a buzzing iPhone from his pocket, the screen crowded with messages.

I watched as Tom sighed and repocketed the phone, then stared into space. It struck me that I knew *next to nothing* about the man I'd been kissing only hours ago...yet the very thought reanimated the thrilling pleasure-ache of those kisses.

The chime rang through the cabin, signaling that we had arrived and were free to go our separate ways.

Tom bolted up, clearing a path for me to come through to the aisle, and at last we were standing face-to-face for the very first time. I was struck by his height, the elegance of his stature, and seized with self-consciousness at my smallness, the rattiness of my clothes. Then the crush of humid bodies forced us toward the cabin door.

Inside the terminal, we were jostled in the direction of Passport Control. Trying to keep close to Tom, I was distracted when a text from Pippa popped up.

Pippa More: Have you seen the tabloids?!

Alex's engagement. How odd, I'd almost forgotten.

Jane Start: Alex and Jessica. Ugh.
Pippa More: NO! YOU AND ALFIE!

She'd attached a link: Cheating All Love heartthrob Alfie Lloyd gets lovey with mystery woman!

I stopped, dead in my tracks, and read on:

Trouble for All Love pop star Alfie Lloyd when photos surfaced of him getting lovey with a mysterious woman at an upscale Las Vegas hotel on the eve of All Love's sold-out world tour. Social media was atwitter with speculation as to who the mystery woman might be. Alfie is linked to a hometown girlfriend in Sydney. One wonders if she is feeling any love from her All Love lover now!

I scrolled quickly through a series of fuzzy photographs taken in the lobby: Alfie with his arm draped familiarly around my shoulders, my face somewhat obscured and thankfully unrecognizable to anyone besides me. And Pippa. And Alfie. And his brother Nick. And potentially even Alex. Oh, sweet revenge.

Ding!

A text from "Alfie FromOz." *As if I knew a whole bunch of Alfies.*

Alfie FromOz: Uh oh 😅 😵 Hope u arrived safely in London Maggie May. Your mate, A

My phone died as I was debating how to reply. The concourse, I realized, was empty. Where was everybody? Where was Tom?

I broke into an all-out run toward Passport Control, ending up at the back of a painfully long line, teetering on tiptoes to scan the vast, congested room.

And then I glimpsed him. Tom was in the line farthest away. His taut angular form, the sharp outline of his profile stirred me even from this distance.

I watched helplessly as he was called forward, slid his passport to the agent. He glanced over his shoulder, his eyes roving...for me? I waved, frenziedly, but I was too small, too far away.

At baggage claim, *no sign of him.* My heart sank—only a few dinged-up freight boxes and my battered rolly making lazy circles around the carousel; mercifully, the customs man waved me through.

I spied a lone driver, in a waterproof mackintosh, holding a card with my name, and sighed, grateful: Pippa had thoughtfully organized a car. I followed, sprinting to keep pace with him. Outside it had begun to pour, drenching Kurt Cobain, my canvas shoes. If I'd known dear Pippa would offer this escape from my bleak straits in LA, I would have packed differently.

"Jane!"

I froze. A plane roared overhead, its bloated shadow sweeping past like a shimmering gray whale. I stood there in the downpour, straining for the voice again but heard only the murmur of engines and rain.

"Miss Start?" The driver was looking at me like I was crazy, from under the cover of the parking structure.

I continued on and collapsed into the back of the town car feeling utterly hopeless. Had I dreamed him? It was as if Tom had vanished like disappearing ink in the downpour.

"Jane." This time the driver, already closing the door, heard it too. "Jane. Wait."

It was him, several feet away, soaked and breathless, his suitcase and beat-up leather bag at his feet, each in its own small pool of rainwater.

"Hi," he sighed. That pained smile, those gray-green eyes gleaming even in the gloom of the carpark.

The driver slunk away to give us privacy.

"Hi," I said, leaning forward, easing open the door to see him better.

"We hadn't said goodbye, properly," he said, stepping closer.

"Yes—no," I said, climbing lightly from the car and gliding to him. "We didn't."

I was damp and shivery, delirious at the sight of him. Any twinges of self-consciousness about my appearance would have to be ignored.

"It's rather strange but I—" He wavered; the sound of a plane rumbling overhead filled the silence.

"Let me give you my number," I said.

"Yes," he said, relieved, and patted his pockets for his phone.

I took it from him, and smiling down, tapped myself into his contacts.

Chapter 8.

SWEATS

"Jane. You need to get up off the sofa *now*."

Pippa was staring down at me, a laundry basket tucked under her arm. "You're meant to be—"

"Writing. I know. The guitar is right there." It lay prostrate on the living room floor, as if passed out drunk, or dead. "But *this,* right now," I said, muting the volume on the TV, "is research. For a song. I did start something I'm pretty excited about." A lie. I had started ten things over the past two weeks, all garbage. But I hated to let her down. She'd flown me here, put me up in her lovely flat—a stylish mix of crisp modern and comfy boho, with an open floor plan living room/kitchen that faced a garden, streaming with sunlight. And yet, here I was with nothing but ennui.

"Excellent," she said, encouraged, and thunked the basket onto the coffee table beside my brand-new copy of *The Paying Guests*. The closest I'd come to Tom since landing in London. There hadn't been a peep on my phone, so naturally I'd had no choice but to binge-watch dark Scandinavian thrillers, edgy 1970s classics, and every extant version of *Jane Eyre*.

Pippa sighed. "Bingeing telly is a known depressant."

"I know," I said, feigning effusive agreement, and switched

it off. "And you're so right. Thanks, again, for letting me stay. Longer than originally planned." She dismissed this with a wave and a smile.

I glanced at my phone, still inert, on the coffee table. "Why did I stupidly put my number in his phone under John Shaft? *Why?*"

She gave me a *Really? Again?* look.

"I'm convinced it's why he hasn't called. I mean *anyone* would find it confusing. But I just thought, at the time, *John Shaft, Jane Start*. Same initials. It was meant to be a clever recall of our first conversation. Can you blame me for thinking someone of his intelligence and higher education would put it together?"

Pippa gazed at me with renewed pity.

"You should have seen his face when I gave him my number. I can't even *begin* to describe it."

"But you have," she said, wearily. "You've rendered him like a police artist sketch. Painted him in oils like a Delacroix or a Vermeer, so vividly I'm sure I'd recognize Tom Hardy, Oxford professor, if I passed him on the street. Or on the wall, at the Louvre. But, *Jane.* You really must begin to think about moving on. And if I'm honest..." She steeled herself with a cleansing breath. "The likelihood he'll call, now? I'll just say it. Very low." The old "two weeks" rule.

"*You* weren't standing there dripping wet in the carpark, witnessing the look on his face. Experiencing *the feeling* of that look. The *frisson.*"

"I know. I do understand. But dare I remind you, that once upon a time, you experienced that same *frisson* with—"

"Alex. Yeah." *Not. Even. Close.*

I thought of the wrap party for Alex's last film. A vulgar downtown club, all metal girders, like a prison. Alex and Jessica had towered over me. I'd wished I'd thought to wear heels. Terrible music throbbed through the sound system, and Jessica's lips were continually close to his ear, murmuring some inside joke. I'd given up trying to insert myself, feeling only the agitation particular to this sort of party and deliberating when I might acceptably make my escape, even if it were Alex's "job" as producer to stay, to banter with "his actress." That was when it had struck me. The way she grasped his arm, with those treacherous, black-lacquered talons, and his easy slouch, hands jammed in his pockets. Their hips were just shy of touching. The familiarity, the intimacy of their body language. When I'd noticed, beneath her fitted blazer, she'd had on Alex's white T-shirt. The one he'd relegated to sleeping in for its obvious red wine stain. There it was, damned spot, in the shape of a pink-petaled peony, splashed across her patently perfect bosom.

When I'd peered up, she was gaping at me, indignant, like *Ew, your pervy girlfriend's staring at my tits.* I'd turned to Alex and witnessed the moment of his realization, when he knew that I knew.

"Jane."

"What," I barked, unintentionally.

"Is there something you want to tell me?" Pippa's brow cinched. She extended me a coffee.

"No." I accepted the mug and slugged some back, still shaken.

"How about we get you dressed and off the sofa?" she offered with the air of a preschool teacher embroiled in a protracted negotiation with a four-year-old. "I've washed and folded your things, because quite simply, I love you. And also, you've been wearing my sweats for days and I really do need them back. I'm off to an appointment with that fab new trainer. And those are my only good ones."

Why does everyone only ever have *one* good pair of sweats?

"But they're so soft and cozy." I snuggled myself deeper into the sofa.

"Jane! Do whatever you want!" She was suddenly genuinely exasperated. "I don't care. Go ahead. Masturbate all day long if you must. I just need my sweats." She planted her fists on her hips.

"Is it that obvious?"

"No," she cried, looking at me like I was insane. "You told me."

"Oh. I forgot. *You see.*" Tapping the side of my noggin. "There is something wrong with my brain." She wasn't having any of it. And it pained me to see her fraught. "I suggest you wash these first," I exhaled, hoisting myself up and slipping defiantly out of her sweats, tugging down my T-shirt to cover my naked lower half. I extended them to her, dangling from my fingertips. "If not, it will be the closest we ever come to being lesbian lovers."

She stared coolly back.

"Perhaps we should?" I said, giving her sweats a little wiggle.

"Might jeopardize our friendship—our work relationship."

I would be dead without Pippa. "Too right," I agreed, a grin creeping in.

"And this new trainer, Lawrence," she said, the old twinkle returning to her eye. "Mmm, gorgeous. And brilliant. Studying for a PhD in international relations." Her gaze drifted south, to the guitar on the rug. "When do I hear the song?"

"Soon. Yup. Very, very soon."

Once she'd departed, I picked up the guitar but found I had nothing to say, to sing. It was as if all of the tender yearnings, all of the epiphanic moments I'd collected, dissected, protected in the hard drive of my brain for this very purpose, had been erased in some cataclysmic user error. And if no reboot were possible, it'd mean the worst. That I'd lied to Pippa, my family, my friends, myself: I *never did* have the goods to write, and never would.

The truth was, I missed it. I missed how I'd felt composing my second record—getting lost in the story, puzzling out the right rhymes, reproducing the pictures that bloomed in my mind. A madwoman sprawled on the floor surrounded by Post-its, scribbled with lines. Music was the beginning, the middle, the end of each day. It was oxygen. It was hope and comfort and love, and *lust*. I found myself musing on rhymes that went with *Tom,* but only came up with *wrong* and *gone* before I decided to get a jump on season three of my BBC crime drama.

"How was Larry? I'm calling him that now," I said, over my shoulder to Pippa, home from her workout. I clicked off the TV and made myself vertical.

"Larry's engaged. Never mind. Sometimes I wonder why I bother." She pitched her gym bag and keys to the floor.

"Oh no."

"Yup. Same old same old. Me essentially humiliating myself in front of some fit gorgeous man whilst he blathers on about the highs and woes of his day, Larry's sudden engagement being a very high high for him. Speaking *of*—a little pot would be nice if I could get my hands on some." She plopped down beside me on the sofa.

"He'd probably be weirdly athletic in bed if it makes you feel any better," I said.

"Exactly. And it *does*. Thanks," she said.

"Definite turnoff."

"It's not bloody yoga."

"I should hope not."

"You don't need to show off. 'Oh, look at me,'" she said, imitating his Birmingham accent. "'I can make my body into a pretzel.' Well, good for you. He's vastly less sexy now that we're calling him Larry," she sighed, and flopped her head to me.

"Yes." I flopped mine to her.

"Gah. Enough about engaged people."

A tabloid with Alfie and his "mystery woman" on the cover stared up from the coffee table at us. Buried inside was the blurb about Alex and Jessica's engagement, and their film, ludicrously titled *Universe Exploding*.

"Yeah. Go fuck yourself, engaged people," I said.

At this very moment, Tom was somewhere on this island,

somewhere in Great Britain. The thought resuscitated a low-down, stirring ache.

"Chardy?" Pippa clapped her palms to her thighs and popped back up.

"Do you even need to ask?"

Pippa clattered around in the kitchen and rejoined me on the sofa with two glasses and the wine. I made a toast, to us, for not being annoying engaged people who droned on about color schemes and diamond rings. She smiled, glowing and lovely, and I thought, *Shame it didn't work out with Lawrence the trainer*. There was no one more deserving of love and companionship than Pippa.

Her mobile chimed and she groaned, stretching an arm lazily out to grab it. "Hello. *Yes?* This is Pippa More." She shot me a funny look. "Who's this?" she asked, our eyes still locked. The color ebbed from her face. She glanced at the caller ID. "Oh. Right. Well, yes. Of course. I'd be happy to speak with him. Why, hello there." She bolted up, wine sailing over the rim of her glass.

I whisked it from her and parked both of our drinks on the coffee table.

She palmed the receiver and whispered, emphatic: *"It's Jonesy."*

What? My heart gave a hard thud in my chest. Why the devil would he call? It'd been a decade since his team had last been in touch.

"Oh, I see. The Royal Albert Hall? November?" She was boring a hole into me. "Right. Well, of course I'll have to check her schedule," she said smoothly.

Impressive comeback. As if my schedule were jammed.

"You'd like to speak with her." She widened her eyes at me.

I waved *NO,* retreating, and thumped, unnerved, into the armchair.

"I'm afraid she's not here at the moment. *Right.* Got it. Top secret. *Ab-so-lute-ly.* Oh—okay—bye now—bye-bye." She peered up from her phone, astonished, and clapped a hand over her mouth.

"Was it really?"

"*It really was!*" She giggled, the shock, the madness—Jonesy *himself* cold-calling her mobile—beginning to sink in. "That *voice*. Unmistakable. I'd forgotten it was so different from—"

"His singing voice. I know, right?"

"One expects, dunno, Dracula, but then, he sounds shockingly adolescent."

I nodded, agreeing, even as adrenaline coursed violently through me. Pippa dashed to grab her computer, and I thought back. There *had* been something shockingly adolescent about him even ten years ago, when he was closer to thirty. Not only his voice, but *him,* as a person. The obvious entitlement, the outlandish bravado—a shrink would have a field day. But also, his cryptic way of talking, the sly insinuating looks. But of course, when things took their turn, *how dare I think he was coming on to me? How dare I think he was flirting?* I'd been left feeling shame, like it had all been my projection.

I had a sudden disconcerting thought: How did Jonesy know I was here, in London, *now?*

I glanced out at the garden, half expecting to see him standing there, expressionless, like a hologram vibrating in a shaft of sunlight. Tall and gaunt, with the pale fragility of a Gainsborough, suited in blue satin. *This was madness.* The thought of Jonesy and me, together in the present tense, had made me faint and faintly nauseous.

That night he'd first materialized to watch me play his song, on the Lower East Side, I'd been invited to celebrate with him afterward. I was whisked to his Manhattan penthouse along with his glamorous entourage. I assumed they'd join us in the private elevator . . . but they froze when Jonesy and I entered, standing blank-faced, like zombies in the marbled alcove as the doors slid shut. Suddenly, it was just him, and me, and silence. I felt tricked, duped. I'd hoped Pippa and my bandmates Alastair and James might join us later but now I was alone with him in that claustrophobic mirrored box, my eyes glued to the numbers rising higher and higher, his image looming from every conceivable reflection, if I dared look.

The elevator doors slid open onto a grand foyer, jerky with candlelight. I followed him into a funereal wall of floral sweetness—he must own the entire floor. There was no party. No murmuring fashionistas in Pucci-patterned silks, no caterers in black, no tinkling trays of champagne sailing past. Only the perfect silence of skyscrapers, of triple-paned glass and wraparound views. Only him, and me.

"I can't believe it, the Royal Albert Hall," Pippa thrummed, jubilant, perched once more at the edge of the sofa and clacking away at her laptop. "Fuck. If only my assistant hadn't suddenly chucked off. Maternity leave. How dare she? Kidding, of course."

I blinked. I was in London, in Pippa's flat, summer sun flooding in from garden doors.

"He wants you to perform with him. Sounds a bit vague, what he has in mind for you to do, but my god, this is thrilling. Ten years! I *knew* I brought you here for a reason." She grinned up, beamy; a second chance, she meant, for success.

"I dunno." I rose and began to pace. "I mean, the likelihood of me being bad at this sort of high-profile show is very high, especially *now*. All it takes is one dodgy moment on stage and you're reduced to an embarrassing YouTube clip you can *never* escape. Something no one ever seems to grasp, apart from internet trolls."

"You'll be brilliant. Of that I'm sure," she said, obviously trying to appease me.

She *knew* I'd battled stage fright my entire career. How would I cope with it there, beside Jonesy, after all these years? His talent was supernatural, intimidating, but it went deeper still: that long-ago night, in his penthouse, when things had taken a bewildering turn. The truth was that I'd never told Pippa, after. I'd never been sure *what* to tell Pippa.

I gulped. I needed to at least appear thoughtful, reasonable: "The truth is, I'm honestly only capable of being good in small venues anymore. I don't have the gravitas, the swagger for a big fancy stage. I never really did, even in the 'heyday.' I somehow managed it, but I'm not, *Bono,*" I reasoned, "or one of those artists who exudes...*bravado*. Who can saunter out and be commanding. Clubs, yes, *those* I can do. You *know* that. But the Royal Albert Hall. *Jonesy.* The complexity of that alone?"

But Pippa did what managers do when their clients have crises of faith.

"Stay calm. Give it a think," she said, evenly. "And for what it's worth I disagree. You mustn't sell yourself short. And anyway, I've bought you time. I'm checking your very packed schedule, remember?" She sounded as staid and resolute as the queen. But then she raised her brows and grinned. "And just when we thought it had all gone to shit."

The toilet paper ad. As if I needed reminding.

Chapter 9.

TINY BUBBLES

The following morning, Pippa and I met up with our dear friends Alastair Ekwensi and James McCloud at a café in Primrose Hill. I'd barely seen them since we toured together a decade ago, and now they burst through the sun-blasted entry with their five-year-old, Georgia. All three were immaculately dressed and preposterously cool: Alastair, in a sky-blue summer suit, which set off his gorgeously dark skin, and James, freckled and suntanned in beachy trousers and huarache sandals, dirty blond hair falling over his Buddy Holly glasses. Georgia had on black leggings and a black sleeveless turtleneck, like Edie Sedgwick, or some cool 1950s existentialist.

Georgia beelined straight for Pippa for a hug, then clambered onto a chair and set about removing art supplies from a tote with great conviction. She seemed not to notice the stranger beside her.

"I'm Jane," I ventured. "You probably don't remember me."

She glanced up. "I don't remember you," she said bluntly, and returned to arranging crayons by color group on the table.

"The polite thing to say is 'Pleased to meet you,'" murmured James gently. Alastair darted a tacit *My daughter's kind of a bitch, hopefully she'll grow out of it* look, and I rose to give first him and then James lingering overdue hugs.

Alastair, James, and Pippa had been classmates at Cambridge and remained close ever since. Pippa had had the intuition to put me together with them when our journey as manager and artist first began. Had she not, "the one song" might never have become "the one song." I'd wanted to radically reinvent the style and feel of Jonesy's lesser-known recording, a stripped-down solo piano ballad about yearning and unrequited love. It had meant the world to me when Alastair and James had endorsed my take: to replace the piano with guitar. To make Jonesy's underlying groove a danceable beat with real drums and a hypnotic bass line. And lastly to slather on church choir harmonies, as if they were the delicious icing atop a layer cake. But it was the duo's brilliant production savoir faire, the sonic snap and crackle they gave to the record, to which I credited the song's success.

Lattes arrived, and conversation turned to Alex, the three other adults exchanging digs to express their indignation and their solidarity. Three weeks ago, it might have cheered me, but I was preoccupied thinking about Tom. His eyes gleaming even in the gloom of the rain. How had he simply vanished?

"Jane? Thoughts?"

Alastair was staring at me in the sharp morning light.

"You're awfully quiet, for you," he said. He always knew. "The studio? Tomorrow?" Clearly repeating the question. "I hear you're working on new songs."

"You're welcome to borrow any of our gear, if you fancy," added James.

"Oh. Yeah," I said, bluffing. "That sounds *great*." Why did the kindness of friends make lying worse?

"Excellent. Now that that's settled, a little birdie let slip some frightfully scintillating news," Alastair said in a silkier tone.

"A recent adventure. With a person of great interest," chimed James.

All three took synchronized sips of latte. I glanced at Georgia, intensely focused, drawing, naturally, a little birdie. So, they were talking in code. Person of great interest. They had to mean Alfie. All Love's song had just leapt to number one in the UK. Alfie and Nick were international heartthrobs, their faces splashed all over the British tabloids. And my face too, if you knew where to look.

"It was really more *mis*adventure. I blame Vegas and *way* too much—" I felt a light kick under the table. Pippa was imperceptibly shaking her head. Okay. So, she wanted whatever happened in Vegas with Nick Lloyd to stay in Vegas. Pippa was infuriatingly discreet, yet this quality spoke to her good character. She had to have been dying to tell them about the Royal Albert Hall, the top-secret Jonesy offer. *I* certainly was, though the mere thought made my heart race. The thrill, *the dread*. But there would be hell to pay with Jonesy if we uttered a word before we'd signed off.

"On the plane ride to London," James clarified.

"Distinguished older chap?" Alastair raised a brow. "And rather more...substantial?" He was coining Pippa's favorite new descriptor.

"Tweed jacket. Leather patches on the elbows?" James adjusted his glasses.

"There weren't any patches," I said.

"And an Oxford don. Spill the dirt, you tiny minx," insisted Alastair. "According to the little birdie, things got rather hot and heavy over the Atlantic with Mr. Tweed. Or shall we call him Patches?"

"I hear someone's joined the Mile-High Club?"

I gaped at Pippa.

"I said snogged," she said vehemently, frowning. "Not shagged."

"Let me set the record straight. I was not, nor have I ever been, a member of the Mile-High Club."

"Ah well, there's a disappointment," sighed Alastair.

Georgia turned to Pippa, her eyes wide. "Have *you* joined the Mile-High Club?"

"Nooo," Pippa exclaimed, reddening. "None of us have, darling. It's not a proper kind of club, like, a soccer club, or a squash club, it's a grownup thing. But not for grownups like any of us." The child appeared satisfied and resumed coloring. Pippa collapsed forward onto the table and mouthed: *Fuck.*

"I didn't imagine it," I said, an unwelcome quaver in my voice. "There was a deep connection. He has my number, but nothing. It's been over two weeks and I know. I know what that means." Pippa, Alastair, and James stared back with pity. My eyes began to well. *Not in front of the girl.*

"Perhaps we should switch to wine, or something stiffer," Alastair suggested, scanning for a waitperson. "It's past noon."

"Finished." Georgia turned to me and held up her drawing. I was touched. So this was why people had children.

"Do you like it?"

"I *more* than like it. I love it." I meant it. The kid had real talent.

"Would you like to trade for it?"

"You mean *I* make *you* a picture?"

"For that," she said, coolly, pointing to my backpack. Her parents began to protest. But her shrewdness had jolted me from woe. Besides, I genuinely adored her drawing.

"Deal. But *first,* let me just empty my things." I flipped the backpack upside down for comic effect and issued a river of junk onto the table, delighting her.

"It's yours, my friend."

She clutched it, beaming, to her chest, then frowned. "It's buzzing."

My phone!—captive in some overlooked inner compartment, and *buzzing!* It was too early for anyone in America to be calling, so it might be him.

Tom Hardy, Oxford professor, calls at long last!

I wrestled the bag from her tiny clutches, tore open the zippers, and grabbed ahold of my phone.

"Sorry, Georgia," I said, contrite.

"Don't leave us hanging," Alastair insisted.

I slid the phone slowly to the center of the table. "Unrecognized number. No caller ID. No voicemail. A call that just so happens to come from"—lifting my palm like a poker player revealing her hand—*"Oxford UK."*

The eruption of voices was pierced only by the sound of a text. We nearly knocked heads diving to see the screen.

Unknown Number: Hi, Jane. It's Tom, from the plane. I hope you're well?

"Sweet Jesus," cried James, flinging himself back, nearly capsizing his chair. "He lives!"

"Okay, if I'm honest," said Alastair, crossing his arms, "I expected something a bit more, scintillating."

"Like what?" demanded James.

"Dunno. Something cerebral, poetic."

"Shut up," Pippa hissed. "Let Jane think. *Every. Word. Counts.*"

Precisely. Every word *did* count. I studied his text: *It's Tom, from the plane. I hope you're well?* Right. Pretty straightforward.

The three adults rose, quietly gathered around me, leaned forward en masse as I clacked out a reply.

Jane Start: I didn't know Oxford professors used text messaging. I thought you sent messages via house owl.

I hesitated, despite their murmured approvals, my index finger suspended over the send trigger. What I'd written was silly. Surely I could do better? I was thrust unexpectedly forward; Georgia had muscled in, setting off the equivalent of a fender bender. My hand slipped. There followed the unmistakable sound of a sent text.

Tiny bubbles appeared on my screen. I felt a rush of endorphins. *Tom Hardy of Oxford writes!*

Georgia was plucked like a kitten by its scruff and plunked onto her chair.

Glued to the screen, I felt as if my soul had detached from my corporeal form. I felt that if this were a movie, the camera would be shooting us from above, as Don Ho's crooned classic "Tiny Bubbles" played. How could I feel this way about a man I hardly knew? How could the music in my head be so right? So perfect? And why, damn it, were the text bubbles starting and stopping, then disappearing altogether, leaving only my embarrassing juvenile joke?

Ding.

Unknown Number: No. But we do wear robes. I have a closet full of them.

"I wonder what else he's got in his closet," murmured Alastair.

"Cor," said James, under his breath.

Pippa was biting her nails, thinking.

Ding.

Unknown Number: Would you like to see?

Oh my.

Pippa emitted a shrill shriek, and the café went eerily silent. "That says it all, doesn't it," she pronounced like a judge banging her gavel. The burble of customer voices began to reanimate.

"Cheeky. I love him already. What now?" said Alastair, gazing determinedly at me.

"Fuck." *My move.* My thumbs twitched over the phone again.

"Someone owes me fifty p," said Georgia flatly, glancing up from another drawing. She was summarily ignored.

I gazed at my phone and suddenly the sun-drenched room seemed to dissolve away, and it was only Tom and me, the purr of engines, the cabin lights dimmed. *Tiny bubbles.* I filled the empty text box with the only two words that made any sense.

Jane Start: Yes. Please.

We tumbled into sunshine outside the café, giddy and animated, even Georgia, who clutched my backpack proudly. And there to serenade us, as if we'd conjured him, was a busker. He had a guitar, and a little drum rig he played with his feet, when a familiar melody struck me. He was doing "Can't You See I Want You."

We stopped in our tracks. How mad, the timing. Alastair shot me a look: *You HAVE to.* On any other day, not a chance, but I was still buzzing with endorphins. A feeling like floating, the promise of seeing Tom again! Thinking of him, I found myself joining in, singing out, for the pure pleasure of it, for this improbable occasion to seize the day, to surrender to the singular focus, to become *her,* a girl who dared to stand on a street corner and belt out Jonesy's song of love and of lust to any passerby who'd care to listen. And the busker was extraordinary. We started to draw a crowd.

"Man, you sound just like her," he said, grinning, once we'd finished and the crowd had dispersed. Pippa darted me a look.

"I've been told that," I replied. But Georgia had sidled up, she'd grasped ahold of my hand. And just when I thought this day couldn't possibly get better.

"Take some of this—I insist." The busker extended his coin basket, now overflowing.

"No, I couldn't possibly." I waved it away. "The pleasure was all mine."

Chapter 10.

FIRST DATE

This outfit was wretched. Rejects from Pippa's closet were heaped around my feet, and I had a train to *Oxford* to catch.

"Remind me," Pippa said from the edge of her bed, studying my reflection, "what you know about Patches?"

I shot her an exasperated look. "Okay, that's the last time anyone calls him Patches." I undid the top button of my blouse and then buttoned it up again. "Stupidly *I* did all the talking. He might be married with four children."

"Or a serial killer," she said. "Do text once you're there so I know you're safe. And if you have the slightest intuition he *is* a serial killer, run, Jane, run. Your return tickets." She waved them and set them atop the nightstand. "And that's the outfit."

"You sure?" I spun around, unconvinced. I wore the fruits of a frenzied Zara shop, and a cardigan from Pippa's closet. "It's not me, trying overtly to look attractive? Or what I think, assume, a man, another human, would find attractive? Also, I hate my underwear. I have no good underwear. *Not* that it's going to matter. *No one* will see." I raised my skirt so she could: frumpy cotton briefs of a vintage floral pattern, at best like something a 1950s ingenue might wear, at worst, your grandmother. But it was a hot summer day and they were breathable, and roomy. "I don't know how you wear those lacy, thong-y, claustrophobic things when you don't absolutely have to." And when no one's around to see, I thought, for it had been ages since Pippa'd had a boyfriend, and she really *did* wear sexy underwear every day. I found that both unthinkable and, honestly, a little aspirational.

"As you wish," she said, a brow raised. "And perhaps avoid using *fuck* and *shit* in place of words which actually describe things and make you sound intelligent. Which you are." She was looking at me like she really meant it. For a second I thought I might cry. I would die without Pippa. "And don't order salad. High possibility of ending up with green bits stuck to your teeth. Trust me, not good."

I was twenty minutes late as I threaded my way through the bustling dining room of the Reading Room Café in Oxford. I was instantly charmed by its bookish Bloomsbury ambience; the luscious gray walls crowded with antique oils, and bookcases cramped with well-worn volumes. But there was no sign of the professor amid the professorial-looking clientele.

Jittery with expectation and a sudden unmanageable shyness, I continued toward a glowing span of windows with a view of a sunlit patio and froze. He was sitting some distance away at a small table, gazing out at a river, so close it seemed to kiss the deck's edge. Visible, too, was an ancient bridge of honeyed stone that arched across tranquil waters, and on the opposite bank, a meadow of emerald green. I could just make out one of Oxford's Gothic colleges, dusky in the distance. Yet even catching only a sliver of his profile, a mere glimpse, my heart did a gymnast's flip. There was something elusive and thrilling even from here…the sleek, sturdy architecture of him.

There he was, the stranger from the plane.

All at once, I felt unhinged. I'd begun to fear I had invented our connection—projected onto him all of my feelings in the wake of our singularly strange and dreamlike night. Yet in this moment, the memory of kissing those lips reanimated—a sensation akin to being swept into the arch of a wave, of weightlessness. But the recollection was too intimate to be having right *now,* standing *here.* I needed to gather my wits about me—to put one foot in front of the other and get my ass over there. How late I was! I dismissed a quick instinct to dash to the ladies' room, to check the status of my hair, my face—hopefully a crop of pimples hadn't time-traveled from adolescence.

Tom rose unexpectedly and was chatting now with a man in an elegant suit, who seemed to have appeared out of thin air. Their exchange intensified, became fraught when the man patted Tom's upper arm, almost consolingly. Looking a little dazed, Tom sank down in his chair. The man was now heading straight toward me, his gaze lowered, texting. But he stopped, sensing I'd blocked his way, and inched aside, half bowed, with a theatrical sweep of his arm, like an old-fashioned gallant, as if to say, *You are free to pass, m'lady.*

A bit perplexed, I approached the table, and Tom, sensing me, bolted up. Instinctively I bounced onto tiptoes as he bent down to give me a polite kiss on the cheek. But it all went a bit wrong, awkward and misaligned.

Well done, right out of the starting gate. Pull it together, bitch.

We gazed at each other for a stunned beat before he whisked out my chair, and in unison, we took our seats.

"I think I may have just kissed the side of your nose. I sort of...overcorrected." I smiled, deciding to tuck my hands between my thighs for safekeeping, but he simply looked on serenely, his eyes searching. I thought I might come apart like a dandelion in a breeze, but then he smiled back. Somehow, it's a much bigger deal when a serious person smiles at you. "I guess I'm a little nervous." There. Said it. Not twenty seconds in.

"I'm nervous, too," he said without hesitation.

I was taken aback. "You *are?* Why?"

"I'm not entirely sure," he said, still smiling. Above the river there were clouds that might have been painted by Magritte, pinned to a crisp summer sky and mirrored in its waters. "Seeing you in the real world. It's strange, rather, meeting someone on a plane. Something surreal about it, up there, suspended above the earth, above the clouds. *Your* theory."

He remembered.

"An alternate universe," I offered, a bit tritely.

"Yes," he said. "And I wasn't sure I'd find you...in this one." I felt the corners of my lips rise and my cheeks color. "I'm glad you're here, Jane."

Oh god. The accent, the smile. The way he said my name. He had no earthly idea how glad I was.

"I'm glad, *too,*" I finally managed.

Glad schmad. I was *ecstatic.* Doing-fist-pumps-in-my-mind-level ecstatic. *Calm yourself, woman.*

Tom cleared his throat, filled our glasses from a bottle of sparkling water. We both took sips, our eyes locked, and there was only him and me, the perfection of this serene pastoral setting.

"FASTER, YOU FUCKING CUNTS!"

Suddenly crew boats were upon us, speeding past from out of nowhere. *FUCKING CUNTS* lingered painfully over our heads long after they'd vanished.

Tom creaked back a little in his chair, as if taking me in, and all at once I was mortified by my outfit. Especially *here,* amid the urbane university crowd. I had on a Peter Pan–collared blouse, pleated skirt, Pippa's navy cardigan, and *Oxford* loafers. Talk about on the nose. How had she let me out of the house?

"You're a perfect fit here," he said. "Perhaps a boater hat and book bag to complete the picture."

"And for it to be 1964." I placed my clasped hands primly on the table because I was wearing a goddamned schoolgirl outfit and would just have to cope.

"Shall we look?" he said, eyeing the menus.

"Yes." I practically erupted with relief.

When the waitress arrived, Tom ordered grilled salmon as I scoured for something vegetarian. ("Today's Specials" were Crispy Terrine of Ham Hock, Cockles of the Day, and Roast Rump of Lamb.) A rogue bead of perspiration originated between my breasts and trickled lazily down, inspiring other like beads to do the same. The lamb special came with a baked potato and salad so I ordered that, "without the lamb." Then I heard Pippa's voice in my head, warning about green bits. "Or the salad. Thank you."

The waitress furrowed her brow. "So... just the potato?"

Tom looked concerned.

"No, I think..." I flipped rapidly through the menu, past some extremely appetizing salads. "I'll just have the cheese pizza. If it's okay to order from the children's menu."

"Yes, ma'am. As you please. Cheese pizza. From the children's menu."

"And we'd like some wine," said Tom. Good man.

Things we discussed before food: Tom's job. Maybe other stuff. I was distracted by a sensation of steam rising cartoonishly and, I feared, visibly from the top of my head for I was still *anxious.* How I longed for things to work out with him. And oh, how *beautiful* he was. *My god, listen to yourself, you desperate fool.* Wagering *everything.* Betting all your chips *on him.* What were the odds we'd amount to anything? And where was the wine, damnit?

Oh. But he was smiling at me now. I couldn't tear my eyes from his. *Why would I?* I could stay like this forever.

At last, the waitress swooped in with a large tray.

"Here you are. Pizza for m'lady, and salmon for you, sir. And *more wine.*" Darting me a covert look of sisterly encouragement, she filled my glass to the brim.

I wasted no time downing a healthy amount before determining the pizza, quartered into enormous gooey slices, was impossible to eat with any modicum of grace. There was nothing for it but to pick up knife and fork.

"In Britain, we eat pizza with our bare hands," he said, watching me saw away. "Like barbarians."

"*Really,*" I said. "In California we use a knife and fork. That's how we do it."

"Very civilized of you. I adore California, by the way."

I stopped, peered up, remembering what he'd said on the plane. That he was "loath to leave." I hoped California *girls* might be one of the reasons, too. (Los Angeles was in fact teeming with British ex-pats. I'd tried to convince Pippa to come west, without success.)

"And I adore England." I smiled, sawing once more.

"Do you? That's lovely. How long will you be here?"

"Not sure...staying with my friend...you know, my manager, Pippa. It's somewhat open-ended." Not really. I'd been in England over two weeks. Pippa was probably booking my return flight home, this very moment. "I'm meant to be working. Recharging my batteries, creatively speaking." Finally, I sectioned off a lady-like piece and lifted it to my lips.

"HARDER—FASTER—STROKE—STROKE!"

The rowers were back.

I followed Tom's cue and attempted to chew delicately as sunlight washed over us, the willows along the banks softly swaying—

"RAMMING SPEED—LEGS—HIPS—TO THE FINISH, BOYS!"

"I had no idea they'd be out today," Tom exhaled, apologetic, once they'd finally vanished. "I hope this doesn't put you off Oxford. More evidence of our barbarism. But you were saying. About re-charging your batteries, creatively. How do you go about that?"

"Good question." *How did I?* I could hardly remember, I'd been blocked for so long. "I guess, at first, I try and make myself still. And I don't mean still as in lying on the couch, bingeing things, mostly dark things, which I happen to be attracted to. What I mean is, still my thoughts. Which have a habit of zooming every which way." I took another drink of the wine, and savored it on my lips, my tongue, feeling its heat all down my chest, and lower still.

"Mmm," he said, resting his elbows on the table, leaning closer. Sunlight streamed over him; his expression, his entire being, was warm and open and inviting, and I couldn't push away a picture of the two of us, dry humping on a plush blanket of wildflowers, in a nearby wood. "Tell me more." He was gazing at me with such soft, penetrating directness.

"Oh yes," I said, and then somehow, *here,* with *him,* it came flooding back. "Well, it's usually a melody that refuses to go away, like it's haunting me, but in a good way. But then, if I'm lucky, words arrive to match the feeling. And best of all, and this is *rare,* is when I braid them together and I'm singing? And it feels almost out-of-body. As if the sound, and the song, has a life of its own, and I'm just the vessel through which it's released into the air. Like freeing a bird from her cage."

And just then, a band of tiny birds winged fast and low across the dappled waters, drawing our attention. How *blissful* it was to be here with him.

"You were saying?"

"Right." I straightened. "When it feels like that, I think *wow,* this one might actually be good." My fingers caressed the stem of my glass. "But then typically self-doubt creeps in, and I just don't want to—" I hesitated, remembering Pippa's caution about swear words. "To blow it."

Somehow in the time I was babbling, he'd managed to roll up his shirtsleeves, and his lovely naked forearms were exposed once more. I felt myself tugged forward as to a magnet, my ribs pressed to the table edge, my whole body canted toward him and the sound of the river lapping gently against the banks. I settled my hands very lightly atop his where he'd rested them on the table, and then skimmed my fingertips farther up, tingling a path beyond his wrists, over the steady expanse beyond. He closed his eyes, his warm skin and sand-colored hairs prickling, his sculpted muscles growing taut beneath my fingers, which made me want to wrap them around his forearms as far as they could go, and hold him firmly for a moment, so I did. He opened his eyes, and in the clear light of summer, his opal irises seared into me, and I retraced my path, to memorize the solid radius and temperature of him, before finally letting go.

"Sorry. I'm sorry," I said, coming to from my trance. "I've been wanting to do that—"

"No," he said, shaking his head. "Please don't be... *Jane*."

But I could hardly contain what his gaze did to me, or hearing him say my name that way. I *believed* him. I hadn't invented our connection. He'd felt it too.

We strolled—*I* levitated—over fairy-tale cobbled streets, blurring past storefronts painted creamy hues and window boxes tangled with ripe summer blooms. The air was faintly tingling, the bells of Oxford ringing an enchantingly dissonant tune. He began to tell me about his youth, the only child to hardworking schoolteacher parents in the north of England—how he'd disappear into books to stave off loneliness. He gently grasped my hand, as if impelled by this sentiment.

I stopped and gazed up at him. Without thinking I asked, "Do you live nearby?"

Oh god, what am I doing?

He held my eyes and a skittering warmth, like sunlight when it dances on a wave or flickers through treetops, scintillated through me.

"I do," he said. Several students swerved past on bicycles, laughing. "Not far from here."

How impossibly, deliciously tranquil he was. *Now look what you've done,* I thought. Yet I couldn't help smiling up at him. He smiled in turn. That wondering expression, like from the plane.

"Would you like to...?"

"Yes," I broke in. "I would. I would very much like to see your place."

He lived in a row house, a Victorian Gothic Revival of brick and stone, one of many that lined the street on either side. There were several steps leading up to a narrow stoop and two doors, one to the left (his neighbor's ground-floor flat, he told me). Tom unlocked the other, lacquered rich black with brass fittings, and ushered me through to a small entry at the base of a narrow, steep set of worn wooden stairs.

He gestured for me to climb first, so I started up, a bit self-conscious knowing he was right behind me, with a direct view of my ass. Yet the wine and walking and sunshine conspired to pleasantly mute this concern.

"Wow, these, my friend, are some steep apples and pears," I managed, winded.

"A very old building I'm afraid. Where did you pick up Cockney rhyming slang?"

"Oh *that.* I've watched *Austin Powers* a few times. And traveled a fair bit. This isn't my first rodeo, Tom Hardy."

"No. I wouldn't have thought so," he said.

"It's a bit hard to assign a number to how many rodeos I've, you know—"

"Ridden?" he offered. I reached the small landing at the top, breathless, jittery with anticipation. Mere *inches* from the *actual* door, to his *actual* flat, and from whatever might come next.

What I felt next was warmth, the gentle impression of his finger-tips on my shoulders, the sensation of spinning, of kissing, and finally, *finally,* of *euphoria.*

Chapter 11.

FIRST SEXT

Pippa flung open her front door and found me standing there.

"I know what you're going to say. *Jane, you ignorant slut.* There. I said it, so you don't have to. I *did* take your advice about salad."

"Hello," she said, and tugged me in, kicking closed the door with her foot and dragging me swiftly to the sofa, where we sat knee-to-knee, face-to-face. "Does this mean you've been a *full-on* ignorant slut?" she asked, beaming.

I nodded, conflicted.

"Yay! So...was he...?" she murmured, raising a brow. She glanced crotch-ward and made a snipping gesture.

Interesting first question. "That's what you want to know?"

She shrugged. "I want to know about *all of it*. The buildup has been merciless."

"Nope." I folded my arms, thunked back into the sofa cushions. "Perhaps I should take a page from your playbook and be a bit more *discreet* about such matters, for once."

"Oh, but that's so boring."

"I *know*." I shot her a look. "But to answer your question, yes, as it happens, but it wouldn't have—"

"Mazel tov!" she cried. "The Silverman-Starts have reason to celebrate."

"We're getting *way* ahead of ourselves. It was only a first date."

And upon saying it, I felt suddenly as if the floor had dropped out from under me. Perhaps I shouldn't have slept with him *quite* that fast? I brushed the notion away and flopped my head to her. "Just so you know, the Silverman-Starts don't care about such things. I could be dating Jesus, and they'd probably be more interested in where he buys his sandals. Or whether he could pop by to do some light carpentry."

"Right," she said, flopping hers to me.

"But since we're pondering the subject, one weirdly does keep a sort of mental record of all of them. Each distinct, unique." I flashed on the various and sundry I'd come to know over the years. I wondered if this went both ways.

"Unless it's been so long one can't remember." She gave her head a little self-fortifying toss. "I'm not feeling sorry for myself, really, I'm not," she sighed. "I could murder a cappuccino, *you?*" She rose, wearing a defeated look, hands on her hips.

"*Yes* to caffeine, and it won't be long," I insisted. "*You*—are a goddess."

"Ha. I'm seriously thinking of joining a dating app," she called over her shoulder, gliding toward the kitchen.

"Why not," I concurred.

I fished my phone from my bag, caressed its steely, toasty surface, and fought off an urge to text Tom, having already restrained myself for the hour-plus journey.

Instead, I replayed the afternoon. He'd ushered me into a large loft-like space. Wood plank floors, a bank of atelier-style windows vibrating with sunlight, and a small kitchenette to the left of the windows, which shared the same leafy street-side view. There was mismatched furniture including a generous sofa, upon which we continued kissing like teenagers until I felt his fingers at the hem of my skirt and fabric moving up, shivery air on freshly liberated flesh, untethering me from any- and everything. The sensation of his warm palms skimming my thighs as if he were studying them, *appreciating* them, his lips simultaneously beginning to graze my neck...too many nerve endings under unbearable luscious siege, the feeling of *him, everywhere.* Then his palm went still in the gap above my knees. Perhaps it was my original intention to behave virtuously, or perhaps it was my staid underwear that impelled me to draw my legs together. Yet he simply eased himself onto the floor and rested his divinely scratchy cheek upon my bare thigh. All of me tightening, melting, at knowing his face, his mouth, were so near. I let my eyes drift shut, let my head sink back into the sofa cushion, let my fingertips trace his features as if blind—bridge of his nose, hollow of his cheek, eyelids, lashes, lips—the pulse of his warm exhalations upon my bare skin, edging me toward a tipping point, a tingling awareness of him easing down the flowery cotton I so didn't want him to see, in a manner so tantalizing—so achingly languid—

"Too spicy?" Pippa was calling out from the kitchen, suddenly cross. "I know how sensitive you are." Apparently she'd been trying to confirm my curry order from our favorite place around the corner.

"No. Spicy is good," I called back, staring down at the hot little device in my hot little hand. I would text him, I must. Yet how to distill this swelter of feelings into words? *Emojis!* They exist for this very purpose. I pulled up our texts and sketched in:

Jane Start: Hi! 🔥 🗡️ 🚀 ◎ 📱 xo j

It was practically a sext.

"I've had another call from Jonesy's people," Pippa called out, over the rumble of the espresso-maker. "They're getting impatient, but on I go, stringing them along." She said the last part in an agitated singsong. "Hilarious. It *is* the Royal Albert Hall. Still top secret, by the way. But you do need to come to a decision before too long."

At the mere thought, a shiver tore through me. *No.* This time, I would stand up for myself. Not until Jonesy had explained precisely what he had in mind for me to do would I say yes, to anything.

But...the Royal Albert Hall would mean I had a reason to stay.

Tom Hardy: Hi! In London safe and sound I hope. Visit me again, soon? Tom x

He must have liked the emojis! And how was it possible a mere lowercase x could be suffused with such promise?

Jane Start: Yes. And yes! Jane x

"*Jane*. It's rude to be texting in the middle of a conversation." I felt Pippa glaring down at me.

"I know. But this is sort of...*sexting*. Which supersedes ordinary texting. I'll be quick."

Tom Hardy: Lovely! I must confess I'm not sure what all the ?s inside of boxes mean. You'll have to enlighten me when next I see you. Let me know when you might be free. T. x

"How adorable." I beamed up at Pippa. "He doesn't do emojis? What century is he from?!"

I was still jabbing at my phone when the FaceTime burble sounded and my own face appeared on the screen, from the most unflattering angle known to humankind, under the chin. My brother's face popped up. *Relief.*

"Hey, what's shaking? How's Great Britain?"

"Great. Not much shaking. Except I just slept with a very nice Oxford professor."

"Jesus, Jane, that was fast. Careful now. I mean after everything with— Nope. I refuse to utter the bastard's name."

I felt a tap on my shoulder. *"Hellooo,"* Pippa whispered, making a face. "A whole lot *is* shaking. *Jonesy.* The Royal Albert Hall?"

"Who are you talking to?" Will asked.

"No one. Hang on a sec." I shielded the phone. "But it's top secret?"

"He's your *brother.*"

She knew full well that Will was a Jonesy *fanatic.* I uncovered the phone, ignoring the pit in my stomach. "You can't say anything, but Jonesy has invited me to perform with him at the Royal Albert Hall, in November. It's all shrouded in mystery and honestly I don't have a good feeling about—"

He cut me off. "Are you nuts? You have to do it."

"That's what *she* said."

"Who said? Mom?"

"No. I mean my other, I mean Pippa." I aimed the phone at her. She froze, a mug of cappuccino aloft in each hand, with a distinct sexy Swiss Miss vibe.

"I'm not mumsy-ish, am I?" She plonked sulkily onto the sofa, unaware her V-neck tee had drifted south, exposing an eye-catching amount of black lace, and cleavage.

"Ahh—no?" Will said. I caught a mumbled "God no" under his breath, which went unnoticed by Pippa.

"Well, thank you for saying so," she said, swiping cappuccino foam from her upper lip.

"Not at all," he said, reddening. "But, Jane, listen. Hear me. You have to do it. The concert. Just get over yourself. Or do it for me. You know how I feel about Jonesy." He glanced over his shoulder. "But hey, I'm actually at work, the only genius at the Genius Bar," he murmured. "So, shit fuck." And gestured, *So long.*

"Paris France," I returned.

"Whoops. One last thing! I found us a decent apartment. Think we could swing it if we were to live on popcorn and very shitty wine. I exaggerate. Sending you the link. The good ones go fast so we need to jump, 'kay? You still game?"

"Yeah—sure—okay."

"Farewell, my lovelies." And his face dematerialized from the screen.

But the thought of checking out some bleak apartment. Of rooming with my brother. Of leaving England anytime soon—

"Jane, you mustn't panic about the concert," Pippa said, reading my face. "Oh, and I meant to tell you this, but his team hinted, via email, that he's planning to put the one song in the set. We could have assumed that. But just think how cool it will be. And how, potentially, easy."

I took a beat. "Nothing with him is *ever* easy." The fact that I'd said it calmly had an impact on her.

She paused and sighed back, "No." Even she couldn't argue with the truth.

I glanced down at my phone.

Tom Hardy: Visit me again, soon? Tom x

"Remind me what that Shit Fuck Paris thing is all about?" Pippa threw her feet up onto the coffee table.

"Oh that," I said. "Just a stupid thing from when we were kids. Will was having a hard time. Getting bullied a lot in school. He used to creep into my room in the middle of the night. And this one time, I was up late reading *Jane Eyre* for the millionth time, and all of a sudden, he sits bolt upright, like he's in a trance, and says *Shit Fuck Paris France,* and promptly flops back down and goes right on sleeping. He didn't believe me when I told him. But it was so *him.* And now, I guess, it's one of those curious memories from childhood you keep alive by reminding each other of it all the time. I used to wonder what he was dreaming about. But right about now, I'd say he's dreaming about your boobs."

Pippa peered up, startled, and faintly cheered.

"I wish I had your boobs."

"You don't," she sighed, and tugged at a bra strap through her yoga top.

"I do."

The fairy lights in her garden blinked on, and she gazed wistfully out. Pippa was one of those people whose features had magically retained the oversized proportions of a child's.

"You're pretty," I said.

She flicked her face to me, vaguely alarmed. But she was. And she needed to know. I didn't say it enough. And it's important when you're having these sorts of thoughts about someone, to tell them. To say it out loud.

"Well, for the record," she said, "I wish I had your lovely olive complexion, naturally glowy all year round."

We exchanged smiles. *I should say yes to Jonesy,* I suddenly thought, *for Pippa.* Whom I had never told the truth about that strange night long ago. And what was I doing—barreling headlong into this thing with Tom, still reeling from Alex? *Work. Discipline. Not sex.* Not another *relationship.* With someone who lives *in England.*

I grasped Pippa's hand. I wanted to tell her: You're *not* mumsy-ish. Only concerned for my welfare. How grateful I was.

"Starting tomorrow, I focus *entirely* on music!" I said, waving my phone. "I'll let Alastair and James know I'll be there first thing in the morning—at the cock's crow!"

Pippa broke into a gorgeous smile, but before she could respond, the doorbell buzzed with the curry and, almost in time, my phone chimed.

Tom Hardy: Any chance you're free tomorrow?

Chapter 12.

SECOND DATE

Calm, cool, collected, controlled, *chaste*. That was my mantra as I mounted the steep stairs to Tom's flat, breathless once more at the landing. I took a beat, reminding myself, the entire purpose of this date was to get to know him better, *as a person,* and for him to know me. I hesitated before knocking, but at the barest touch of my hand his door swung in.

He hadn't heard me. He was at his kitchen sink, gazing out a window, not yet aware of my presence, and something in the quiet effortless armature of him, the broad slant of his shoulders and inward curve at his lower back, in his jeans and T-shirt, disarmed me.

"Hi."

He spun around at the sound of my voice.

"Hi," he said, pulling soapy hands from the water and darting around for a towel. The sight of his face made me suddenly shy, and I stole a sideways glance at his sofa, where so much had happened last time. That should have done something to assuage me...but last time I'd had a lot of wine, and wine has a way of making a stranger seem less *strange*. This time I would *not have any*. I inched closer as he leaned back into the counter, drying his hands, crossing one leg over the other. For a professor of literature, he seemed not in the least inclined to bother with words.

"You cook," I said finally, freezing a discreet distance from him.

"I've made you a potato," he said, simply.

"Oh, thank you." *And oh how I adore you. You have no earthly idea.* "I'm so happy with that. Seriously, I'm a very cheap date," I said, composedly.

"Which one wouldn't expect from a *rock star*," he said, setting aside his towel.

"Oh no." *Oh god.* "You didn't watch the video? Did you?" *Because I'm no longer "her." Or maybe . . . I am! Grrr.*

"Of course. Several times."

"I hate the internet, so I'm going to change the subject." I glanced around, taking in a sweet buttery scent, noticing the fall-out of his culinary efforts: spices, utensils, a chopping board. "I'm impressed."

"It was difficult, making a potato."

We fell again into awkward silence, the molecules between us vibrating like a heat mirage.

"Are you hungry?" he asked, and abruptly swiveled to gather plates from a cupboard, his movements crisp, masculine, in a lean, mean kind of way.

"I'm okay to wait," I said, but stepping closer to him was startled by a warm squishy feeling, down there, that I could actually *hear.* Oh god. Could *he?* Who knew talking about a potato could be so erotic? This must be some animal response. I risked another squish closer.

Tom set the plates on the counter and spun around, and there followed a delicious, attenuated silence, our eyes softly locked . . . and I had the impression of something somewhere softly unraveling, a bolt of charmeuse silk perhaps, in rhythm and rhyme with the sensations rippling through me. Time seemed to drift, or perhaps it simply . . . *stopped.*

And then I was in his arms.

Kissing is underrated, so totally underrated. I became faintly aware of something burning, and an instant later we pulled apart. Tom rushed to check the oven, releasing a cloud of smoke into the room. He sighed.

"I'm afraid we'll have to find you a potato in town," he said at last, shutting the oven door decisively.

We stood beaming at each other through the haze until I could no longer suppress a cough. Tom got to work opening the large window over the sink, evidently jammed shut. Snowy shafts of light were pouring in through the spectacular bank of windows that spanned the street-side wall of the living area, illuminating many uneven pillars of books on the floor, like sandcastles. A jewel-toned rug that looked antique, and expensive, stretched over beat-up wooden floorboards; two worn leather armchairs faced the now-familiar slipcovered sofa, faded a pinkish color from basking in bright window-light, and on either side, a couple of Moroccan side-tables with hammered metal tops stood guard in place of a coffee table.

"I like this room," I said. "Very much."

He smiled like it mattered what I thought, and I spun around to take in the opposite side of the space, which I hadn't had a chance to appreciate the first time I was here.

"A bit of a mess," he confessed, eyeing a narrow farm table, cluttered with books and papers; the wall behind it a pleasing jumble of paintings, drawings, and posters hung salon-style. There was one noticeable, lonely rectangle of empty space, craving the perfect thrift-store treasure, and I fantasized unearthing it for him. I thought of Alex's pristine midcentury modern, which he kept oppressively ordered; even the magazines on the coffee table had to be strictly aligned.

"It's *great* this way." Like an artist's loft inhabited by an artist, as opposed to a spoiled wealthy dilettante impersonating an artist.

"Would you like to see the rest of the place?" Tom offered. "We didn't get round to it, yesterday."

No, we most certainly didn't.

He inclined his head toward the unexplored territory, and I felt fluttery, and unready.

We made our way across the living room and into the mouth of what turned out to be a dark and windowless passage lined on either side with floor-to-ceiling bookcases, like stacks in a gloomy old library, the air at once chilly, as if all the warmth and sunniness of the front room had been sucked out.

"You have *a lot* of books," I said. "That figures, the whole professor thing. I thought you might have a ship in a bottle somewhere."

"My parents had one of those, so no," he said. *Duly noted.*

There was a small utility room with a washer-dryer on the right, and beyond it, midway down the hall on the same side, Tom pointed out a good-sized bathroom. I poked my head in; it was cheerful and bright thanks to a small skylight, and had crisp white tiles, a clawfoot shower-tub, and a simple farmhouse vanity and sink. No fancy salves on the counter, merely a staid square of soap in a simple ceramic dish. It was as if Tom didn't realize he was handsome. Refreshing, especially after narcissistic Alex, a serial subscriber to overpriced face potions.

"Nice." I smiled back at him.

We continued on toward a closed door at the far end of the passage whose edges seemed to pulse with light, and which creaked loudly when he opened it... *the bedroom.* Surprisingly ample and flooded with sunlight—a nice reprieve from the creepiness of the hall.

There was a set of large bay windows with views of breezy treetops on the street-side and, tucked in the alcove they created, a writing desk, which faced, oh yes, his bed. It was very neatly made, as if he had taken particular care.

I experienced an unexpected relapse of shyness and quickening of heartbeats at the thought of what might come next. I wondered if *he* was thinking what *I* was thinking. But church bells began to chime, drawing me toward the windows, and I sought out the dreaming spires of Oxford off in a gauzy distance. When I turned back, Tom was still hovering by the door, quietly watching me. What was it about him that undid me so? A gravitas, his mysterious restraint. Always thinking, but saying little.

I feigned a kind of academic scrutiny of the room, taking in the wall of built-in closets on the far side, no doubt teeming with professorial robes. Tucked in the corner, a cool Danish-modern console table.

"That's called a record player," Tom said dryly, referring to the one sitting atop it.

He gave the door a nudge and it clicked shut behind him, exposing built-ins devoted entirely to vinyl. *Now we were in his bedroom, with the door closed.*

I glided over to the shelves for a better look. "I'm guessing lots of Bach, and Beethoven."

"And the Beatles."

"Really?" I darted a quick smile over my shoulder. *Yes,* alphabetized: loads of Beatles, but also Big Star, Blondie, James Brown, Kate Bush, the Byrds. *Unexpected.* So, he too had an affinity for music from the 1960s, '70s, and '80s. A man after my own heart. I'd grown up with this music, a staple in the Silverman-Start household. I snuck a glance at the *J*s, curious to know if Tom really was a Jonesy fan. My heart gave a lurch; there beside Etta James and Grace Jones were the Jonesy records. I felt the need to deflect. "I have to ask the question. Beatles or Stones?"

"Both," he smiled, "but I think I'd have to say I love the Zombies just as much."

The Zombies? He'd had me at hello, and now *this.*

I crouched before the *Z*s. He wasn't kidding. More Zombies albums than I knew existed. He knelt beside me and slid one out.

"Want to listen?" Our faces were close. He smiled. *Oh god.*

I popped up, but where to sit? Only the one chair at his desk, and that didn't feel quite right, so I had no choice but to perch a bit awkwardly at the foot of his bed.

Tom set the record on the turntable and when the needle sparked the vinyl, a soft swell of feeling washed over me. This beautiful sound, it was the answer to everything. He sidled close, our hips and thighs warm and touching, both of us transfixed by the shimmering disk spinning round and round.

I'm going to love you in the morning, love you late at night. It was as if Tom was beaming his thoughts straight into me, wrapped in the raw-silk purr of Colin Blunstone's voice.

And suddenly his very real body entangled mine.

"Jane—I don't know what you do to me...but it's good," he murmured into my hair, and I wanted to tell him I felt the same, but I couldn't, too rapt, too wrapped up in the sensation of him, the rustle of crisp cotton in my ears, the cadence of his breathing like music, his skin, his warmth, a thousand soft suffusions—petals loosening and fluttering down, stirring a smooth watery surface and rousing it to ripple and dilate.

I couldn't contain the pleasure of it; it had nowhere to go, so I just felt it, and that was all I had to do.

The next morning, I was in his bed, naked, and he was fast asleep beside me. I remembered my earlier determination not to sleep with him, nor had I intended to spend the night. Yet there wasn't a single thing wrong with this picture except, *How was he single?*

When he'd shown me around, I'd noticed, too, the absence of photographs, as if his past had been erased. He certainly wasn't on social media—I'd checked. I sort of loved not knowing, starting only with the now. Since that seemed to be what we were doing? Not telling each other our sad stories. Like in *Jerry Maguire.* In fact, maybe it was perfect. Why would I want to bring up Alex's rejection, and risk permanently marring his perception of me? If I could simply clear my history, like on a web browser, and delete that chapter of my life, forever, *I would.*

I found myself wondering about the sofa; if it had been an ex-girlfriend, an ex-wife, who had slipcovered it in pink. Well, who cared? And what absurd gender stereotyping on my part. He could very well be a bachelor who liked pink. I liked pink. Loads of people liked pink. And if I was being honest, I did sort of love that he remained *the stranger from the plane. I* could be the stranger from the plane, for him, too. How liberating to reinvent myself entirely. To be the girl I'd always wanted to be. Fearless. Daring. Unabashedly sensual. Continuously *musical* . . .

Tom stirred, blinked open his eyes, and gazed at me, as if he was suddenly remembering, *She's here*—and he seemed pleased by this.

"Hi," I said, feeling caught, but also swooning from the sight of his ocean-colored irises, the magnificence of a singular sturdy shoulder poking from beneath the crisp white sheet, tanned and faintly freckled, the palpable sense of the rest of his solid, simmering body so near.

"I'm enjoying watching you think." *Busted!* He hoisted himself onto an elbow and grazed his fingers lightly over my cheek, then left them to linger on my bare shoulder. "Like weather systems, moving across your face. Stormy clouds and lightning and, very often, lovely sunshine."

This was too good. His being so interior, yet willing to express himself this way. The fact that he intuited the constant tumult in my head, yet didn't seem to mind. And, fuck *me,* the sexy British accent. I had no comeback.

I spied his T-shirt atop the covers. It was such a pretty color, faded from deep blue to something an interior designer might call Thistle. I had a deranged, intense urge to drape it over my face and huff it like a glue-head. *Too soon,* I thought. Instead, I asked, "Can

I wear your shirt?" In truth, I wasn't yet ready to traipse around stark naked in front of him in the cold morning light.

"Please do," he said.

I slipped it on; it was so soft I nearly groped my breasts through the fabric, *right in front of him*. But I slid out of the covers and ambled over to the desk, relieved the T-shirt fit like a short dress and covered enough.

Something somewhere began buzzing. Not *my* phone; it was still charging in the outlet by the record player.

Tom leaned over the side of the bed and wiggled a buzzing iPhone from the pocket of his jeans on the floor. How handsome he was, I thought, swooning a little again. But after a quick downward glance at the screen, his expression darkened before my eyes.

I remembered this face from the plane. Where did he go? And who was it that made him go there? The phone buzzed again and I felt suddenly like I shouldn't be here at all.

"It's okay," I said, "don't mind me." I grabbed up a weathered, leather-bound book from his desk and buried my face in the pages. He seemed not to hear.

From over the book, I glimpsed him still staring at the phone, and when it buzzed again, he gave it a decisive jab, and stuffed it into the top drawer of his bedside table.

"Ooh what's this?" I said, coyly. "You read Latin?"

When he glanced up, his face was eerily blank. Then he seemed to finally *see* me, and sighed. He'd come back. I felt myself flush.

"Of course you do," I murmured. "What does this say?"

He slipped on his jeans and came over, plucking the book from me and dropping into his rolling chair. I leaned against the desk edge facing him so that now we were eye level. He looked happy again.

"It's Ovid. Amores. Someday I'll translate it for you." And he snapped shut the book with a flourish, and canted toward me, his bare chest grazing my breasts, as he set it back down on the desk.

"I'm *impressed*," I managed, tingling.

He furrowed his brow as if this was a silly thing to be impressed by, and rolled the chair closer, so our knees were just shy of touching.

"What would you say to a little excursion? This weekend, or even...this afternoon?" He inched the chair closer still, capturing my bare legs between his knees. *Yum.* To be trapped this way, his body heat radiating through the fabric of his jeans.

"Excursions are good...and *I'm* good, with *any of those options.*"

What would Pippa think? She'd worry I was lovesick, acting on impulse. *So, what if I am?* Because now he was rocking his knees back and forth, with mine imprisoned. *Distracting.* And pleasurable, but *distracting.* "What did you have in mind?"

"Perhaps we could take a drive? To Devon, or Sussex, or Cornwall." Each of these mystery places murmured into my neck, my ear, the nape of my neck, eliciting little shivers. "And by the way, you look very cute in this shirt. Keep it if you like." Now running his hands featherlightly over the front of it, as I'd willed him to do, my nipples having no choice but to reinvent themselves as eager, ready confections, on the verge of discovering their true purpose, begging to be—

"Shall I take you there?" he said into my hair.

The Staples Singers had begun singing in my head...the sexiest gospel song in the history of...ever...

"Where?"

"The English countryside," he whispered, his lips skimming downward over the front of the shirt. *He reads minds!*

The feel of him yanking the T-shirt impatiently up and over my head—

"Just you and me. Somewhere *lovely.*" His words were now mumbled and muted, apparently giving up on this talking thing altogether in favor of far more important things...

But then somewhere, I could hear it. The faintest buzzing; his phone again, from where he'd buried it away, inside his dresser drawer.

Chapter 13.

NO SECRETS

We were out the door the next morning. I was in charge of tunes and came prepared. As soon as Tom and I hit the open road, I played "Fly Me to the Moon" and felt as though he would. Julie London sang, "You are all I long for, all I worship and adore." And then Chris Montez: "The more I see you, the more I want you." So what if the lyrics were a bit on the nose. Isn't that the great thing about songs? They give voice to thoughts and feelings and urges one might hesitate to reveal some other way. And besides, there was no room in my head to fret. The car windows were open, the crisp air tingling my skin, undulant green spreading out as far as I could see. I sensed his gaze. He'd turned his head. He had one hand relaxed and confident on the wheel, and he was smiling at me.

I cued up the romantic theme from the 1960s French film *Un Homme et Une Femme* as we drove through Devon. Rain began to dapple the windshield, refracting the streetlights cinematically like in the movie, as if I'd willed it.

The hotel Tom had booked for us was even run by a French family. At reception, a man with a thin mustache greeted Tom warmly—"Monsieur 'Ardy, welcome back"—and lingered on me a little too long, frozen in a pinched smile. Clearly Tom had been here before with— No, I stopped myself from that line of thinking. Who cares who with. He was here with me now, and that's what mattered. And if things were reversed, and he were in America, I'd want to steal him away to all of *my* favorite haunts.

Over the weekend we took ambling drives, meandered the countryside as if we were the only inhabitants of some alien planet. We lounged in our small bright room, rambling on about everything or nothing at all. I told him about LA. My fascination with the city's noir side, its *Day of the Locust,* Black Dahlia underbelly, always darkly thrumming beneath the ever-sunny veneer.

As usual, I said more and he said less, but he did tell me a bit more of his childhood. How as a teen he'd scribbled the start of what was to be his great novel, only to let it languish. At Oxford his studies had been all-consuming, then came teaching, his students, the same story. He was *substantial,* as Pippa liked to say, and so different from preening boyfriends past. The only time I'd seen him even glance into a mirror was to shave. I listened to the satisfying synesthetic *scrape scrape scrape* of his razor, the slow pulse, the lazy summer heat seducing me to close my eyes. And when I opened them again, he was there at the edge of the bed, and in a single heartbeat of that swimmy liquid moment I knew only that I *adored* him, and that I didn't want to wake up from this dream, if it was one. How could I ever explain this swell of feeling to anyone? I had an instinct to grab my phone and capture a fleeting image of him, like a hunter. But it was a melody, and words I craved. It was a song I needed to write, to sing, about *him* . . . the feelings his mere quiet presence aroused in me.

And I would.

As he drifted away to dress, I scribbled stealthily on a leaf of hotel stationery, and then, before doubting myself, tucked it safely into my bag.

*   *   *

On our last afternoon in Devon, we relaxed in a courtyard of sun-scrubbed stone under a brilliant sky. Perhaps it was the undulating rise and fall of nearby surf, the sultry breeze caressing my bare arms and legs, or the *many* glasses of wine, but I was thinking how much nicer this was than it had *ever* been with Alex. Or Dick-Actor (as he had become known), the one before Alex, who had once let slip that the person who'd set us up had suggested he dispense with dating actresses, and "try a rock chick." I literally ticked a box for Dick-Actor. He "tried" me like someone might test-drive a car.

I realized Tom was looking at me over his wine, a smile threatening to erupt, hopefully not reading my mind. *No.* I wouldn't tell him about Alex or Dick-Actor. Not when he was gazing at me like that.

"Your students," I found myself saying, starting to graze a fingernail slowly up his toasty, sun-drenched forearm. "They must all have mad crushes on you. How do you resist, *you know*—"

"That's a line one mustn't cross, ever," he said, and I could tell, by the nuanced change in his expression, he meant it.

"So, you were never tempted?"

He didn't answer, only wove his fingers through mine and gave me a squeeze, then pulled our clasped hands to his lips and let them linger there, our eyes locked. I enjoyed imagining his temptations, his lusty unbridled urges, while at the same time I sincerely appreciated his integrity and good character.

"There was *someone*," he admitted, after a beat, releasing my hand. "She wasn't a student."

"Ooh tell me more." I nestled expectantly into my chair.

He contemplated me, possibly wondering how to get out of this, then filled his glass with the last of the bottle.

"Her name was Monica, Monica *Abella*. Actually, it was when *I* was a student. She was—my *tutor*," he admitted reluctantly. "But, nothing happened, until, essentially, the end of the term."

Essentially? I tried to suppress a smile. "So you were, what, twenty-one? And she was—?"

"Thirty-seven," he said, taking a choked little gulp of wine, as I leaned in, intrigued. "A lovely woman really. Brilliant in her field, a scholar, Romance languages..." He trailed off, aware of the irony.

"She'd sent me a note, rather casual, at the end of the term. *Might we meet for lunch?*"

I pictured the two of them now. Same café. Same table by the river where we'd had *our* first date. "So then?"

"Her husband was having an affair, and she was rather desperate for a shoulder to cry on, and somehow—" He faltered, his focus turning inward that way it did sometimes.

"And somehow...?" *Out with it,* I wanted to cry. The suspense was killing me.

"I don't know really," he said, coming back to me. He sighed, and gave an almost shrug, then shifted in his seat—tried and failed to get comfortable. "We were briefly together, before she headed to Rome, where she summered."

"Mmm. *Monica.* From *Roma,*" I said playfully, rolling my *R.* "Who summers in *E-talie.* She must have been *extremely* alluring." This was all so titillating, imagining Tom, so full of resolve and then *not*—surrendering to his sensuous Italian tutor. "I'm conjuring up an image of Monica. *Monica, Monica, Monica,*" I said.

I decided to read his searching expression as, *How marvelously refreshing Jane is. So open. Clearly not the jealous type.* And how very *cool* was I, for being so splendidly unruffled.

"Sooo," I prodded, "was she more like Monica Bellucci? Or Monica Vitti?"

Yet he remained strangely mute, fidgeting in his chair like a hostage.

"Wait," I sputtered, the ground slipping out from under me, "does she *actually* look like Monica Vitti? Or Monica Bellucci?"

"She did rather, a bit. Like Monica Bellucci," he said gravely, tossing back the last of the wine.

The heat was suddenly unbearably cloying. I thought I might get sick right in front of him. This was all my fault. I'd basically *demanded* he tell me about his past lovers. But one fling didn't a fetish for bodies like Monica Bellucci's make, *did it?* And don't you dare, Carly Simon, start playing in my head: *Often I wish, that I never knew, some of those secrets of yours—*

"Jane," he said, concerned, "you look awfully pale."

I closed my eyes, but saw only huge bouncing breasts as on a vixen warrior running in slow motion toward me.

"It's very hot, have some water," Tom murmured, and I felt the gentle press of a glass to my lips. I took a sip, not yet ready to risk opening my eyes. "Monica Abella is a colleague, a friend. And you have nothing to worry about, with regard to me and my students. As I said, it's a line I would never cross."

"I'm not worried," I said. *I've had too much wine.* And dare I admit, *I'm envious.* But he looked at me with such genuine concern and kindness. "I mean, unless it's your *thing.* Your *type.*"

"I don't have a type. But I do most emphatically have *a thing.* For you."

Oh god. There it was. I thought I might die of elation. "Who cares about the past, anyway," I said.

There was a beat, our eyes locked.

"Not when we've got now, and it's *this.*"

"Sure you won't come back to Oxford with me?"

It was nighttime. We'd journeyed back and were idling in Tom's old Saab in front of Pippa's.

"Pippa's expecting me, and I need to … do my laundry, and other important things, like writing."

"Write in Oxford."

I smiled back, loath to move from here, so close beside him, and into the shivery dark of the London street. How swell he looked in the gray cashmere sweater with its tatters and moth holes, its frayed crewneck collar. But it was *inside* his head I craved access to. Where his most private self was filed away. To rifle through his secrets with my fingertips as a spy might do. To touch the lava-flow of his desires. I imagined his past lovers, lithe ones, zaftig ones who might have flung that very sweater over their naked breasts on chilly mornings, and whose nipples stiffened at the feel of such tantalizing fabric.

And yet it only made me desire him more.

My strange jealousy earlier had been replaced by a stirring, a warmth between my legs, as we considered one another. If only I could distill this feeling into song; a euphoria, akin to flying, like we do in dreams. Song ideas were lurking, percolating in me. It had to mean something. Something *good*—

"Penny for your thoughts?"

Did he read minds?!

I bit my lip. "It will cost much more than that, I'm afraid."

He took my hand. "If you must do your laundry in London, then don't stay away too long. Come back to me soon, my sweet." And he pressed his lips to my fingers as if we were in an Austen novel or a movie inspired by an Austen novel. "There's a lovely little room at the far end of my flat, with a pretty view and a desk and a comfy chair. Very quiet. Good for writing. It can be all yours. And as it happens, we do have washing machines in Oxford."

I was watching him drive away, regretting it instantly, when my phone dinged.

Will Start: Fancy a roommate in Old Blighty? Happy to couch surf with anyone who'll have me! Promise I'll make myself useful! Dust gear at James and Alastair's studio! Manny services for Georgia!

Tech support for anyone who needs it! I can even alphabetize the professor's books? Think of the fun! You and me! We could learn to play shuttlecock?

Oh no. He must have been fired again. And judging by the mad number of exclamation marks, truly desperate.

Will Start: Staying with Parentals for time being. I have no money. No job.
Will Start: Help.

Fuck. I couldn't deal with this now. In fact, I could barely turn the key in the lock at Pippa's, my fingers barely cooperating because: *Did Tom just invite me to move in with him?*

I poked my head in Pippa's front door. "I'm baaaack. From Devon. Loads of songs percolating."

I tried to still my heart despite wanting to break into a soft-shoe in her darkened entry. *Obviously,* it was way too soon to move in with him. On the other hand, how could I ignore this floaty feeling? This intoxication?

In the stillness, it occurred to me that Pippa might have gone out for a drink with a candidate from her new dating app, or was already in bed for the night. I ought to have texted. I was a terrible houseguest, and she'd put up with me far longer than originally planned.

But then I saw her, perched on a barstool at the far corner of her kitchen counter, hunched predictably over her laptop, a pair of large noise-canceling headphones clapped over her ears.

I set down my carry-all and scurried over. She seemed not to notice, bopping a little to whatever she was blasting. I lightly tapped on her back and she jumped out of her seat, ripped off the headphones, and flailed them across the room.

"Bloody hell, you scared me," she cried, gasping. An instant later, her eyes darted back to her laptop, which she abruptly slammed shut.

"Sorry!" I said, in earnest, yet found myself eyeing the computer, which began to hum, the way they do when overtaxed. "What were you doing?"

"Nothing. Working," she snapped.

"O-kay."

Pippa was twirling her hair dissociatively. Not a good sign. "Just boring work stuff," she muttered.

"I feel like you're hiding something. In the spirit of manager-client transparency, please show me."

"If you insist," she said, sulkily, dropping onto the barstool and whipping open her laptop. The screen filled with images of Dominic West.

"What's all this?" I asked, dragging another barstool over. "He's gorgeous, that's for sure." On closer inspection, there was a common feature throughout, a feature clearly outlined through the fabric of sweats, shorts, swim trunks, slacks, possibly even a *kilt.*

"*This* is what you've been working on?" It was hard not to grin.

"Clickbaited into it. So sue me. Fancy some chocolate?"

"Always."

We slouched side by side on her sofa, with chocolate. I caught her up on Devon, omitting the usual details, having a sudden instinct to treasure those in private. And Pippa seemed a little low, a little lonely. Here I was, off playing hooky with Tom, when the point of her bringing me here was to write. Her disappointment was palpable.

"Have you ever noticed there are way more sad love songs than happy love songs?" I said, after a silence.

"No," she sighed, "but I've never done a tally. I suspect you're right, though."

"Which might explain why I haven't come up with anything great yet, songwise. But I *am* trying. I'm beginning to think happiness as an emotion may be anathema to songwriting. Did I just use 'anathema' correctly? It's one of those words that can suddenly feel wrong. Like 'pulchritude.'" *Excuses, excuses.* Oh, who was I kidding. If that were true Alex's betrayal would have reaped something.

And there was that scrap of paper, from Devon, in my purse.

"I have no idea," Pippa sighed, morose. "But then it's great news you've returned to dreary old London, where you can now pine away."

"I know, but, *interestingly,* Tom has just offered me a little space in his flat... in which to work," I said, gingerly.

Her brow furrowed. "But he lives in Oxford."

"I know what you're going to say." I straightened up. "But things are going *really* well, just for the record."

I witnessed her jaw slowly drop, her thoughts plainly written all over her face:

Are you telling me you're moving in with him, already? But you've only known him two weeks!

Okay, yes. But if you count back to the day I met him on the plane, more like three and a half weeks. Ish.

But you had no contact with him for two of those, so my original calculation was spot on. Jane, I cannot condone you moving in with a man you've only known for two weeks.

But I feel like I know all I need to know about him. I know that sounds crazy!

Because it is *crazy.*

At this point I stopped arguing with Pippa in my head and took in the actual Pippa, who was staring back impassively.

"I know you disapprove," I said, rotating to face her, "and worry I'm being impulsive. But historically, my impulsivity has worked out a decent percentage of the time. I took the plunge with *you,* instead of heading straight for grad school. That was akin to running away with the circus, and look how well that turned out."

Slam dunk; a success story thanks to *her!*

"If you'd rather stay with Tom in Oxford then I have no objection," she said, her tone a bit flat, but nonjudgmental.

At this I felt the old tightening in my throat, a feeling that I might burst into tears. I hadn't realized Pippa's blessing would mean absolutely everything. I owed Pippa so much. She'd even given up her fantasy shagging holiday in Fiji to fly me here. Had she not, I'd never have met the man I was so recklessly infatuated with.

"I mean, what do *I* know about relationships?" she sighed, flinging her head back into the sofa cushion. "Look at me."

Oh no. I searched my memory for the last time she was in a *real* relationship: *the hot activist guy from Mumbai.* But then he became more friend with benefits. One of those dating apps could be precisely the thing.

"Just promise me you'll take care," she insisted, looking suddenly worried. "And know you can come back here on a moment's notice if things don't—" Her phone buzzed. She groaned at the sight of the caller ID, flipped the phone on its face, and ignored it.

"Leopard Pants?"

"No. But Jane, *listen,*" she said, desperately. "There's something I *really* need you to do for me."

"*Yes. Anything.* And for the record, you have *immense* pulchritude. Inside and out. Pulchritude means *beauty,* which it doesn't sound remotely like—"

"Jane. No more deflecting. I need you to sign off on the Royal Albert Hall. *Commit to it,* once and for all. Jonesy's people are hounding me incessantly and honestly, I'm rather coming undone. I can't even play proper phone tag with them, now that my assistant decided to have—*a baby.*" She was practically in tears.

"I know. And that sucks. I mean, not the baby part. You not having any help."

Of course I had to say yes. But it was so hard to actually *say the words.* To *Jonesy.* Yet harder still to see Pippa unraveled this way. "Done. I'm in. You can tell them."

A nanosecond later: Steep plummeting regret.

Pippa appeared too stunned to register relief. Her hair was mussed and sticking up, somewhere between Bride of Frankenstein and a sexy, bedheaded Julie Christie from one of her British New Wave films. Chocolate was endearingly smudged across her cheek.

My phone vibrated. It was Will, of course, melting down.

A lightbulb idea! *Will* could temp as Pippa's assistant. At least until after the Royal Albert Hall in November.

Which would mean, *oh yeah,* I might as well linger in England until then too.

And since Tom had invited me to stay with him in Oxford, I wouldn't even be in Pippa's way. Will could take my place here, or better, shack up in James and Alastair's guest cottage.

I clutched Pippa's hands in mine. "I have an idea! A *brilliant* one."

PART TWO

Dirty Mind

Oh honey you turn me on, I'm a radio.

—*Joni Mitchell*

Chapter 14.

SEXUAL HEALING

The train sluiced into the Oxford station, and a glimpse of Tom, windblown and sunlit, slid past my dust-dappled window. *Was this a dream?* I wondered moments later, clutching my suitcase and guitar as I glided toward him on the platform. He held my eyes softly as travelers swirled around us, dissolving brushstrokes on an impressionist canvas until it was only him and me, the empty train platform, a rose-colored sky. Inside his flat, we undressed in the dying light and climbed into bed. The cool sheets, the swelter of his skin, the softness of his lips as they grazed my thighs and belly and breasts and neck, leaving a tingling wake and then melting into mine. *I hadn't dreamed him.*

We were in Oxford together. For some indeterminate length of time. And time was but a construct, I thought, as rain gently tapped the windowpanes.

That first week, a routine took shape; Tom leaving early for his "rooms in college" to prepare for the autumn term, and me, learning the town. Nosing around antiquarian bookshops and print sellers, fingering illustrative plates in faded secondary colors. Pippa would invariably text. She was desperate to visit and meet Tom. I deflected, somehow afraid of breaking the spell. Instead, I prodded *her* to share the profiles of bachelors pinging her dating app. It was endlessly entertaining; the pretentious mission statements, the unseemly selfies meant to entice but instead sending us into fits of laughter.

But mostly we fretted over Jonesy's radio silence. I'd accepted his challenge: what now? What was expected of me at the Royal Albert Hall? It was nearly October; we honestly needed to know.

The following Monday, I was making espressos on the brand-new machine I'd splurged on (thank you, Gentle Caress) and was gazing out at a decidedly gloomy British sky when I had an admittedly regressive thought: I wouldn't swap this dreary view for Alex's sunny panorama any day, because the *man* I was bringing coffee to in bed wasn't an adolescent fuckhead, but a very brilliant, very British, *very sexy*—

"Hallo."

Startled, I spun to find an elderly woman standing just inside the door. She had on an overcoat and a plastic rain bonnet, and Tesco bags dangled from the crooks of her arms. She let the bags thud gently to the floor, all the while squinting in the vicinity of my crotch; okay, so I was wearing only Tom's T-shirt, but how was I to know we weren't alone? And now she was peeling off her coat and hanging it on a hook by the door.

"Hello, I'm sorry, *who are you?*" I said, tugging the shirt down just as Tom gallantly rushed in to drape me with a bathrobe.

"Jane, I'd like you to meet Mrs. Taranouchtchenka," he said, beaming at her. "Back from summer in Bulgaria visiting her son. Mrs. Taranouchtchenka comes Monday mornings to tidy up"—he gave me a tight, robotic smile—"and she does an exemplary job keeping things round here *spit spot.*"

Despite my embarrassment, I couldn't help delighting that my new boyfriend said things like *exemplary* and *spit spot.*

"Pleased to meet you, Mrs. Taran-chu-la—?" I looked to Tom for help, even as she glared.

"Taranouchtchenka," he said with an easy smile, like it was nothing.

I made another botched attempt, and she offered stonily: "Mrs. T. You can call me Mrs. T."

"Yes, great, very pleased to meet you, Mrs. T." I extended my hand, which she ignored. She simply nodded sullenly, like *We worked that out, no need to go all crazy.* I glimpsed her narrowing her eyes disapprovingly at Tom, who gamely volleyed back with an expression of warmth, to which she returned a look that seemed to say: *Okaay, Professor. If you like having this naked little tramp in your house, okaay.* Game. Set. Match?

"I start laundry now," she announced grimly, at last removing the plastic bonnet. She re-anchored her wiry gray hair into a low bun, then trudged toward the hallway.

"Cool," I said to her back with relief, but then realized: The bedroom was *no place for Mrs. T.* I barreled past her and quickly shut myself in, leaving her frozen midway down the hall with a look of confusion, as if paused by a remote.

I am a grown woman and I am not intimidated by Tom's housekeeper. But actually I was. I concluded the schoolgirl outfit I'd worn on our first date provided the best hope of rehabilitating Mrs. T's impression of me and, thus chastely transformed, took a moment to survey the condition of the room. The bed was a complete mess, as if sex-crazed humans had *very recently* been sex-crazed on it, the sheets not only rumpled, but, skimming my hands over them, a little *crusty.* A double tap at the door and Mrs. T inserted her head.

"Hallo, miss?" And before I could protest, she'd nudged it open with the laundry basket.

"*Oh,* just a moment, Mrs. T!"

But she was moving with great purpose toward the bed.

"Excuse me, I like to wash sheets now," she insisted, clunking past. I darted in front of her and prostrated myself on the bed, scrabbling them up before she could get her hands on them.

"It's okay—I've got this," I hollered, hoping the volume of my voice would make her understand. But apparently it wasn't working, because she'd dropped the basket and was toddling toward me, hands reaching, like a zombie. "It's okay, Mrs. T. *Really.*" Now I was clutching the bundle to my chest and backing away. "I'm very happy to wash them myself." I really was. I honestly enjoyed doing laundry.

But she wouldn't take no, and we wrestled briefly with the sheets before she said, "My job," with a final, forceful jerk, and I had no choice but to surrender.

Later, with Tom departed for work, I sought shelter in his promised writing room. It had been a week and I'd yet to pick up my guitar, though I'd felt its presence every day, eyeing me critically from a corner of the bedroom. But what to sing about? What to say? Those heady glimpses of inspiration in Devon had all but faded away, leaving fear and doubt and memories of last time. Those songs I'd loved. The echoing silence that followed, and in its wake an apprehension that persisted in haunting me.

But with Mrs. T bustling away, and out of excuses, I forced myself into the alcove just off his bedroom. Frankly, there was something a bit ominous about the space. I felt a shiver each time I set foot inside. Tom suspected the room had been tacked on ages ago, as evidenced by the oddly narrowed doorway of the secret-passageway variety. As I sank into the creaky chair, I thought, *This was where the children lay,* in iron cots, with fevered cheeks, afflicted with consumption.

Silly me. The desk was simple, of a Shaker style. The window view, leafy and lovely as Tom had promised. I chalked my premonition up to procrastination. Lack of confidence. I would finish the song I'd started.

But first a sudden imperative to open my phone, to check on the status of things, generally, in the world.

My breath caught.

They'd done it. Jessica's Instagram page was overflowing with proof. They were Mr. and Mrs. Alex Altman. Honeymoon photos in Turks and Caicos; how glamorous, how realized, how *well documented* their life was. I felt a tightening in my chest, a disconcerting numbness in my fingers. I sat bolt upright and shakily googled: "what are the signs of a—" But I stopped myself. I knew where this led.

Instead, I returned to the coziness of Tom's bed and made a rare call to my parents.

While the phone rang, I pictured the old family home, the Eichler-inspired creation my parents had designed, nestled in a canyon close to the Pacific, now battered by sea air and leaks, with its faint, persistent, mildewy scent. I imagined the quiet of the living room, dust motes dancing beneath a slant of ceiling with a skylight cut in, morning sun washing over the white leather Eames chair, the art books arranged by color on low walnut shelves, the large woodblock prints propped against the hearth. The four jumbo trash bags I'd hastily stuffed when I'd bolted from Alex still languishing on the floor of the dank childhood bedroom I dreaded returning to. Four years with him had fit so precisely in four—

"Tootseleh, cookie, it's *you*," my mom answered groggily. I'd forgotten how early it was in LA. Or how long it had been since I'd made a desperation call of this stripe. "I'm waking up Dad."

"No, don't—"

"Jane?" he murmured, yawning.

I explained my symptoms. My dad asked how much coffee I'd had, and I said, "Don't ask." He prescribed listening to "Ripple" by the Grateful Dead, three times, stat. "You know what else works, kid? Pick up your guitar."

They don't realize I'm a fraud, who got lucky, *once. And it wasn't even my song.* But it was the reassuring tone with which he'd said it, and the gentle smile I imagined on my father's face when he did, that was almost a cure.

There was a rustling of sheets. Lulu plucked the receiver from Art Start.

"Write a song *for me,* your mom, who loves you," she cooed. "And you're *not* dying. Not today. Definitely *not* today!"

I pictured her sparkling bright teeth, her tanned freckled shoulders and storm of honeyish hair. My dad's rich olive skin, his Pacino good looks, his Modigliani smolder.

I thanked my parents profusely and they thanked me for getting Will out of the house to work with Pippa, who in turn had organized a place for him to stay in James and Alastair's guesthouse. I promised I'd try them again, at a more reasonable hour. As soon as they clicked off, I remembered a story my dad liked to tell me when I was an anxious kid. There were two Buddhist masters who, upon meeting for the first time, sat together in a garden for many hours without saying a word. Finally, one of them laughed, pointed to a tree, and said to the other, "And they call that a tree?" The other master considered this, and he began laughing, too.

My philosophical father was saying silly humans have a compulsion to label things, including themselves. *I am a loser who can't write. I'm a love addict who moved in with the new boyfriend recklessly fast. The idiot who was triggered by an Instagram post of her cheating ex.* And they call that a tree.

I tried in earnest to contemplate silence like the monks in the story, hoping I might burst out laughing at the absurdity of some reductive label. *And they call this a bed. A lamp. A vagina.* Which they also call a pussy, a snatch, *a very special place.* Not that last one, but they really should. I took a moment of gratitude for mine.

Almost immediately I found myself wondering if Tom had invited *other* women to stay here as quickly and easily as he

had me. Like Monica, his sultry Italian tutor, and then his *lover.*
Ha! I wondered if she'd stashed bountifully cupped bras and
skimpy underpinnings in the nightstand where I kept my ho-hum
equivalents. Then I wondered if I should upgrade to something
deserving the label *underpinning.* Then I began to fantasize about
Tom and voluptuous Monica entangled in various positions on this
very bed. Feeling stirred and a tad criminal, I peered guiltily into
his upper bedside drawer, where he'd hidden away his phone that
time, but there was nothing but a few innocent pencils and a bit
of loose change. Feeling more brazen, I moved on to the next: a
syllabus for the Romantics, a shiny travel brochure for Greece, his
flight itinerary for the trip to California when we'd met! A stab of
guilt seared through me for snooping. But I'd gone this far. Surely
a cursory peek in the bottom drawer wouldn't hurt.

Books, predictable, yawn. Atop the stack was a small old-
fashioned leather-bound volume, no title, no author, nothing but an
intriguing classical bust embossed on the cover, somehow familiar.
The Venus de Milo. Could be a journal. If so, back in the drawer
it would go. *But* more than likely, it was some dry academic
book about the Venus de Milo, whom I knew nothing about and
probably should.

I let the pages fall open at random; thankfully the words were
printed.

*The chamber maid slipped discreetly through an unlocked
door to find the handsome officer awaiting her, sprawled
upon a luxuriant bed, his red military jacket slung over the
rail, his plain linen shirt flung open to reveal a smooth, sun-
kissed chest. He watched, wanton, as the comely maid untied
her apron, petticoats, and drawers, and let them fall brazenly
to the floor. Wasting no time, he lifted her to him, lowered her
gently to his taut, bare abdomen: firstly her silken thighs, then
her tender bare intersection, quivering like a beating heart*

upon his warm pulsing muscles, her ample bosom heaving, as he fumbled to free her from the tangled laces of a corset, until at last, the creamy fullness of her breasts tumbled free and he buried his face in them hungrily.

Overcome with lust, he seized the plush curves of her buttocks and guided her farther up, her warm fluttering place, its throbbing heart, grazing lightly o'er his chest, his neck, and higher still—its delicate honey'd sweetness caressing the rugged landscape of his chin until, finally, he lowered her gently to his waiting lips. The chamber maid, overwhelmed with paroxysms of passion, hardly noticed mysterious muffled moans behind her, and grasping a bedpost for ballast, whilst the Officer delivered her unspeakable flicks of pleasure, she craned round to spy the sultry new scullery maid from Barcelona, skirts lifted, easing herself upon the officer's proud cock, and began to ride him, as the moans and sighs of the three converged in a symphony of carnal pleasure——

Ooh la la. Better stop, but what fun. I returned the book to its rightful place in Tom's drawer, sweetly touched he had a book of cheesy Victorian erotica stashed away, when I caught sight of a few other enticing artifacts I hadn't spied hitherto: a couple of faded *Playboy*s from the last century, perhaps sentimental treasures of his youth? This little stash was frankly adorable and titillating to me, and I became aware of my own warm fluttering place beckoning, insistent. I slipped my fingers (aha! no longer numb!) beneath the waistband of my ho-hum underpinning, and *why not take care of myself.* It was arguably a form of meditation, as it required a rather single-minded focus, though perhaps not the kind the monks had in mind.

The doorbell rang and then continued to ring shrilly and persistently. Might Tom have forgotten his key? Might he have telepathically intuited my condition and decided to come home early? *Perfect.* I couldn't be more ready for him. I dashed barefoot along the passage, through the living room, and down the stairs, where I flung open the front door and was blinded by sharp afternoon sunlight, through which the blurred silhouette appeared.

It was not Tom but a stranger with a handsome face and fashionable mop of dark hair, dressed in a sleek bespoke navy blue suit. He had the foppish mien of a British aristocrat straight out of central casting, which made him seem vaguely familiar.

"Why, you must be Tom's new friend Jane," the man said, tapping a riding crop absently into the palm of one hand. His stance, attitude, accent, the *crop*—all screaming, *I'm very posh, and once was a naughty schoolboy.* His gaze slid blatantly down my bare legs.

"Yes," I said, crossing them; normally, I wouldn't be caught dead in a dress this short, this *sheer*. Plus, now the sun was hitting it. I sincerely hoped my nipples weren't apparent, or my underwear, or what I'd just been up to, upstairs.

"Extraordinarily pleased to meet you, I'm Freddy Lovejoy," he continued rather smugly, as if surely I'd heard all about him.

Nope, had not.

"Popped up from London to return this to the old boy," he said, extending the crop rather than his hand. "I'm quite sure you've done something egregious to his brain, which is generally very keen— you see, Tom never misplaces things." He cocked a brow.

Funny, Tom hadn't mentioned riding. I grasped ahold of the crop but Freddy refused for a beat to let go, proving out my Naughty Schoolboy theory.

"I mean that as a compliment, an acknowledgment of your charms, your wiles," he said, releasing it to me at last. We fell into awkward silence, which he seemed to relish. "Would you mind terribly, Jane, if I popped up? For a quick sippington?" He did a gesture with his fingers that did not compute. "Before making the long journey back to town. Hmm?"

But I did sort of mind, for lots of reasons, most particularly that I'd prefer to go back to masturbating.

"Of course. Please, pop up."

He gestured for me to go first and bowed, like an old-fashioned gentleman might, and it struck me. *He* was the man at the café on our first date. He'd done that same gesture on the patio, when I squeezed past him. Okay. At least I hadn't just invited a serial killer up for a quick sippington, whatever that was.

As I started up the stairs, I had a sudden horrifying awareness that there might actually be a damp spot at the back of my dress, precisely eye level for him. I couldn't exactly reach around and check.

Luckily, Freddy made himself at home immediately, commandeering the sofa; his arms splayed across the back cushions and his long legs stretched out as if he owned the place.

I gingerly set down the crop, excused myself, and raced down the darkened passage for the bedroom, shouldering on Kurt for cover. I took a moment to compose myself before returning serenely to the living room.

Freddy looked me over, head to toe, with a bemused smile. I'd forgotten to slip on shoes.

"Tom's been frightfully guarded about you, and that's saying a lot. The man's perpetually guarded. Such a bore really, a little goss never hurt anyone. Though I must say, I've never seen him happier."

"*Oh*. That's ... so nice. To hear."

"I was simply desperate to clap eyes on Tom's mystery woman, incorrigible old gossip that I am." He grinned, but then looked suddenly bored and yawned shamelessly into his fist. I pretended not to notice, instead easing myself into the leather wingback opposite him and steeling myself for what might come next.

"Might I trouble you for a spot of tea? It's after four." Tapping a large Rolex as if I needed proof. "'Fraid I can't string two words together."

"I should have offered." I sprang up like a jack-in-the-box and darted to the kitchenette.

"Lovely. Builder's will do. Ta."

I got the kettle started on the stove and rifled through drawers for tea—Earl Grey. English breakfast. Harney & Sons Celebration—trying to remember what builder's was. I chose at random: *You get what you get, Old Sport.*

"As I was saying," he went on, "Tom's been frightfully hush-hush about *you*..." I managed only to half listen, banging around for a proper teacup, as surely a mug wouldn't do.

"P'raps owing to the timing of it all. So very sudden. And on the heels of such Sturm und Drang—"

The kettle whistled shrilly, obliterating his voice. I grabbed it, scalding myself. Shoving my hand under the cold tap, I strained to follow him.

"I can still see Tom as he was then, as freshers, long hair the color of hay falling over his eye, skulking about the college juggling great stacks of books, intent on learning. *Shocking.* Who gives a fig about Lord Byron? Apparently *he* did, *Tom,* from Yorkshire. The rest of our class were mostly overindulged public school reprobates. Myself included." He laughed. "I must confess I rather turned into the green-eyed monster when *he* was the one to snag Amelia Danvers, the girl *everyone* wanted." There followed a pregnant pause. "But now, he has *you,*" he finished brightly.

Amelia Danvers. The girl everyone wanted. I wheeled around. Caught him yawning, again, and remembered the tea.

"Here you go." Carefully passing the delicate cup and saucer to him. He gaped down. Did I do it wrong?

"Trouble you for a bit of sugar? Some milk? Go on, ruin it, then," he said, peering up, a bit wickedly.

"Sorry. I'm from America. We're bad at the whole *tea thing.* You'd probably like a crumpet or a scone—some clotted cream, wouldn't you."

He simply cocked his head and narrowed his steel-blue eyes at me, upper lip curling into a smile. The rock star hair doing nothing but looking perfectly rock star. If he and Tom were side by side at a party, most people would pick Freddy. But not me.

"You *are* an American girl, aren't you," he chuckled. "No need for crumpets, Jane."

But as I scrounged for sugar, I had another thought. This Freddy didn't strike me as the sort of person Tom would have as a friend. Perhaps I didn't know Tom as well as I thought I did. A shiver ran through me. Truth was, I hadn't met *any* of his friends until now. But then again, *I* hadn't introduced him to mine either, desperate as they were to meet him. We'd just been hiding out here, the two of us, not mentioning the girl everyone wanted in college. Amelia Danvers.

I returned with milk and sugar, but without a coffee table had nowhere to set them and found myself kneeling slavishly at His Majesty's feet, placing them on the floor before returning to the wingback chair, where I sat, hands primly clasped in my lap.

Freddy smiled at me, his dainty teacup held aloft. Somewhere, a clock ticked. It felt, suddenly, like we were playing a theater exercise, waiting for the other to instigate a new behavior, until he mimed a stirring gesture over the cup.

I rose and returned with "One silver spoon." Surely he was born with one in his mouth? Hopefully I hadn't just made a terrible gaffe.

"You really are so very different from—" He broke off, stirring his tea. "All I can say is you're having quite an effect on Tom." He seemed to make a decision. "I'm glad. I take it you'll be riding with us at the week*end?*"

Riding? At the week*end?* I shook my head. "No, I don't ride."

"No?" he said, scandalized. "But now that you're in England you *r'ally* must. Tom rides like a Yorkshireman. Atrocious. We've tried to teach him to do it properly. But you, my dear, would be a

quick study, I'm quite sure." And he drew his teacup to his lips, pinky out, and peered at me over the rim.

"I think not," I said, shifting in my seat. "I can't really picture myself, at this point—"

"Mounting a stallion? Galloping off into the sunset? Pity," he murmured, a wry twinkle in his eye. Never in my life had I been more desperate for a pithy Katharine Hepburn comeback.

But Freddy tossed back his tea and leapt up, newly energized.

"I must be off. You're lovely, Jane, and thank you ever so much for this," he said, raising the cup and saucer, and depositing them in the sink. Then he snatched up the riding crop from the sofa and proceeded to give me a soft bop on the head, like a blessing, or the casting of a spell.

"I do hope you'll join Tom and me at the weekend, and henceforth I shall be on a mission to get you into the saddle. Now my dear, I bid you goodbye."

Before he could do his Gentleman's Bow, I gave him an old-fashioned curtsey, which he seemed to appreciate, and which left me feeling vaguely triumphant. And like that, he departed.

Chapter 15.

I WANT YOU TO WANT ME

An hour later, I heard the door at the base of the stairs clap shut, and Tom's footfalls as he bounded up. He found me waiting at the kitchen counter, still hopped up from the afternoon's discoveries. Freddy's unwashed cup languished in the sink. The riding crop was hidden behind me amid the detritus of the tea operation.

"Hello," he said brightly, just inside the door. "You look happy. Productive day?"

Not exactly. Unless you count snooping in your drawers, checking out your porn, and hanging out with your nosy friend.

"I *am* happy. But utterly unproductive." An image of the student Tom, hair the color of Yorkshire hay falling silkily over his eye, a copy of Lord Byron in his pocket, morphed onto the forty-year-old Tom gliding toward me.

"Your friend *Freddy* popped by to return this," I said, whipping out the crop and twirling it suggestively. "I didn't know you were into riding." Tom stopped dead in his tracks, his demeanor visibly altered. "Don't worry, I won't be going all *Fifty Shades* on you. Unless...you want me to?"

He stepped closer, a hint of a smile, but I sensed something other, underneath.

"Freddy told me you'd met as students."

"Did he?" He was looming now, the air suddenly charged, our eyes locked.

"Yes. As 'freshers.' I'm getting the lingo down."

He plucked the crop from me and flung it blindly away, led me by the hand to the sofa, yanking me almost on top of him. All very playful, yet a different Tom than I'd experienced hitherto; perhaps he *was* into *Fifty Shades*. He jerked my legs into his lap and began skimming his hands lightly over them, like he'd missed them, terribly, all day at the office. Yet he seemed distracted. Or like he was trying to distract me. But still, it felt *good*.

"He made fun of the way you ride, 'like someone from Yorkshire.' How *dare* he," I said.

Tom's hand stilled; he studied me. It was impossible to tell what he was thinking. Late-afternoon sun caught the amber flecks in his irises arranged in their dandelion pattern. I experienced a sudden quickening sense that he might be a complete stranger. Who was he, really?

But I flashed on his endearing stash of old *Playboy*s and thought, *He's just a person.* A person who was private. Extremely so. And the fact that he was reserved actually turned me on, *intensely*. Except I shouldn't have snooped.

"And well, the Brontës were from Yorkshire," I murmured a bit nervously, one shoulder raised.

He smiled. "Yes," he said, and gave my thigh a solid, righteous squeeze, triggering another part of me to squeeze back in return, whether I wanted it to or not.

"He also mentioned Amelia," I said offhandedly.

Tom froze at the sound of her name. "Freddy, he's a gossip," he said in a low, unfamiliar voice. "I wouldn't take anything he says seriously."

And then, he gazed out, at nothing, and began to caress my legs again. "And I don't use a crop when I ride, that crop belongs to him. I'm sure he just…came by…to get a look at you." I placed my hand, cautiously, over his, to still it—hoping to draw his attention back.

"*But* you *are* a bit of a mystery?" He'd promised to show me his office, but still he hadn't. "I learned a lot in twenty minutes with Freddy."

"Did you?" He fixed his gaze, strangely empty, on me. And though he didn't flat-out ask *Like what?* I felt compelled to say, my heart galloping, "There was a girl, Amelia, who you dated in college, and who rides, I'm guessing, very well." I searched his face for the slightest glimmer of reaction, but he gave no hint of one, so I continued. "And I'm guessing is good at lots of things. Like, making an excellent spot of tea. Perhaps hunting? Or, say, fishing?" I shrugged. "Things that *I* don't do."

I'd brought up his past! We weren't going to do that. I felt faint, yet exhilarated, too.

"*You* do other things." He swept my hair from my face, grasped it into a messy ponytail, and held it, securely and pleasingly, in his fist, in a *Me Tarzan—you Jane* sort of way.

"And you *like* those other things I do?"

"I *love* those other things you do." At which point, he released my hair so that it fell messily back around my shoulders.

I stared down at my tattered frock, like something a Victorian orphan might wear. "I'm afraid I'll never be posh," I said, "nor will I *ever* hunt an animal. And my emotions can be"—I shrugged—"unbridled, unruly. Essentially, I'm the antonym to what you British refer to as stiff upper lip."

His whole being seemed to soften. "Why would I ever *want* you to be any other way? And how could I ever resist…these impossibly sweet"—kissing me—"impossibly lush"—kissing me more—"American lips?"

And there was suddenly no need for further discussion, only

need for kissing. I should have been grateful there had been other women. After all, wasn't I the beneficiary of all that mileage in the sack? And who was I to talk. My dance card had more names on it than I cared to remember, including one...well, I remembered his first name...but Tom was pulling me into his lap, and I was facing him, wrapping my legs around him, melding, soldering myself to him.

I wondered if Tom had kissed her the way he was kissing me. And I wondered where she was now. Amelia.

"I feel I haven't shown you round Oxford properly."

Tom lay propped on a couple of pillows. "I like it right here," I said, astride him. I grasped his wrists and took his big man hands and cupped them to my breasts; he was now my puppet. I skimmed his fingers lightly over my face and lips and hips and everywhere I wanted him and felt him stiffen beneath me. Oh, the power of it.

What was it about him that made me feel so pretty? So worthy. So *naughty*. So strong and assured, and even defiant. And so *constantly* turned on.

He pulled me to him, all heat and muscle and *man*-ness. "We could just stay here forever, the two of us, couldn't we," he murmured into my breasts. Pleasure rippled through me, at the brush of his lips, his softly suctioned kisses. I could hardly stand it.

"Why don't we," I said, and we were rolling around when I suddenly remembered. "Oh! My brother is coming to England. You can take me—us—to that pub in Oxford, the one Tolkien used to go to."

"The Eagle and Child."

"My brother is Tolkien obsessed. He'll want to go there and get righteously drunk."

"We shall, then. I'll even get righteously drunk with you, and your brother." We were lying very close, on our sides. He searched my face. "You have this funny way of—corrupting me." I almost said sorry, except I wasn't. "But now I'm afraid I must work for a few hours."

"Ooh, on what might that be?"

"Nothing *scholarly.*" He sounded a bit reluctant. "The novel actually. I'm"—he hesitated—"well, I'm back at it."

There was something in his eye that made my breath catch. *"Oh really,"* I said, trying to contain a rush, a tidal wave of feeling.

"Perhaps nothing will come of it, but lately…" He inclined his head. "I've been *inspired.*"

I beamed back and thought, *This, right now, is what* happy *feels like.*

"You're disciplined." I snatched his tee from atop the duvet and draped it over my face. "This is me working," I said from under his shirt, enjoying its clean, peppery scent. "Research. For a song, quite possibly, about *you.* But don't mind me."

There was the rustle of him slipping into jeans, padding barefoot to his desk. The wheels of his chair groaning over the wooden floorboards.

Things could have gone so differently. I could have easily ended up in some squalid, once glamorous Hollywood bungalow, with my *brother* for a roommate and Baby Jane living next door.

"Can't you at least…clothe yourself, minimally?" The T-shirt was still over my face. "It's difficult to concentrate—knowing you're there—like that…the things I could do to you."

I sat up and smiled at him. And the things I could do *to you, mmm.*

He sighed and flipped open his laptop, began to type, but it didn't last long.

"Either you must leave this room immediately"—he pointed to the door—"or, come here."

I slipped on the shirt and rose. His desk was an island between us.

I'd wanted to tell him I loved him a thousand times, practically on the plane, which was madness! In Devon for sure, but this time was worse. I was a person who brazenly, even carelessly, threw *I* *love you*s around. And yet I'd sensed a strange discipline in both of us *not to say it*. Our arrangement was still unspoken, undefined. We were taking it a day at a time. Even the Jonesy concert, my official excuse to linger in England, was a genuine secret, and I dared not reveal it, even to the man I was crazy about. The man—

"I love—"

Tom straightened, his eyes wide, gleaming with expectation. He leaned forward, his palms flat on the writing surface.

"I love—that you just said I was corrupting you." *Oh god.*

I squeezed myself into the gap between his chair and the desk, our faces level, and rested my cheek against his warm scratchy one. We stayed like this for I don't know how long, but until our breathing aligned.

"So, there's something I need to tell you," I murmured finally. "I don't...know how to ride horses. I'm actually afraid, of falling, and breaking an arm. A guitar player thing...silly, I know."

"I don't care," he said.

We pulled apart. I searched his face.

"But I can watch. I can tag along and watch you and Freddy go riding this weekend."

He took my hands, his brow adorably furrowed. "Okay! But Jane, the thing of it is, we generally...get on our horses, and ride straight off into the countryside. I'm afraid we'd be out of view very quickly. Not much for you to watch."

"Oh, right," I said, feeling ridiculous.

But he pulled me close, murmured, "But I'll be glad you'll be there," and the words *I love you—I love you—I love you* reverberated in my head, in perfect time with his heartbeats.

Chapter 16.

WILD HORSES AND RED LIPSTICK GIRLS

"A quick shower and we're off?" Tom poked his head into the living room from the mouth of the passage and set his equestrian boots on the floor. It was the following morning, thus "riding at the weekend with Freddy" was on the books for today.

"Perfect, take your time," I chimed innocently back from the sofa, my computer searing a hole in my lap, the name *Amelia Danvers* blinking up from the search bar.

He disappeared down the hall, happy and unsuspecting.

Oh god I shouldn't be doing this. It was sneaky and wrong to exhume his past when he was so private, and things were so good. It was just that I had this nagging premonition we'd run into her now that I was entering Tom's life. And it was too irresistible, not to at least sneak a peek.

I heard the shower running, my index finger trembling a little as it hovered over the image search—*I shouldn't, I really shouldn't*—and then I clicked it.

She was arrestingly gorgeous. Her hair as black as coal, very long and straight and striking against the flawless alabaster of her skin. And she was statuesque, broad-shouldered, standing at even height beside her father (listed as the Right Honorable Lord

Geoffrey Danvers), both of them appearing very serious and very posh. But it was her dark eyes, her frosty, imperious stare for the camera in *every* photograph, that sent a shiver through me.

There were photos of her at the Derby. The Regatta. The Prince's Trust. Wimbledon. With her parents, her sisters, various dukes and duchesses with royal-sounding names and endless hyphenates. And one of her on a yacht, in which she appeared supremely elegant behind oversized designer sunglasses, a drink dangling from her long fingers like an extension of her toned and braceleted arm, the way tumblers of whiskey hung from the Rat Pack. I spied Freddy in one of the many photographs, but Tom, to my relief, was nowhere to be found. Maybe his thing with her was indeed a thing of the past.

But I continued flicking restlessly through, my curiosity piqued. When it struck me: Amelia Danvers had on red lipstick in every photo.

Tom had dated a Red Lipstick Girl.

It took swagger to pull off red. Femme fatales wore red lipstick. This was such a striking disconnect from my sense of *him,* as a *person,* that I was dumbstruck. Seeing Amelia Danvers triggered the same disconnect I had intuited upon meeting Freddy. And for an instant the room skewed, off-kilter like a phone screen swinging between vertical and horizontal orientations.

But hold on. If Tom were to google Dick-Actor, or Alex, and scroll through photos of him with Jessica, what would that say about me? Best not to cement judgments based on a Google search. Or relationship mistakes.

I felt suddenly ridiculous, but I couldn't help zooming tighter and tighter until her face became fractured and pixelated, the impenetrable coal eyes aimed, point blank, at me, until I could stand it no longer and tore my eyes from the screen—

Tom was so close, I nearly gasped. He was there at the edge of the passage, casually leaned in its frame, a towel around his waist, sweetly oblivious of his ex's face blown up on my screen.

*   *   *

"Let *me* drive."

The words had escaped without warning, but I needed something to distract me from my online stalking. I felt giddy, unhinged, but driving and road trips always steadied me.

Tom froze by the old Saab and studied me, his brow cinched.

"But you don't know how to drive on the left side, do you?"

I gave him a smile. "I'm an excellent driver in America."

He considered, not giving anything away, and I took a moment to soak in my surroundings; the Victorian brick row houses framing him on either side, the obligatory pub on the corner, its owner watering pink geraniums in black painted boxes.

"Okay. Why not," he said, a bit soberly, unlocking the driver's side door and placing the keys in my palm. *Baby you can drive my car?* I thought thrillingly of the Beatles song.

I made the necessary adjustments to seat and mirrors, and when I glanced at Tom, his face was calm, watchful.

"Ready?"

"Yup. Hmm, the gearshift's here." I wrapped my fingers theatrically around it.

"Yes," he said evenly.

I shifted into gear and proceeded to pull the car from the curb. "How odd, everything is reversed." And yet surprisingly intuitive.

"Eyes on the road, Miss Start," he said, not wanting to encourage this sort of thing.

I let him coach me, until I really did get it, negotiating us smoothly through yet another series of turns and feeling pretty ace.

"By George, I think you've got it," he said, and then playfully: "And once again, where does it rain?"

"In *Spain.*" I sang out in full voice, and then again, the words ringing, clear and bright and unbridled, Broadway-style, surprising even myself as I whirled us neatly through a tricky right turn. My cheeks flushed at the audacity of breaking into my "musical theater voice," particularly after resisting singing for him, *hitherto.*

"How the devil did you just do that?" he murmured, astonished.

I hadn't, actually, sung in front of him before. Giddiness swept over me. I grinned inwardly. It felt as though the car might suddenly spurt wings and take flight. I sensed his eyes on me but kept mine tight on the road ahead.

"It just kind of *poured out* . . . of its own accord. It's *nothing.*" I raised a shoulder. "I sang along to the soundtrack of *My Fair Lady* a lot as a kid."

"Do it again, would you?"

I shook my head, yet he continued to entreat. He was doing a damned good Rex Harrison. It was tempting.

"What do I get in return?"

"Everything," he said.

It took me a moment to recover my breath, hearing him *say* that. *Everything.* How could I not sing the whole song through?

Soon, we were gliding through Oxfordshire, my hands upon the wheel, rolling green unfurling around us. Velvety meadows of wildflowers and whitewashed hamlets half-hidden beyond hedgerows and apple orchards, a crisp bright sky with feather wisps of cirrus cloud, far as the eye could see.

I snuck a glance. His head was resting against the passenger window, and his eyes were closed. An exquisite imprint of his features remained: a ridge, a hollow, a curve, a sweep of eyelash merging with the road, the sky, the lush green borders blurring past, and when he stirred, something quickened deep inside of me, the feeling again of being swooped into the arch of a soaring wave, and I had to grip the steering wheel to hold it steady because my fingers were trembling—

"I love you."

There. I'd said it. Finally.

From the corner of my eye, I saw him swiveling, the words seeping into his sleepy consciousness and dilating like a drop of watercolor on linen paper. I felt his eyes on me but kept mine fixed on the road ahead.

"I do," I said, "I just—*do*." There was relief in the welling silence, the sense of him so near, of his beating heart, caged beneath muscle and simmering skin. The purr of the engine. Wind humming through an unsealed window. "But I don't want you to feel any pressure to say it back. *Zero* pressure. And it's okay if you don't. I'm honestly okay with just me loving you. One hundred percent. Well, maybe more like, ninety-two percent, but truly—"

"Jane," he said. "Pull over."

I did. Along the grainy shoulder, my hands still clamped to the wheel, my face frozen ahead, unable to look directly at him.

Outside in the meadow, a couple of sheep were bleating. They lifted their heads and gazed at me with wide vacant eyes, and when I twisted back, the sight of his face, *his face,* undid me, and I thought I might cry, because he began to look blurry—

"*Jane*—I *love* you," he said, and he was so blurry now. My lips parted, but no words came, only the taste of my tears. "I'm *in* love with you, and I love you, madly. *I do.*"

Tom took over the driving. The roads narrowed, and we began to creep down a sinuous forested lane, passing through gauzy columns of fairy-tale light until we rounded a sharp bend, which opened onto a wide, sunlit vista, and a stone manor rose up, majestic and intimidating, before us.

Tom explained that the estate and stables, where he and Freddy rode from time to time, had recently been acquired by an old class-mate of Freddy's from Eton: Lord Hamish Hancock and his wife, Lady Beatrice. And indeed, as Tom craned back to park, a tall, elegant woman in full equestrian costume skipped down the steps of the manor. I spied Freddy some distance away, leaning against the hood of a vintage sports car as if he were James Bond, while the woman strode confidently toward him, arms swinging. My pulse quickened when she began to remove her riding hat—I was steeling myself to see *her,* Amelia.

To my relief, the woman was now giving her blond bob a kitten-ish ruffle, leaning close as Freddy lit her cigarette. No red lipstick there. If body language counted for anything, the two seemed to be wildly flirting. They continued their stolen looks, their excuses to grasp and touch one another lingeringly even as Tom and I approached and were introduced to Lady Beatrice. I began to wonder if she and Freddy were having an affair. She was dryly witty, and fun, in that upper-class way—saying things in multifarious musical inflections, like: "Oh, Perdita's been bonking Dickie *for ages*—neither of the spouses could give a toss, *naturally,* but can you *blame* them?" And "Oh, *do* come to the Regatta—the so-and-so's and the *dreadful* so-and-so's are sure to be there, kicking up the *usual mischief*—"

After tea, in the *drawing room* (which was textbook *Masterpiece Theatre,* complete with a bowing staff person), Tom, Freddy, and I stood at the foot of a riding path and watched Lady Beatrice gallop off on a gleaming dark horse to see about a gamekeeper or some such on her large estate.

Freddy turned to me, ran his palm along the twitching muscles of the much smaller dappled horse he'd had the stable boy drag out, a last hope I'd join. "You're quite sure you can't be persuaded?"

"Quite sure," I said, peering down at my summer frock; having expected his insistence, I'd come prepared, wearing my excuse.

"Then I must get over my disappointment at once," he said, returning the reins to the boy, who led the horse away. "Enjoy your walk. There's a lovely path just there." He pointed to a range of low hills beyond the stables. "But beware the wood sprites and witches."

Tom darted me a little look. I wondered, again, if Freddy wasn't one of those friends a person outgrows but doesn't have the heart to reject.

"Shall we meet back at the cars, say, nineteen hundred hours?"

Catching my stymied expression, Tom made a discreet seven with his fingers, like a catcher to a pitcher. *Math.*

They mounted their horses and Freddy started off, but Tom lingered long enough to slip me a look, contained within it the brightly shining memory of the two of us by the side of the road, as if it were a photograph in a locket.

I headed for the hills, scurrying past the corral in case of... what? The girlfriend from college might pop out and say boo? Yet I couldn't stop myself from glancing over my shoulder, sensing I was being watched.

I was relieved to be away from it all and on my deserted path, taking purposeful strides like one of the Brontës might, just me and tangles of wildflowers, the heathered English countryside spreading out around me. I listened over and over to the Cure's "Friday I'm in Love" and the Pretenders' "Don't Get Me Wrong"—almost tipsy, replaying again and again, "Jane, I'm *in* love with you, and I *love you, madly...* "

Then the music blaring in my ears abruptly stopped. My phone had died.

I looked around. No idea how long I'd been walking, or what time it was. Only that the sun had slipped below the ridge and the sky was growing dark. Tom and Freddy must be waiting by the cars already, wondering what had become of me. *And what has?* I thought with a jolt of panic.

On the horizon, a flock of birds alighted suddenly from a distant oak—an undulant black swarm in the deep violet sky. I started to sprint back, finding it harder and harder now to make out the path. As I crested a small hill, my panting breaths merged with a low rumbling, like an awakening earthquake before it kicked into gear, a vibrating suddenly underfoot...the foliage around me beginning to tremble, the roar growing louder and louder until it threatened to overtake me. For the first time I felt real fear—I'd seen no one else out here, not for hours. I stumbled, lost my footing, and tumbled into brush just as a dark horse thundered past, kicking up dust. I locked eyes for an instant with the rider—caught a glimpse of a face, craning back, ghostly pale, framed by the absolute black of an equestrian hat, and a slash of searing red across her lips.

Chapter 17.

X MARKS THE SPOT

"Welcome to the old haunt," said Freddy brightly, meaning here, the Silent Woman pub, in the quaint stone-clad village of Lower Slaughter, in the Cotswolds. Above his head creaked a wooden sign of a headless woman, eerie in the flickering gas-lamp light. His vintage Jaguar hadn't started, naturally, so it remained parked at the lord and lady's estate, and we'd traveled together in the trusty Saab to grab a bite and a pint.

I stole a glance back at Tom, his hands clamped on the wheel, still idling at the curb. He lifted his fingers, an acknowledgment, not quite a wave when he felt my eyes on him. We gazed at one another, and I thought: *No, I won't tell him about the woman who nearly mowed me down—he'll think I'm crazy, paranoid.* Who would *intentionally* do that? This was me willing bad things to happen just when my life was unexpectedly perfect, some lingering aftereffect of Alex's betrayal. I would not let him poison my innate belief in the goodness of humans. And, anyway, if Amelia were there, we'd have seen her back at the stables. It must have been Lady Beatrice, not expecting someone to be stumbling along the dusty path at twilight. Perhaps she put on red lipstick to go riding.

As Tom drove away to hunt for parking, Freddy announced, "*You,* my dear, look like you could use *a drink.*" I was startled to find him scrutinizing me. He arched a brow, grasped my hand, and whisked me into a wall of humidity and boisterous voices.

The room fell silent, soon as the door clicked closed behind us. A waitress seemed to freeze too in the midst of filling a pint. As did a grizzled man taking aim at a dartboard. In fact, the entire clientele went stock-still and stared blank-faced at us. I tried not to think about that scene in *An American Werewolf in London.*

Freddy, unperturbed, led me coolly past the bar, the waitress following us with her eyes as we swept past. It wasn't until we'd slid into a back booth that the room began to reanimate and a shadow fell over the table, thudding down two pints before us. The barmaid hovered, glowering at Freddy as ale dripped down the sides of the glasses. She looked to be in her forties, with a handsome, ruddy face, full lips, and very large breasts straining the buttons of a tight flannel shirt.

"Long time no see, *sir,*" she said, her accent definitely not BBC. She darted a leery glance my way and fixed again on Freddy, whose arms were splayed somewhat arrogantly across the bench back. He was grinning up at her.

"Well, hello to you too, Maureen. How the devil have you been?" She narrowed her eyes. "Right. And we'll need another for Tom, who shall be along shortly." He said this slowly and de-liberately, tipping his head toward me, then taking a self-satisfied swig. Translation: *I am not sleeping with the woman sitting across from me.*

"Ohh, I thought…well, bollocks," she mumbled, playing ab-sently with a shirt button.

This day just got way more interesting. Especially after all the touchy-feely action with Lady Beatrice, the sexually loaded lighting of cigarettes. *What an incorrigible dog you are, Freddy,* I thought, with a mix of warmth and disgust.

"What would you like to eat, then," she said, recovering yet not quite able to ditch the scowl.

I snatched the plastic-coated menu, snuck a peek over the top to see if I might discern the story line between this unlikely pair.

"I rather fancy some of your world-famous fish and chips," said Freddy meaningfully.

"Do ya," she said, her color rising. "And for you, miss," she muttered, still intent on him.

"Umm, the same. No. Sorry. Just the chips if that's okay. Thank you."

She wheeled slowly to me, her expression a mix of confusion and contempt. Was it the American accent, or the "just the chips"?

"And for *Tom?*" Where *was* Tom?

"Fish and chips for Tom, never mind your world-famous," Freddy said cheekily. Finally, she grunted and swaggered away. "I think Maureen was frightfully baffled by *you,*" he said sotto voce, sprawling forward.

"By *me?*"

"Well, yes. As you may have guessed—" He hesitated, perhaps thinking better of admitting to something. "In point of fact it's been quite some time since we've gone riding. What with Tom's work thingy in California. His abrupt about-face on his return, the fallout, such scandal with—" He broke off as a dark shadow fell over the table. *Tom.*

Freddy jerked up, bumping the low pendant lamp and splashing jags of light ominously around the booth. "Dear me," he sputtered. "Don't just loom, man. Sit."

Tom grasped the edge of the fixture and stilled it. His expression was blank, almost stony.

"We've nearly finished our—"

"Have you?" Tom murmured, eyeing our nearly full pints. A

shriek from across the room—"Bull's eye an' you're pissed as a fart, you saucy bint"—made us turn, but the hoots and cackles seemed to defuse the tension.

Tom sidled alongside me and pulled me close, his thigh firm and toasty against mine, his body faintly vibrating from all the riding or from being miffed at Freddy for gossiping, or from sheer unbridled joy because today we'd professed our—

"Cheers!" Freddy called out, raising his glass as Maureen swooped in and deposited Tom's ale.

We toasted and drank, and I was relieved the mood was breezy again. Freddy held court, ranting about the trials of being a wealthy banker bachelor in London. Models throwing themselves at him. What to do? Which to choose? It was disgusting but fascinating. I wagered he never gave head. Or he was terrible at it. Or maybe he was great at it. He liked to be spanked. To be tied up. To have his balls tickled with an ostrich feather by a dominatrix in pleather. Or not. *The mind races.*

Mostly, I marveled at Tom's deliciously dry comebacks to Freddy's self-aggrandizing bluster. *En garde!* The parries and ripostes. Screwball comedy repartee between British men. Hadn't we all had a friend like Freddy? Someone we loved simply because we'd known them forever.

Under the table, Tom's warm, newly callused palm found its way to my knee, then under my skirt. He proceeded to give my thigh a good sustained squeeze—

"Why so long to park, old chap? Has the town been overrun by some music festival or another?"

Tom's hand stilled. "No—I...got a call. Not important." He sounded flustered.

But then he very confidently slid his hand farther up, along the tingling flesh of my inner thigh, and I didn't stop him. How amazing it was that my new boyfriend could converse with his improbable friend and take casual swigs of Guinness with *one hand,* while simultaneously, surreptitiously, doing what he was doing to my leg *with the other*—now easing apart my thighs, now beginning to graze a single, renegade finger upward. I rested my head on his shoulder, let my face tip into his chest—to feel the hypnotic vibrations when he spoke—to marvel at his acute knowledge of the map of my body—finding the fastest route, but not rushing, nor speeding, but rather gliding deftly—del-i-cate-ly—just shy of hovering, over the thin cotton of my underwear, until he reached his destination, the pin of my map, the X marks the spot, where he parked it, save for an almost imperceptible twitching pressure—

And Maureen reappeared.

She set down generous platters of fish and chips for the men, and a meager side plate of chips for me. She was probably hoping I'd wander out onto the moors and get mauled by a werewolf.

The black eyes, the brutal red lips, the ghostlike pallor, thundering past on her gleaming dark horse.

This was absurd. Ridiculous. Pathetic. Yet somehow the fleeting thought was enough to kill my appetite.

I pressed closer to Tom, slipped a palm into the gap between his thighs, which he tightened, on instinct, knowing I'd wanted him to.

Music began to play somewhere. A guitar and a man singing. This was a pub, after all. I craned out and discovered the dulcet disembodied voice belonged, incongruously, to the grizzled dart player. And that his saucy lady friend was playing guitar, and incredibly well.

"Oh, I love this song," I announced without thinking. It was John Denver, "Take Me Home, Country Roads." Then mumbled, "But they need *someone* to sing the harmony."

"Go on then," Freddy chuckled, flapping a hand at me. "Join in. Promise we won't snicker."

Tom shot me a look, and I knew in that instant he hadn't told Freddy what I did for a living. Not that I actually made what you'd call a living from music these days. But wow, Freddy was right; Tom *was* discreet.

Tom slid out of the booth to make way for me. I skated quickly over and stood watching them play until I couldn't stop myself from singing out the high harmony, not merely because Freddy'd challenged me to, but because someone had to! That harmony was the humble puzzle piece that went unnoticed but, to me, made the song. Perhaps it had something to do with "The Rain in Spain" in the car earlier, but I surprised even myself when the notes rang out, clear and bright and free; they seemed to have a life of their own, as if my voice belonged to someone else. I felt a surge of exhilaration, and in my chest, a sensation akin to flurried beating wings, as of a captive bird that'd been sprung from its cage.

And though I sensed Freddy and Maureen in my periphery, as well as a few phone screens held aloft, when I locked eyes with the dart player and melded my voice to his unpredictably honeyed one, everything else disappeared. I was *her,* that other girl, who lived inside me, the one with the pluck, the audacity to burst into song in a roomful of watchful faces. And then there was only singing, and music, and I thought, *Here it is! Here it is, at last.* What strange magic it was, that a song could connect perfect strangers this way. There was nothing better. And nothing better than singing in a pub, where I could drink in every smile, feel the tangible warmth of real human communion; I'd take this over a big fancy stage any day.

And it was suddenly so clear! Some people aren't meant to be pop stars. And some, like Jonesy, just *are.* Could it be the life I wanted was the one in England, with Tom? To write, record, perform in small venues—a folk singer's life? I'd never yearned for the spotlight, only the music, only to strive to give others what music had unwaveringly given to me. An outpouring of love, of expression, of connection.

I caught Tom's eye as I sang the final notes, and he beamed at me. And when it was over, the dart player gave a shout-out to the "young lass," "for lending her sweet voice." I smiled and gestured my thanks back. As I returned to the cool dark of the booth, Freddy, beaming, blocked my path. He gave me a salutary clap on the back and said: "You could be a singer. I'm not kidding, seriously, *you could.*"

Chapter 18.

MONDAY, MONDAY

With Tom departed for work, and with Mrs. T *everywhere,* I found myself unable to accomplish anything on a Monday morning beyond making myself a few more espressos. I perched at the edge of the sofa and stared, totally jacked, at the rain; its rhythmic patter on the rooftop commingled with distant pealing church bells, a sonic cliché of Oxford, which a person a little less jacked might find soothing. A person a little less stuck might pluck from the air to use in a song. My phone chimed. Pippa. Naturally.

"You near a computer?"

"No?" I had a sudden plunging feeling. "Has something *terrible* happened? My brother, right? He's just got here, and he's already fucked up." The job had been my idea, so this was all my fault. I leapt up and began pacing.

"No. He hasn't," she said. "In fact, he's been *great.* Why do you always think that? It's something good. Get your computer."

"That's going to be a challenge," I said, lowering my voice to a whisper. "I'm hiding from Tom's housekeeper. She's cleaning the bedroom and the computer's trapped in there with her."

"You're not *really* hiding from Tom's cleaner?" she murmured, incredulous.

"Oh yes. I am." I tiptoed toward the closed door, light vibrating around its edges, steeling myself for Linda Blair.

"But why?"

"Dunno. She has a kind of prison matron vibe. And I can just tell, she *really* doesn't like me."

The door was very slightly ajar. Through the narrow crack, I spied Mrs. T, eyeing the odd configuration of pillows stacked up on Tom's side of the bed.

"You there? Jane?" Pippa's voice pealed from the speaker. Mrs. T snapped her head back; for a hot second, our eyes met. She sighed and began stripping the bed, so I swooped in, snatched up my laptop, and slipped out.

"I'm *baack*," I whispered, scurrying for the living room.

"Thank god. Now google yourself. You're *everywhere!*" Pippa chimed. "The show's been announced! *Sold out! Already!*"

"*Really?* Wow," I managed, my heart careening. It hadn't seemed real, until *now*. Fear. Panic. *Jonesy*. The Royal Albert Hall. It was real. All of it. I flung myself onto the sofa and booted the computer. "Amazing, and phew." I feigned calm: "And now I can tell *Tom*. It's been torture keeping this whole thing a secret, and he's such a *huge* Jonesy fan…" *Right*. There was that. "He'll be *so impressed with me…*" My voice trailed off.

Oh no, the photos. Basically, same as ever. Embarrassing screen shots from the "Can't You See I Want You" video. And .gifs. The most widely circulated: me doing my ignominious homage to Sharon Stone's crotch flash.

"Jane?"

"One sec"—*fuck*—"just looking at this *Daily Mail* thing…"

Onetime sultry songstress Jane Start to join Jonesy as his very special guest at the Royal Albert Hall, 20 November, causing speculation that this once hot pair are hot once more. Jane

Start had her 'fifteen minutes' a decade ago when she burst onto the music scene blah blah blah. *Recently spotted in the U.K.—rumored to be dating—*

"Noo!" I nearly knocked the laptop from my knees.

"What?"

"Tom. They've written about him!" But how could they possibly have known? And why did the press always assume Jonesy and I were lovers? But I knew the answer: It made the better story.

I scrolled down, clicked on the link with the sound muted, suddenly queasy. Me, singing in the pub, and Tom looking wistfully on.

"'Don't get your knickers in a twist, ladies,'" I read aloud, dismayed. "'Not *the* Tom Hardy. This one's an Oxford professor specializing in Romantic literature, *naturally.* Perhaps he's writing a love poem for Miss Start this very moment. But what will happen when the retired songbird reunites with former flame Jonesy at the Royal Albert Hall...'"

"Retired? Rubbish." Pippa fumed. "But Christ, I better get you a work visa, and fast, gah."

"Ugh. They've included a headshot of Tom from the college website." There was a silence on the other end of the line.

"He's lovely-looking. Which you've left me *to imagine,*" she said, pointedly. "Please tell me you're not keeping him from me *intentionally.*"

Busted.

"I know I speak my mind, but I have your best interest at heart. You know that, darling, and sometimes, well..."

"My judgment sucks?"

I flashed on all my terrible choices: Dick-Actor, Alex, the Soup Stalker. (I'm really ok, I remember texting him, after finding yet *more soup* on my doorstep, long after I'd recovered from a little cold, hoping he'd get the message.) They appeared in my mind as in a police lineup. I pictured myself turning to the detective and saying: *It's* all *of them. They're* all *bad.*

In the silence, the vacuum hummed down the hall.

"Jane? You still there?"

"Yes. And I haven't kept you from Tom intentionally. We've just been...busy? Oh god"—glimpsing his face again on my computer screen—"Tom's a private, serious person. He'll *hate* being linked to this garbage."

I slammed shut the laptop and began to pace again in front of the bank of windows. *I* hated being linked to tabloid garbage. And the whole "former flame" thing. *If only it was that simple,* I thought queasily, wringing my hands. From the corner of my eye, the *Sun* and the *Daily Mail* peered from the tops of Mrs. T's Tesco bags. What would she think if she put it together?

I plunked onto the sofa.

"No. Surely he'll understand," Pippa said unconvincingly. "But here's the crazy thing. The phone's been ringing off the hook. Requests for *you.* Breakfast TV! Even a guest judge thingy on *X Factor*!"

Breakfast TV?

And I was suddenly there. In the past. In the future. *Poised at the edge of a white leather sofa, beginning to sweat under hot studio lights. I'm in the requisite short skirt—have to look sexy, keep up appearances. Yet a man can look sexy in a suit. An insistent makeup person has just slathered my legs with bronzer. I fear I may be inadvertently flashing my—I place my hand inconspicuously over the triangle of shadow where my skirt ends and the tops of my slippery, freshly oiled thighs have left a gap—whoops. I'm being asked a question by a gleaming-toothed TV presenter, wearing even more makeup than me (and I'm practically in clown-face). I'm perspiring now, my thighs so slippery, I feel myself slow-motion sliding off the edge of the sofa, potentially leaving behind a misinterpretable bronzer stain.*

I hear myself saying: "Sorry? Can you repeat the question?"

"Right, let's try this again." Laughter. Canned. "Do tell us, Jane. Is Jonesy as wonderful at lovemaking as he is at music?"

"Jane?" This time it was Pippa. "The press offers are honestly a fabulous opportunity."

Groan. "It's only because people think Jonesy and I—"

"You're wrong. People like you, genuinely. But I won't lie, the gossip isn't hurting to put you back in people's minds again."

Did I *want* to be in people's minds again? This way?

"Take a breath, relax, give it a think," Pippa said calmingly.

I did as she suggested, conscious of the whir of the washer, the oscillating hum of the vacuum down the hall, and that the rain had subsided. As Pippa conferred in the background with Will about visas, I thought: *I love music, that fact is indisputable.* Music, listening or playing, had saved me, day in and day out, the entirety of my life. But the music *business* was another story altogether. Was this the dance one had to do, to not be relegated to the Where Are They Now bin? Like poor Spinal Tap, who deserved so much more?

But then I thought of the great Bobbie Gentry, her brilliant "Ode to Billie Joe." How one day, she just, walked away...

Pippa was back. "Now, before I ring off, I do think you ought to seriously consider the guest judge thingy on *X Factor.* Could be jolly, no?"

So. Not. Jolly.

The great span of windows stretching nearly the length of Tom's living room transformed into bright sheets of mercury; the sun had finally broken through. A sign! The only reality show I wanted to take part in was the one right *here,* with *my guitar,* and with *him. I would find a way to express myself in song, I would.*

"I know your heart is in the right place, but I just can't," I told her. "For so many reasons. For one, somebody always gets humiliated on those shows, and why would I want to do that to

anyone? And why does everything have to be a *contest?* Isn't *life*
contest enough as it is?"

"Sleep on it?"

"Leopard Pants wouldn't do it."

"He *has,*" she said, "he's done them all."

Chapter 19.

REBEL REBEL

One hour later, it was pissing down rain again. Mrs. T was hunched over the dryer, folding my underwear. I'd been tinkering quietly on guitar, hoping a melody might magically wed with the lyrics I'd jotted down in Devon. But honestly it was impossible to sing with *her* here.

"Hi! Just letting you know I'm running out"—*because if I stay imprisoned in this flat with you one minute longer, I'll lose my*—"to do a few errands," I said brightly. "And thank you, very much, for doing my laundry."

"Okay," she mumbled, retrieving another pair from the small mountain; her folding technique was mesmerizing, like origami.

"Is there anything you need? I can pop by Tesco and pick something up?"

"No," she said, flatly. But as I turned to depart, she added, "Thank you," in a more conciliatory tone.

"Cool. Well. I'm off."

"You need umbrella," she said, still on task. "Can borrow mine if you don't have. It's blue one, at bottom of stairs." Her nimble fingers were working a floral pair into the shape of a crane.

"Oh, but that's incredibly kind of you. Thank you so much."

She responded by way of a grunt, yet I had the impression Mrs. T and I were headed toward a détente. Perhaps she'd gained new respect for me, seeing I favored Soviet-style underwear.

Moments later, I was on the damp stoop, pleased that the rain had subsided. I was buttoning my coat, vexed that the video clip of Tom and me at the pub could have landed at the *Daily Mail*. Had Maureen the waitress sent it? Or Freddy? He *was* a gossip.

I jumped at the sharp clap of a front door. Tom's neighbor! In the time I'd been staying here, the place had seemed utterly deserted.

"Imbecile postman strikes again!" cried an elderly man of small stature, his eyes cast down, shuffling through a large stack of mail. Yet I had the distinct impression he'd addressed his comment to me.

"Oh! But you're not—?" He gasped, peering up. He inched closer, scrutinizing me through thick round spectacles that seemed to magnify his surprise. "Why, I simply assumed you were—"

"I'm Jane." I bowed somewhat ludicrously, but his hands were occupied, and also there was something of another time about him.

"Well then, hello, Jane, who gave me a *start*," he said, a bit charmed.

Ha. One day I'd tell him my surname. "Sorry for that."

"It's quite all right, my dear. One of Professor Hardy's new students, I presume? Then you won't mind seeing he gets his post, as you're at his door."

He pressed the letters into my palm and began maneuvering his thinning tufts of faded copper hair into some semblance of order. Perhaps it was better to impersonate a student than admit I was his girlfriend, last seen on the internet flashing her—

"Romantics or Victorians?" he asked, and then thankfully before I could concoct a response: "Either way Professor Hardy is a marvelous tutor and you will *love* him. *Love him.* I'm quite sure of it."

If only he knew.

"Professor Tobias Thornbury. Classics. Magdalen College. How do you do." He thrust out his hand, finally.

"I'm—well? And you?"

He gave me a moist lingering squeeze; we stood at even height, his round face and round magnified eyes recalling a baby owl. Except old.

"I won't *lie,*" he murmured, suddenly confessional, releasing my palm. "I am rather disconsolate after three glorious months in *E-tal-ee,* slaving away at my latest commission." At this, he flung back an end of his wool scarf like a gallant. "How I shall long for the sunshine. The wine. Bronzed gods and goddesses traipsing about in their summery attire. And to think I traded it all *for this?*" He opened his palms to the sky and made a little Pagliacci frown. "This gloom, this frigid clime? Alack and alas, the life of an Oxford professor." He adjusted his spectacles. I could have sworn he was working out that I wasn't one of Tom's grad students.

"Actually. Professor Hardy isn't home. He just this moment dashed out."

"Well then perhaps I'll take those back, my dear—our postman is rather daft. Can't make out the difference between our flats. You see, the numbers are the same, but the *letters?* Professor Hardy's *A* and I'm *B.*"

I shot him my best "idiot postman" look, still clutching the letters. I ought to admit I was *living* here, but he kept right on.

"Most annoying. I daresay some of that post dates back to the start of summer. I pray there aren't too many unpaid bills just there or Professor Hardy's electric will get shut off and I daresay he'll be forced to peruse his many rare volumes *by candlelight.*" He thrust out his palm, like, *Fork over the mail, psycho schoolgirl, I'm officially done confabulating with you.* "I'll pop back this evening, shall I? Press them into the professor's hand myself?"

Just then it began to drizzle.

"Yes, of course." I was returning the stack to his moist little paw when something caught my eye. *Amelia Danvers.* Handwritten in formal cursive on the upper left of the envelope, the ink bleeding a little from the rain.

Surely it didn't matter that Tom was still in touch with Amelia. Or that she wrote him physical letters, *in cursive.* The British do cling to tradition—they've still got a monarch, for god's sake. But I wished I'd caught her address before handing Old Owl Eyes back the stack. I was guessing she lived in London, based on the number of posh events she attended there. But why did she bother if they were no fun and she never smiled? Maybe the frosty stare was simply her camera face. Some people are extremely committed to camera face. No one from the 1800s smiled for photographs. Perhaps Amelia Danvers was like that.

Back from aimless wandering, still disquieted, I watched Mrs. T set off, from Tom's windows, trudging down the rain-slicked sidewalk in her overcoat and her plastic rain bonnet, until she disappeared from view.

I was sure mail with my name on it still landed in Alex's box, and soulless, honorless Jessica was right now dumping my beautiful issue of the *Paris Review* in the trash so she could flip mindlessly through copies of *Shape* and *Self.* I thought of the old professor below these very floorboards, perhaps napping, perhaps aroused, dreaming of Gina Lollobrigida, wearing only an apron, feeding him pasta straight from a copper pot. Lonely old geezer. My heart broke a little for him.

Unable to shake my mood, and with an unsettling sense of foreboding, I experienced a *genuine* urge to pick up a guitar, if only to mollify myself, and found myself in my creepy writing nook at long last, beginning once more to pluck out chords. This time I felt myself getting somewhere; there were sparks, there was warmth, a growing nearness, as if to simmering coals, and firelight. The melody took shape before any keeper lyrics, with the quality of a lullaby that might twinkle from a small antique music box and which I hoped might soothe me. Yet against the gloom, the gloam, the rain, my sour state of mind, it sounded *too* sweet. So, I switched a few of the notes to dissonant semi-tones and there it was... a feeling, like yearning, like when your heart turns over in your chest, or butterflies dart around inside you but you can't catch them. Love was fleeting. We can delude ourselves, but—

"That's beautiful."

I startled. Tom was at the far end of the bedroom, listening with that unnerving stillness. I felt suddenly shy, caught.

"Don't stop," he said softly, but I leaned the guitar against the desk and moved toward him. "Sorry I interrupted. That was so lovely, and rather haunting. Do you know the song by the Left Banke? It's *not* 'Walk Away Renée'—" he broke off, searching for the name.

"'Pretty Ballerina.'"

"Yes," he said, beaming.

He'd put it together before I had. All the while I'd been humming my little sketch, I'd visualized a ballerina figurine twirling creakily inside a music box.

"It's just a start—nothing really," I murmured, somehow jittery and flushed. "But thank you. Now I'm inspired to finish it." *Let it be true—if by luck, or magic.* I smiled up at him. "And really, I want to hear about *your* first day."

I experienced an overwhelming rush of gratitude for him. He knew the Left Banke! A band that deserved more recognition than they ever got. I pictured Tom and me, hands clasped, strolling the Left Bank in Paris. How dreamy that would be. "I met your neighbor this morning. Professor Thornbury."

"Did you?"

"Yes. He's like a character from Dickens, or maybe George Eliot."

"You're *right,*" he said, like this was some great revelation, and I felt suddenly very clever, except I still hadn't finished *Middlemarch.* Had anybody?

"He's been here a very long time, a bit lonely I suspect. Makes a good neighbor. No loud parties. Away most summers."

"Well, he has a big stack of your mail, which he was *adamant* you pick up. Something about an unpaid bill—"

Tom shook his head. "I don't get much mail here. Nothing of importance."

Huzzah. That must include Amelia Danvers!

"He assumed I was one of your students. I'm not sure why, but I was afraid to correct him." I hesitated. Tom's expression was disconcertingly serene. "And actually, I have some bigger news," I continued nervously. "Maybe you saw? It's been, um, online. I've got a job, a 'gig.' I'll be performing with Jonesy, at the Royal Albert Hall. In November—"

His eyes widened. "Jane, that's *incredible.* You must be thrilled! My god, congratulations!"

"Yes—thank you," I stuttered, a little thrown. It *was* thrilling, for a Jonesy fan. But for me (though I was most grateful for the job) it was nerve-racking, panic-inducing. If only I knew what Jonesy expected of me. Yet knowing, after ten years, this was my last chance for a comeback. *Please let me not fuck it up.* "I wanted to tell you for ages, but I was sworn to secrecy. Jonesy was adamant, *to say the least.* But the thing is, today it was officially 'announced.' And well, there's also *this.*" I held my breath as I pulled up the *Daily Mail* piece on my phone, scrutinizing his face as he read. I knew how this could go. He hadn't signed on for tabloid bullshit or for being pitted publicly against an enigmatic rock star, or for .gifs circulating of his girlfriend spread-eagle on a chair.

He finished reading, his opal eyes inscrutable as he looked up. "I've never been part of a love triangle," he said, with a delicious trace of a smile, and I felt suddenly so lucky to be here with him. That he didn't care about the tabloids. That I'd started a song that might even be good.

"But I take issue with the word 'onetime.' 'Onetime sultry songstress'...It should say irresistibly sultry. Infuriatingly sultry."

"Stop." I reached up and covered his mouth with my palm to prevent him from going on, color flooding my face, but he very gently tore it away.

"Ruinously sultry. That's it." And he smiled again, satisfied.

I was smiling back when his phone buzzed. He sighed, our eyes still locked, but a downward glance at the screen and the color ebbed from his face. He stuttered, rattled, that he was needed, *a work emergency,* and promised, "I'll race home to you, darling, just as soon as I'm able."

I chose to ignore his pallor, a glint of rising panic in his eye— because he'd thought to string "home" and *me* together in the same sentence, *the same breath.*

Soon as the door at the base of the steps clapped shut, I picked up the guitar and began writing in earnest.

It was finally Friday night and we were late, negotiating a maze of pedestrians choking the High Street en route to Magdalen College. My official entrée into Tom's world: an evening chapel service, to be followed by "High Table," a formal dinner in which the faculty sat literally at an elevated table and apparently ignored the students dining below. *Jeez.* Surely that wouldn't apply to Tom, I mused; he was so clearly devoted to his. And besides, I felt giddy, intrigued. I'd already fallen in love with Oxford the city: its great swaths of honey-hued stone and endless array of vintage book sellers. The cozy cafés painted creamy-rich macaron colors. Yet a nagging apprehension had persisted; the University of Oxford as portrayed in, say, *Brideshead Revisited,* which made the place out to be insular, classist, and snooty? There was also the pesky issue of the tabloid frenzy still circulating online; surely Tom's colleagues were strictly consumers of academic scholarship and highbrow lit and wouldn't have stumbled across any .gifs?

"Careful!" Tom called out suddenly and wrenched me up to the curb as a peloton of cyclists sped past. I'd been lost in thought, and only now did I take in Magdalen College's bell tower, looming in all its stony Gothic enormity directly across from us. I felt a shiver and wondered if Tom was nervous, too.

Inside the chapel, a choir of young men was already singing, and we slithered quickly up a set of stairs and secured seats just as the chaplain began a reading. As he droned on, I found myself feeling not only extremely Jewish, but fearful I'd never fit in here having been raised by a couple of beatniks who eschewed formality and convention, fascinating as this brand was.

I became intrigued with the older gentleman to my left. His wire-framed Jeffrey Dahmer–style glasses were held together with tape, and a Waitrose bag was tucked between stained Wallabees, as if he'd simply been out for groceries and thought he'd pop by for a spot of religion. His beatific openmouthed smile transfixed me until a whiff of his breath forced me back to the sermon and dais.

"Almighty and most merciful Father, we have wandered and strayed from your ways...we have followed too much the devices and desires of our own hearts."

At which point most everyone in the joint dropped to their knees and started in on some hardcore praying, heads bowed, hands clasped. I immediately regretted using the prayer kneeling cushion as a footrest for my slightly muddy shoes. Tom's head was bowed too; sensing me, he glanced my way. There was a little smile in his eyes, which I took to mean: *Don't worry. I'm not really praying, just being polite.* Or alternatively: *Whoops, you caught me in the middle of "Dear God, please let Jane not do anything* embarrassing *in front of my colleagues tonight."*

I smiled weakly back, bowed *my* head: *Dear God, please don't let me do anything* embarrassing *in front of Tom's colleagues.* I figured I'd give it the old college try, but then gazing out at everyone else, I couldn't help thinking that surely some of them must be distracted by other thoughts, like *CHRIST, did I remember to clear the porn history on the old iPad? Or chuck the cum-encrusted tissues left wadded up on the nightstand?* That sort of thing. Yet it was amazing to consider: Most everyone here was thinking exceedingly *personal* thoughts, all together in such a public place, which I had to admit was rather cool.

"Let the wicked abandon their ways, and the unrighteous, of their thoughts."

I knew it. Here was the stuff about guilt. I wondered what Dahmer Glasses was guilty of. Perhaps his wife couldn't handle his breath, but his neighbor's wife was more forgiving?

Jesus. Now *I* felt guilty for *my* thought about a sweet little old man who couldn't even afford new glasses. It wasn't his fault he suffered from halitosis.

"Father of our Lord Jesus Christ, we confess that we have sinned in thought, and word, and deed."

"I have a confession," I whispered to Tom, feeling suddenly *very* hot for him. I nestled closer, resting my cheek against his warm scratchy one, his smile palpable against mine. "Soo, I was looking for a pencil, figured you'd stash one in your bedside drawers, and I *inadvertently* stumbled onto one of your books? The one with the Venus de Milo on the cover? And I feel just terrible—"

"Did you like it?"

I was arrested by his swift, nonjudgmental response. "I *did.* Very much. Excellent book. I mean...not the prose exactly."

"I'm glad you enjoyed it. What's mine is yours." And he

smiled, so luminously the whole gloomy place brightened, and I was seized with an almighty powerful urge (what a great fucking onomatopoetic word, *urge*), the same rogue urge Julie Christie's character had in the movie *Shampoo,* when she blurts out at the uptight Republican dinner, "What I really want to do is—" Then, whoosh, she disappears under the table and surrenders to it with Warren Beatty's character.

Instead, I placed my palm on the firm curve of Tom's upper thigh and I prayed. *I shall not feel guilty about my urge and I shall continue to* worship *that scene in* Shampoo.

As soon as the service ended, Tom took my hand and we dashed like teenagers out the doors of the chapel, through the deserted stone cloisters, and up a set of stairs to his "rooms." His robe was required, apparently, for the formal High Table dinner.

"It's odd you haven't shown me your office until now," I murmured, in the cool of the stone hall, as he dug for his keys.

"I know. Why is that?" he said offhandedly.

You tell me, man of mystery.

Perhaps inside there would finally be photographs of the special moments in his life, with his friends, his parents, things I knew nothing about. Or at the very least, some enticing clues.

And maybe it was the autumn chill, or simply this thought, which sent a shiver through me: You can *know* a person, know their body intimately (all the subtle places to touch, all the things you can do with your hands, your lips, your tongue), yet at the same time recognize they're still a complete stranger.

"Here we are." He smiled over his shoulder as he opened the door, gesturing for me to step in first.

The room was bathed in dusky amber light, which streamed in through a pair of spectacular leaded-glass windows, and possessed a faint, pleasing, woody scent from the many books lining the walls.

There was a sofa covered in a rich caramel chenille, and mismatched chairs arranged around a large coffee table. A mini-fridge hummed, atop it a plug-in teapot, boxes of PG Tips, and a bottle of scotch. No photographs, I noticed with a plunge of disappointment. Yet, I found myself eyeing the sofa again, wondering if Tom had ever had sex there. Maybe I'd seen too many movies? Or maybe I was simply perverse, these dirty thoughts a reaction to all the talk of righteousness, of wicked ways and deeds.

Still, I flashed upon an imagined Monica, draped over that very sofa back. Tom was behind her, pressed into her, his palms softly cupping her ample breasts, relishing the arousing weight of them. Her eyes half-mast and her full lips parted, *his* lips grazing her neck, his hand pushing aside the skimpy satiny underpinning so he could thrum his finger where it counted most as they moved together— I could almost feel the pleasing pressure of the sofa back against her abdomen and had instinctively rested my palm on mine when the real flesh-and-blood Tom racked into focus. He'd thrown on the robe we'd come here for in the first place and was leaning now into the desk edge, one long leg crossed casually over the other.

"I don't know how to tell you this?" he said, furrowing his brow. *What?!*

"No," he said quickly, reading my alarm. "It's just that, at Oxford, I'm afraid we call these things gowns, not robes, like in—"

"Harry Potter." I finished his sentence. Our first text exchange! He hadn't the heart to break it to me then. *Oh, Jesus fuck, how I adored him.* "Well, thank you for letting me know." I played it cool, given my whipped-up state. "And good timing. I might have gone up to one of your colleagues at dinner and said something stupid, like, 'Nice robe.' And by the way, I love your office. And your *gown.*"

For an instant, he seemed sad. But then I realized it was only that particular smile of his, a smile imbued with feeling, of being stirred in some way. That smile had a funny way of tormenting me, especially here, seeing him in his professor gown, for the very first time.

I felt my lips part, my skin prickle. "I *wonder*. If *Monica*...ever visited you here?" It just slipped out. A giddiness swept over me, but I didn't let it show. "Or perhaps *you'd previously* had a 'tutorial' in *her* office?"

Tom didn't so much as move a muscle. Mostly I sensed his surprise that I'd even clocked her name. But he took his time before answering.

"Yes. I suppose she did," he said finally.

Oh.

We gazed at one another, and a gathering warmth, a sensation akin to a mounting tropical storm, surged within me. Tom was so deliciously impossible to read, I could hardly stand it. And all at once I *imagined* myself saying in a deep, sultry voice: *Text her. Invite her here to join you with your new American girlfriend whose mind is roaring with dirty thoughts. And tell her to bring the satiny things.*

Ha! What was happening to me? Had he hidden a wand beneath his professor gown, and covertly cast a spell on me? Was this some form of madness? I truly only desired *him*.

He reached out, as if he'd been reading my mind all along. I stepped closer until his fingertips made contact, until he was grasping and tugging me to him, wrapping the gown and his arms around me, burying his face in my neck in a ravenous way, his warm panting breaths and the rustle of silk in my ears almost too much to bear—

"Jane, what's happening to us?"

"I don't know, but I suppose we must get control of ourselves."

"Must we?"

"I think we must. High Table, formal dinner—which is it?" I said, wanting to press every inch of myself into him and doing my best to accomplish this goal. "Why can't you British decide on the name?"

"I don't *bloody care* about formal dinner," he murmured, his face in my hair, his hands everywhere, pinpricks of pleasure all through me. "Let's skip it."

"I'm all good with that," I murmured back. Oxford formalities could wait. Truth was, I was only hungry for this.

I took hold of his wrists and clapped his palms crisply and meaningfully to my ass, so that he knew in no uncertain terms it was his to have, to hold, to love, and to cherish, which it was, exclusively. Both of us were messy-haired and glassy-eyed, a couple of panting dogs. The thought of him, prim on a dais, surrounded by self-serious pedagogues seemed suddenly absurd.

And then I tugged one of his hands free and walked us directly to the sofa, and positioned myself, as I'd fantasized Monica, because whether or not he'd had sex in his office with her, he would certainly have sex in his office with me.

The following Monday, I had just set a pile of Professor Thornbury's misdelivered mail before his door and was preparing to dart away when—

"Oh, Jane—*it's you.*"

Bespectacled eyes peered from the little window cut in his door; he began fumbling with the various bolts as I shivered out on the stoop, trapped.

"Daft postman strikes again," he said, ushering me in. "Toss them there, if you would, dear," gesturing to a desk to my left, already shuffling ahead. "I'll put the kettle on, shall I? You simply *must* try the ginger-poached pears from the Covered Market. You won't be the same once you've sampled them, *life-changing,* they are," he chimed over his shoulder. "That is my promise to you."

"Okay, yes," I said, but he'd already disappeared, and now I really was stuck. Tom was right, the old professor did seem terribly lonely.

So, this was what lay below us. Thornbury's flat was painfully dank and dreary by comparison, almost subterranean; it had a decent number of windows, but with views of gnarled tree trunks and only scant natural light. The decor, the expected professorial clutter: books and *objets,* worn furniture draped with wooly afghans, framed sketches of Corinthian columns and caryatids, faded photos of him smiling toothily beneath a floppy sun hat at the Parthenon or the Colosseum, in all of them alone, probably snapped by some tourist he'd handed his camera to.

"Welcome to my humble surrounds," he said gaily, tottering back with a tray. "*Flattery* will get you everywhere."

"It's wonderful, Professor Thornbury. I can see"—scraping for something nice to say—"you've traveled. A lot."

"Why, thank you, and quite right." He grinned, placing the tray on his coffee table. "I have indeed. Sit, sit, *please,*" he insisted, jutting his chin at a lumpy armchair. "It's very good to see you, my dear, and do call me Thorny. Everyone does." He gave me a wink, dropped onto the sofa, at a right angle to me, and began pouring out tea. "I shan't prick, *unless provoked,* but now, you simply must try some pear." He inched a chipped Wedgwood plate toward me and leaned forward in anticipation, observing me keenly.

"Mmm." I smiled, taking a small bite. "It's sort of like…eating perfume, except *delicious*." He appeared to be hanging on every word, so I went on. "Buttery. Yet textured. And, wow wow *wow*." His eyes widened; how easy he was to please. "There's suddenly a whole new set of flavors. A *second act,* if you will, which is all about spice and zest."

"You see!" He gave a salutary clap. "What did I tell you! You shan't ever look at a pear the same way after today." No, I didn't think I ever would. "I knew fast friends we'd be, Jane, but *you,*" he said, brows raised, spearing himself a big bite, "Professor Hardy's *inamorata?* What astonishing news. And I thought perhaps I'd see you at High Table, Friday last?"

Whoops. But did he just say *inamorata?!* Hilarious. "And *you* thought I was one of his *students*."

He protested, mouth full of pear. "Professors and their students," he mumbled, chewing, dabbing the corners of his mouth with a napkin. "No, my dear, this is *Oxford.* Founded in 1096. You'd hardly be the first. It's simply that Professor Hardy and his *former* consort kept company for so long they might have well been chiseled in marble, Orpheus and Eurydice, such handsome creatures both. I had *no idea* the two had broken it up. *I* used to stay abreast of all the college tittle-tattle, but alas and alack, consumed by my work." He sighed and took a smaller bite. "I knew them as students, and *she,* in the heady bloom of her youth, so *statuesque,* so *fine of figure,* skin of lily, cheek of rose," he said with reverence. "I daresay *Amelia Danvers* reduced everyone to a puddle." He winked at me, speared more pear, and began chewing with relish.

Amelia. They'd been together so long they might as well have been chiseled in marble? My stomach plunged. I flashed on the recent letter, from her to him, when Thornbury's face came into focus, his eyes magnified through his thick spectacles.

"Have some more pear, dear, lest I devour them all," he said, suddenly contrite, intuiting, and pushed the plate closer.

"That's all right, I had a massive breakfast." *Lie.*

"If you insist," he said, impaling another. "You're very kind, Jane. *And* lovely." The latter so obviously tacked on after gushing about Amelia. "I expect I shall see you at the faculty dinner forthcoming, on Professor Hardy's arm? You should be safe," he said, leaning conspiratorially. "Professor Danvers is off to Harvard this term on a grant, I hear."

Professor Danvers. I nearly choked. *No one* ever mentioned she was an Oxford professor! The photos online made her out to be a *socialite.*

"Or, was it *Princeton?*" He blew his nose into a napkin, quick and sharp. "Somewhere with ivy-covered walls I'm quite sure. At any rate you should be spared any awkwardness amid so many of our colleagues, *thrust together,* in one large but *very stuffy room,*" he said with an air of scandal.

But his face flushed at the sight of mine, draining of color, the ginger-poached pears rising most inconveniently.

So. She was his college girlfriend, who was now *also* an Oxford professor, and Tom had apparently dated her all that while?

I glanced at Old Owl Eyes. He was chasing a sliver of pear around his plate. Perhaps he was senile? Or simply out of the loop, remembering them as student sweethearts from years ago.

Then a sudden sense sent my heart careening. Had Tom kept me from attending High Table *deliberately?*

I'd determined I would pry a bit more out of Old Owl Eyes by casually inquiring how long he'd lived here when my cell rang. Pippa.

I darted an apology to Thornbury, but he flapped his hand for me to take the call and I scurried to the window, my back to him.

"Hi," I said, under my breath.

"Hiiii, Jane, I haven't wanted to bother you with businessy things while you're writing, but something rather urgent has come up and I thought I really must ring. How are you, by the way?"

"Good question," I said, searching out a patch of sky through the gnarled branches, a view of storm clouds dividing like bad cells before my eyes.

"Uh-oh. Then perhaps it's best I rip the Band-Aid off straight-away."

Chapter 20.

DIRTY DANCING

"I'm such an *idiot*," I groaned to Pippa, a minute later, on speaker, bounding up Tom's stairs two at a time. *This was very bad news.* "I mean I could have just reached out to them and said, 'Look, guys? Let's all make a pact never to upload the old skeletons to the old inter-webs.' Ugh. This is the worst day ever."

I was already freaked out about *Professor* Danvers, Tom's long-time girlfriend, about whom no one here could stop gossiping. Except him.

At the top of the landing, I hunched, panting.

"Worry not," Pippa insisted, "I've got my solicitor on it. She's organizing a cease and desist thingy as we speak."

I slammed the door behind me and stormed through the living room.

"Okay but *fuck fuck fuckity fuck.* Let me just get to my computer and see how hideous it is—"

I came to an abrupt halt by the laundry room, newly aware of the whir of the washing machine and the Tesco bags lining the hallway.

"Trapped again with the scary housekeeper?" Pippa bellowed from my phone. I stared at Mrs. T and Mrs. T stared back, a pair of my underwear dangling from between her thumb and forefinger.

"Sorry," I mumbled, "I've just got to...do something."

I sped off for the bedroom, leaving Mrs. T frozen there with my underwear.

Tucked safely in the privacy of the bedroom, I told Pippa I'd call her right back and flung myself onto the bed with my computer, my heart hammering.

Calm down. And they call that a tree. Right. Nothing means anything, I reminded myself, waiting for the page to load.

I closed my eyes, prepared myself with a cleansing breath, and opened them again.

"Jane Start college 'Art' film hacked! LINK to video: Jane Start stoned and stone cold naked." I clicked on the link and was muting the sound when my phone trilled. It was Pippa again.

"*Jane?* You okay?"

"I don't...know." My soul had left my body and now hovered like a vapor overhead as my screen filled with a close-up of a pretentious young art student blowing a mouthful of bong smoke straight into the lens of a camera. When the haze cleared she began doing the Robot, naked, to "Rockit" by Herbie Hancock played at trippy half-speed, the dance bizarrely in sync with the slow-motion lope of the film footage. It was meant to be an homage to Warhol! The Factory! Or at the very least, only a pretentious college art film.

"Jane. I just want you to know I've read the comments, and the vast majority are *extremely* complimentary. I know this feels like a disaster of the highest magnitude, but I'm serious when I say this, people really *like you*. And this will be *gone, expunged,* from the internet very, very soon. I promise you. Jane?"

I could only manage a groan, the taste of sour pear still lingering on my tongue.

"Oh, and this just in. A text from Alastair. He says"—she took a beat, cleared her throat—"he doesn't want to bother you, in a moment of crisis, but wants you to know, *quote:* 'You are the coolest girl ever. Be brave. Chin up. And if I were ever to play for the other team, I'd fuck you in a heartbeat.' Jane? You still there?"

I couldn't stop the tears, Alastair's text sending me over the edge.

"*No.* You mustn't cry. It's going to be fine. You were *young,* everyone knows that. And honestly it's—"

There was a pause.

"Charming," she said.

Was it? "Well, it wasn't supposed to be 'Rockit'! I couldn't help it! I just…spontaneously broke into the Robot. It's Pavlovian. Naked or no."

"Of course, you would. Anyone would—well no *I* wouldn't. It seems a uniquely *you* thing to do. But we'll get it all sorted. I promise. Oh, and one last thing. Still there?"

"Mm-hmm." But I wasn't really. I was thinking how stupid I'd been to let one of my college cohorts film me naked for *their* art project.

"On an entirely different subject, the boys have suggested we do a little brunch at the weekend. We're happy to come up to Oxford if you fancy. We still haven't met your professor! And you haven't seen Will yet. He's shaping up fabulously as my new temp!"

"Of course." I muted the sound on my laptop and clicked the link again.

"*Lovely!* And please don't fret, darling. In the meantime, turn off your computer. I don't want you stressing over this. I'm getting a bleep. Ooh, it's the solicitor! Must run, love you!"

I had been a pretentious idiot, but I wasn't bad at the Robot. The freshman five added a nice bit of extra bounce in the boob department. Feeling them now—solely to compare, though if I were honest, it was comforting, too—

That was when I realized *Mrs. T was reflected in my computer screen.* She was standing right behind me, watching me dance naked in the clip while, in real life, I fondled myself.

I slammed shut the laptop. A nanosecond later, the familiar clap of the front door rang through the flat.

Tom was back.

In cases like this, I supposed, this being my first, the best course of action was to pretend like absolutely nothing's happened.

I rose slowly, set my laptop gingerly on his desk, and smiled weakly at Mrs. T, whose expression was her standard illegible squint...which *could* mean she needed glasses, and had no clue whatsoever that was actually me—right?

Mrs. T. released a heavy sigh, trudged to the bed, and began stripping the sheets.

"Thank you, so much," I said, tiptoeing backwards, "for doing that." I spun on my heel and sprinted down the passage to freedom, stopping shy at the edge of the living room, at the sight of Tom, not yet aware of my presence, making espressos, all sturdy beams and joists, the familiar chiseled angles and planes of his features in profile. He sensed me and twisted around.

"Hello, you," he said.

"Hi," I murmured, and glided toward him, wanting very badly to blurt out, *Why didn't you tell me Amelia is an Oxford professor?*

But I didn't. Because I prided myself on not being the jealous type and because I hadn't disclosed the unabridged history of my exes either. If I did, Tom would never think of me the same way, ever again. So I didn't say any of it, because he was reaching out his hand. Because the *now* with him was so much more compelling than the *then*. Because when I saw him, even after only a few hours of *not* seeing him, I was just so crazy about him.

"I've been thinking," he said, weaving his fingers through mine. "There are quite a number of events I must attend for work, and I wouldn't want you to feel obligated to join me. I imagine many of them would be rather onerous for you." His brow was endearingly furrowed. "Though I'd *love* to have you with me every minute." He swung my hand gently back and forth. "But I leave it entirely to you, which of the onerous things you'd be willing to endure. As a matter of fact, I wondered how you might feel about attending—"

"The upcoming faculty dinner?"

"Yes," he said, thrown. "But, how did you—?"

"Thornbury told me. I brought him his mail this morning."

"Ah. That was kind of you."

"It was nothing. He served me tea. And pears. *Life-changing* pears."

"Really. And were they?" He searched my face as Thornbury's words crept back into my head: *Amelia. So fine of figure. Skin of lily, cheek of rose. You should be safe my dear, amid so many of our colleagues, thrust together in one large and very stuffy room.*

Her name formed on my lips.

Not now. Not when Tom was looking at me this way. Not when he was waiting for me to say I'd be his date for the faculty dinner. Besides, there were more pressing things to discuss. Like the fact that I was all over the internet, smoking weed, doing the Robot, stark naked. And I still hadn't responded to his query about the pears.

"I'd love to go to the onerous dinner with you. And the pears. They were, genuinely, life-changing."

Yet, by Saturday, I was thinking how I could be bingeing a Scandi noir about serial killers, or filling an Amazon cart with stuff I didn't need and would never end up buying, or doing any number of equally pleasurable things besides applying makeup for an intimidating faculty party I should never have agreed to.

"You're an angel. Thank you for coming. You all right?" Tom called out to me from the bedroom. He was dressed and ready to go, and I wasn't even close.

Ding!

Pippa: Internet fuckwits have uploaded video again. Contacting solicitor now.

What a week. "Fantastically calm," I called back, returning to my reflection in the bathroom mirror, having just hideously botched my eyeliner. Surely Oxford academics didn't watch clips of naked college girls on the internet? *Ding!*

Pippa: Interestingly, Strictly Come Dancing have seen it and would love to have you on. They've assured me you can dance fully clothed. Give it a think?

Ding!
Why did I always get texts in the middle of eyeliner triage? I decided I might actually hate intimidating parties. I set my phone to vibrate.
Buzz.

Pippa: I take it your non-response means you'd like me to politely pass? Either way I recommend you sleep on it.

Buzz.

Pippa: PS. Strictly Come Dancing have viewing audience of kajillions.

Buzz.

Pippa: PPS. I'd really love it if at least you'd acknowledge receipt of these texts. I'm not angry I'm lonely. There, I've said it. Gah. Stumbled upon Instagram of my ex's latest conquest, receptionist at a spa apparently—all come hither selfies naturally—she's twenty-five years younger than him!!! AM I OLD AND UNFUCKABLE? AM I PUT OUT TO PASTURE? SORRY, TOO DEMORALIZED TO TURN OFF CAPS LOCK.

That was it. I couldn't blame her for being panicked about approaching forty. Or triggered by an Instagram page. I threw down the eyeliner and dashed off a jumble of typos: how she was literally *the* most fuckable woman I'd ever known, and fuck spas, fuck selfies, fuck men who fuck women half their age, harrumph. Pippa deserved only the best. I felt suddenly, wretchedly guilty. How was it possible I had this great boyfriend, and *she* was alone? *She* was the beauty! *She* had the brains!

I heard Tom's phone ding from the bedroom. Lucky men. They don't have to bother with makeup. They can wear the same suit over and over, and no one judges.

"Jane?" Tom called out. "Would you mind terribly meeting me at my office? It appears I'm needed. A quick meeting with a student. A very anxious young woman. Fresher of course—"

"No problem," I shouted back.

"Occupational hazard I'm afraid."

"As long as you don't have sex with her. On your desk."

"Got it." A beat. "The sofa?"

I love him.

"Off-limits too," I called back, when a shadow fell; I startled, and my heart gave a thud. Tom was suddenly right *here,* looming, in the doorframe. Somehow, no matter how familiar he was, he also wasn't.

Tom dug out his phone. "From Freddy. To you. Quote"— he peered up, his eyes smiling—"'Tell Ms. Start she mustn't get her knickers in twist re: the faculty dinner. Those cadavers would rather watch David Attenborough documentaries on the sex rituals of bowerbirds. I on the other hand enjoyed her video very much and have given it an excellent review which she can find in the comments, under the pseudonym Bong-Hit Jane Lover.'"

Good old Freddy Lovejoy.

"He's right, about all of it," Tom said. "Especially David Attenborough." But he suddenly leaned in close, scrutinizing my face.

I twisted back to my reflection. Somehow, I'd made one eye look totally different than the other. "I swear I wasn't intentionally going for Picasso."

He smiled. "See you very soon, darling, and mind how you go. Take a cab. It's dark and rainy."

Now I seriously had to rush. I set an alarm on my phone and opened the hot tap in the shower (who says you can't steam a dress while wearing it) then began excavating through my collection of useless makeup in the vanity drawer for the only two drugstore lipsticks that together made the perfect nude-pink. Frustrated, I unhinged the drawer and dumped the contents onto the floor, when something leapt out: *the iconic interlocking Cs of a Chanel lipstick?*

Definitely. Not. Mine.

I recoiled, heart hammering, then looked closer.

RED! Like a foghorn going off in my head. I knew it was hers. Had to be.

The edges of my vision went black, closing in like an iris shot in an old movie, the floor shifting suddenly out from under me. I grabbed the edge of the sink and closed my eyes. And when I opened them, I was dangling her lipstick over the bin. But it was as if *she* was somehow watching me.

Slowly and meticulously, I instead set the lipstick on the sink edge—conscious now of the steam everywhere, the mirror completely fogged. Time seemed to be decelerating, unwinding ...and I was shutting off the tap...and I was on my knees on the cold floor tiles, sweeping everything into the upended drawer. And I was noticing a small envelope, Tom's name scrawled across it, stuck to the very back of the drawer. And then I was standing, staring down at it. How was it possible a mere slip of paper could feel so weighty? A tissue sheath sailed soundlessly to the floor, leaving bare her name, Amelia Danvers, embossed on the card stock, over an image of a black stallion. Her perfect, sinuous cursive:

Tom darling—
I adore the trinket. Meet you seven sharp for drinks with parents.
Don't forget to dress for the opera. And please, don't be late.

Amelia x

When I gazed up, it was *her* face, glacial and ghostly in the mirror. I uncapped the Chanel.

"Tom darling, I adore the trinket." I slowly twisted the base. "Meet you seven sharp for drinks with parents. And please, don't be late." The lipstick's faint perfume wafting as I ran it over my lips. "Jane. x."

Only the *drip—drip—drip* of the faucet. The color on my lips was so very much like blood.

But Tom must like it, I thought, staring hard into the mirror, leaning closer and closer into my reflection. The alarm on my phone blared like the closing bell of the New York Stock Exchange. I jerked back and the lipstick skittered across the clinical white floor tiles, leaving ugly red gashes like the aftermath at a crime scene.

I did my best to scrub them out and hid the rest with a bath mat. I returned the note to the drawer, the drawer to the vanity, and tossed her lipstick decisively into the bin. Then I bolted for the living room and paced and paced, waiting for the cab. When it arrived, I bounded for the front door, desperate, almost rapturous to flee, yet something stopped me.

And suddenly I was sprinting once more down the gloom of the passage, compelled to return. I retrieved the lipstick from the bin and tucked it safely away in my purse.

Chapter 21.

POLITE INTERCOURSE

We hesitated at the edge of a raised foyer, taking in a sea of professors and their guests. The faculty party was already in full swing. A string quartet played Vivaldi's "Four Seasons." Naturally.

Tom turned to me and smiled. I caught him subtly studying my face; either he hadn't quite put together what was different—or he had. *The red lipstick.* I felt suddenly cold, cunning, morally ambiguous. Like some femme fatale, like Jessica.

"Shall we?" Tom said, still eyeing me a little funny. He extended his arm.

"Yes." I smiled innocently back, sliding mine through, and we plunged in. We threaded our way through schools of well-dressed older people, nearly all of the women wearing silk-shantung suits in autumnal colors, as if a memo had been passed between them. I was the only person in funereal black, apart from the catering staff.

A tray slid into view. "Angels on horseback?"

Tom declined quickly, perhaps too anxious to eat with Bong-Hit Jane by his side, in this crowd. But honestly, he appeared utterly calm. *I* was the anxious one. *I really ought to put something in my stomach,* I thought. I'd hardly eaten all day.

"Oysters wrapped in bacon," the caterer explained, tilting the tray for me to get a better look at them.

"Oh—*no*. I'm good. But thank you."

He bowed, and I whisked up a napkin and discreetly wiped off the lipstick when Tom was conveniently angled away. A woman, mistaking me for staff, handed me her empty glass, which I stealthily deposited at the base of a potted plant.

"It's just like I pictured," I chirped to Tom, "but maybe *a drink?*"

"Your wish is my command," he said, swiveling back, sweeping a champagne flute from a tray sailing past. "Oh no," he sighed. Professor Thornbury, some distance away, appeared to be ranting up at a tall patrician-looking fellow who drew back as drink slopped over the top of Thornbury's tumbler. "That's Graham Crankshaw. Rival Classics Department don. They dislike each other intensely. Crankshaw's just been made head of the department, a position Thornbury coveted. Ah well."

"Poor Thorny. He really does prick when—"

"Hello! Tom!"

We swiveled in the direction of a woman's voice and found ourselves before a group of younger people, similarly earth-toned but less conservatively dressed than the senior set.

"*Sooo* pleased to meet you. Gemma Chang. Psychology," the woman said, shaking my hand effusively. She was pretty, with a quick bright smile, perhaps a few years older than me.

"And this is Vikram Sunda, DPIR," she went on, clonking her shoulder into the tall, dark, and very handsome man beside her. "Politics and International Relations," she added, before he got a word in. So, a couple, *check*.

"Lovely to meet you," said Vikram Sunda, *Politics and International Relations*. His voice was the molasses baritone of a late-night DJ. We politely shook hands.

"Cyril Chissell, Physics." I was shaking hands now with the epitome of an English schoolboy: round blue eyes, mop of tousled blond hair, and evidently a prodigy, as he surely wasn't old enough to be a professor.

"Hiya. I'm Bryony Obaje. *Not* an Oxford tutor, *his* friend," the gorgeous girl beside Cyril, *Physics,* said with a laugh. Thank god I wasn't the *only* non-professor in the house!

"Hi," I managed, overwhelmed. "I'm—"

"*We know* who you are," Gemma Chang, *Psychology,* burst out. "We're all really big fans!"

"Cy and I've got tickets for *Jonesy* next month," said Bryony, in a lovely husky voice. She slipped her arm through Cyril's, gently caressing his forearm, while he maintained the same stiff smile, and stance, his hands jammed into his pockets. *Cute.* Cy the Cyborg. That's how I'll remember their names. *Cy and Bry—*

When it hit me. *The concert. Jonesy.* Was it only a month away?

As I kept my own smile plastered on, I placated myself with *Oh, calm down. How hard could it be? You've sung "Can't You See I Want You" ad infinitum.*

Except…this was *with* Jonesy. And at the *Royal Albert Hall.* And he still hadn't shared any details. Jonesy was known for his keen sense of theater…perhaps he was cooking up something *mad.* He'd want me to descend on a wire, like Peter Pan, and sail breezily over the audience, with my guitar—who the fuck knew?

Jonesy did, I scoffed inwardly: *He* knew.

But the earth-toned professors came into focus and Gemma, *Psychology*'s lips were moving.

"I thought *Vikram* was snagging tickets online, and *he* claims I was meant to? *Anyway. Blew that.* Sold out," she sighed, rolling her eyes.

Vikram remained quiet, a resigned, slightly amused look on his face.

"But wow, here you are," Gemma murmured, still in gushy-fan mode. "And *Vikram* was *in love* with you." She batted her eyes cheekily.

"Everyone was," he said, in that creamy deep voice, and smiled apologetically.

"Umm—*thank you,*" I managed back. There is literally no good rejoinder to this sort of statement. As the group of them stood silently grinning at me I thought it might be as swell a time as any to ante up on my buzz. I downed my champagne and was grabbing another when a bell chimed somewhere and a hush fell over the crowd.

"Good evening," intoned a voice across the room.

"Julian Davies, president of the college," Tom whispered to me.

"I wish a warm welcome to faculty and friends," Julian Davies, *President,* continued, as I strained to locate the disembodied, ultra-posh voice, over the heads of Vikings. "Dinner shall commence shortly. I urge you all to enjoy a last preprandial before sitting down to table."

I was following his instructions *to a tee,* getting to work on my current preprandial and considering stockpiling another for good measure, when I found myself face-to-face with Professor Thornbury and a woman of about his age and size, with cute spiky white hair in a pixie cut.

"Honora Strutt-Swinton, Anthropology," she said, officiously, thrusting out her hand. She reminded me of Judi Dench, solid and curvy, in a rust tweed suit, plus the awesome hair. "It's an Honor-ah," I replied, bursting out a little Elizabethan curtsey, for no good reason except that Dame Judi had played the queen a bunch of times and the champagne had kicked in. "But everyone probably says that." Nothing. Nary a smile. "I'm Jane," I said, straightening, extending my hand like a normal person.

"Yes. I know," she said, fingering a necklace of chunky amber beads and forgoing the handshake altogether. She raised a brow: "Professor Thornbury's filled me in on *all the grisly.*" She swiveled to Tom, murmuring: "Can I have a word?" And proceeded to show me her back, leaving me to hover awkwardly, eavesdropping on snippets like "He's in pretty high dudgeon. In his cups already I'm afraid." Something, something, something, and "Polite intercourse? Is it too much to hope for?"

Tom darted me a quick *Sorry, I'm stuck* look, as she continued offloading to him, in hushed tones. Finally, Professor Strutt-Swinton turned to Thornbury, whose nose was in his drink, slung her arm through his, and said, "And how are we, dear?" And he grumbled back: "Positively tigerish."

Who *were* these people? I kind of adored them. They reminded me of the professors on the show *Inspector Morse:* outrageously imperious, and sometimes even *arch.* Oh god.

The dinner bell chimed.

The dining room was paneled in gloomy dark wood with large oil paintings of landed gentry dressed in jewel-toned finery, looking bored or miserable, despite their obvious privilege. I thought it rude. At least have the decency not to glower down at the rest of us.

I was next taking in the fancy china, the goblets, and the vast array of silverware, and working out which was for what when I felt a hand on my shoulder. It was Bryony. *Relief, a plebeian, one of the hoi polloi, like me!*

She crouched and whispered, "Fancy nipping off to the loo?"

I glanced at Tom being harangued by a wizened old professor with breathtaking Albert Einstein hair.

I turned to Bryony. *"Yes."*

Soon as we'd exited the dining room, we exchanged the unspoken look of outsiders and without so much as a word took off running down the deserted marble corridor, our shoes clattering. We began to laugh like unruly schoolgirls, escapees from the stuffiness of it all.

We ducked into a small powder room and, panting, caught our reflections in a gilded oval mirror over the sink, our faces close, like in a cameo. I experienced a sudden warm dilating sensation of hope, a distinct intuition she and I would be friends. I realized I had longed for a *friend,* a *girl* friend, here in Oxford. I missed Pippa. I would encourage her to make the trek up next weekend.

"I've brought something. But only if you fancy," Bryony said apprehensively, withdrawing a joint from her clutch. "Not *just* because of the video. We've seen it, *Cy* and me"—she began to stutter—"and think it's incredibly cool. And Gemma and Vikram"—she gulped—"they do too."

Freddy was wrong about professors, then.

"Oh no," Bryony murmured, seeing my face. "I've put my foot in it, haven't I?"

Truth was, I realized, I was basically too sloshed to give a fuck. "Nooo. Don't *worry,*" I said, waving off her concern. "It's a *nightmare,* but, blahhh." I shrugged and grabbed the joint, mostly to make *her* feel better. Interestingly, I hadn't smoked weed since making the "art film," and for damned good reason. But since this dinner was as stuffy as I'd feared, and as I was *now* for all intents and purposes "Bong-Hit Jane"...

Bryony smiled, relieved. She grabbed a candle and I leaned in, lighted up like this was old hat. *I've got this,* I thought, going in for a measured hit and passing it back to her.

She closed her eyes and took a looong drag, giving me a chance to study her incredibly adorable face. My brother would go *bonkers* for her. I could introduce them. *Oh wait.* She had a boyfriend.

"I can't believe I'm in the toilet," she squeaked, holding in smoke. "Sharing a joint with—"

There was a knock on the door.

"Bollocks," Bryony whispered, and exhaled a huge plume in my face, which I had no choice but to inhale.

The knock came again. Panicked, Bryony thrust the joint at me and began batting away the residual smoke with her clutch.

I wasn't sure what to do with it, except risk another quick puff—after how many drinks on an empty stomach? *Math.* Oh fuckity. I took a drag while there was still time—

"Uh-oh." Bryony pointed to the doorknob, rattling like in a horror movie.

Holding in smoke, I chucked the joint in the toilet as Bryony nervously unlocked the door, tucking herself behind it as it creaked open.

"Jane Start, it's *yooou?*" Professor Thornbury cooed, toddling right into the cloud I'd exhaled.

"Oh hi-lo," he said, craning back as Bryony materialized timidly from behind the door. I glided over and joined her.

She and I stood shoulder to shoulder, watching protectively as the obviously hammered Thornbury weaved toward the commode.

"A bit of drinks-taking he has, wee little gnome," she rasped under her breath.

"And now—he's *wasted,*" I said, under mine. We tried not to giggle and bolted for the dining room.

"Just in time," Tom murmured into my ear, as I slunk, self-conscious, into my chair. He inhaled. "Is that—?"

Luckily, there was the chime of a knife on a glass, and the din shrank to an expectant hush. I caught sight of Bryony, across the table, convulsing with weed giggles as her boyfriend patted her arm. *Shit.* Those were highly contagious. I quickly averted my gaze.

Fortuitously, all eyes were now fixed on the head of the table. Julian Davies, *President,* had risen and was giving a welcome toast. Finally in my view, he was attractive, with stiff, straight, silver-streaked hair, which he wore acceptably longish like a Parliamentarian. Now he was introducing his English rose of a wife, named, naturally, Rosamund, whose cheeks pinked as she attempted to rise while cradling her ginormous pregnant belly, as if the baby might accidentally whoosh out right onto the table.

"This makes number three for us." Davies smiled up through a loose forelock, resettling Rosamund into her chair. "And almost upon us, as you can well see." This triggered polite British applause. Weird, the things people clap for.

Parrrties arrrrre fun!

The president's speech was a bit of a snooze, but the meal was *yum-tastic*. And I'd been having *polite intercourse* with Professor Reginald Kennish, *Maths* (why the "s"?), for ages now. He had the most spectacular mutton-chop sideburns. I was convinced he was secretly a member of Emerson, Lake, and Palmer, and had time-traveled here from the seventies. I mean, who had those? I'll tell you who! Civil War soldiers and Reg Kennish, of Emerson, Lake, and Palmer *and Kennish.*

Oh hello. Gemma Chang, *Psychology,* was waving from across the table. I busted out some little Robot moves, in my fancy chair...*because I was high as fuck.*

Whoops. Honora Strutt-Swinton had set down her fork, looking pinched. I could actually hear her thinking: *Why the devil is Tom with the silly American girl?* Surely *Amelia* wouldn't have smoked pot in the loo or worn *boxers* under her party dress. But what Ms. Honora Strutt-Swinton, *Anthropology,* didn't know was that *my* vagina preferred fresh air and gentle breezes. No crotch imprisonment in Lycra for it! Or me! *Amelia* might have sashayed into the party, elegant and refined, with her Chanel red lips and her long black hair swinging, just like that woman over—

It was *her.* The real flesh-and-blood Amelia.

I seized up at the sight of her. She sensed me staring, her head turning slow motion in my direction as the room began to swim. I grasped the table edge and averted my gaze to my lap.

"*Jane,* you're so pale, like you've seen a ghost." Tom had leaned close, and I felt the warm weight of his palm on my thigh. "Perhaps we should get you some air?"

"No—I'm fine—it's just—there's a woman over there," I said, sneaking a peek up. "Dark hair, red lips—is it—"

"The wine sommelier?" Tom offered.

I saw that the woman was refreshing a glass for a guest. *Why did I smoke pot?* It had made me paranoid and crazy.

"I'm sure she'd love to pour you more wine, which I think..." he said, gently, sliding his coffee to me, "might not be the best idea."

"May I assist?" It was a woman's voice from behind me. The accent posh, the tone assured, a bit pompous, and all at once recognizable: *Honora Strutt-Swinton.*

"Jane's feeling a tad under, I'm afraid."

"Must be going round."

I couldn't resist peeking up. Thornbury was slumped in his chair, dozing. The raven-haired, red-lipsticked sommelier assessed the situation and skipped over him to refill Vikram's glass.

"Perhaps your friend would like to visit the ladies'?" Honora suggested.

"Let me," said Tom, starting to rise.

"No, no, sit, Tom, *r'ally*. I'll have her back in a jiff."

In the cool quiet of the corridor, I felt better, but experienced a pang of guilt for my bitchy thoughts earlier. It was kind of Honora to check on me.

"Oxford can be a rather overwhelming place for *newcomers,*" she said, taking my arm. We began to amble. "I remember when I first arrived—"

"I *love* Oxford," I protested. "I do." I stopped.

She studied me. "Yes," she said skeptically. "You are so strikingly different from—"

"Amelia."

She widened her eyes, a bit taken aback. "Right. Well," she said, and we resumed walking, her arm still slung through mine. "It's quite clear you're having a marvelous effect on Tom."

"I've been told that, too." There was a beat. I could almost hear her thinking: *Cocky little thing.* But I wasn't. Far from it. Freddy had indicated as much that first time, at the flat. And I sensed the same from the younger professors, tonight.

"He's been known to be a bit *gloomy,* our Tom, but he seems *lighter, looser,* these days. And here we are."

We stopped outside the powder room, a skunky hint of reefer still discernible.

"Would you like me to go in with you, dear?" For a split second, she was someone's kindly grandmother.

"No, I've got this. Feeling much better already, but thank you."

She gazed back—a bit puzzled, not quite sure what to make of me.

"I'll be waiting right here," she said, and stationed her staunch little self by the door.

I started to say there was no need, but something told me she wouldn't take no for an answer. And in truth, I was touched to know she cared.

Later that night, back at the flat, I was curled up in bed with my phone, too restless, too happy, to sleep. Tom was in the living room, working on his novel. I couldn't see him, only the faint luminescence from his laptop at the far end of the dark passage.

I'd done it: I'd made friends and influenced people. I hadn't let uptight, vainglorious Oxford conquer me. Bryony was most definitely a new friend, and she, Gemma, and I had gone so far as to make a lunch date. Even haughty Honora Strutt-Swinton had warmed to me. Plus, she'd said I was having "a marvelous effect" on Tom! And see here: We'd inspired each other to write! How marvelous it *all* was.

Feeling giddy and impulsive, I clacked out a gushy text message to Tom, with some of my reflections on the night, and jabbed send, without so much of a thought to proofread it.

Shit. I was still very drunk.

His phone dinged, from the living room. It made me smile. In fact, I could hardly contain my glee. I felt like a schoolgirl who'd just passed a note to the person she had a crush on.

A beat later, my phone illuminated.

Tom Hardy: I'm glad you made a new friend, Bryony's lovely. And I'm not at all surprised my colleagues took a shine to you. Darling, how could they resist? I know I can't. x

Again the heady feeling, because *tonight*—to the tune from *West Side Story*—"*the world is full of light*—because this is where I live, this is where I sleep, with him!"

I'd never ever have to return to my dreary childhood room with the garbage bags, with all that reminded me of my past life, of Alex. They ought to be burned in a ceremonial effigy. Or better, donated to Goodwill. So they might be enjoyed by someone for whom no dark memories lingered.

On the heels of this liberating thought, I experienced a lurching of euphoria, of *kvelling* (being extraordinarily pleased, bursting with pride!), even *schvitzing* a little (perspiring, but let's call it glowing). Why were my thoughts suddenly in Yiddish? Mama, can you hear me?

I texted Tom a song link: "Miracle of Miracles," from the *Fiddler on the Roof* soundtrack.

Ding from the living room again. I could hear him listening to it on his phone speaker. *Oy.* I've reminded him I'm a theater nerd. But it's *Fiddler,* for fuck's sake—when I heard the song's swirling intro, those ecstatic violins, I could barely contain the thrill, picturing him listening in the dark as I lay writhing in expectation, for the precise part of the song that encapsulated my feeling about him. This miracle, that the universe had given Tom to me.

There was a silence. He was done listening. I froze. My phone vibrated and I unburied my face from the pillow. I hadn't heard him come in but here he was in the entry. He had that quiet, unaffected smolder, that wordless way of undoing me…now a suggestion of a smile, his lips faintly parting to speak.

But I raised an index finger and checked my phone.

Tom Hardy: Bob Dylan. "To Be Alone with You."
Tom Hardy: His Nashville Skyline voice, I know…

A bold, out-of-the-box choice. How adorable, I thought, calling Bob out on the *Nashville Skyline* voice, which frankly divided people. I wanted to blurt all of this out, but instead texted back:

I. LOVE. THIS. SONG.

Ding.

Tom pushed himself off the door with his shoulder and glanced down at his phone, his hair falling *sexily* over one eye, and began texting. He was standing a foot away. A beat later my phone vibrated.

Tom Hardy: Wanna listen. Together. In bed?

"I'm afraid I don't know her," said Bryony, picking at a *pain au chocolat* with endearingly chipped painted nails. "I've been living with Cyril for nearly two years, is it?" She smiled, her voice scratchy but soft, like mohair. "I work at the library, the Bodleian, so I'm round loads of tutors, but we don't much mingle with them. We mostly sloth about the flat, bingeing telly. We do *definitely* get out to see bands whenever we can, but no, sorry, I've not met her. Amelia Danvers, you said?"

"Yes," I affirmed, feeling all at once fluttery and faint; I hadn't intended to grill Bryony about Tom's exes.

We were seated across from one another in a trendy Oxfordian café, peopled with academics, elegant septuagenarians sporting white Beatle haircuts in tweedy sportscoats *with patches,* glowering fashion-forward hipsters, mothers with toddlers, some seated in groups at community tables of unfinished pine. It reminded me of the old haunt in LA: how different the world seemed now than when I'd last gathered with my—well, Alex's—friends there.

"Hello, women." Gemma swooped in, collapsed into the seat beside Bryony with an air of familiarity, as if the three of us had been friends for ages. "Tutorial ran over, like they do," she cooed, and wriggled out of her wintry layers, depositing a large, overstuffed satchel on the floor before flagging a server to order a pastry and double espresso.

"Jane was just digging for a bit of gossip on Tom's past women," said Bryony, dipping her face demurely into her cup.

"Well, there was really just the one, wasn't there," Gemma said with a scowl. "*Amelia.* Amelia Danvers. Gone off to Harvard. Or MIT, was it?" Bryony shrugged; she wouldn't know. "Except no. Yes. No—I could have sworn I saw her the other day? But it couldn't have been... but *wow wow wow.* You and Tom!" she said.

"Living together," Bryony murmured.

"Crikey. That was fast."

They both stared at me.

"Y—*eess,* I guess? Yep. It was." I felt my cheeks flush; I was a *fast woman.* It was official.

"Sometimes you just *know, though,* don't you," Bryony posited, darting me a little rescue smile, but my stomach had already dropped. Gemma was right. It *was* fast. And impulsive. And *could* she have seen Amelia? Here, in Oxford?

"Vikram and I think it's *super* Tom's with you," Gemma said, overcompensating. "I mean, gah, *Amelia*—" She hesitated, frowned, began to pick absently at Bryony's pastry. "She's something of a fixture round here." Her tone became circumspect. "I didn't read at Oxford, but some of my colleagues started here as students and never escaped, like Tom. Like *her*." She raised her brows. "I mean, the Danvers legacy goes back generations. I think she's even related to the royals somehow. Oh god, I'm boring you. Just tell me to shut it."

"Not boring, I promise." *So. Not. Boring.*

"It's just that she and Tom never seemed quite suited. I mean, Julian Davies, *he* had this *huge* unrequited thing for her. Now there's a pair that made sense." She popped a crumb absently into her mouth and scowled. "Word is she broke poor Julian's heart. Nearly crushed him, but now he's blissfully married to the Baby Machine. Christ. How many babies do they need? The world's overpopulated enough as it is. There are children starving in—"

"Pain au chocolat?" The waitress was hovering with Gemma's pastry.

"Ooh yummy, ta," she cooed, snatching the plate, tearing off a generous bite. "Where was I? Amelia, right, well. I feel *wretched* saying this about Amelia, because obviously she's brilliant and *gorgeous* and has courtside seats at Wimbledon, *the bitch.* But it was like, Tom was never good enough, or posh enough, for her. And the way she dumped him? *Ruthless.* She's just very...*questy.* And Tom's just...not." She shrugged.

Bryony darted me another encouraging look.

"But honestly, here's the thing," Gemma said, leaning in, conspiratorially. "Amelia doesn't have many friends among us 'ord'nary professors.' I mean she hardly remembers my name, or Vikram's or Cyril's or anybody's. Really bad form if you ask me. Too busy swanning about in London with her royal-adjacent friends or frolicking in Ibiza with her fabulous beach bod and the earl of whatsit, with the yacht. You know?"

"I don't...follow...royal things," I stuttered. Now there were two pair of eyes awaiting my response. "I can't quite picture Tom with someone like that. He's so, well, kind of humble. Even his flat—I mean, it's *far* from fancy."

"Tom lives in a flat? I would have guessed they—he—lived in a big renovated house by the river." Gemma was genuinely flustered, stammering. "He's been here so long. But perhaps he hasn't..." At which point she suddenly decided to shut it, all on her own. No prompting from me.

"He hasn't...*what,*" I prodded.

"Oh, you know. Scratched and clawed his way up the academic ladder. Or published much. Or reached beyond Oxford like Vikram with his consulting work—and stuff." She trailed off, biting her lip. "But Tom's extremely popular. Everyone always says what a compelling lecturer he is. I've wanted to sit in on one of his talks for ages, and, well, some professors do truly love the teaching part. I mean *I'm* utterly pathetic at publishing too. Still noodling away at my latest. Feels like I've been working on the bloody thing since the Middle Ages. I probably have been. That's how bored I am with it. Bad sign, actually," she sighed, and ripped off another corner of her pastry.

But this was sort of a revelation. I *had* assumed Oxford dons lived in actual houses. But then, once I'd seen Tom's flat, I'd never questioned it. And Thornbury lived there, too!

"I envy you," she said wistfully. "What I wouldn't give to be in the honeymoon phase all over again." She puffed out her cheeks. "Oh god, why did I order this? *My thighs.*" She pushed away her plate. "But honestly, Tom's brilliant to keep things cheap and cheerful. Houses are *nightmares.* We've just finished the most hellish renovation on ours, and all I see," she said, looking pointedly at me, "are the mistakes."

Her phone dinged, and then mine and Bryony's in quick succession. We locked eyes, warily: Had some dictator just launched a warhead? But an instant later, we were simply another gaggle of humans, staring down at our devices, sucked into the vortex.

"Oh, Christ," Gemma exclaimed. "I've left the plumber waiting! Sorry, girls, next one's on me, I promise!" She shouldered on her coat, wrestling her bloated satchel up, and off she went.

"You all right?" Bryony said. "Gemma going on about Tom and that?"

"Oh, I'm fine," I said, a little stunned, but not by Gemma. "I just didn't expect a text from—well, someone I don't know all that well. It's this guy, he's in a band. Alfie Lloyd?"

Bryony's jaw dropped. "Not *the* Alfie Lloyd, from All Love." I nodded. "You're joking! Their music's a bit bubblegum, but my god, he's *gorgeous*. And clever. I'd run off with him in a heartbeat."

"What about Cyril?"

"Cyril would too, given half a chance. Cyril's not—*my boyfriend,*" she explained, reading my confusion. "Cyril's into boys. Mostly. He doesn't put a label on it. I'm not, actually, 'seeing' anyone at the moment," she added offhandedly, gazing steadily at my phone.

Ooh, I *could* introduce her to Will. I pushed my phone center table so she could read the text.

Alfie FromOz: ♪♪ Wake up Maggie I think I've got something to say to you. I'm back in Sin City ☺ Any chance you're here? Where are you! Wot you doing Maggie!

"Like I'd *ever* be in Vegas if I didn't absolutely have to," I mumbled.

Bryony glanced up. "Maggie May? Like, the song?"

"*Kinda.* It's my tour name. You know, for hotels and such."

"And," Bryony said, impatient for me to get to the Alfie Lloyd part.

I explained about the dodgy bachelor party gig and how my manager and I shared a rather long, and rather debauched, evening with the Lloyd brothers.

"You mean—?" She sprawled forward.

"No!" I said, speculating she meant some polyamorous orgy, the stuff of All Love fan fiction no doubt.

Bryony gestured for me to go on.

"Okay, so I *did* end up in Alfie Lloyd's room. Where we engaged in...what you might call...heavy petting."

"Crikey." She palmed her cheeks schoolgirlishly.

"I *know. Exactly.* And it was just before I met Tom. So crazy?" I thought, reflecting. "But, I'd been in a very dark place." And not wanting to go there, I nudged her my phone, with Alfie's text yearning to be answered. *"You* do it," I said.

"Wot? Nooo—*really?"* She stared back, chewing a nail.

I nodded. She snatched up the phone. "Okay," she said, uncertainly, beginning to type. "I've oft dreamt of our night of heavy pet—"

I lurched for my phone. "Kidding," she said, clutching it to her chest, proprietarily. "You're in England," she typed, "preparing, for your upcoming performance at the Royal Albert Hall, with *Jonesy.* A bit expository?" She crinkled her nose.

I nodded for her to launch it.

Alfie's response was immediate: PLEASE TELL JONESY I AM TRULY HIS NUMBER ONE FAN. I'd kill to be at the show. I'm seriously thinking of quitting my band so I can come. Don't tell my idiot brother.

But I experienced a jolt of panic, so sharp and stinging it was like Aunt Lydia from *The Handmaid's Tale* had jabbed me with the cattle prod. The Albert Hall was only three weeks away.

I needed to call Pippa, to insist Jonesy's people tell us exactly what he expected of me at the show. I couldn't face him again, not knowing.

"Ugh," I said to Bryony. "It's slipped my mind, I'm meant to be on a work call." It was mostly the truth. As I rummaged for my wallet, I made contact with something else. An icy chill slithered down my spine. Amelia's lipstick. "This belonged to Tom's ex. I found it in a drawer," I explained, extending it to her.

"It's Chanel," she said, widening her eyes. "You don't . . . want it?"

"It's yours," I said, and set it decidedly into Bryony's palm.

Chapter 22.

DEAD THINGS

Finally. *Pippa.* At long last my London friends and my brother had made the trek up, and were biding their time in Oxford's Museum of Natural History for the sole purpose of clapping eyes on my mysterious stranger from the plane. And Tom was an hour late. I kept a close watch on the entrance, praying for him to appear.

Young Georgia was off in the distance, looking smart in a black velvet suit and tie; she was gazing up at a series of enormous skeletal sea creatures suspended like mobiles in the winter light that streamed in from the vaulted glass ceiling. Gemma, Vikram, Cyril, Bryony, Alastair, James, and my brother, Will (clearly battling social anxiety), hovered nearby.

"I'm beginning to think he doesn't exist, your mysterious Oxford professor," Pippa teased. "All this time. Merely a figment of your imagination?"

"Not funny." I shot her a look. "And this is not like him." It really wasn't. His meeting must have run over.

"I want to believe you, I do." Pippa grinned. "But seriously, I must thank you for sending me Will. He's sorted the WiFi, upgraded the whole streaming hoo-ha, *and* fixed the pesky front door lock. Handy. You wouldn't know it to look at him, but he gives excellent phone—not *quite* the panache of my last assistant, but he'll do."

"Thank god." *Seriously.*

I caught sight of my misanthrope brother conversing awkwardly with Cy and Bry. Bryony ruffled Will's hair and I could almost feel the heat of him blushing on my own skin. If only Bryony would fall madly in love with him, all would be right in the world.

"Oh, and this just in. Georgia insists on being called George from now on."

"Got it. Cool name. What I wouldn't give for that suit." Pippa and I smiled at the fashionable kid, who was now taking in the museum's pièce de résistance, an enormous sperm whale jaw shooting fourteen feet high. She'd begun sketching, as the adults in our entourage happily chatted away.

"Something like that would be perfect for the concert. Still nothing about what they want me to do? We're two weeks out. This is madness," I sighed, riled.

"Actually, there is."

I turned to her, eager.

"Sudden rumblings of a Jonesy *world tour,*" she said, wiggling her fingers theatrically, her gaze still clamped on our little group. My stomach dropped. And was this a ploy to avoid eye contact? "But what you're meant to do at the Royal Albert Hall is still shrouded in the usual Jonesy mystery." As if it were a mere annoyance. "Oh, look," she pealed, and darted off to join the others.

I stood there paralyzed, my thoughts racing. World tours can go on for a year, *more.* And world tours aren't for the faint of heart, or for their significant others left at home waiting for the phone to ring, until they *stop* waiting. Of course, there are musicians who do truly love the road: the fun, the camaraderie, the partying, the booze, the god knows what else. But what about the having to pee into Dixie cups, crouched behind some RV with a stopped-up toilet in Canada, in a freezing fucking field, mere moments before you're meant to be on stage for one of those outdoor festivals? And there you are traipsing around with a steaming cup of your own urine, wondering where to dispose of it, plastering on a smile for the various crew personnel rushing past, when you're meant to be strapping on your guitar, shoving in your in-ear monitors (don't get me started on those), and getting into show mode? Small annoyances, in the grand scheme of things, I knew. And I *knew,* I was damned lucky to have had those opportunities. And a cup, on such occasions, to piss in. And I'd left out the wondrous part: the *music.* The magical connection with an audience. The euphoria that came from that *oneness*—that inexorable bond with other humans who loved music as much as you did, who suffered Porta-Potties and mud and hopefully not drug-laced treats, just to experience it.

I'd had a couple revolutions around the sun riding the wave of my one-hit wonder. But then a swift death. End scene. Curtains.

And surely I was getting ahead of myself. Surely Jonesy'd have no interest in dragging me along for all that.

"So sorry I'm late." It was Tom, wintry air washing over me as though he'd brought the chill inside with him. "I got stuck," he said, breathless, raking his hair roughly back.

"Just glad you're here." I was.

I grasped Tom's hand, but it was ice. His hands were always toasty, no matter the weather. His phone began to buzz. I released my palm so he could answer, but he ignored it, color draining from his face.

"You can take it. It's *fine,*" I said, eyeing him. Our group was still gathered around the enormous jaw, Alastair crouched beside his daughter, who was showing him her sketch. He must have sensed me looking; our eyes met.

"It's all right," I heard Tom say. A chill slipped down my spine. He smiled, a bit weakly, and said, "Let's join the others, shall we?"

*   *   *

Introductions were hastily made. Alastair, James, and Will darted me stealth approving looks; Pippa grinned ear to ear, babbling away with Tom. Yet I felt sour, off—I couldn't seem to refresh the page.

"I'm sorry I left you hanging. It was good of you to put this thing together," Tom said, as George sketched on, determinedly. "She's adorable and so adorably serious," he added as he rested his arm across my shoulder. Somehow it felt heavy and cloying.

Pippa approached and slapped on what struck me as an obsequious smile. "*So sorry to interrupt,* but might I borrow Jane, for just a tick?"

Soon as Tom was out of earshot, the smile faded.

"Jane. Listen. I'm so sorry. After all the years with Leopard Pants, I thought I could handle anything. But this Jonesy business. They've been impossible. So bloody cryptic about everything. But the world tour—"

"This is bonkers. But I've got it." It was Will, dashing over. He waved his phone at us.

Jonesy Assistant 3: Rehearsal information forthcoming tomorrow.

He typed back.

Pippa More Assistant 1: Excellent. We eagerly await.

Will had offered tech support to one of Jonesy's assistants and that had done the trick. *What a relief,* I thought, but my stomach dropped. This meant the show was *real.* All this time I'd been silently praying it would go away. *What's wrong with me!*

"Let's just hope Jonesy Assistant Three is true to her word.

This one," he said, tipping his head, meaning Pippa, "needs a new laptop." It seemed he might actually excel at this new gig.

"Do I?" She scowled. "But thank you, Will. Excellent. Brilliant. Well done."

Will blushed from her sudden attention, and her beauty, I'd have wagered.

Off in the distance, Tom was crouched before one of the displays as George chattered to him; in the foreground, a cacophony of dead things seemed strangely alive in the vibrating sunlight.

"A lot of professors over there," Will said, apprehensively. "But Tom's great. Most definitely a grownup." He elbowed me. "Good job." I flashed on Alex's Hot Wheels car. *No car should be yellow.* It's not right. "So, uh, I guess I'll just go hang. With them all," he muttered, intuiting Pippa and I wanted to be alone.

We watched him amble reticently toward the group.

"Finally, news," Pippa sighed, relieved. "It's hard, this thing, being a manager *and* a friend, but, Jane, I—"

"What have I missed?" said a posh voice behind me. Freddy! Why was *he* here?

Pippa's color rose; clearly, she was not immune to his dashing looks. She pressed her palm instinctively to her décolletage like some blushing maiden, drawing his gaze to it.

"Tom's over there," I said, pointing a little rudely, so he got the picture to *scram.* Unruffled, Freddy smiled, bowed, and departed.

"Don't say it. He's gorgeous," I said, before she could.

"A stunner," she agreed, watching him. "But the way Tom looks at you." She turned to me. "*That's* the thing."

I sought him out across the large expanse of room, through a series of warbling pillars of light, and the ghosted impressions of children darting through them; Tom *was* gazing at me, concerned.

"I've been kind of *off* today. I should go over there, pull myself together—"

But Pippa was hypnotized by something else, her face flushed and beaming. George being spun around by the arms by my brother, like our father used to do with us, when *we* were little.

I found Tom's eyes again, and smiled, if a little tentatively, at him. And when he smiled gently back, I thought, *Everything will be okay. We have each other, don't we? What more do I really need?*

Chapter 23.

PREGNANCY BOOBS

Another week of unsettling silence from Jonesy had passed, but with Tom away on a field trip in London with his students, I decided I'd finish the song he'd heard me working on tonight if it killed me. I was ready. I could feel it. Tonight was the night. After some procrastination, plumping pillows in the living room, lighting candles for creativity, I swiped open my phone for a bit of the old inspo—

Instagram. Jessica's selfie at the top of the feed, one of those *Here's me looking unintentionally bodacious in a sweaty tank-top, post yoga* shots. Then I read the comments: Nice pregnancy boobs 👍. Your new hubby must be having fun with those. 😜

She was *pregnant. Already.* I did the math or tried to. Could Alex have knocked her up when *we* were still together? Honestly, what did it matter. He'd been having sex with her for who knows how long behind my back.

The day he'd left his laptop at home and I'd dashed it to the set. I rewound the memory like an old videotape. Alex's assistant was on headset, pacing, as if exiled, outside his trailer. She paled at the sight of me bounding up the metal stairs, like she wanted to stop me. The trailer lounge was vacant, the door to the bedroom shut. I figured he was on set already. Or perhaps he was napping. They'd just wrapped a week of night shoots.

Adrenaline shot through me now. What would I have witnessed had I casually flung open that door? The two them together, in the throes of—

Feeling grim, I tossed my mobile to the other side of the sofa. Then I lurched for it, reopening it so fast, Jessica was still glowing sultrily at me. So I did what any self-respecting masochist would and sought out another Instagram page guaranteed to make me feel worse: Alex's. And guess what? It did. A photo of him kneeling worshipfully, his lips pressed to her exposed baby bump. Then I unfollowed them both and felt *great*. Liberated! Free!

But it only lasted a moment. And feeling desperate for actual human connection, versus *THE INTERNET,* I tried Pippa's cell, then Will's, then Bryony's. No luck reaching anyone. There was no one else I could think of to offload to. Obviously not Tom.

For half a second I thought to try Freddy, just to rag with someone who clearly loved ragging. But I still hadn't revealed the tale of Alex's infidelity to Tom. I'd kept my exes a blank slate; I'd stayed the course, as had he, except for what I'd prised out of him about Monica. Plus, ragging, as an outlet, only makes a person feel worse. And now it could get tricky. Pippa was meeting Freddy for drinks "Friday next" at the Groucho, an exclusive "members only" club in London. I didn't want to be a downer but honestly, I needed to warn her that Freddy was trouble.

Pippa finally answered, coughing.

"Sorry, did I wake you?"

"Nooo." She giggled. "I've just smoked some—"

"Weed." Of course. "My brother, right?"

This annoyed me. Everyone else in the world was giggling and high or glowing and pregnant. Or able to write a truly good song.

"When is he moving to James and Alastair's guest cottage?"

"They've hired a live-in for George so—no—can—do," she said, laughing as if this was funny somehow. "Shit timing, I know." She sniffed, attempting to rein herself in. "It's *fine,* I can tolerate the intrusion. Though—" She dipped down to a whisper. "He is a bit *odd.*"

"I warned you. But it's only temporary. And thanks for giving him a job. Really. I appreciate it." My voice went suddenly wobbly.

"Jane. I know how you worry about him. Or are you upset still from yesterday? The Jonesy business?"

"No. I'm fine. It's nothing. It's just that, okay, yes, I'm *extremely anxious* about the Royal Albert Hall and also, *Alex is going to be a father.*"

"Ugh. You'll be faaaabulous. And Alex was never right for you."

I remembered an evening when Alex and I had just begun dating, the look on his face when his phone vibrated and he glimpsed the caller ID. The emotionless "Hey" as he answered. I'd sworn I could hear muted sobs as he'd eased himself out of his sliding-glass doors, sealing me inside a vacuum of silence, the lights of the San Fernando Valley beyond, a bowl of jewels you could scoop with your hands.

Of course. Despite all his denials, Alex had cheated on his then-girlfriend with me. And then on me with Jessica. A *serial* cheater! I hadn't trusted my instincts. Never would I let this happen again.

"Jane? When do I hear the new songs?" Pippa was coughing a little; I could pick up 1960s samba faintly tinkling in the background.

"Very soon," I told her, and begged off—because a wave of panic swept me up, churning me in its wake and then spitting me out. And there was only one thing left for me to do, to assuage this desperation, this yearning for something to believe in, for *someone* I could count on, to love and trust with my *whole heart,* or what was the point of *anything?* I stopped pacing, and eyed my guitar, down the long dark tunnel.

And so I sealed myself in the gloomy writing room and recorded the little music-box tune Tom had heard me playing into an app on my phone. This time the words tumbled out and maybe they were right and maybe they were wrong, but it was a start. And you have to start somewhere... And then the room flooded with light.

I hung over the narrow desk and peered out the window into a moonless night. A black sedan idled below, in the middle of the road, its headlights making snowy beams in the mist as fog rolled in, thick and Jack the Ripper–ish. All at once I had the distinct feeling I was being watched, illuminated in the window by the glow of my phone.

I ducked down; an instant later the little room went dark again. I waited, crouched, my heart thumping, and risked another peek. No car. *Phew.* I'd watched too many crime shows. Probably some drunk idiot looking up the address of a hookup.

I clicked on my recording with trembling fingers and must have inadvertently grazed the tempo meter, as my voice oozed out in a woozy, haunting half-speed.

The windows blazed with light again.

Instinctively, I dropped once more, inched around the desk and stole another peek. The black car had returned. It didn't help that my song, still playing, sounded demonic. I stared hard into the driver's side to see if I could make out a face, but caught only my own, reflected in the glass. Which meant... whoever was out there could definitely see *me.*

I skittered back and sent the guitar crashing face-first onto the floor with a dissonant groan. For a paralyzed instant, I was convinced the driver had heard it too. Ridiculous. Impossible. I jabbed at my phone to make the song stop.

I ran to the bedroom, ducking so my silhouette would not be visible in the bay windows, and switched off Tom's desk lamp. A split second later the headlights were killed too, as if the driver were sending a message. *I see you. I know you're in there.*

Oh god, stop being dramatic. There must be some logical explanation. Surely this had nothing to do with me.

The unmistakable clap of the door at the base of the stairs rang out. My heart practically burst through my chest. Tom wasn't due back for hours. Who else had a key? Besides Mrs. T. Was he home early?

I forced myself into the dark passage.

"Tom? Is that you?" I crept forward on groaning floorboards. The living room ahead flickered like jumpy film stock, erratic with candlelight. "Tom?" I called out again, freezing in place. Yet my voice seemed to trigger only more creaking, coming from the stairwell.

It came closer still, from the landing, just beyond the door.

"Tom?" The creaking stopped. Oh god…I began to tiptoe backwards.

The doorknob to the flat began to judder. There was only one way in and out of this place. I was trapped!

I spun around, tore back toward the bedroom, and sealed myself in. But no bolt! No way to lock the door! The room was dark, and cold, and now I was desperate for my phone—where had I left it? I whacked into the bed, then scrambled to Tom's desk and searched wildly around, books thunking off in the dark, when I made out a familiar metallic clunk on the wood floor and fell to my knees. Oh sweet iPhone, glowing to life!

I heard a slam, so close the vibrations reverberated through me. The door to the flat! I sat on the floor, quaking, waiting, but there was another slam, this time from the door at the base of the stairs. And finally, the crisp sound of a car door. White light splattered the walls, tires screeched. Then eerie silence, except for my thundering heart.

I steeled myself and ventured back out, my head swampy, fumbling to call Tom but poking at all the wrong buttons. Led Zeppelin's "Rock and Roll" suddenly wailed from the phone's speaker. I was jabbing to make it stop when an ear-splitting shriek ignited the passage like a firebomb. I slipped swiftly inside the laundry room, where I crumpled to the floor and pressed my back to the door in the pitch dark.

Crashing sounds! Whoever it was had begun tearing apart the flat—my fingers were so trembly I could hardly dial 911. But it wasn't 911 in England. And then I remembered: Thornbury. He'd given me his number.

It rang once, twice, *Oh please pick up,* the ghoulish glow of my screen in the dark—

"Yes, hello, Professor Thornbury, Classics Department, Magdalen College—" He sounded groggy, disoriented.

"It's Jane," I said in an urgent whisper, "please come quick. Someone's broken into—"

"Who calls? Hello? Who calls at this late hour—"

"Shhh, it's Jane, from upstairs—"

"Oh, hello, dear. Speak up. I can't—"

"I need help—"

"Jane? Hello?"

But I couldn't catch my breath, couldn't make my mouth work. My whole body seized up; a scratching, so close it was practically in my ear, like a taunt—*there was someone just on the other side of the door!* The phone slipped from my fingers and into my lap, and through the pounding of blood in my ears I could still hear Thornbury calling out from the tinny speaker. The door thudded hard into my back, as if someone had kicked it, and that's when I became aware of the smell of smoke.

Chapter 24.

SMOKE GETS IN YOUR EYES

I had no choice but to get out. The passage was dark, smoke oozing in from the living room where I glimpsed—

—the rug was on fire, a handful of low flames dangerously close to the sofa. White light seared in—a car speeding past—and at the entry to the living room I beheld a black cat, its back arched, eyes glowing like embers, hissing.

The cat screeched, catapulting straight for me. I darted out of its path and sprinted for the kitchen sink, aware of broken dishes crunching underfoot in the dark. Fortunately, I had on shoes, but there was no time to lose before the flames reached the sofa. I flicked on a light, grabbed the large pasta pot, and managed in three trips to douse all the flames.

At last, I became aware of pounding sounds drifting up from the stairwell. I rushed down and found Thornbury barefoot on the stoop, shivering in a short flannel robe. And with him was *Honora,* wrapped in a coat, *her* feet bare too. Before we'd exchanged words, she was barreling through the door and up the stairs, Thornbury lagging behind.

Thick haze met us as we entered the flat. I switched on more lamps, only now absorbing the extent of the damage. It looked like the place had been ransacked. The rickety Moroccan end tables upon which I'd set candles had been knocked over. Each of the candles now lay on a charred patch of rug. The cat, in a panic, must have upset the tables, sent candles flying, and then pounced onto the kitchen counter, wreaking havoc with the dishes lying about.

Honora hastened straight for the window over the sink and unstuck it with a few good thwacks, while I got started sweeping up the mess of broken china on the floor.

"Good god. Shall I call the police? The fire services? What's happened?" It was Thornbury, winded, hunched in the doorframe.

"Fire appears contained, just smoke now," Honora said over her shoulder, impressively calm. "But mind, there is broken glass. Tobey, be a dear, won't you, go down and grab my shoes?" He was staring down at his feet in a stupor. "Tobey?"

"Right. Go down. Grab your shoes," he said robotically, and shuffled off.

"And remember to put on yours. Tobey? Do you hear me?"

"Right you are, right you are..." His voice was fading down the stairs.

Honora took a moment, scanning the room, her fists planted on her hips. Spying the overturned end tables, she squished barefoot across the soggy, singed rug, gooey with candlewax, and righted them. Then one by one, she scooped up the candles and deposited them in the bin. What a woman.

"My dear girl, tell me what happened," she said, craning back, taking me in. "Oh, you're shivering."

I was trembling, in fact. Honora came over, placed her palms on my shoulders, and searched my face.

"Here, take mine," she insisted, unfastening her coat, but stopped short, whisked up a nearby throw blanket, and draped me with it. "Now tell me everything," she said, in a gentle voice.

"Someone broke in, left it here, a cat, but I thought it was...I didn't know what it was at first? It was shrieking, going crazy, knocking over furniture—the candles fell onto the rug, and started the—"

"The fire, yes, there, there," she said, rubbing my upper arms.

"And it's still *here*." I pointed shakily to the passage. "Down *there*."

"How very strange," she said, glancing over her shoulder. "And have you rung Tom?"

"There was no time, and he's in London, with students. On a class trip. A museum. And then a film."

"Ah, I see. Well, I'm here now," she said, soothingly. "And you weren't harmed, by the intruder?" I shook my head. "Good. I'll go down there and see what's what, shall I?" I nodded, just as the downstairs door clapped shut.

"Back with your shoes, Honora," Thornbury called up. She looked at me and sighed. We waited until Thornbury, panting, galumphed over, her flats dangling from his fingers. *Funny,* I thought, him in that robe, bare-legged and sockless, now in his clunky Clarks. And Honora, I suspected, with *nothing* under that coat?

"Apparently an intruder entered the flat and left an animal, a cat," she said, one hand on Thornbury's shoulder for balance, explaining how the fire had started as she slipped on her shoes. "And Tom's in London with students. Can't be reached."

"How very curious." He adjusted his spectacles, eyeing the burnt rug. "And the smoke alarm didn't sound?" He sniffed the air. I shook my head. "Must have that seen to posthaste, my dear."

Suddenly there was plaintive meowing coming from the hall. We swiveled in unison just as the black cat emerged, hazarding its paw delicately over the threshold. Seeing us, it raised its backside and hissed, then charged straight for me. I yelped out of its path. It simply shook itself out and padded nonchalantly over to Thornbury.

"Oh, hello, *pussy. I know* you, don't I?" he cooed, and crouched, his robe gaping. I averted my eyes and Honora failed to repress a

212 · SUSANNA HOFFS

snort. "And what a very sweet pussy you are," he said, gathering the purring thing up. "Now what the devil are you called?" He looked to me, like I would know. I shrugged.

"Surely there must be a tag," offered Honora.

"Surely there must be, hmm?" said Thornbury, rooting around the cat's vibrating scruff. "A-ha! Ophelia! Yes, of course. Mad little pussy come back from the dead."

Chapter 25.

WHAT'S NEW PUSSYCAT?

"You're quite sure you're all right?" Honora repeated, wavering at the base of the stairwell, as the two old professors prepared to leave. There was still no sign of Tom. I had called, texted, but no response yet.

"Yes, I promise, I'm fine, truly." This was not entirely true. Tom was MIA, and Psycho Cat still prowled around upstairs. "Really, I can't thank you enough."

Honora smiled beneficently, her softly weathered face close, and I thought of Japanese raked sand gardens, mesmerizing and lovely, though I'd only ever seen them in photographs. Thornbury, half-asleep in the crook of the door, yawned.

"But do ring tomorrow, let me know how you go, dear, won't you?"

"Yes. I absolutely will." I showed her my phone, her number freshly entered.

"Well, this is us, old boy."

The two codgers shuffled out and I made my way, exhausted, back up the stairs and perched myself at the edge of the sofa, a safe distance from Ophelia, who was lapping water indifferently from a bowl Thornbury had set out below the sink.

214 . SUSANNA HOFFS

I'd never been good with cats (*understatement*) and honestly, who named one Ophelia? Tom had never mentioned having a cat, yet Thornbury had implied it was his. And it did seem to know its way around. Now it meowed and began to stalk toward me, all vertebrae, claws, bad intentions—

"Don't even think about it," I said.

It stopped, extended its paw daintily, *evil ballerina,* then sat erect, tail swishing. Good. It appeared we'd reached some kind of understanding—*I don't have to like you, and you don't have to like me*—when it jetéd straight for my lap. I shrieked, bolting up, and the cat went sailing and landed splat on the burnt rug.

Oh Christ, had I killed it?

The room flashed suddenly with light, and thankfully the creature roused, darted to the entry, both of us now keenly attuned to the watchwork clicks at the base of the stairs. The sound of Tom vaulting up. *But what if it wasn't him?* I watched the rattling doorknob, paralyzed, heart hammering, until the door burst open.

"Jane, darling, are you all right? I smelled smoke in the hall. What's happened—my god." His face was anguished, his eyes roving the crime scene and coming to rest on Ophelia as she wrapped herself around his leg, purring, ecstatic.

I told him as quickly as I could: The strange car idling in the road. The sounds of mayhem as I hid in the laundry room. The cat going bonkers, upsetting the candles.

"I didn't realize she still had a key. *Amelia,*" he said, mortified. By now we sat close on the sofa, the cat curled between his feet.

Christ, it was *her*. Here. Tonight. Even still, just hearing him utter her name, so often repeated in secret in my head...*Amelia... Amelia...Amelia.*

"So brainless of me. I'd never have thought she'd show up like that, let herself in, leave the cat, without so much as a word. I'm so sorry, Jane." He turned to me, racked with apology.

"At least she's not an arsonist," I said, weakly.

"I'll speak to her, first thing. This is unacceptable." He straightened and grasped my hand. "And I shall have the locks changed at once."

"Okay. Yeah. I mean, probably a good idea." A better idea months ago, but still. "And—the smoke detectors. They need new batteries."

"Yes, of course," he said, squeezing my hand. "I'll take care of it. All of it. Oh god, Jane, I feel wretched. This should never have happened." He wrapped his arms around me, pulled me close. Over his shoulder, I scanned the still hazy room and thought, wickedly, *So beautiful, brilliant, questy Amelia wasn't so perfect after all?*

The cat meowed. "Did *you* name her Ophelia?" We pulled apart.

"God no." He made a face. That's what I'd suspected. "Amelia discovered her, lost and starved in her garden. *She* named her." And apparently had retained custody until now?

Just then, she lolled onto her side, crossed her paws like some sultry odalisque, and gazed longingly up at Tom. *Oy vey, what a flirt.*

"Sorry to break it to you, but this cat has questionable taste in music. She doesn't appreciate Led Zeppelin." I filled him in on her response to "Rock and Roll" blaring from my phone.

"Appalling," he said, and rose, grabbing a bottle of whiskey. He held it up for my approval.

"Yes."

He sidled close again and poured each of us a shot. We touched glasses, knocked back our drinks, and he quickly followed with another, before allowing himself to sink deep into the back cushion.

"And what will you do about *her?*" The cat was splayed across his shoe, massaging herself. He seemed not to notice: clearly a cat person. *Adorable, honestly, even though...* "I'm actually a little *uneasy* around cats." The way they stalk and pounce and dig their sharp claws unexpectedly into your flesh. "Especially...black cats."

"*No*. That can't be true." He sounded faintly amused. But it was *not* funny, especially after what had happened here tonight. All at once, I was authentically riled. The whiskey was partly to blame, but mostly it was his dismissiveness.

"I'm not quite sure you understand just how horrible it was earlier. When I was here, alone, and the cat was shrieking, setting the place on fire, and I thought there was someone with bad intentions inside the flat, and I was trapped, and couldn't *reach you*—"

"Jane." He straightened, turned to me. "My darling. I'm so terribly sorry. My phone ran out of battery." He grasped my hands and kissed them, in that nineteenth-century-novel kind of way.

But he couldn't simply dismiss my anxiety. He couldn't sweep all of this under the rug, which just so happened to be burnt beyond repair. Though it struck me: Was it possible Amelia knew nothing about me, or my relationship with Tom? And why would it matter? *She* was the one who'd ruthlessly dumped *him* and was now hobnobbing with royal-adjacents and doing fellowships at Harvard. *Or was she?* A trickle of panic slid down my spine. Was this the beginning of the end? Had it all been too good to be true?

"Let's go to bed," he said.

Not so fast, Professor. "You still haven't answered my question. What are we going to do about her?"

I found myself strangely glued to the creature, engaged in some play-fight with an invisible frenemy, darting beneath the wingback chair, peeking out every few seconds.

"Well?"

But he'd popped up from the sofa and was reaching out to me. He clasped my hands, a little smile in his eyes, and began to gently hoist me up, though I ever so slightly resisted.

"What's new, pussycat? Whoa whoa whoa."

Really? This was his diversionary tactic?

"Pussycat, pussycat, I love you, yes *I do*—" But he stopped, serious. "And I'm so sorry you were frightened. I *will* talk to her."

I had to give in. Our hands clasped, he began taking backwards steps toward the *bedchamber,* towing me along.

"You do a questionable Tom Jones," I said. In truth, he was pretty good.

"You and your *pussycat lips,*" he sang on, not caring in the least. "You're *so close* to being in tune."

He shrugged, our eyes still locked. "You and your pussycat *eyes.*" And we kept going, into the mouth of the passage; I wasn't exactly resisting.

"You mostly sing when you're drunk, don't you."

"Yes," he said, pulling me gently past his many books and goddamnit I loved him. "You and your pussycat...*no-o-ose.*"

We stopped, finally, at the threshold to the bedroom, and the way he looked at me, I loved him. I did. Which had to mean something, didn't it?

I sat bolt upright in the dark. There was something crawling on me—then I felt pinpricks of pain. I scrambled out of the covers and thudded hard onto the floor. It was cold and dark and I couldn't stop shivering.

"Jane—you all right?" Tom was stirring.

Purring. Rolling waves of it. *The cat.* Amelia's cat was on the bed, purring for its master.

"Sorry, darling," he said, groggily. "Thought I'd shut the door. Come here, you little thing, you."

I could just make out his silhouette in the dark as he scooped her from the bedcovers, tossed her gently into the hall, and closed the door. I clambered back under the duvet but twisted away, toward the closet.

The creepy black car, idling in the middle of the road, was alive again in my mind—red steam curling up from the taillights like in a horror film.

The mattress dipped. Tom was climbing back in.

"I've been thinking," he ventured in a soft voice. "Perhaps we could disappear over the holidays?"

We could. By then I'd be done with the Albert Hall. *Oh,* what a relief, just to think of it.

"We could meander north through the countryside. Misty moors and quaint B-and-B's all the way to Scotland. Just the two of us. We could write?" He placed his palm gingerly in the hollow between my shoulder blades.

Oh god, that sounded divine. But nothing more, about the cat, the fire, his ex showing up in the middle of the night. He waited a beat for me to respond, and when I didn't: "Or you could just— sing to me?"

I could, couldn't I?

And I pictured the two of us flying down some ribbon of highway, winding through emerald green, past stone-clad inns and thatched roofs...yet I couldn't shake it, a haunted, disquieted feeling, the sense that something bad was about to—

Tom had inched closer, he was dovetailing into the back of me, pulling me tightly to him until we were perfectly fitted puzzle pieces. His skin was intoxicatingly toasty in contrast to the chill of the air.

"I can always tell when you're feeling sad," he murmured, and settled his lips, his fingers, on my bare shoulder.

He began to smooth his palm languidly from there, into the dip of my waist, and up, over the swoop of my hip like a sculptor; it felt so crazily good, yet part of me wanted to rip myself from him.

"I wonder...if you and the cat have a bit too much in common to make good friends," he said, softly, intuiting, and swept my hair gently from my neck. "Afternoon nappers, both," he went on, beginning to graze his lips featherlightly over the freshly freed skin; I could hardly contain the pleasure of it. "Unabashed, unapologetic sensualists—no complaints here." His voice velvety and warm in my ear, he abandoned the trail of tingling flesh to start a new one. "With sharp nails for scratching"—tracing a delicate path down my spine—"metaphorically speaking, and only when necessary..." He suddenly grasped hold of my ass and I couldn't help pressing and arching myself into him. "You're both a bit— *sly,*" he continued, slipping his hands around my waist, "and it's not at all difficult to make you purr"—gliding them upward, and softly cupping my breasts, his fingertips skimming lightly over my nipples—"in fact, it's an *absolute pleasure*"—grazing one hand down, slipping his fingers between my thighs—"to pet you in all of your favorite places." And he was, he was doing that. "And though I rescued the cat—*you, Jane,* are an accomplished, independent woman, a tiny powerhouse really, who needs no rescuing." And he pressed his body firmly into mine. "Yet there is something tender and alive and wild in you that *drives me a little mad*"—warm tingling blasts on my skin, his lips *somewhere, everywhere...* "And sometimes I want to—I want to gather you up and keep you with me always—because I *do*—I *do* want to take care of you."

A bolt of panic seared through me. I broke free and swiveled to face him.

"We've got to get rid of the rug."

He looked at me, startled, confused, our faces close in the dark.

"It's ruined," I pleaded, "burnt beyond repair. We'll never be rid of the smoke. It's *everywhere.*"

Okay, so, the rug was a metaphor. But if the cat was going to stay, the rug had to go.

"Now?"

"Yes."

"How do you have such a tiny face?" he asked, like this was a sincere question.

I shrugged. No idea.

He sighed, cupped my face in his hands as if he were measuring it. "Okay. Right, then. We'll do it."

We slipped into T-shirts and sweats and set about moving the furniture in the living room, and together we rolled up the rug. He grabbed an end, but it was immediately clear I couldn't possibly lift mine. So I crouched and pushed and he pulled and we got the thing out and onto the landing. After some debate, it was decided Tom would continue to take backwards steps down and all *I* had to do was maintain my grip and not let go.

And after a brief moment while we caught our breath, Tom hovered at the precipice at the top of the landing, his face to me, his back to the plunging stairs; never had they appeared more steep or treacherous.

What was I doing? This was *madness.*

"Okay. Let me know if you need a rest." He took a moment to adjust his shoulders, to re-anchor his grasp. "Right, then, here goes."

We started down in silence, the old wood treads groaning loudly from the weight of the rug. Tom's labored breaths merged with the ominous *thump, thump, thump* as it thudded over each and every stair like in a film noir.

"Are you thinking what I'm thinking?" I managed at last.

"Don't say it," he said, but he was having the same thought: It was like we were disposing of a dead body.

Halfway down, I glimpsed his broad shoulders through the thin fabric of his shirt, strained from the weight. In the gloom, with his head lowered, I couldn't make out his features, and I thought for an instant he could have been anyone.

Who *was* he, *really?* There was so much I didn't know. He could have been a stranger. He was—the stranger from the plane.

The sky was pale violet when Tom flung open the front door. He grabbed up his end now, and together we lugged the thing into the back alley, and managed with some effort to heave it up and into a dumpster.

The following afternoon, with a primly worded text, Honora inveigled me to meet for tea. We sat across from one another at the Ashmolean Museum's café, a spectacular space that seemed to float above the city, with splendid sweeping rooftop views through floor-to-ceiling glass. I felt my spirits rise, despite the unsettling events of the previous night.

"Tom made it back from London, I assume, and you're all right, my dear?" Honora queried.

"He arrived not long after you left," I reassured her. "And I'm fine, *really,* thanks to you and Professor Thornbury. We'll need some new dishes. The rug, I'm afraid," I said pointedly over my tea, "is *toast.*"

Tom had revealed somewhat reticently, after we'd chucked it, that the rug had been a gift from Amelia. Somehow this didn't surprise me. Poetic justice.

"What a shame, and such a lovely rug," Honora mused. "And how are you and Ophelia getting on?"

"I'm beginning to make good friends with her. Tom is quite attached...the things we do for—" I wanted to say *love,* but stopped myself. "For our *friends.*"

"Yes, quite right," she said, sipping some tea. "Perhaps now might be as good a time as any to segue into—well—" She cleared her throat, set the cup circumspectly into its saucer. "As you may have surmised, Professor Thornbury and I have begun a little... *affair.*"

Affair? Hot damn, woman. I was suddenly struck by the newly incarnated Professor Strutt-Swinton: the visible glow, the clingy wrap dress that highlighted her curves and décolletage, set off by her requisite strand of amber beads.

"It all began at the faculty dinner, when he was rather *inzuppato.*"

She coyly fingered her beads; I smiled like I knew what that meant. "Rotten. Lathered."

"Right," I said, remembering I'd been pretty *that* myself.

"Hence, I made it my duty to see him safely home. He was frightfully indisposed—I don't know how he would have managed had I not been there, to help him out of his clothes, into bed and so on. Thus, I found myself rather drained and thought, if only I could make myself horizontal, if, but for a moment, regather my strength? I curled rather innocently alongside him and drifted off. And when I awoke, I was in for a wee surprise." She slurped some tea. "Or rather, a *big* one."

Oh, shit.

"Truth be told, it had been rather a beastly drought in that department for the both of us," she said, eyes a-twinkle. And as if to punctuate her disclosure, Honora Strutt-Swinton tore off a bite of a donut, leaving a dash of powdered sugar on the tip of her cute button nose. "Suffice it to say, we've been making up for lost time and it is rather like riding a bicycle—one simply climbs aboard, and zoom zoom off one goes, ever so invigorating. But I suppose I ought to spare you the concupiscent details."

Gosh, maybe.

"We may no longer be in the bloom of youth," she continued anyway while I tapped the tip of my nose meaningfully. "But that hardly means one has a Closed for Business sign hanging over one's respective...well. You'd never know, to look at him," she went on, leaning in, sotto voce, "but Professor Thornbury is rather a satyr—astonishingly frisky for an old coot. I suppose he was simply bursting with all manner of passions waiting to be expressed. Alas, I am the grateful recipient of such zeal. And good god, for such a little fusspot one wouldn't have guessed he has an *extraordin'ry* appetite for—"

"Ha! Wow! That's so *cool*," I interrupted clumsily, recalling the ginger-poached pears.

Honora gave me a Cheshire smile. "Oh dear. And I thought you Americans were so open about such things. Land of the Kardashians and all that."

"No, we are, and it's all extremely wonderful, you two . . . hooking up. Though that doesn't sound . . . quite right." I grimaced.

"On the contrary," Honora Strutt-Swinton said brightly. "I think hooking up is *precisely* what we're doing."

I walked briskly home in the cold listening over and over to "There She Goes," by the La's. Tom had texted me the song and said it reminded him of me, not only the lyrics, but the chiming guitars and tambourines, which "seemed determined to brighten every-thing." And how he didn't miss the rug as there was something fresh and hopeful about all the wood unadorned, and that *I* was all the adornment he'd ever want or need!

Beaming, I stood chilled and thrilled by the door to the flat and texted him back. Simply the song link to "Norwegian Wood (This Bird Has Flown)" by the Beatles.

My phone rang almost immediately. *It's him,* I thought, jabbing blindly, giddily, at my screen.

"Hi! Jane!" Pippa trilled from the speaker. "Rehearsal's officially on the books!"

"Oh, *wow,*" I stuttered, thrown, processing.

"Saturday noon, the day before the Royal Albert Hall. I shall be there with you, *every inch of the way,* so not to worry," she said calmingly, intuiting my first response would be panic. "We're eking out more details, but it looks like it *is* just the one song. I'll have a definitive answer imminently. Oh! And Alastair has offered a fab guitar and amp for you to test out once you get to London!"

"Oh good," I exhaled. A guitar to clutch and cling to. A security blanket of sorts.

"*And,* Team Jonesy have arranged a lovely hotel room in London for Friday through Sunday nights. All is falling into place!"

"Okay, good. Yes."

Except I was trembling. The Royal Albert Hall was no longer a date scribbled in a calendar. It was *real*.

"Oh, and a bit off topic," Pippa added, piquantly. "I finally had drinks..." She paused as if waiting through a drumroll. "With *Freddy!*"

"Oh." *No!* I'd let my guard down for only a moment!

"Yup! At the Groucho. How gorgeous and hilarious is he? And he knows *everyone*. But darling, Freddy's simply *desperate* to come to the concert," she purred. "Is that all right with you? Oh fuckity...I'm getting a bleep—more soon..." And the line went dead.

Shivering, I dug for my house key, craving the warmth of Tom's flat, wanting to curl up in his bed, to bury my head beneath the covers, when my phone sounded off again.

"Brace yourself." It was Will, in an urgent whisper. "This is a bit palace-intrigue-y but Pippa's on the line with Team Jonesy...and wait for it. You've officially been offered the tour. She'll wanna be the one to tell you, but I couldn't resist. Sister, you're a star. Yes you are, yes you are, yes you—" And the line went dead.

Above my head, a jet rumbled. Shivering, unable to look away, I watched it arc gracefully out of view.

PART THREE

Once in a Lifetime

Music is a conspiracy; it's a conspiracy to commit beauty.

—*José Antonio Abreu*

Chapter 26.

FIRST CLASS

I was seated beside Jonesy on the plane. We were en route to Tokyo—or was it Sydney? Sun struck the chiseled peak of his cheekbone. There was no denying he was beautiful, like a painting from another time—the satin-blue eyes, the see-through skin, the pale blue vein pulsing faintly at his temple; his hair a blinding platinum, cropped at the back but sleek and longish over his eye. Yet I felt dread. He turned suddenly to me, as if he'd been reading my thoughts. Caught, I glanced quickly away.

His bodyguard hovered at the threshold of a curtained galley like a young Brando: the white T-shirt, the pugilist features, the sculpted biceps imperceptibly twitching as he chatted up a pretty flight attendant.

There was an ominous metallic groan and the cabin began to quake. "You don't have to worry," murmured Jonesy. "This plane won't crash—it can't." His eyes were strangely vacant. "You know why? Because I'm on it." He wrapped his long cool fingers around my wrist a little cheekily. "I've got you now." He tightened his grasp.

I laughed nervously and, without meaning to, peered down at my wrist and back up at him. *Okay, now you can let go,* I thought. He smiled serenely back.

The plane made another terrible groan. The nose dipped sharply, and we began a steep descent, Jonesy still shackling my wrist.

In panic, I watched his bodyguard slide down the galley wall, attempting to anchor himself on the floor. The flight attendant crawled to her jump seat and fumbled to strap herself in. I searched her face for reassurance but it was ghostly pale. I didn't find any. We continued to slip through space until the shrill bleat of a warning alarm became audible through the cockpit door, repeating with the horrible regularity of a heart monitor in a hospital, and oxygen masks dropped from the ceiling and swung jerkily, but I still couldn't move my hands—

And then it was Tom! Beside me, in bed.

The doorbell was ringing shrilly.

"Jane—stay here," he insisted. Rain pummeled the roof, slapping the windows.

It was only a dream. Tom was slipping on jeans.

It was five days to the concert. I was not on a plane with Jonesy. "What's happening?" I finally managed.

"Not sure," he said, jamming a T-shirt over his head. "Stay *here,* Jane, all right?" He darted me a serious look.

"Okay—yes."

He shut the bedroom door and started down the hall, the doorbell still screaming.

I put it together—it was Amelia! It had to be. Unless it was Thornbury, something to do with the storm? The doorbell stopped. I felt the small quake of the slamming of the entry door.

I slipped quickly into my nightgown, a girly sleeveless Victorian thing, and threw on Kurt for warmth, then tiptoed over and cracked the door. The passage was dark, the living room darker still. There was thudding now in the stairwell, the murmur of voices as Tom and the mysterious visitor entered. The visitor's voice, unfamiliar. Female. It *was* her! Amelia!

I strained to follow them through their clattering sounds. Tom had flicked on a lamp. The kettle shrieked, and the cat, Oskar Wilde (I'd taken to calling her that, a Norwegian pronunciation on Oskar), darted between my legs from out of nowhere. I nearly yelped but managed to cover my mouth, trembling a little, and gently closed the bedroom door. Footsteps approached from the hall.

I collided with the bed and perched erect at its edge, preparing myself for anything. The cat sat at my feet, focused and watchful, her tail swishing. Tom slipped in and closed the door gingerly. His face was drained of color.

He seated himself beside me, took my clenched fist in his, but stared out at nothing, as if he were mustering courage to tell me something awful.

"Amelia never left, did she?" I whispered, frantic. "She won't leave, she won't leave us alone."

He flicked his head to me. "No," he whispered back. "It's not *her*." He searched my face, a little desperately. "It's Monica."

Chapter 27.

HERE SHE COMES AGAIN

I was a terrible person, eavesdropping on Monica and Tom from the darkened hallway in my nightgown, tucked covertly into a gap between bookcases, cross-legged on the floor. I couldn't quite make out what they were saying, but I could catch a fairly generous slice of the living room as his former tutor paced in and out of frame, and glimpses of her in profile: dark, rain-soaked hair, pretty features, queenly brows, sultry sun-kissed skin. But it was her physique—her tiny waist, her curves so voluptuous, so willful, they appeared barely constrained by the feeble fabric of a white tee and jeans—which exceeded even my own carnal imaginings. She really did resemble an Italian movie siren.

I watched as Tom moved through the frame too, with a throw blanket, and soon after, Monica wore it draped across her shoulders. Tom lowered himself to the sofa and listened, compassionate, shrink-like, elbows to knees, chin to fists, as she paced and murmured indecipherably. When she began to sob, he bolted up and returned moments later, offering a box of tissues. As she blew her nose I felt a stab of guilt for snooping. Yet not enough to remove myself.

I'd begun to pick up snippets of what she was saying, her voice

rising with agitation: "Devastated . . . gutted . . . utterly heartbroken."
Yet her voice remained mellifluous, her accent seductive.

Briefly she turned, giving me a perfect full-length view of her
in profile.

"And after giving *all* of myself. My *heart!* My *soul! My body!*"
she cried. As if to make crystal clear her point (*This body, this
killer body you see before you!*), she skimmed her hands over the
front of her shirt, down her hips.

"Not *her* of all people, *not her!*" she wept.

Wait—who?

"It's all so humiliating—I just want *to die.*"

She was wailing now, yet somehow managing not to sound
strident; even in tears her voice was whispery, the edges smoothed
like sea glass.

Oskar tiptoed over and settled with a bored huff into my
lap. We listened as Tom tried to comfort Monica. She sobbed
dramatically into her hands as he gave her a staid sort of hug, but
she wasted no time pressing her breasts into him, at which point
he politely released himself, coaxed her to the sofa, then left her
there, whimpering. But then she glanced around for someplace to
discard the tissues, and when she twisted toward me, I feared for a
panicked instant that she could make me out in the dark. But she
simply thrust a hip upward and shoved the used tissues into the
front pocket of her jeans, giving me the first unobstructed view of
her from this angle; her gorgeous face, but also her large honey-
colored areolas and erect nipples standing at attention like mighty
soldiers of Eros, plainly visible through the wet T-shirt. *No wonder
Tom had draped her in a blanket.* Those would be distracting
to anyone.

He reappeared with her tea, then sank into the wingback, a safe
distance away, cropping my view of him at the knees.

"His *mistress,*" Monica seethed, elevating the cup to her pretty
mouth. "How could he go back to her!" *Ah-ha! So this story*

didn't involve Tom at all! She began keening again, attempting, simultaneously, to slurp tea.

Oskar, sensing my relief, perhaps trying to follow the story, looked up at me, and I gave the top of her head a caress.

"He told me he *loved* me...and that I was his soulmate...his *goddess of lust,* per sempre, *for always,*" she blubbered as she managed to unburden herself of the cup, placing it gingerly on the floor before prostrating herself across the cushions, like Eleonora Duse.

Tom covered her once more with the blanket, but she sprang up, wild-eyed, blanket sailing, and flung herself at him, ruffling his hair, caressing his face, cupping it between her palms as she murmured and moaned in indecipherable Italian. To his credit, Tom gently dislodged himself, yet she triumphed in keeping her face glued to his chest, tears and snot getting all over my favorite Thistle tee. Alas, he finally surrendered, and let her grieve on him, trying his best, with a series of gentle pats to her back, to send the right signals. At which point I scooped up Oskar Wilde and pressed my lips to her warm furry head.

I tiptoed away, to give them privacy, feeling a sudden comradeship, and empathy for her grief. I'd been there too. How lucky I was to have found in Tom someone ethical and kind, as opposed to some self-involved serial cheat! All my angsting about Amelia struck me suddenly as petty, pathetic. Why invent problems when there were none?

Chapter 28.

FRIDAY ON MY MIND

It was 7:15 a.m. on Friday. Two days until the Royal Albert Hall. My little rolly was packed and ready by the front door, my train ticket to London resting atop it, along with an itinerary and hotel information for the weekend, reserved under the old tour name, Maggie May. I'd face rehearsal tomorrow. And presumably, with it, *Jonesy.*

To calm myself, I imagined my future creative life in Oxford with Tom. My very own Rochester, except not rich, or arrogant, or twice my age. I was dreaming about the promised road trip to Scotland when I glanced out the window and caught sight of the postman bopping down the sidewalk, headphones clapped over his ears. My chance!

I barreled down the stairs singing, "Wait a minute, Mr. Postman," hoping to introduce myself and explain once and for all that Thornbury lived *there,* and Tom and me *here* (the latter sending a shiver of astonishment straight through me), but by the time I'd made it down, Thornbury's mail (mostly travel brochures) had already slid through the slot. Perhaps the old professor was planning a holiday with his new *inamorata?* How touching. I'd hand-deliver his post. I knocked on his door.

"Oh, Jane, it's you, my dear, come, come—quickly, out of the blasted cold." Thornbury slammed the little window in my face and fumbled endlessly with the locks before tugging me in.

"Not again," he cried, eyeing the stack of mail. "Miscreant. Oh—but I've something for *you*." He yawned; I must have woken him. "Do forgive me for not bringing it round sooner. I daresay this is what end of term at Oxford can do to a man." I noticed he was barefoot, and also that his fly was open. I tried not to stare, but once you get it in your head not to look, it suddenly becomes the only thing.

"Honora castigated me, cracked the whip she did—Tobey, she said, you simply must organize. How can you cope with this Augean mess of yours?" He gestured to the mountain of papers and books at his feet. "And do you know what?" he sighed, a faraway look in his eye, "Ms. Honora Strutt-Swinton is a woman of many gifts. Intelligence... wit... acuity. Not to mention tenderness, ardor, *sensuality*."

"Shall I help you look? For the, the thing?" I broke in, fearing where this was headed.

"No, no." He raised a hand in protest. "Now, where was it—ah-hah!"

He was now attempting to jimmy a small box from a great stack of papers and books but succeeded only in toppling the entire pile.

He winced, touched his chest. "Indigestion." He shrugged.

"Let me help you—"

"No, no, my dear, it's nothing, for *I* am a lucky man! I gather you know, about Ms. Strutt-Swinton and me?"

"I do," I said, coyly, splaying out the glossy travel brochures like a fan. He ceased scrabbling in the landslide to grab them greedily from me.

"We're planning a last-minute getaway over the winter break," he said, his eyes agleam. "Someplace *hot*." But as he pored over the images of azure waters and sun-soaked villages, his glee seemed to fade. "I've oft dreamt of sharing my favorite places with a companion." He tore his eyes from the pictures and fixed them on me. On the wall behind him was the framed photograph at the Parthenon, him alone. We let a wistful silence pass.

"I have something for you too, Professor Thornbury." I reached into my pocket. "It's called a Jazz apple. And once you've breathed its honey aroma, tasted its intoxicating blend of sweet and tart, I daresay you'll never be the same."

For a moment he appeared faintly alarmed. "A life-changing apple, is it? Why, thank you, my dear." His eyes were suddenly moist, and as I extended the apple to him, *my* throat tightened too. He placed his little paw appreciatively over mine, then closed his eyes and inhaled the apple's scent, savoring. "But please, none of this Professor Thornbury business. Do call me Tobey from now on, won't you?"

"Okay, Professor Thornbur—I mean, *Tobey*."

I gave him a quick peck on the cheek, scooped up the little package where it lay abandoned on the floor, and slipped out.

I nearly tripped over Mrs. T's Tesco bags on my way in. Oh right. She'd swapped days this week for personal reasons. She was vacuuming at the other end of the flat, so I didn't bother to announce myself; instead, I set the box on the kitchen counter, Thornbury's response to the apple still vivid in my mind. How important it was, I thought, to take a moment to be *grateful*. And I was suddenly aware of all *my* little things, scattered about the living room, commingled with Tom's: Kurt Cobain flung over a stack of his books. The museum-card mobile I'd made faintly spinning, casting shadows on Tom's unsorted papers across the dining table.

I glanced once more at the mysterious package I'd set on the counter. It seemed to be staring back. It was addressed to OM HARDY; the T concealed beneath packing tape, which all but held the battered cardboard sides together. I picked it up and gave it a little shake and heard the faintest rattling sound, grazed my fingers over the pretty jewel-toned mystery stamps. *Who had sent it?* The return address was patched over with brown tape, which had come loose on one end, so if I *juust* pulled it back a titch—

"Hallo, Miss."

Startled, I flung the box away, realizing too late the packing tape was still tethered to my fingers like an umbilical cord.

"Sorry—didn't mean to scare," Mrs. T said, and with a crisp, surgical karate chop, freed me from the box. She balled up the tape and stuffed it into her apron. "I like to tell something to Mr. Tom. This year I need extra time, over holidays. My son, he's getting married and—"

"Of course." So Mrs. T had a son? Somehow I'd never pictured her as someone's *mom.* "No problem. And congratulations, Mrs. T—to you *and* your son."

Instinctively, I stepped closer to give her a hug, the air between us charged with our usual awkwardness, but fuck it. I was going in. I tentatively put my arms around her. To my amazement, she reciprocated, still holding the box in one hand.

"Thank you," she said, as we pulled apart. "I am still here next couple weeks."

Back to business, just like that. "Yes—right. I'll be sure to let Tom know." I was trying not to grin, but it was hard.

"Okay," she said. She was now eyeing the espresso machine. "Can I?"

"Yes, please, help yourself." I laughed. "Mrs. T—*you don't need to ask.*"

She smiled warmly, maybe for the first time ever, and placed the box into my hands.

"And you can call me Jane," I blurted. "If you like."

"Jane," she said, nodding slowly. "And I am Rosa."

Mrs. T was somebody's *Rosa.* Their sweet girl. Wife. Mother. You think you know a person. We considered one another for a moment. Then she got started on her coffee.

"Your song—I like," she said over her shoulder. "Catchy. Good for dancing."

She *danced.* But even more astounding, she knew my song.

I suddenly pictured her in a sequined dress tearing it up at a disco. For all I knew she was on TikTok, too.

I was smiling to myself as I glanced down at the box and my breath caught. With the tape gone, I could see it was addressed to MS. AMELIA DANVERS AND MR. TOM HARDY.

"Okay, well—I'll just…" But I was already skating quickly toward the hallway. "Go down there and—"

I broke into an all-out run and sealed myself in the bedroom, heart thumping, hands trembling around the package. *This was nothing,* I thought, beginning to pace. *Nothing.* I was sure Alex and Jessica still got meaningless packages addressed to me. But I was wishing, really wishing, I could make this one go away—

—when I noticed something shiny, *and silvery,* through a tear in the cardboard.

I hesitated a split second before ripping open the damaged edge. Some sort of decorative gift wrap? With a pattern…of *wedding bells.*

Without thinking I hurled the box from me like it was radio-active. It slid to a stop at the base of Tom's record shelves, leaving behind a typed card, dangling from a withered piece of tape that had tethered itself to my fingers:

Dearest Amelia and Tom—
May your love remain sweet and fresh and lovely, always.
 To our favorite couple—you beauties. Damn you for being so perfect and gorgeous. Sorry we can't celebrate your

nuptials in person but imagine we are there, on the church steps, throwing rice at you.

With love and cheers and soap, because you can never be too clean…

Rupert and Bumble x

P.S. Dinner at Morton's over Christmas? By then you should be fully honeymooned out, and we'll have returned from the third world, a little worse for wear, but glowing from so much do-goodery.

P.P.S. Amelia! It took us ages to track down that mill in France—only you, goddess of taste and class.

Chapter 29.

THE LION, THE BITCH, AND THE WARDROBE

I had the feeling there was no oxygen left in the whole world. My heart hammered wildly, violently in my chest.

Why—how—had he kept this from me? True, we tacitly avoided talking of our pasts. Yes, I'd been desperate to bury the ghost of my bitter breakup. But they—they were going to be *married*.

I approached Tom's desk and lowered myself, apprehensive, into his rolling chair. I eased open the shallow center drawer: pencils, paper clips, innocuous Post-it notepads, nothing more. I closed the drawer, considered his closet. Next thing I knew, I'd flung open the doors and was standing before his fleet of Oxford gowns, the rest of our clothes haphazardly mingled, the tall and short of us.

Above them, a high shelf: stacks of books. His riding hat and boots. And two unmarked packing boxes I'd never paid any notice. But why would I? I had a savage compulsion to look in them now.

I couldn't stand on the rolling chair, so I'd have to dash to the living room and drag in one of the dining chairs. But Mrs. T—Rosa—was still here, and I couldn't bear the thought of facing her. Now it hit me. The way she'd scrutinized me with utter disdain that very first day. It made total sense. Tom was engaged, *to be married,* to a "goddess of taste and class," and there I was, half-clothed in his living room, traipsing around in his shirt like I owned the place.

How could he have kept this from me? I flashed suddenly back: Freddy, when he first appeared. *No wonder* he was curious. He had no idea Tom had kept me completely in the dark. And yet Tom hadn't corrected me that very afternoon, when I asked him about *Amelia,* "the girl you'd dated *in college.*"

His desk chair came back into focus. It would have to do.

I rolled it over, and clambered up, steadied myself by gripping the metal clothing rod. It quivered, unpromisingly, and the gowns began to swing. If I stretched, I'd just be able to shimmy one of the boxes forward and to flick off the top with the tips of my fingers.

The box contained nothing but a pile of innocent winter sweaters. I nudged it back into place, disgusted, hating myself. But now the other box beckoned... it was practically begging and if I didn't look, it would keep *on* begging until I went mad; but this one was heavy and obstinate, and I was forced onto tiptoes to coax it forward. I managed to upset the top, and tip down the front for a peek—*PHOTOGRAPHS!*

The memory of our second date here, when Tom showed me around and I noticed their absence. Only books and records. We'd listened, together, on this very bed, and somehow that was all that had mattered.

Adrenaline was searing through me. I *had* to look at the photos or they would haunt me—taunt me—leave me incapable of all other thought.

I was lengthening as far as I could and nudging the box forward when the wheels slipped out from under me and the chair sailed backwards, smacking into the side of the bed as I catapulted onto the floor.

After a stunned instant, I became aware of the doppler hum of the vacuum down the hall; I was still in one piece and Mrs. T was none the wiser.

And the box was miraculously upright on the floor, staring back at me almost indifferently, like, *Get on with it already*.

Chapter 30.

SKELETONS

Moments later, a sea of photographs fanned around me on the bed. *Who was he, really?* Stirring images of a teenage Tom, his flaxen hair messy and longish like some *Tiger Beat* heartthrob, the kind of boy I secretly yearned for in high school, the kind who never gave me a second look.

A lonely image of him on a drab olive sofa, glancing up from a book, caught in a moment of surprise, his blurred hand sweeping hair from his eye. And there was the ship in a bottle, in plain view, the one he'd scoffed about his parents having when he'd given me the tour of his flat, before I'd ever set foot in this bedroom or slept in this bed.

And photo albums. A small tooled-leather one filled with Oxford students in freshers gowns, gathered on risers on the college lawn. I found him in the center of the back row, Freddy beside him with that signature naughty grin.

But *she* must be here somewhere. Squinting...scanning the faces over and over when my heart stopped—*Amelia,* in profile, her raven hair knotted in a loose bun, at the far end of his same row...and she was staring at him! Tom.

My hands began to tremble...Amelia was the only one in the

photograph not looking at the camera. He was her obsession *even then.* A shiver tore through me. And now he was—I was afraid even to think it—now he was mine. *I should stop this minute.* I should slam shut the album.

Instead, I turned the page. Amelia on a black stallion, stunning in her equestrienne gear, her head cocked, a suggestion of a smile. Amelia gazing flirtatiously over a champagne glass, bathed in candlelight. Amelia on a beach, model-tall, and chic in a floppy black hat and black bikini. Flipping faster now—Amelia— Amelia—Amelia in London—Amelia in Oxford, under the arched cloisters, carrying a briefcase, wearing her formal gown—Amelia in a spectacular floor-length sheath dress on a dance floor. I was beginning to feel sick—dizzy—*I needed to stop.*

Yet I returned to the box, possessed, until I'd plumbed its depths and reached a stratum of crumbly-paged paperbacks—*Love in the Time of Cholera, The Diary of Anaïs Nin, Atonement*—a tattered *Oui* magazine, a record collectors guide, and at the bottom, a set of weighty leather encyclopedias and what looked like a black scarf jammed along the side, its label sticking up like a tiny flag: *Loro Piana* in gold thread. Something so lovely ought not be entombed in a packing box.

I was struck by the softness, the delicacy of the cashmere in my hands, and the intense desire to try it on, when I realized the scarf was knotted around something solid.

It took only a moment...a half-hearted gesture to loosen the knot...for a small blue box to tumble free and onto the bed: *Smythson of Bond Street* printed on top; the slightest flick of my nail to upset the lid, to set sailing the sheath of crisp white tissue paper, revealing what lay below.

Chapter 31.

WEDDING BELL BLUES

Lord and Lady Geoffrey Danvers
request the honour of your presence at
the marriage of their daughter
Amelia Sophia Danvers to Thomas Hardy
Son of Edward and Clara Hardy
The fifteenth day of September, 20—
four o'clock p.m.
St. Oswald's Church
Widford, Oxfordshire
Reception and dinner following the ceremony

The box was empty save the one.

September fifteenth. How was it possible? I met Tom in the middle of August. We were in Devon by September. The hotel clerk, the Frenchman with the thin mustache, his face still vivid in my mind: "Monsieur 'Ardy, welcome back."

He was surprised because I wasn't *her*.

Yet none of it made sense. The timeline made *no* sense—

"I go now." It was Mrs. T, just beyond the bedroom door!

"Don't want to disturb, I see you Monday, laundry is here."

I heard the thunk of the plastic basket, followed by her trudging away, and felt a wave of nausea so intense...but I *wouldn't* get sick, I *couldn't,* not with his photographs everywhere, not after Mrs. T, *Rosa,* had ironed the duvet with the lavender water I'd bought on *that* trip to Devon. *Oh, why is this happening.* I didn't understand.

Oskar meowed loudly from the hall.

I started for her, but something stopped me, *a feeling,* a presentiment, which drew me to Tom's bedside table, the bottom drawer. There was the book of erotica I'd confessed to stumbling upon. I found my fingertips sweeping over its buttery leather cover again, the embossed outline of a Venus di Milo, and flipped open to the flyleaf, having never thought to do so, and there it was, plain as day, a faded, penciled inscription in Tom's hand, the date, February 14, 20—, *Valentine's Day...*

For Amelia Sophia, T. x.

I covered my mouth to stifle a gasp, burying the book back in the drawer, and peered down at my own trembling hands, expecting to see blood.

Were there other clues I'd overlooked? I began rifling through the drawers I'd missed, in a frenzy, leaving no stone unturned. There was nothing in the shallow top one, and in the middle, the same familiar things: the class syllabus for the Romantics, his flight itinerary from August, a travel brochure for Greece, which I grabbed up, remembering this, too.

Oskar meowed obnoxiously.

"I'm *coming,*" I said, and dropped to the edge of the bed, hypnotized by the brochure's gleaming cover. An image of the Aegean, the impossible *blue*ness of it, and the crisp white of jumbled dwellings scattered along a sharply rising cliffside—what must it feel like, to actually *be* in such a place? I began ripping through the pages, insatiable for more...more flushed skies at sunset...more hot pink bougainvillea tumbling wild, when a ghostlike slip of paper fluttered down and settled gently into my lap—

Mr. and Mrs. Hardy Travel Itinerary for Santorini, Greece:
16 September–23 September, 20—
London Heathrow to Santorini Airport
Hotel, Canaves Oia, Honeymoon Suite.

There was only one person I could think of to call.

Chapter 32.

STRANGER ON A PLANE

"You look ghastly, Jane. And you're *weeping*. What's happened?"

Freddy took my elbow and led me swiftly to a table in the far corner of the deserted pub, the Bear Inn, an Oxford landmark. He maneuvered me into my seat, made a stern "stay" gesture, and headed to the bar. The only other customer here was a bleak-faced old man draped over his pint. I wondered what sorrows he was drowning, alone at a pub this early in the day, and had a sudden overwhelming compulsion to run—but Freddy must know *something,* and he was already traipsing back with ales.

I sank back down and debriefed him: Wedding gift from Rupert and Bumble. The invitations, the travel itinerary for a honeymoon in Greece.

"You *have* been a clever detective," he murmured, unable to tamp down a burbling titillation. "But my god, I thought *you knew*—about *her,* the engagement. When Tom broke it off so suddenly, so frightfully close to the wedding date, I thought, Tom, you rapscallion, surely you've been bewitched by some minx, some wily homewrecker who's cast her carnal spell upon you."

That was *Jessica*. And Gemma had told me it was Amelia

who had dumped Tom, not the other way around? She'd said nothing about an engagement. No one had. *Tom* hadn't! But had I known...

"I didn't know he was *engaged*. I'd *never* be a homewrecker. *Ever*. It's not who I am. You have to believe me!"

"I *do*—but steady on, drink your medicine like a good girl." Freddy slid my glass closer, watched until I'd forced some down.

"But how could Tom have kept something *this big* from me? We made a point of not...dredging up our sad stories from the past, but—" *If I'd had less pride.* If I'd just been upfront about Alex from the start, might he have told me?

"You did seem rather *in the dark* when first we met," Freddy said. "I thought, well, p'raps he's been *light on details*. I need hardly tell you the man's discreet, infuriatingly so, but I thought surely you knew he'd called off his *wedding*. How can one as clever as he be such an absolute fuckwit? Shocking—" He stopped short, seeing my tears. "There, there," he said, reaching across, patting my hand awkwardly. "I thought you knew, Jane, honestly I did." His voice more subdued now: "I'm only sorry I didn't sit you down and tell you the whole tawdry tale, unabridged, myself."

Speechless, overcome, I managed only a shrug.

He sighed, leaned back in his chair, and downed some ale. "To be perfectly honest, I chalked the whole thing up to Tom having a midlife crisis. Why not a little romp with a musician after all the histrionics with Amelia? A little rebound whatsit, ignites in an instant and burns out just as—" But he stopped, seeing my face, recognizing his gaffe.

Was it all a rebound? For him and for me? I looked down at my tearstained cardigan. Why was I still wearing Alex's ratty old sweater?

"Frankly, I didn't think it would last," Freddy exhaled. "No slight on you of course. I simply assumed they'd make it up. As they had done hitherto. But here you are, aren't you? Lovely as ever, though

rather swollen, and blotched...and you've got a little...just here."
He tapped under his nose and offered his napkin to me. "Truth
is, Jane, *I* thought it a *wretched* idea, Tom and Amelia getting
married in the first place. And on the heels of them breaking up
and spending—what was it, nine, ten months apart last year?"

I shook my head. "I have no idea," I said morosely. The only
thing I was sure of was that the man I thought I knew had left his
bride-to-be virtually standing at the altar.

"Right. Well, that's when Tom had the short-lived fling with
the sultry Italian ex-tutor. Amelia was none too pleased, but can
you blame her?" He cocked a brow, some part of him relishing the
scandal of it all. "But his tutor, you see, was like a starved alley
cat...one sets out a bowl of milk and then one can never get rid
of them. And Tom has too much heart not to offer up his shoulder
to every stray cat, every panicked student, every ancient professor
jawing on. He's made himself too available. The man can't seem
to say no, or set boundaries. He's a good egg, a compassionate
fellow...but *Freud* would have an absolute field day with him.
This need, this *compulsion* of his to rescue every lost pet he finds
meowing at his doorstep. Not that you're a pet, darling. He's so
terribly happy with *you*."

But had I appeared to him like that, on the plane? In the carpark
at Heathrow? Some lost kitten caught out in the rain? I thought
he'd seen through my tipsiness, my chaos. I believed he'd seen the
real me shining through. *The artist. The fighter.*

The future soulmate.

Freddy sighed, creaked back in his chair. "On paper, you see,
they made the perfect pair. And Amelia, so desperately in love
with Tom. From day one."

I flashed on that picture of her, gazing longingly at him. I
couldn't bear it.

"And yet scheming, always scheming," Freddy said, suddenly
riled, "to make him over, to extirpate every last shred of Yorkshire

from the man. To dress him in the family tartan, install him in the family compound, decorated within an inch of its life, by her."

He grunted, petulant, and swigged the last of his ale.

"What I could never understand is *Why Tom?* when she had so many suitors. The president of the college eating out of her hand, and *he* practically an earl, or a viscount."

He began ringing his empty glass at the lone barmaid across the room, who was staring dully at her phone.

She ambled languidly over and Freddy ordered fish and chips.

"Dear me blathering on and you've hardly got a word in," he said, eyes trained on her tush as she sashayed away. "But you look rather peaked—the food will—"

I was going to be sick. "Sorry." I bolted up, practically knocking over my chair as I darted for the loo. This had been a bad idea, calling Freddy.

I hovered over the toilet until the feeling passed, then splashed water on my face and began to pace... What I needed to do was talk to Tom. But I couldn't! Not yet. Perhaps I could find Bryony. At the library— But *no*. I'm meant to go to London, tonight! The concert. This weekend. *Fuck.*

"Jane?"

I seized up. It was Freddy, just outside the door.

"Jane, I must prevail upon you to have some lunch. Please don't make me come in after you. Because I will." I didn't put it past him.

Back at the table the waitress appeared with fish and chips, and Freddy sized her up. She seemed not to notice, her face completely deadpan as she lingered, arranging condiments on the table as if she was working out an elaborate puzzle; she couldn't have been more than twenty. I made a mental note to warn Pippa again about him.

"You must understand, for Amelia, for everyone in her circle, her family—Lord and Lady Danvers, the sisters—Tom had dragged his feet, stringing the old girl along for far too long. Then all at once, out of the clear blue, they announce they're tying the knot. Huzzah, I thought, well finally, at long last." He harrumphed and dove into his fish and chips.

"It was almost September when I met him. He said *nothing*. How is that possible?" I cried.

"No earthly idea," Freddy sighed. "I only know things imploded *the instant* he returned from California." He raised a calculated brow. Was he implying *I* was to blame? The thought made me want to leap out of my own skin. "I don't suppose I'll ever know what transpired there. Never could wrestle it out of the old boy—believe me, I've tried," he said, darting me a faintly lascivious look.

That kiss, on the plane. I was the one who had instigated it. *I* had kissed *him. Oh god.*

"Alas, the old girl's not doing very well. Her hopes, her dreams so abruptly dashed. The humiliation of it all. She didn't last long in Boston. No. Hobbled back, devastated, a complete wreck—when was that?" he considered. "I'd met you by then, hadn't I. *Why, it was the day we went riding.*" He straightened. "She'd called me that morning in tears."

"Wait—*what?*" A chill slipped down my spine.

That was the day I told Tom I loved him. And *he* had told *me*. He couldn't have known she was back. But he'd taken forever to park, been shaken at the pub, saying he'd been delayed by a phone call. Had it been her? Had it been *her* thundering past on the horse?

I remembered the day Freddy had shown up to the flat with the crop. He'd assumed Tom had told me about Amelia. In fact, he seemed bent on gossiping about it.

And that same afternoon, when I brought up her name to Tom. He'd gone eerily quiet, dark. I'd referred to her as *the girl he dated in college*. He hadn't corrected me. Instead, he'd deflected.

Gemma'd had it wrong at lunch. Amelia hadn't mercilessly dumped Tom. *He* had dumped *her*.

I felt sick. The specter of her was everywhere. *That day at the museum.* Tom was late, different. Had he seen her then? Had he been seeing her this whole time?

"Why did she leave her cat at Tom's flat in the middle of the night?"

"*Her* cat?" Freddy slammed his pint on the table. "She *loathes* that cat—loathes it. Wanted rid of it the moment it whined at her doorstep. Tom begged her not to take it to a shelter. But that's Tom. Rescuing animals, students. Waifs on aeroplanes." He arched a brow at me, pointedly, and my stomach flipped. "And then she names the cat Ophelia. So clearly a veiled threat. *I'll keep the loathsome creature on the condition you marry me, or I shall throw myself in the river*—that's how desperate she was for him. There was even a time or two she downed a handful of pills with Daddy's expensive wine from the cellar and gave us all a good scare. And why do you think Amelia demanded she keep the cat after they'd split? Out of spite. To hurt him. She knew full well how terribly attached he was to it. Really, Jane, none of it is any of my business except that I feel such a great fondness for you. And for Tom. I only hope you all resolve this sooner than later."

Please no, not again. Had this all been a terrible delusion?

"For all her brilliance and beauty, Amelia lacks...How shall I say it?" He puffed out his cheeks. "*Warmth*. Something you have in heaps. Tragic, really. She really does love Tom, frightfully, and I believe he loved her. Though not in the way he loves you, I daresay. Not in the way he loves you."

He gave my hand a squeeze of sympathy, perseverance, perhaps even genuine friendship.

"Well, there it is. Right," he said, letting go, slapping some bills on the table—what looked like an enormous tip. I followed his gaze to the bar; he'd locked eyes with the waitress, who peered coyly up from her phone. How different she was from Lady Beatrice, or Maureen, or Pippa. An equal-opportunity playboy.

"Funny thing, life," he said, turning back to me. "All those years, Amelia waiting for Tom to come round...he *finally* commits, and they're on the brink of her fairy-tale wedding." Freddy's blue eyes were searing into me, like that first time, on the stone steps outside Tom's flat, when everything was hopeful and bright. "And what does he do? The old boy falls head over heels—with a *stranger*. On a *plane*. I mean, honestly, what are the odds."

Chapter 33.

WHO'LL STOP THE RAIN

Tom burst through his door whistling "There She Goes," a small bouquet of wildflowers in his hand. A sweet sendoff before I headed to London. Oskar leapt from my lap and wrapped herself around his leg.

He caught sight of me on the sofa and smiled brightly, approaching, until he took in the small silver-wrapped wedding gift, the invitations box set beside it. I watched the color drain from his face. He stuttered, dropped into the wingback chair, his leather bag slipping from his shoulder and onto the floor, the flowers drooping in his hand.

"Jane," he said, desperate, as Oskar crumpled between his feet, but she was invisible to him.

I tasted hot tears on my lips but swabbed them quickly away. I'd resolved not to cry but hearing him saying my name was too much.

"The card." My hand trembled as I extended it to him. His anguished eyes fixed on mine for a terrible beat. Finally, he rose and took it from me, then sank back in the chair. He gave the faintest groan as he read.

"The gift?" I held it up, offered it to him. I knew this would hurt him. He slumped over his knees, squeezed his head in his hands.

"I want to burn it," he said to the floor, his voice low and unrecognizable, full of self-loathing.

"And there's this." I inched forward the invitations box, wanting to get it all out and over with. I'd never seen him like this, utterly wretched and broken.

"I want to burn them too. I want to burn my entire life before I met you." His voice caught in his throat. It was horrible to see him this way, there was no consolation in it.

"When were you going to tell me?"

He tried to speak. "I know what you must be thinking, you must despise me," he said finally.

My heart squeezed in my chest. I shook my head. "*No*. I could never feel that way about you—don't you know that? I feel, I don't know, deceived. You could have just told me. You *should* have."

The church bells began to chime, and on instinct, we both turned to the bank of windows. The sound of weddings, of celebrations, of birth and death and funerals. Of Oxford. But there was nothing to see. Only night, descending.

He sighed. "I kept *trying,* over and over to find a way to—to explain all of it, but the longer I delayed, the harder it was. And then I got it in my head, if you knew—" He broke off. "If you knew, you would *leave*."

"I don't even know what to think—I'm just—" I shook my head, confused, scared of what all of it meant. Being with him had brought me back to music, to happiness. But my fairy tale had shattered hers.

"It was pure cowardice." He leaned sharply forward, his elbows pressed to his knees, his eyes pleading. "Can you forgive me for it?"

Yes! I forgive you! I love you! I didn't want to tell you my sad story, either!

But the words were only in my head.

Tom was still waiting.

"It's true," he sighed, resigned. "When I met you, I was engaged."

He went on to tell me everything, his real story, the one I hadn't wanted to know, starting with the things I already did. They'd met as freshers, stayed on at Oxford to become tutors, fellows, in a relationship that had been on and off for years. He told me he had loved her, and she had loved him, and I thought, better that than him being with her all those years for some other reason— her family's wealth, the posh society she ran with. In fact, he'd kept himself at a distance from her London life, and *that* had been an ongoing source of discord. It also explained why there were no pictures of him in any of the society photos I'd found online.

He told me they had reconciled this past March, after having been apart for close to ten months; the caveat being that Tom agree to an ultimatum: If they were to stay together as a couple, they would marry and start a family right away, as they'd both just turned forty. No more slumming like students, back and forth between flats. Amelia had been driven half mad over the years, watching her sisters and friends marry, have children, set up in lovely houses. So, on that chilly night in March when Tom agreed, and Amelia began planning an extravagant wedding, with fervor, set for September, he told himself it was time to stop resisting. He'd made it harder than it ever needed to be. In time, it would all make sense.

I listened in silence, but Tom was now awaiting some response. It had grown dark, the two of us mere shadows, rain beginning to tap the windowpanes. I had missed my train to London and wondered if there was another.

Tom rose at last, Oskar following his every move, as he flicked on a small lamp and returned to the frayed leather chair. A sallow glow washed the dinged-up kitchen cabinets, the chipped farm sink, the mismatched flea-market furniture. I saw his place through her eyes, Amelia's, but it didn't make me like it any less.

"Amelia stood by me all those many years when I was depressed,

unhappy, remote to her. It wasn't fair, but I let it go on like that…
on and on," he murmured to the floor, his hands tensed, gripping
the arms of the chair.

Depressed, unhappy? I didn't know this Tom. What I saw, what
I felt, was only his iron self-restraint in constant conflict with a
smoldering core, his preternatural calm always beckoning me in,
to get even closer to him—

"*Jane,*" he sighed, anguished.

I thought of Jessica, how she stole Alex's heart in an instant, and
felt sick. How could I want Tom this way, knowing Amelia was
out there, despairing, having been replaced so suddenly by me?
How would I *live* with myself?

"Are you okay? You don't look well. And you're shivering."

He rose and stood before me at the sofa, our bodies close. And
for a breathless instant, my skin prickled. I closed my eyes, every
nerve, every cell, waiting to be gathered into his melting warmth—
longing to run my cheek shamelessly back and forth along the
edge of his forearm, to rise and rest it flush to his chest, to feel
my heartbeats sync with the steady double throbs of his own, to
know everything would be okay, to forget everything that was
not *now*—

But he only draped the throw blanket over my shoulders, still
smoke-tinged from the night of the fire, faintly scented with
Monica's perfume. Yet still I was shivering, and seeing this, Tom
tugged the gray cashmere sweater I so loved him in up and over his
head. Careful to keep his distance now, he stepped back, offered it
out to me, his eyes searching. Once I'd slipped it on, he lowered
himself to the edge of the armchair, again, his hands clasped, and
I was aware of the steady heavy thrum of rain coming down,
washing everything away. It was as if we were back on the plane,
wrapped up together in white noise, "suspended above the earth,
above the clouds," as he had said, that afternoon by the river in
Oxford, our first date—

"*I* kissed you on the plane." The words tumbled out before I could catch them.

Why *had* I? It was stupid, and impulsive and *selfish*. I'd desired him. It was an act of free will, not that of a woman awaiting her cue from a man. But had I not? Everything would be different. They would still be together, married, perhaps a baby on the way. His life would have remained intact.

"I wanted you to," he said. "I was *dying* to kiss you." He was looking straight into me, his eyes gleaming. "It was as if I'd been sleeping, for years and years, and then suddenly *to feel* something I hadn't even known was missing. I didn't want that feeling to end. I'd glimpsed something bright and hopeful...another life." He looked at me with such love.

And my heart careened: *How could we possibly continue, knowing what we know? That our love, our bliss, meant pain and heartache for another?*

I had no words, only a terrible ache, a crushing weight on my chest. He began pacing, agitated, speaking rapidly, his gaze to the floor. After we'd parted at Heathrow, he told me, practically the instant he'd returned to Oxford, things fell apart. He only knew for certain he couldn't go through with the wedding, because somewhere inside him he'd known all along he could never be the person Amelia wanted him to be. And yet he'd *stayed*, he'd led her on, selfishly.

She was rightfully furious. She told him she never wanted to see his face again as long as she lived. She insisted he not breathe a word to anyone—that *she* would do damage control. In the days that followed she told her family, her friends in London, a few select colleagues, that it had been her idea and hers alone to call off the engagement. Tom left her flat the night they broke up and heard nothing until Freddy rang him a couple of days later. Freddy seemed to know, but he was close with Amelia, so perhaps she'd confided in him. Amelia had asked him to gather a few of her things from Tom's place, some clothes, a small oil painting, and a few framed photos.

So, there *had* been photographs.

Adrenaline seared through me. I gazed up at the mysterious blank patch on the wall. All this time, it had been staring me in the face—like the book of erotica, the honeymoon itinerary, the Chanel lipstick, her note left in the vanity drawer. Had those small things simply been overlooked in his haste to move on? Or had he *wanted* me to find them?

Maybe all we'd ever been was two wrecked people, blinded by infatuation.

"When Freddy came by, he told me Amelia had been granted the fellowship and was off to Boston. That she was doing well— thrilled to be rid of me."

This had all taken place my first weeks in London, when I'd been *pining* for him to call; it was obvious now why he hadn't— and right of him *not* to! If he had, it would have been far worse. But now he seemed desperate, unhinged, trying too hard to sell me on this notion that his broken engagement had all been tied up with a neat little bow when it so obviously wasn't. And there was some- thing bleak and pathetic and Willy Loman about his desperation, which terrified and pained me.

"I should have told you from the very start. I owed you that—I owed you *the truth.*"

Yet I hadn't been truthful either. About Alex. About Jonesy. Out of pride.

"In those weeks after it all fell apart with Amelia, I thought of you *constantly,* I listened to all of your music. I listened to 'The Only Living Boy in New York' over and over and thought, how could she have known what I was feeling?"

"You remembered?"

He nodded. On the plane, I'd told him about Pippa—how she appeared in my life at the exact right time, the exact right place.

"'Let your honesty shine.'" The song again. "But I hadn't in *years*. I was desperate to contact you, but it was too soon. But then I began to panic, because I didn't know how long you'd be in England. I just wanted to be *near* you, to *know you,* and after we were together, I couldn't *stop*. It was a dizzying kind of vertigo but wonderful, indescribable. I wanted to tell you I was mad for you, but on the heels of— Well, it felt wrong. I don't know. I stopped myself."

And I'd stopped myself, too.

"I've been cowardly and selfish ever since, afraid if you knew, I'd lose you."

"She called you, that night in the Cotswolds. After riding with Freddy. That's why it took you so long to park?" I felt my heart quicken.

"Yes," he admitted. "She'd fallen apart—she'd come back, to England."

What were the chances it had been her, thundering past?

"And you saw her, didn't you, that day we all met at the museum?" She had to have been the one calling him incessantly, when he was ignoring his phone.

"Yes," he said, mortified. "She appeared out of nowhere. She knew that I, that you, that *we*—she'd seen gossip, in the papers, and that's when she began to unravel—"

And who could blame her, I thought. "And after she left the cat, you *still* didn't explain to me what was going on."

"I keep trying, to help her move on, see reason, but each time I think she has...She can't seem to let me go."

This would never end.

Suddenly he was before me, desperate, grasping my hands. He rested his head in my lap, slipped his arms around my waist, and I wanted to fuse myself to him, knowing only that I loved him inexorably. My palms hovered over his back, over the rippling waves of heat rising from his body.

"Marry me, Jane."

My whole body went rigid, shot through with fear. *Was he mad?*

"Jane." He was frantically searching my face. "Jane, please say something, I can't—the only time I can't read you. Tell me what you're thinking. What you're feeling."

That it's too late. That we can't go back. That she'll never let you go. That I'll never be able to trust you. I thought of her, as broken as I was when Alex left me. No. I'd never do that to anyone. I went cold, and numb, and instinctively extricated myself from him.

"You do know. You know I have to leave."

"But—? Why?" he blinked.

Because it happened to me. *I* was *her.*

He stared, stricken, as if reading my thoughts.

"No." He slipped lower, resting his cheek on my thigh, his tears warm on my skin and soon mingling with mine. I couldn't stop myself from running my fingers through his hair—

"I have no idea what I'm doing," I said, folding myself onto him. I found his cheek with my own, the sensation wakening every nerve ending. I grazed my lips over his damp eyelashes, the straight bridge of his nose, breathing him in, memorizing the details of him.

"Whatever you're doing, don't stop—don't ever stop," he murmured, his head in my lap. "All the sweetness in the world is here, in you. *Please don't go.* Please don't leave me, Jane."

But, Reader, I did.

Chapter 34.

COMING CLEAN

It was now well past midnight. I'd managed to catch the last train to London but couldn't face the thought of an empty hotel room. There had been no way to warn Pippa, my phone dead, my charger abandoned in my frenzy to run. I let myself quietly in, parked my rolly just inside the door, slipped off my shoes, and stood paralyzed in her foyer in the dense nocturnal silence, the faint glow of electronics like scattered stars. I'd left Tom despondent, his head in his hands. All the pretty wedding soaps from Rupert and Bumble, little cubes stamped like children's alphabet blocks, scattered about his feet. Oskar Wilde had worked open the box from Amelia's special mill in France. Their scent was his, his skin. Even *this* had belonged to her.

I pictured him rising, drifting down his dark passage, past his many books until he reached the bedroom. I pictured him freezing at the sight of the photos of him and her fanned out across the bed, and a bolt of panic seared through me. I stumbled through the living room and into the pitch dark of Pippa's hallway, feeling the walls for the guest room door and for Will. Once the concert was over, he and I would leave England, start over together, home again in LA, like he'd wanted us to, back in August.

But I froze outside the door. It reeked of weed. I could hear the whir of his white-noise machine. He was clearly asleep. It was Pippa I wanted, anyway, and I turned to her bedroom, thinking I wouldn't wake her, only ease in soundlessly alongside her. In the morning, she'd know what to do. Calm, clearheaded, brilliant Pippa.

I quietly opened the door to her master suite and, skimming the walls blindly, wound my way through the L-shaped entry until my bare feet sank into the plush carpeting of her bedroom. I could just make out a thread-thin glow beneath folds of heavy blackout drapes. I crept hesitantly toward where I knew her bed to be, my eyes still struggling to adjust, when a faint outline bloomed before me, like a photo emerging in a darkroom.

Pippa. The back of her. She was facing away, toward her headboard, sitting upright in bed as if in some sort of trance.

But wait! She was naked, her hourglass form gently rocking, her hips *undulating—oh Christ!* There was someone beneath her!

I shielded my eyes and backed away fast. Please *not* Freddy— but now there was creaking, and moaning, and rustling of sheets— the headboard thumping—

I bashed blindly into the wall. "Shit. *Fuck.*"

The creaking stopped.

"Paris France."

For a confused instant I scrambled to place the voice. Then it came to me. *My brother.*

"I *know,*" Will sighed, moments later in the living room. "I shoulda come clean, *we* should have." So now they were a "we"?

He was standing, with his hands planted on his hips, skinny and barefoot and incredibly annoying, dressed only in jeans. Pippa was refusing to leave the bedroom.

"Well, now I'm scarred for life, having witnessed you and her." I waved my hand in the direction of his crotch. This was actually *worse* than Freddy. "Your fly's halfway down, by the way."

He scoffed, but swiftly zipped himself up.

"Sit," he commanded, suddenly the big man. "Don't move. I'm making you tea." He swaggered toward the kitchen. Now he was someone who swaggered, ugh.

I plonked down, stewing, listening to him clunk around. How hard was it to make a cup of tea?

"How long, if you don't mind me asking, has this been going on?" Will glanced over from the kitchen, appearing a bit more contrite. "Was it the night of the museum?"

I could tell from his face I was right. So, while Tom and I were dragging Amelia's rug like a corpse down the stairs, *they* were fucking their brains out. And neither of them said a thing. Pippa had even gone on about her date with Freddy a couple days later.

I turned, fuming, and crossed my arms. How could she be so deceitful—how could they? Obviously, it was none of my business. But if Pippa had simply admitted it, I would have *thanked* her! I would have cheered: *Huzzah!* This is a *mitzvah* for the entire Silverman-Start family! But most especially for my lonely, horny brother. Was I that clueless? I was the person who routinely guessed lines of dialogue before characters in movies said them. So then how had I missed Alex sneaking around with Jessica? How had I missed Pippa and Will? How had I missed Tom's hidden life?

How could every person I knew, and loved, have deceived me?

"Jeez," Will said, after I'd calmed down enough to reluctantly catch him up. "I still can't believe it. Tom seemed so forthright." He sipped his tea. "Never thought I'd have occasion to actually use that word." But seeing my face: "*Sorry.* I'm truly sorry, Jane."

"I can't even blame her for hating me. I'm *her,* Jessica, now—that's how this woman thinks of me. And all this time I'd convinced myself my paranoia was childish and irrational."

"Just slow down, 'kay?" He jutted his chin at my tea and I forced some down.

The clues were *everywhere*. Why didn't I just ask? "I honestly thought *this time* I'd *finally* gotten it right." How could I have been so blind? "I don't know, I just—*I want Pippa*."

"Me too," he sighed. "Sorry. She's mortified."

I would be too, if I were her.

But somehow I couldn't resist asking: "Do you guys *always* do it in the dark? I mean, that was like *Elvis*-level blackout curtains. Like aluminum-foil-lining-the-windows *dark*."

"Not *always*," he sputtered. "She's bizarrely insecure about her looks. Which is absurd. She's Brigitte Bardot for Christ's sake, but obviously"—he cleared his throat—"I want *her* to feel comfortable."

"She looked pretty damned comfortable to me. Insecure my foot, like having a great rack like that is a bad thing?"

He choked on a laugh. "I can't believe you just said that. But yeah, my god, *exactly*."

He slouched back and ran his hand through his hair, his legs a little man-splayed. Now he was someone who man-splayed. Ugh.

"Truth is, I'd be quite content to do nothing but sit around all day gazing at her, preferably naked." I made a face. "*Her*. Not *me*. I've been madly in love with her for years, you have to have known. But I oughta have told you it'd become real—I mean, at this point, she's practically my girlfriend. And she spent all last night worrying about *you*. How worked up you are about the concert. Your old nemesis must be stalking you right about now."

My heart flopped in my chest.

"Not Jonesy," he clarified, reading my face. He meant stage fright. I couldn't argue with the truth. My expression told him as much. "Look," he sighed. "She's desperate for everything to go smoothly. I was just trying to help her un*wind*." He raised his palms like an old vaudevillian.

She's practically my girlfriend.

"Go right ahead, fuck yourselves silly for all I care. Have all the

fun in the world! You both deserve someone amazing. I'm happy
for you"—my voice was suddenly wobbly—"because you're both
so special to me."

Beginning to blubber all over the place, I curled into a ball,
hiding my face inside the collar of Tom's sweater, which I'd stolen
and which smelled clean and peppery like him, and which made
me feel worse. As did the thought of Kurt Cobain, abandoned in
the little writing room in my desperation to flee.

"I'm so...sad. I don't know how to think straight or what to do
except run. From everything."

"So do it. Pull a Bobby Fischer. But *after* the show. You gotta
do the show."

I peeked out. Will was staring at me with those soulful dark eyes,
his smooth olive chest glowing. He was the image of our father, a
young Art Start in his Jack Kerouac phase, when he used to tinker
around the yard inventing things in the bleached sunshine amid the
lime trees, shirtless in Levi's and huarache sandals.

"Don'tcha get it? You *can* disappear, it's within your rights, and
you're obviously not a misanthropic dick like Bobby Fischer...My
point being, it doesn't really matter, Jane...life is but a dream,
except it's a lucid dream and you've got the oars." My crazy but
wonderful brother. He was getting keyed up now, at the edge of the
armchair. "Okay, so maybe you're in some tiny wooden rowboat
in the middle of a great big ocean, but you can still *steer* the thing?
You can go anywhere. Do anything."

His eyes were gleaming with hope, and I realized it was morning. I could hear the sounds of London waking, black cabs on
damp pavement, a passerby's cell phone going off, a whole other
world outside.

I sat up, too agitated now for the fetal position. Will's gaze had
drifted. He had this huge implacable grin plastered at something
behind me.

Pippa, full of apology, a reluctant smile dawning.

"Pull a Bobby Fischer," she said, raising a shoulder and cinching her robe. "Go to Paris France. It's high time you two just bloody went. As long as you do it *after* the Royal Albert Hall."

I suddenly saw Will through Pippa's eyes. He was seriously kind of a heartthrob. Sheesh.

"For now, we gotta get you right," he said briskly, changing gears. "You're a mess. And you've got a show to do in..." He looked at his watch. "Shiiiit. Thirty-six hours."

Chapter 35.

JUST WHEN I THOUGHT I WAS OUT, THEY PULL ME BACK IN

It was a gallows atmosphere at Pippa's as the clock struck five. Rehearsal had been postponed repeatedly, surprising everyone *but me,* and we were now at T-minus twenty-seven hours and counting till *showtime.* Alastair, James, and young George had encamped for moral support. Everyone was hushed, tacitly avoiding the subject of—

"Is Tom coming?" George inquired, perched cross-legged atop Pippa's kitchen counter. Bored, she plonked her chin into the heels of her palms.

James poked his head around the opened fridge door. He and Alastair shared a look.

"Tom is busy teaching," James deflected in a tight voice, "teaching at Oxford." He zoomed past, with a drink, and settled himself on the sofa.

"What does he teach?" George drawled, circling a lazy finger on the Corian countertop. The kid was nothing if not intuitive.

"The Romantics," said Alastair and grimaced, apologetic, at me. "And this is the song Jane will be singing with Jonesy, *very soon.*" He clapped a pair of noise-canceling headphones over her ears.

But my heart had lodged in my throat. Jonesy still hadn't

officially confirmed what precisely I was meant to do at the Royal Albert Hall.

I darted an anxious glance at the clock, then to Alastair's guitar and amp by the front door. George was bopping her head intently, listening. Over the agonizing hours she'd consumed Jonesy's entire oeuvre, studying the album art and wondering why he looked so different in each. Her parents had explained that he liked to transform himself into various personas, so naturally she now found him fascinating. Who didn't?

Alastair hopped up onto the counter beside her and whipped open a newspaper. The image of the two of them side by side made my throat tighten. I tipped back my head and was attempting to tuck in the tears—everything seemed to set them off—when I caught sight of Pippa frowning down at her phone screen.

"Who are you texting with," I insisted, steeling myself.

"No one," she snapped. Rattled by her own harshness, she gently added, "And not Tom," followed by a *No calling him, you promised* look.

I shot back a wordless *Fuck's sake, I'm not going to*. After a beat, we both resumed pacing.

I was dying to know if he was coming to the show; the not knowing was killing me. Yet the thought of this performance, this moment without him there, it was crushing. But if he did show up, what would I say, or do? It was all too much to grapple with now. I'd been given a strict mandate from everyone to maintain radio silence at least until the performance was behind me, a mandate I knew was sensible.

"Then is no one *them?* Team Jonesy?"

"Not *them* either," she said crisply. "No one is no one you have to bother with."

This was getting very confusing, but Pippa was eyeing me funny, like there was something wrong with my face.

I know. There was. My eyes were swollen and red from no sleep.

This crying business would have to stop, for *real,* because crying and singing are mutually exclusive.

My eyes welled again; there had never been a worse time to break up with a boyfriend than now.

Pippa sighed and resumed pacing, so I followed suit, picking up snippets of conversation from the kitchen. "Crikey, Jonesy's thirty-nine?" There was disbelief over the length and girth of his Wiki page, his towering list of accomplishments. "Good god, Jonesy was only seventeen when he wrote, produced, and played *all* the instruments on *Jonesing for You.*"

There followed effusive declarations about how amazing the concert was going to be, Jonesy and me "reuniting after all these years!" I appreciated the effort, but honestly, it came off as compensatory, given how severely underprepared I was. And no one in this room knew what I did: that the last time I'd seen Jonesy still haunted me to this day. I was left feeling ever more anxious.

I glanced at the clock. Jonesy's stringing me along felt tactical—his pathological need to manipulate every*thing* and every*one* in his orbit. His keeping me in the dark bordered on cruel, *nefarious*.

"You're wringing your hands, little bird," Alastair sighed, peering over the top of the *Times*. He hopped off the counter and began to massage my shoulders. I was too tense even for this, but didn't have the heart to stop him.

"Just when I thought I was out...*they pull me back in.*"

"What was that?" Alastair paused, craned his head to me.

"*Godfather Three.* Al Pacino," James called out from the sofa.

Alastair shrugged and went back to massaging.

"Where's *Will?*" I croaked, panicked.

This was going to be like one of those dreams where you suddenly find yourself on a stage, blinded by a spotlight, with no idea what you're meant to do or why you're not wearing any underwear. That would be *me,* twenty-seven hours from now. I glanced at Pippa's clock. Twenty-six hours.

Well, not the underwear part, obviously.

"Will's running a very important errand," Pippa snapped. "But he should have been back by now." She crumpled beside James on the sofa and hugged a pillow as if she was having cramps.

It was quite possible I was being paranoid, and Jonesy was simply running late. Because he *was* a perfectionist. Oh god, that's right—he was a *perfectionist*. I had to be *perfect*.

I released myself from the massage in order to resume pacing.

Pippa rose and beelined for the kitchen, until noticing she was still clutching the pillow, which she then lobbed over her shoulder. Alastair deftly intercepted it before it reached James's unsuspecting head, then sank beside him and pulled him close. I wished *my* boyfriend were here to do all of that. The lump in my throat reemerged. How was I to sing? If the mere *thought* of Tom dared enter my consciousness, I'd be toast. And what if he decided to show up? It was infinitely more terrifying to sing in front of a person you *knew* than zillions you didn't. Oh god: zillions. And oh god: Freddy was on the list, and Bryony and Cyril, and Gemma and Vikram...

The front door clapped shut. Everyone turned.

"It is I," Will said brightly, tearing off headphones from which Jonesy's voice seeped audibly.

He fumbled to silence his phone. Pippa, grim-faced, rushed over and ripped a small white bag from him, then disappeared down the hall. Perhaps she did have cramps and Will had dashed to the pharmacy for pain meds. Now George was insisting Will give her a spin. Had everyone fallen for Will?

"Okay, kid," he exhaled, after a few whirls. "Keep that up much longer and you'll turn me into a muscleman." He set her down with an exaggerated huff and flexed. She gave his biceps a little punch.

"Any word from His Royal Highness?" He peered up. "Rats. Maybe let's pretend the show has already happened and it went great, and *today* is actually *tomorrow*."

He grinned, quite pleased with himself, and settled into the chair by the sofa, giving its arms a self-satisfied thwack.

"I think, though, you mean day *after* tomorrow, technically," James corrected him. Alastair patted his knee, like, *That'll do.* James nodded solemnly and pushed up his cool nerdy glasses.

If only I could have skipped ahead to which*ever* day meant it was all behind me... or skipped backwards to my life before yesterday, to Oxford, and Tom.

"Let's skip down to the *juicy* part, shall we?" Alastair said. He whisked the laptop from James, scrolled down the Wikipedia page.

George arranged herself tummy-down at Will's feet, face buried in her arms, and continued her Jonesy deep dive through headphones.

"Right," Alastair began. "It seems Jonesy divides his time between Manhattan and Paris, and has recently split with influencer Fleur Amour. He's romantically linked with oodles of celebrities including"—he looked up, gaping—"one Jane Start. Says so right here, and we all know Wikipedia's *never* wrong." He raised a brow, chuckled, trying to make light. "Have you been keeping something from us all these years?"

"No. I haven't." *Yes, I have.* And Jonesy clearly wrote his own Wikipedia page. *He* included me on the list.

All at once I felt faint—the smell of vanilla and gardenia so overpowering, I could practically taste it, chemical, on my tongue. *His penthouse, ten years ago, sputtering with candlelight. I was following him out of that elevator, sinking into his carpeting, thick and plush and white, my ballerina flats leaving footprints like tracks in deep snow. Why was I here? He had a girlfriend—he had three. Jonesy stopped, his back to me. He was gazing out at a sweeping arc of the Manhattan skyline as if posing for a magazine cover. His fingernail click-clicked on the polished surface of a baby grand. The skin at the back of his neck was pale, vulnerable, like a child's, when he turned abruptly and faced me.*

"Reunited and it feels so good."

It was Will, singing under his breath and fiddling with the laces of his Converse. "Sorry," he said, reading my face. "It just popped into my—"

"Peaches and Herb couldn't be more wrong in this moment," I scowled, shutting him down, when Pippa glided back in like a princess, a cloud of perfume in her wake.

We eyeballed her for news from Team Jonesy, but she sprawled silkily onto the sofa and took her sweet time before murmuring, "No. Word. Bastards." There was a chorus of groans, and then everyone realized they needed fresh drinks.

Except Pippa, who closed her eyes and shook her head sultrily to decline.

"*You* seem rather *relaxed,*" James cooed at her. "Have you been clandestinely nipping drink in the back room?"

"I have been clandestinely smoking cannabis," she announced glassily. "It's been a very challenging week." An understatement. Could anyone blame her? Apparently, Will's *very* important errand was not to the kind of pharmacy I'd assumed.

But when her phone rang shrilly, she sprang up, extremities flailing.

"*Gah.* It's *them. How do I make this thing work!*"

Will grabbed the phone, swiped it open, and returned it to her palm.

"Hello, this is Pippa More," she thrummed in a low Marlene Dietrich voice, suddenly impossibly cool and collected. *How did she just do that?*

An instant later, she collapsed over her knees, phone smashed to her ear, and thumped her fist to the sofa to keep from laughing.

"Yes. I see. Oh right. No. This number is *perfect.* Correct. Lovely. Thanks ever so much." And jabbed viciously at her screen a few extra times, to be sure the call was ended. When she turned to me, her face was grave.

"Get ready. Jonesy is about to call you."

Chapter 36.

WHAT THE FUCK

The phone was ringing, yet I couldn't quite bring myself to grab it. Pippa was mouthing, *Take it for fuck's sake* and wagging it in my face. One more ring and it would go to voicemail, so I snatched the thing at last and put it on speakerphone.

From the periphery of my vision: Pippa, Alastair, James, and Will, leaning in, watching me keenly. George remained under headphones, oblivious.

"Hello?" I could barely get above a peep.

"I've got Rod," said a deep bass voice, reverberant, through the tinny phone speaker. "For Maggie. Maggie May."

Will mouthed, *What the fuck.*

A pause when I didn't answer. "Is this Jane Start?"

"Yes?" I said.

"Hold a moment. Oh, and what size shoe are you?"

What the fuck looks from everyone.

"Umm—six, and a half?"

"Thanks. Hold a moment."

No one breathed, especially me.

"Hey." This time it was *him*—Jonesy, the voice resonant yet shockingly adolescent, not at all deep. And familiar, but like *groggy from a dream* familiar, thus vaguely disconcerting.

"Oh, hello," I replied, stiffly.

"You somewhere private?"

Alastair cued me with an affirmative nod, then mimed zipping his mouth shut. The others zipped theirs, too.

"Yes. Totally alone."

"Good," Jonesy exhaled. "So...I think it's better if we just, you know, *let it happen* tomorrow night."

What? No rehearsal?! "Okay—*cool.*" But it *wasn't* okay, *or* cool!

"Excellent...what are you doing, then? Right now?"

Alastair calmly pointed to his wristwatch and mimed eating, and I realized I was panting into the phone like a deviant.

"Oh—I was about to grab dinner."

"Me too," he said, almost before I'd gotten the words out. "I've rented a cozy little place in Regent's Park. We could have it together."

Have it together. At his cozy little place. I couldn't think of anything less cozy, but was this—a *date? No. Nope. No way.* It would be just as unsettling as last time.

"Oh, that's so—nice," I stuttered, my eyes superglued to Alastair, who pulled James close, miming eating again, and James, flustered, did his best to mime along too. "But, um, I've actually got *plans*...to go to dinner...with my boyfriend. So, that might be..."

"Might be what?" Jonesy said coolly, his voice flat. Suddenly there was an awful silence on the line. What had I done? I'd blown off *Jonesy.* Who probably had zero interest in me *that way* and I'd just acted like *I* thought *he did.* Embarrassing, presumptuous. For all I knew he was back with his It Girl. And I didn't even have a boyfriend. My heart squeezed in my chest—

"Kiss me." Jonesy's voice pealed from the phone speaker, suddenly cute and pint-sized, yet simultaneously commanding, the great and powerful Oz.

Kiss him? Over the phone?

Pippa shaded her eyes, unable to watch. Will mimed steam coming out of his ears, James had clapped his palms over his mouth. Even Alastair was stumped.

Will finally signaled me with a swirl of his hand: Go on.

Who the fuck asked a person to *kiss them* over the phone?

But I knew the answer. Jonesy did. So I took a deep breath, puckered up, and delivered a kiss into the speaker, because I didn't know what else to do.

"See you tomorrow," he said, and with that, the line went dead.

Chapter 37.

THE ROYAL FUCKING
ALBERT HALL

"You're awfully quiet," Pippa remarked.

I had no words. No way to express my reaction to the skintight black catsuit hanging from an otherwise empty metal wardrobe rack in my dressing room. The catsuit appeared at once lonely and intimidating, a designer tag dangling from the lowest point of the plunging neckline, *For Jane Start* sharpied across it. Neatly lined up on the floor below were a pair of three-inch stilettos, size six and a half.

Pippa, stationed beside me, cleared her throat. "Jonesy's tall, so perhaps his stylist thought—"

"I'm not Lady Gaga," I interrupted. My voice was calm, steady. "Or someone like that, who's talented enough to perform teetering around in heels—which requires tremendous focus and energy not to fall over, and means having to splay out your legs and tense your thighs." I demonstrated by way of a Tina Turner pose. "All the while balancing a guitar. It's completely and utterly counter-intuitive to singing, which requires relaxing so the sound can flow out." I pantomimed manically. "When in reality, as you can probably tell, I am *not* relaxed. I am panicked. I can't multitask. It's going to take *all* of my focus, *all* of my energy, to be good on the music part. Versus the *fashion part.* And the *looking tall* part."

"Are you quite finished?"

"Mm-hmm." We both stared at the costume again.

"But it sounded so promising," she said, disappointed, "having a stylist for once, presenting you with designer *options.* Plural. Perhaps we should open that."

She pointed to a bottle of Dom sitting atop the pristine makeup counter, alongside a sumptuous arrangement of white roses and a silver tray with energy bars.

"Perhaps," I agreed.

"A long way from dressing rooms past, at least." She ran her finger over the sparkling, dustless surface and held it up with a plastered-on smile.

Dressing rooms I wished I could un-remember, in moldy basements, with saggy sofas, and unsettling stains best not to dissect.

"Soooo," she said, working open the champagne. "Apparently the tech crew have been dealing with some *issues.*"

Pop. The cork shot up, pinged the ceiling, and rolled to a stop between the stiletto heels. Pippa extended a glass to me, but I was still steeling myself for the *issues.*

"Right. So here it is. They've had to scrub your sound check, his ran way over. First night of his tour and all that. And they need to open the house doors soon. *But don't panic,* they've done an extremely thorough line check and have assured me you've got killer monitors, dialed in *exactly* the way you like them." She kicked back the champagne she'd just poured for me.

No. Fuck. That was like a pilot being denied the opportunity to inspect her instrument panel before takeoff. *And Jonesy knew it.* "But I need to at least check the guitar and the amp Alastair lent me. I need to get a good sound."

"But here's this other thing," she said, turning her back to re-up her glass. "*Ap-pa-rent-ly,* Jonesy has a very precise vision for the performance, which in *this* case means you can focus *entirely* on *singing?*" She said this over her shoulder, offhandedly, re-snuggling the bottle in ice, but our eyes locked in the mirror.

I frowned, not quite processing. "Focus *entirely* on singing?"

"Exactly. No need to worry a'tall about playing guitar," she said, breezily. "So no worries about the stilettos!" But a little grimace was threatening to erupt.

She knew: I felt naked without a guitar. I'd gleefully trade this dustless gem of a dressing room for one of those dilapidated dungeons with a suspiciously stained sofa and a flying phallus graffitied upon the wall if it meant I was performing *with* a guitar.

"After yesterday's rehearsal debacle, I know how *desperate* you are to get a sense of things, and for a proper sound check," she said, swiveling to face me. "Especially after *Kiss-me-gate.*"

I pretended to laugh at her joke. This was *not* Pippa's fault. *Welcome back to the music business.* It was a shitshow. And managers and agents were the ones stuck shoveling the shit. For *us.* I was lucky to have her. Pippa was brilliant, wise, ethical, good at her job. I was her charity case. Besides, this was *Jonesy's* show. The superstar. The iconoclast. I should have assumed they'd run out of time for my sound check. I began auditioning nuclear options in my head: *Expired tofu induces debilitating illness.* Virtually impossible to sing and vomit at the same time.

"Jane, you look...well, you look exactly how you must be feeling, so I'm going to let you in on a little secret. Leopard Pants is coming! That's who 'no one' was yesterday—I've always told you he was a fan! In a blink of an eye, this Royal *fucking* Albert Hall business will be over and done with, and we can all go celebrate! Darling, you're going to be brilliant. Trust me."

Was she still high? I was nearly incapacitated from nerves. But back to the other problem.

"Do I really have to wear *that?*" I pointed to the catsuit, which stared arrogantly back, like any second it might start meowing. "I could just wear this," I said, indicating the dress I had on, my long-time, utterly uninspired stage uniform of cheap black shift dress I hoped wasn't made in a sweatshop, with black tights and battered old ballet flats. It had been delusional of me to think Jonesy's stylist would have provided options, plural, with at least one choice I'd feel comfortable wearing. I caught a glimpse of Tom's sweater, peeking from the top of my bag. My throat tightened. *No.* I would not entertain even the slightest thought.

"Let's just give it a shot?" Pippa offered.

And then I was shimmying into the catsuit. To my utter surprise, it felt like a reassuring hug. The fit so confident, the fabric and craftsmanship so fine. Why was Pippa staring at my butt?

"What?!" I burst out, unnerved.

She furrowed her brow. "There's a little problem with—"

"Panty line." I'd caught my reflection in the mirror.

"*Little House on the Prairie* knickers just won't do," she said, making a face.

"*Ugh.* I'll just have to go commando, I guess." I threw my hands up, exasperated, and began wriggling out of the catsuit. *"Oh god."* I stopped short, gaped at Pippa. "This is the dream. The nightmare I pre-visualized yesterday. When you were busy texting Leopard Pants. I'm about to be on stage, with no earthly idea what I'm meant to do, and I won't be wearing any underwear. *Mother fuck.*" I stumbled out of the catsuit, and jammed my Laura Ingalls Wilder underwear angrily into my bag.

Once re-suited, it was back to my reflection in the mirror. If only my boobs were bigger, my waist narrower, my butt... Well, no one had complained thus far. I was pretty proud of my butt, actually. But I really needed a guitar to feel a little less naked.

Ugh. *Jonesy.*

"Give me your jacket," I said, wriggling my fingers at Pippa's reflection.

She set down her champagne and shouldered it off. A moment

later, the two of us were lined up once more in the mirror. Pippa looked smokin' sans blazer, in a white silk blouse with the top buttons effortlessly undone and a bit of bra peeking out. And me? Well, the blazer matched the catsuit.

Pippa cocked her head. "That's it," she said. "You've successfully joined the ranks of Chrissie, Patti, Sofia, and other such badasses." She grinned, went to grab the stilettos when her phone jingled.

"Pippa More. Oh, right. I'll come at once, shall I?" She thrust the shoes at me, clapping a hand over the speaker. "I need to turn in the guest list, sort out the tickets. *Leopard Pants,* can you believe it? *Driving* in from Sussex—you're finally going to meet him, darling. I'll be back in two ticks!" And she slipped out the door.

I stood with a stiletto dangling from each hand. No way was I teetering around in these. Except *Jonesy* wanted me to. He wanted me to look *sexy.* I stared at the champagne bottle; it stared evenly back. *I'm here to help,* it seemed to say. *And what's wrong with sexy?*

I slipped on the shoes and proceeded to pour myself a big, fat glasseroo of Dom, and as I nestled the bottle back into the ice, my eyes fell on a small card addressed to me, damp and stuck to the inside. Pippa had overlooked it.

Heart thudding, I peeled open the envelope:

Happy Anniversary, Baby. Ten years ago today.

My breath caught. *Baby?* What was happening?! I felt sideswiped, the floor skidding out from beneath me as the room began to spin. I grasped the edge of the makeup counter to steady myself.

It suddenly all made sense. Why he'd asked me here. Stupid me, for not putting the timing together. But Pippa hadn't either. I reread the card, and my heart began to gallop.

Can't you see I want you? He'd scrawled it on the back, alongside his logo, a peace sign with wings.

Can't you see I want you? Baby? I flashed on his "Kiss me." The invite to a "cozy little dinner." Had Jonesy seen the humiliating press piece about Alex dumping me for Jessica and known I was single? But I *wasn't* single!

Oh god, I *was*. Without thinking, I clapped a hand over my mouth.

Jonesy must have seen the tabloid blitz about the show, in which Tom was mentioned, and in some creepy Spidey sense way, known that my relationship with Tom had imploded. Had he sensed a window of opportunity to strike?

A paranoic shudder rippled through me. I grabbed my champagne and knocked it back so violently, I was seized with a fit of coughing, even as there came a fierce set of knocks at the door.

It was him. Jonesy. It *had* to be. Perhaps merely to say "Break a leg, *baby*." Which I was very likely to do tottering in these preposterous heels, which ought to be banned if not for safety reasons, then for cruelty. Heart thundering, steeling myself for his towering inscrutable presence, I scrambled to manufacture some rejoinder to his bizarre flirty note as I flung open the door—

"Good evening, Miss Start. It's time I take you to the stage."

I exhaled. *Not* Jonesy, but a staid-faced older gentleman with a clipboard and headset, his accent BBC, his delivery clipped. The stage manager. But I was not due on until later! Three quarters of the way through the set! The show hadn't even started.

"Oh, okay—" I stammered, hugging the door for balance, "but I—just a second, one second." I slammed it right in his face. Unintentionally, but still.

I spun around to my reflection. I'd slapped on a bit of the old greasepaint earlier, believing I'd have oodles of time to jazz it up, but now I speed-tottered back to finish the job. I upended my bag and sent a deluge of cosmetics cascading across the countertop. My phone skated off the highly polished surface and crash-landed face-first on the floor, making a very bad sound.

With trembling fingers, I got to work, but now I looked like a clown. Lipstick haphazardly smeared, kohl pencil smudged crudely around my eyes.

I crouched to pick up my phone, groaning at the cracked screen, to find a flurry of missed calls and texts from basically everyone— *including Tom—TOM!* Oh god, was he here? Luckily, a text from Pippa slid through.

They're not letting me back! Some confusion with my pass! If I can't sort it out break a leg! Have fun! You'll be brilliant! AND THIS JUST IN: THEY ARE FILMING THE SHOW! THOUGHT YOU SHOULD KNOW IN CASE IT AFFECTS HOW YOU DO YOUR MAKEUP. 💄🖌️🎨👹

Surely the ogre emoji was a mistype. Or did she mean Jonesy was an ogre for not telling us? I agreed.

A battery of impatient knocks set the door vibrating.

Fuuuck. The stage manager again. But I hadn't had a chance to do my traditional pre-show pee. I wasn't an ogre; I was a *clown.* A clown trapped in a designer catsuit, who slightly had to pee.

The stage manager led me brusquely through a circuity of corridors. It was near impossible to keep up in the heels (blisters erupting immediately, my toes already going numb). Then all at once we were very near the stage, weaving through bodies along a claustrophobic hallway, cartage cases lining the walls, painted "Jonesy blue" (and with his name stenciled in his iconic font, the O a peace sign with wings). A few wildly dressed influencer types stood out amid crew rushing by in standard-issue black. A couple of cameramen weighted down with gear unintentionally thumped me as they sped past.

At last, we entered a dark tunnel erected of heavy scrim through which a gladiator might make his entrance into a colosseum—to fight or *die.* I felt a thrumming awareness of the stage beyond, and the legions of Jonesy fans stretching into the darkness, murmuring in anticipation.

We'd reached the mouth of the tunnel. The stage manager gently positioned me for the best view.

If I craned my neck, I could catch a glimpse of the hall, glittering like a tiara of rubies and gold. It was more intimidating than I could have possibly imagined. A sound check would have at least prepared me for this daunting view. It had been eight years since I'd approached a stage of this grandeur and scale, and now I was only too aware of how many small technicalities could go wrong tonight and conspire to undo me, to compromise my performance, even if there'd been a rehearsal *and* a sound check to sort out all the bugs!

It would almost be better if I died, I thought. Expired right here and now, my meager legacy at least intact, rather than humiliating myself in front of all these people. In front of *Jonesy.*

"I've been instructed to bring you here to watch the show. Just moments away now," said the stage manager, who'd been murmuring into his headset and was now preparing to leave me.

"Excuse me." I grasped his arm so tightly he peered down at my clenched fingers; embarrassed, I swiftly withdrew them. "But— can you tell me when my song is happening?"

He eyed me, flabbergasted, like, *You don't know?* "Just here," he said, using his penlight to scroll down the set list all the way to—*the encore?* My stomach plunged. *No pressure.*

"We'll be resetting the stage just prior, for your number," he said slowly, scrutinizing my face to be sure I comprehended.

I may look like a clown. I nodded: *Capeesh.* Satisfied, he stepped away.

So. It was real. I knew it. Jonesy had savagely kept me in the dark, and now he expected me to stand here in the wings, watching *his* brilliance, while my stage fright festered into something truly insupportable. And damn these stilettos, I could no longer feel my toes.

Happy Anniversary, *Baby.*

I began to creep backwards toward escape but thumped right into a gorgeous woman wearing a low-cut silk wrap dress and fedora. She had to be close to six feet tall, all angles and cheekbones and cleavage.

"Who are *you with?*" She frowned down at me, fingering her all-access pass; her voice was deep, the accent German.

"Myself?" I responded, thrown by her tone, when all at once a crescendoing roar erupted from the audience. Jonesy, tall and elegant in a blue sharkskin suit, his blond hair slicked back, strode to the lip of the stage, already shredding on guitar, but *coolly,* shrewdly. The stray lock falling mysteriously over his eye was amplified to majesty by a massive screen at the back of the stage. The audience had jumped to their feet, but their roar was quickly subsumed by a tsunami of beautiful sound. The band behind Jonesy lit up and kicked in, and they were off.

The fedora-wearing beauty and I watched, mesmerized, as Jonesy unleashed hit after hit with raw, carnal energy, saying little beyond a quip or some cryptic pronouncement before returning to the business at hand: his mass seduction of everyone here. At times his voice was urgent, rasped with emotion. Then soothing, enveloping. His moves erupted from some deep place within him, part Jagger, part Bowie, part David Byrne. He had a striking Viking quality, the bearing of a Cold Conqueror, mixed with fragility, a rascally boyishness. I could hardly comprehend the sheer range of his abilities. *He's grown up,* I thought. Never before had I witnessed a musician in such consummate control of the stage, the audience, *the moment,* conducting his ace band with mere glances and sly grins. I stood riveted, feeling equal parts rapture and blind fucking fear.

He started in on a song I didn't recognize at first as one of his, his guitar tone inconceivably crunchy and delicious, and then it hit me. He was doing a cover of "Jeepster." His own sultry, souped-up version of the impossibly cool T. Rex song from the seventies!

"Girl, I'm just a vampire for your loove—" Jonesy was nearing the end of the song when he raised his guitar overhead as if it were light as a feather. Like some deity, he seemed to stop time, to will every person in the place to hold their breath. But as a T. Rex fan, I knew he wasn't quite through with us yet.

"And I'm gonna *suck ya!*" he growled, his voice reverberating through the vast hall as he flicked his head stage left with the precision of a tango dancer, his eyes shining preternaturally straight into mine.

Then a spotlight blasted on and Jonesy was reduced to a stark silhouette. An instant later, it snapped off and he vanished like a magician's trick, leaving the audience stunned, and mute, until a roar of applause erupted. The stage went dark, triggering frantic commotion—crew members sprinting, jostling past me—

"I will take you to your mark now."

It was the stage manager. I couldn't seem to make my mouth work, or recover my breath, but he'd already grasped my arm and was hustling me up and onto the darkened stage.

It was then I knew: There was no escape.

Chapter 38.

MY WAY

Showtime. The stage manager stopped abruptly, center stage; there was an X of masking tape faintly glowing at my feet. I could just make out the dim outline of a wooden chair.

"Sit here, please," he whispered. I felt for the seat and lowered myself into it. "The mic is *live,*" he warned, kneeling, placing it solemnly into my sweaty palm. "All right, then?"

I started to whisper "No, not really," but he'd hurried off, because it was a rhetorical question and he couldn't care less if I was all right and *please no, not another handheld mic.*

But this wasn't Vegas. This was as far from Vegas as anywhere could be. I dared myself to peer up, and out, into the venue, a glittering inside-out wedding cake of velvet and jewels— 5,272 Jonesy fans staring back, wondering what I was doing here. *Fuck you, Google, for insisting I search the seating capacity of this venue.*

In the eerie stillness, a cough reverberated through the vast grandeur and a cell phone twinkled from one of the opera boxes miles away. There was a soft *click-clack*ing, like sugarplum fairies arranging themselves in the nearby shadows, and I felt my heart thumping preposterously, like an animated cartoon—bursting red and rubbery and bulbous through my ribs, my flesh, the catsuit. *Relax…just a little pressure and we're done.*

Biblical rays dawned from a lighting rig on high, and light sputtered behind me.

I twisted around. An enormous screen had illuminated at the back of the stage, filled with *me* looking terrified, a hostage trapped on my little wooden chair.

I jerked back to the audience, my palms so slick with fear-sweat the mic sailed off, releasing a shriek of feedback as it slid to a stop at the foot of the stage. A groan, deep and resonant, rose like a vapor from the audience. *This was not happening.* Oh god, *Tom* might be out there. And Will and Pippa and Freddy and Bryony…and the professors. And Leopard Pants. Not to mention reviewers *reviewing,* and a film crew *filming.*

I darted a sideways glance for help but found only the stage manager, his headset dangling, rubbing his ears, his face contorted. I'd deafened the stage manager. Somewhere a sound man was hating me too. Everyone was.

It was becoming obvious I was on my own to retrieve the mic, so I hunched low and skittered for it as the biblical rays on high began their automated sequence, zigzagging like prison lights, capturing me in their beams, triggering merciless titters from the audience. *I should walk off this stage,* I was thinking, *and never set foot on one ever again,* when voices like angels drowned the laughter.

I straightened, not having reached my mic. A women's choir had emerged from the shadows. They were singing the harmonies on my recording and making them…*better.* Then came the soft sizzle and crack of a snare drum; I followed the sound to my right, and a pool of light illuminated Jonesy's drummer. She smiled at me. When the bass fell in, I spun left; Jonesy's longtime bassist materialized beneath a shaft of vibrating light; he nodded, acknowledging what I'd begun to put together. They were playing the song *my* way. Copying the sounds and style of *my* recording.

But there was no time to wrestle with disbelief or gratitude. I heard the familiar velvety growl of a guitar, and Jonesy himself swaggered out. Instinctively, I retreated until I whacked into the hostage chair and tumbled onto it. The audience exploded with laughter. So I *was* a clown. He grinned, like, *Whoops, but isn't this fun?*

I flashed back to his voice on the speakerphone: "Let's just let it happen." Whatever game he was playing, it was clearly at *my* expense. And yet he was re-creating my record, live, in front of a sold-out crowd at the Royal Albert Hall, and that might be the nicest thing a fellow musician had ever done for me. Plus, he'd added the secret ingredient missing from my record all along—the sound of *his guitar.*

Except when was I supposed to sing? The only singing was the choir behind me. I needed a microphone. Mine was still lying at the foot of the stage, but when I started for it, Jonesy shook his head. He played a new, unfamiliar riff, bending the notes almost coyly, his head on a tilt—he was giving me a prompt. *A dare.*

What did I have to lose? I'd been hiding from this, from him, for years. If this was my swan song, I might as well make it good.

Jonesy repeated the riff. I locked eyes with him; there was still some fight left in me. But if we were to go mano a mano, I needed to be on even footing. I needed to lose the stilettos. I kept my gaze fixed on him and removed them one at a time, slung them toward the foot of the stage, where they thunked to a stop. Jonesy widened his eyes and shot me a cheeky, indignant look: *You didn't just do that.*

I widened mine back: *Oh yes, I did. No rehearsal. No sound check. No guitar. And what was that "Kiss me" shit? And for the record I'm not your baby. I'm nobody's "baby."* I flashed on *Tom.* A lump formed in my throat. Pull it together, bitch, it was now or never.

I decided to be gracious. I gave him a little samurai bow,

my palms pressed together, to say, *I humbly reject your offer to look sexy.*

He grinned, shook his head dismissively, and repeated the riff.

To which I unveiled a pair of jazz hands. *Take that, Jonesy, you controlling motherfucking genius you.*

He answered with a new riff, a slinky one.

I replied with a little shimmy and a *bang-bang* with my fingers—blew out the imaginary smoke, spun my imaginary pistols and stashed them in my imaginary holster. He seemed to enjoy this, too. As did the audience, whose laughter rose and fell like distant surf, and buoyed me.

We carried on this way for several rounds, me ceding power, him playing me like his marionette until I turned the tables and *my* moves began to inform *his* on guitar, before he even realized...and when he did, a knowing smile dawned across his face and we eased into our own kind of tango—control sliding seamlessly between us, until one of the choir singers stepped forward and handed me a microphone.

Finally, *I was singing!*

It felt out-of-body at first. I only *knew* I was, because I could hear my voice, dipped in reverb, bouncing back to me from the farthest row of the Royal Albert Hall.

I began to relax into it. To love it. To love the caress of the notes, vibrating in my throat, the exhilaration of setting them free, letting them sail into the air. The best kind of flying—no seat belts, no turbulence, only clear blue skies.

And then Jonesy was singing, too, in perfect harmony. We were singing together, and there was suddenly *nothing else*—only focus, and uniting—only melding our voices—only the unfolding present tense of this synchronous act—until it was time for Jonesy to launch into one final, blistering solo, and my little hostage chair glowed to life. There upon it was a pink wig, phosphorescent, beneath a precision-cued spotlight, and though I wanted to drop-kick the thing to the nosebleed seats, a murmur of recognition from the house rolled stage-ward and I understood what needed to happen next. In some ways, hadn't I always known it was coming? That this wig—this dance—and I would meet again? I strode across the stage without a blink and wriggled it on.

Jonesy threw me a look I hadn't even known I'd been dreading until now. It was "the order"—a kind of implicit command to perform the burlesque from my video. Why he'd given me a catsuit to wear, to spare me flashing my underwear. Decent of him, I supposed.

I had danced my entire life, from ballet lessons as a girl, to the company at Columbia. It was my dance. I could do this. There was no more time for thinking, only for complying, for the choreography—the blueprint of those dances returning miraculously to me, via muscle memory. So I surrendered, and I danced, because what else was there, really? There was a freedom in letting go—of ceding control—of giving over to him completely. Of being... *her*.

There was, wasn't there?

Chapter 39.

I WANT TO HOLD YOUR HAND

And then it was over.

A heartbeat of darkness and blinding lights and a roar like wild surf.

I was struggling to catch my breath, still my heart, when my hand was swept up and raised high. Another wave thundered over the lip of the stage. Then Jonesy took off, tightening his grasp, and we flew into the tunnel and out the other side, swerving around corners, weaving in and around a crush of bodies diving out of our path. We sped past the fedora-wearing woman—who appeared crestfallen—and then Pippa, James, Alastair, Will and young George, and *Leopard Pants,* beaming with expectation, outstretching his be-ringed hand, expecting Jonesy to stop and greet him, and then from the shadows, Tom slipped into view, his form quietly elegant, devastatingly familiar, his face luminous with apology.

Tom.

Our eyes locked for a confused, irresolute instant, but Jonesy wasn't stopping to say anything to anyone—he wasn't stopping until we'd rounded the corner, until we were in my dressing room and the door was closed and he was pressing his back firmly against it, the two of us panting, my palm still shackled to his. Adrenaline coursed through me, all of my senses heightened, a post-show sensation I hadn't experienced in a very long time. A feeling of free fall, of exhilaration. I longed, though, to feel grounded again.

I eased my hand free and began gesturing effusively as if to prove I needed the use of it. "Thank you, wow, just thank you," I said, backing away.

"Thank *you*," he broke in, mildly amused and still anchored to the door. Up close, he had the innocent features of a pretty child, satin-blue eyes, a rosy pout, even a smattering of sweet freckles on the bridge of his nose.

"No, no—don't thank *me*—" I waved this off. "That was just— so unexpectedly fun." It *was,* I thought, surprising myself.

"Unexpectedly?" He furrowed his brow.

Shit. "Expectedly. Expectedly fun." Ugh.

"Jane. I haven't seen you in a long time," he said, with a small smile. I steeled myself for him to say "Happy anniversary, *baby*." What would I counter with?!

I realized I was still wearing the wig and tore it off. "No. Right. Yes. Agreed—it's been a long—"

"I like seeing you, hearing you sing"—he cocked his head— *"watching you dance."*

"Really? I mean, *thank you*. Thank you very, very, much." I might as well have grunted all of that. *Pull it together, woman.* If he didn't insist on the enigmatic cult leader vibe, he might even be lovable. "And *I* really enjoyed hearing *you* sing, and watching *you* dance." This was bad. I stared, stricken, down at the wig, scrunched in my hand.

"Did you?"

I peered up, my cheeks burning. "Definitely. *Yes*. You're, well, you're *you*—the one and only. And your guitar playing's not too shabby either."

He laughed, which seemed so totally wrong on him. He peeled himself from the door and stepped closer.

Instinctively, I stepped back. "To sing your song again—tonight, with you, and your band. Well. It was indescribable."

"You," he said, gliding toward me, "took a song no one cared about and *you* made it special." The room was starting to feel claustrophobic, a car with all the windows sealed, and very little oxygen. "It's been a while, Jane Start."

"I know," I said, agreeing. I began to make myself look busy, slipping on shoes, collecting my things, sweeping cosmetics, my phone, my dress, and Tom's sweater into my bag.

Tom. He was out there.

I glanced up and locked eyes with Jonesy in the mirror. He was right behind me.

But I was saved by a knock at the door. Pippa, surely!

When Jonesy cracked open the door, I could make out a swirl of people I didn't recognize.

"This is us," he said to me. "Time to go. Time to *celebrate.*" He eyed the champagne on ice, the bottle sweating, as if in solidarity with me. Then he reached out his hand like he was Fred Astaire.

I hesitated, and, not knowing what else I could possibly do, took it.

I had to. It was Jonesy. I'd just performed with him at the Royal Albert Hall! As his special guest! I couldn't very well say, *Thanks for the offer, but nah. I think I'll just head home, throw on a pair of old sweats, and hang with my* real *friends.*

We slipped out and four bodyguards encircled us, one taking the liberty of unburdening me of my bag, and we were hustled down the long corridor.

I craned back to find Pippa, Will, Alastair, James, George, Leopard Pants, and Tom rounding the corner and screeching to a stop, in front of my dressing room, abandoned but for the pink wig awry on the counter.

I was desperate to call out, desperate to let them know I was being whisked to some party, and desperate, once more, to break free of Jonesy's grasp, but I hadn't the guts to, lest I appear rude or uptight or ungrateful or just plain *rejecting*. And I realized my phone was in my bag, which was in the possession of the most intimidating bodyguard in the bunch.

As if hearing my thoughts, Jonesy tightened his grip. My last hope was that the gorgeous German model with her all-access pass would be waiting in some amber-lit nightclub booth and Jonesy would disappear into it, and her, and I could discreetly make my escape. We neared the outside door, and I twisted back, glimpsed Tom one last time. I could tell that he saw me, leaving with Jonesy, holding his hand.

Chapter 40.

INCURABLE ROMANTIC SEEKS
DIRTY FILTHY WHORE

The SUV drew up to a stately manor, looming at the crest of a wide sloping lawn. This was Jonesy's cozy little rental. Again, I'd naively assumed the celebration would take place somewhere public, at some swank after-hours club, and felt suddenly queasy, naked without my bag, my *phone*. I would have texted Pippa on the way here, and engineered a swift, stealth plan of escape after a polite celebratory drink. I was wishing, too, that I wasn't so intimidated by Jonesy, who'd seated himself up front and hadn't uttered a single word to me since leaving the dressing room. He'd spent the ride yukking it up with his bodyguards.

I was helped out of the Range Rover into darkness and brisk night air, ushered swiftly beside Jonesy along a shadowy path. Suddenly, there was commotion, a shout from one of his team, "Get zee fuck out of 'ere!"

Jonesy pulled me to him as we were doused in the acid brightness of camera flashes and rapid-fire shutter clicks; a moment later, we were in the house, my eyes still struggling to adjust.

Jonesy had hastened ahead, and a bodyguard swept in behind us, dusting himself off and locking the imposing, ornate door.

"Just zee paps," he explained in a thick French accent, unfazed, his voice echoing in the marbled, high-ceilinged foyer. "I am Sayid, but zay call me Boo-Boo." He grinned and pantomimed a few boxing jabs.

"I'm Jane."

"I *know*. I remember you from before."

"Oh?" I studied his face. *Right.* The Brando features, the pugilist nose—he'd even appeared in my dream, the night Monica had turned up at Tom's flat. He'd been with Jonesy for years.

"You're all grown up." I smiled up at him.

He smiled back and said, "You, too," before gesturing for me to follow him through an entry alive with flickering candlelight and masses of vased gardenias. A floral sweetness stung the back of my throat like a hit of cocaine and icy panic slid down my spine; drug lords and underworld types rented palaces like this. *I need Pippa.* It felt unsettlingly wrong to be the only woman here. I spied my bag with my phone on the credenza and was able to snatch it, embarrassed, suddenly, by this flurry of paranoid thoughts as we crossed into an elegantly appointed living room, warmly lit and brimming with beautiful art. Jonesy was there, a work of art himself, posed aristocratically with one arm resting upon the mantel and gazing into the roaring hearth. I was certain he'd carefully staged this tableau. A painting was perfectly aligned above his head, an incredible Harland Miller watercolor I'd only ever admired in photographs, painted in the style of a vintage Penguin book cover with drippy washes of hot pink, the faux book title: *Incurable Romantic Seeks Dirty Filthy Whore.* Which of us was the *Incurable Romantic* and which the *Dirty Filthy Whore*? His display struck me as preposterous. I bit my lip not to laugh.

Boo-Boo showed me to the sofa, where there awaited champagne and french fries in fancy silver julep cups. He and Jonesy exchanged a look and the bodyguard proceeded to open the bottle, handing each of us glasses before slipping out. We were left in painful silence, me on the sofa, Jonesy by the hearth, the fire marking time with snaps and crackles while I auditioned gracious ways of saying "One drink and I'm outta here."

Anniversary or no.

Ten years ago, in Manhattan, we'd set a similar scene. *Jonesy's back to me as he posed at the baby grand, thirty stories high, wrapped in night sky, the pale of his swan neck, the channel through which so much resonance and beauty had been bestowed upon the world... then he'd turned. His face had been illegible, eerily vacant. He took a single step forward. On instinct I took one back.*

Tiny moves on a chessboard. How pathetically skittish I'd been. Yet that step, that singular step, seemed to change everything. I could never erase the absent look in his eyes as he considered me, considered my rejection. He'd then turned his back, skating wordlessly away, to leave me standing there, ashamed—wondering what offense I'd made. It was Sayid he'd sent in to ferry me home. And I'd been wondering ever since. I was still wondering, here, tonight.

"Penny for your thoughts?" Jonesy sharpened back into view. His eyes were unblinking pale blue pools that shone in the firelight. His innocent-child features only faintly weathered.

"Yum," I said, feigning composure, dipping my face in my drink. "That's what I'm thinking. How delicious... is this... champagne."

Lie. I was thinking about my escape. I was thinking about texting Pippa to come rescue me. And I was thinking about Tom. How he'd come to the show, and what did it mean? Thanks to a conveniently placed cushion, I'd managed to tunnel discreetly in my purse for my phone.

Jonesy disengaged from the mantel and glided toward me— perhaps to refresh my drink, or because he fancied some french fries?—but instead he lunged and snatched up my bag, raised it high like a naughty child, then disappeared down a hallway at the opposite end of the room.

Thirty-nine-year-old Jonesy was still up to his old tricks.

I prepared myself by kicking back two additional champagnes in quick succession and did what I was meant to, *this time*—I followed him.

The hall flickered in candlelight, until I reached an alcove embellished with ornamental molding, creating the frame for yet another of Jonesy's artfully composed tableaux, starring himself. He was effortlessly slouched in a midcentury womb chair in what appeared to be a small library. In his lap was nestled an acoustic guitar and my bag.

On the coffee table there was some portable recording gear, and his signature candles in all the right places, washing him in warm Rembrandt light. I used my hands to make a frame, like a film director auditioning a shot, mostly because I was buzzed, but it made Jonesy smile, and I steeled myself to venture over the threshold and onto his set.

He straightened, leaned the guitar against a chaise, and extended my purse, forcing me to cross the room to get it. And just as I made contact with the canvas strap, he jerked his arm back. *Wait, I'm not done fucking with you.*

Jesus. I sighed, "Come on," and held out my hand.

"I wonder what's in here?" Ignoring me, he began to rifle through my things. I had the most mortifying thought: *MY UNDERWEAR! My* Little House on the Prairie *Laura fucking Ingalls Wilder,* worn *underwear. That's what was in there.*

"Uh-oh." He peered up at me with mock alarm.

No! I could hardly bring myself to look...but he withdrew my phone. My relief lasted only an instant. He aimed the cracked screen at me, and face recognition did the rest, revealing a barrage of missed calls from—

"Who's Tom?" Jonesy's long slender fingers caressed the phone's edge.

"He's—he's—" Why was I hesitating? "He's my boyfriend." *Was* my boyfriend. My throat tightened. I felt sick. Why had I hesitated? But I knew why, to spare Jonesy feeling rejected.

Jonesy rose, his face blank. He plunked the phone in my bag and handed it coolly back as he swept past, then stationed himself at a small keyboard, his back to me, and began to tap out a little melody, almost absently, the notes minor, and haunting.

"Who do you like better—" He stopped, then murmured over his shoulder, "Your boyfriend or me?"

I swallowed hard, at a complete loss. But now Jonesy was staring at me, and from where I stood, his ego looked massive and fragile all at the same time.

"I don't really *know* you," I said. Better to go for *clever* than potentially offend.

"You know everything you need to know," Jonesy said easily. In other words, *What you see is what you get.* He glided past and splayed himself across the chaise longue and began to tinker magnificently on guitar, in case it wasn't clear *exactly* who he was.

Yeah, I knew. You were rich and powerful and successful, you were an *extraordinarily* talented person who'd helped my career immeasurably, therefore I *must* like you better, never mind the dysfunction...but I could almost *see,* almost visualize, the line he'd drawn. He was waiting, expectantly, for me to cross it. That drowning feeling returned, of *no oxygen left in the world.* Would *I* ever dare pose a question to *him* like that? Would I dare whisk *him* away from his friends—disarm him of his personal effects, and then rudely, audaciously, rifle through them? *Never!*

All at once, it was as if I were watching the whole scene play out from above, but *I* was the director. Jonesy had stopped on guitar. He was still waiting for me to tell him who I liked better, my boyfriend or him.

"I *like* you. Very much," I said. "But my boyfriend? I'm in love with him, and I love him, madly." That was the truth. Broken up or not.

Jonesy gazed back, his expression betraying nothing. For all I knew, he was insulted and angry, but my heart was hammering, and my hands had begun to tremble. Then he shook his head incredulously, like, *You've got some balls, girl.*

Actually, I had no balls, only a sudden, distinct awareness of how lonely he must actually be, despite the girls and the fans and the bodyguards and the team. His talent was so immense, it was quite simply isolating. How exhausting it had to be to keep all of *this* up.

He'd risen, he was offering the guitar. "Your turn," he said. "Show me what you can do, Jane Start." He held my eyes, and what began as a mischievous grin blossomed into a big sparkling smile, and *Wow,* when he offered it up like that.

Yesterday, my whole life was in shambles, and tonight—this lonely dysfunctional genius was smiling like that, waiting. If I really *had* balls, I would play him the song I'd started in Oxford.

"You mind?" I said, inclining my head at the bottle of champagne, but Jonesy had already begun plugging in cables, fiddling with his recording gear.

He glanced up and chuckled. "Be my guest."

In the most painful of silences, he pressed record on his portable machine. I started in, strumming too fast at first as it was impossible to tune out the fact of him, *Jonesy,* mere inches from me, or the vulnerability of the moment. Nor could I tune out the evil twin in my head insisting the song was crap, not even close to finished. The red light on the machine reflected in Jonesy's eyes, cool, dispassionate.

"Sorry—I got this." I slowed myself down, remembering finally to breathe, and all at once I was singing out the little music-box theme I'd started at Tom's, and I found myself melting, melding into the melody, following the road map of the song, my hands on the wheel. Near the end of the verse came the haunting chord, the unexpected left turn, and my voice sailed free—seemed to ripple and resonate effortlessly through me, and I saw Jonesy straighten at the pleasing surprise of the sweep and swerve of that turn, and it felt good and right to have taken it—*right* to have sung out, unbridled and tremulous and free. Jonesy was listening keenly, and there was only liberation now in beaming out the emotion, in releasing all that was tangled—all that was yearning and longing for love to be solid and true and 100 percent fuckup proof—all that was possible and impossible in this life.

Jonesy swept up a guitar and suddenly there were walls and beams, a roof and a steeple to my song. He was building a little church for my music-box melody to shelter in, and as I sang and his fingers danced over the strings, he did the thing only he could do...he made his guitar ring out like a bell, and then, like many.

Chapter 41.

THERE'S GOT TO BE A MORNING AFTER, OR WE CAN WORK IT OUT

"Oh, Jane, I've been so worried," Pippa cried, flinging open her door.

It was dawn. I was shivering on her front step, my bag clutched to my chest, still in the costume from last night, with Tom's sweater over it. I gave a wave to Boo-Boo, still idling in the Range Rover to be sure I was safe.

As soon as she pulled me in, I beseeched her, "Tom was there?" I was exhausted, and breathless, but finally, I was here.

"Yes," she said, her brow furrowed. "Jane—you disappeared. All night. What's happened?"

"First, please tell me about Tom."

She stared back, at a loss, then started in. "It was all rather *fraught.* He'd reached out, the day of the show, devastated, clearly holding out hope for a rapprochement, and I should have told you, but honestly, I wasn't sure how to. And I feared it might throw you off. You were so terribly anxious. And still very much despairing." She grasped my shoulders and drew me close. "I know, I *know* he was wrong to hide his past. But I don't believe he's a philandering fuckwit like Alex. And obviously you're not some heartless hussy like Jessica. It's not like me to say this, I'm usually rather hard-nosed about such things, but Tom's stayed the night in London and I think you should go see him." She sighed, her eyes gleaming. "He loves you so."

My heart squeezed in my chest at those last words, *He loves you so*. Pippa's opinion meant everything. I trusted her. She would never steer me wrong.

"He's fucked up. Royally. But he's a good man," Pippa insisted. "Life's too short. I would never judge you for trying to work things out with him. He didn't cheat. He wasn't two-timing, he was just a damned fool. And his ex, from the sound of it, is off her trolley. Tom's clearly been muddled up in a very messy situation."

He has, hasn't he.

"The name and address of his hotel," she said, pressing the scribbled note into my palm. "I can put you in a cab straightaway— but where *were* you all night?"

Oh, that. "Jonesy took me to his house." Her face paled. "It's not what you think. We ended up playing music, or rather, I think I may have finished a song—something I started in Oxford." Pippa's eyes widened, intrigued. "Weirdly, the night was...well, it was kind of good? *Very strange,* but good. And he recorded it. The song."

"She lives," Will proclaimed, shuffling in from the hall with a severe case of bedhead. "Excellent. My god you were good last night," he croaked. "Your singing. All of it. Moxie. That's what you've got. I'd shower you with more effusive praise but I'm nursing a pretty shitty hangover, if you must know."

"Wow, *thanks.* That means a lot. And join the club."

"I've ordered a cab," Pippa informed me, looking up from her phone. "It's one minute away, go—go now!"

Tom's hotel resembled a charming Georgian row house. There was even the de rigueur house Labrador snoozing by an informal front desk. My heart constricted, thinking of Tom splurging on this place.

"I'm sorry, miss," the clerk said, looking me over apprehensively. "I'm afraid Mr. Hardy has already checked out." His hands slowed on the papers he'd been shuffling. "You look a bit...*wan.* Let me fetch you some water."

"No. It's okay. Can you just tell me the best way to Paddington Station?"

I snaked my way through the crowded train car and managed to snag an empty row as we jerked to a queasy start. Overheated from running, I peeled off Tom's sweater and buried my face in it. My eyes stung with tears. Sensing movement, I peered up and was met with the openmouthed stare of an innocent child who'd flung himself over the seat back in front of me, his rosy-cheeked face so close I could smell the sweet decay of apple juice on his breath. He eyed me, curiously.

"I'm a superhero," I murmured, gesturing to the ridiculous Catwoman getup I still had on. The boy's eyes widened with wonder. "A superhero who's had *no* sleep. Who's just broken up with the love of her life, which makes *me* a very sad, very lonely, *very desperate,* if I'm honest, *superhero.*" The boy cinched his brow, unconvinced. "I *know.* And you're absolutely right," I said, gesturing to my notable lack of cleavage. "I don't have the figure to be Catwoman. But it wasn't *my* choice," I insisted, hand to chest. "The people in charge of superheroes— *they* decided it." At which point the kid's mum yanked him down.

I was on the brink of losing my resolve and messaging Tom when a dizzying number of texts slid across my shattered phone screen.

Pippa: YOU'RE ALL OVER TWITTER!!!

Oh god, not again.

She sent a series of screenshots:

@TheGuardian: After some cringe-worthy fumbles, in which we may have all lost a few decibels of hearing, Jane Start found her footing.

Photo: Me on the chair with my legs spread.

@TheHerald: After an awkward start, Jane Start won our hearts.

(Essentially, the same photo.)

@theTelegram: Start starts with a stumble but proves she is no non-starter.

(Apparently there was only the one photo.)

@TheSundayMirror: The resurrection of Jane Start by none other than Jonesy. Out of the Where Are They Now file and into the Royal Albert Hall. Jonesy rescues ex-gal pal from obscurity at his sold-out show.

(Definitely the only photo.)

@Jonesylover: He will dump her again soon. The slut can't even dance thats obvious. And how dare she sing his song for a toilet roll advert on telly. Shitty of her if you ask me, ha ha.

Oh god. I'm sure Pippa didn't *intend* to include the cruel comment at the bottom, and there was absolutely nothing to be gained by reading this sort of thing, so I wouldn't, I definitely *would not* launch Safari and plunge past the review, and headfirst into the cesspool of the *comments* section…

@Sexybeast13: He's having it off with her but she don't deserve him. She'd be nuffing if not for his song the little slag.

"I'm not a slag!"

My voice rang out in the silence. An elegant gentleman in a mac, an actual bowler hat in his lap, peered up from his newspaper. He tipped his head to a sign, which read, *This is the quiet car.* It was frankly a relief. It meant I couldn't call Tom, even if I wanted to. Even if I knew what to say. What I felt…what I hoped for.

And suddenly, there was only one thing to do to distract myself from what might await me in Oxford. That was to google myself.

The Daily Mail.

The caption: *Jane Start reunited with superstar Jonesy for sexy after-show sleepover at Regent's Park mansion.* And a photo of Jonesy and me in an embrace, his palatial rental manor looming decadently in the background, captured the instant he'd pulled me to him, startled by the paparazzi's flashes.

And there were two additional photos taken with a telephoto lens the morning after. *Reunited lovers share passionate kiss at dawn.* But it was only a goodbye hug, yet the camera angle suggested more!

And finally: *Jane Start starry-eyed, basking in the afterglow of torrid tryst with sexy rocker.* The photo showing me not *starry* but *bleary*-eyed. I scrolled quickly to the comments section:

—Jane Start is using Jonesy to claw her way back. What does he see in that flat-chested nothing anyway?

And the comments to that: Shut up your just jealous obviously no model but she has a nice voice. I still love that video to.

—Jonesy wake up she's using you mate.

—Why's Jonesy messing about with her when he could get with anyone.

—Good for Jane Start snagging him. Always thought she was kinda cool. Fancied her for half a sec way back when.

—Exactly. Because she pranced about naked in a video you wanker.

I planted my phone facedown in my lap and fought back tears. *All the shit that fits.* What the hell was I doing, reading about what a slag I was when there was absolutely nothing to be gained from it? But my phone was burning a hole in my lap. I began furiously scrolling through texts, blurring past messages from Bryony, Gemma, Will, Freddy—*Alex.* How transparent he was. It took me trending on Twitter for him to suddenly reach out. Is that all he ever cared about? Me in a pink wig, on a chair with my legs spread? I wasn't even tempted to read it, and hit delete.

Finally, there was a text from Tom. Sent before the show, which seemed a thousand years ago—

Tom Hardy: You are a bright star, tonight and always—yours, Tom x

The Keats poem. The final stanza, it slayed me, it did.

Pillow'd upon my fair love's ripening breast,
To feel for ever its soft fall and swell,
Awake for ever in a sweet unrest,
Still, still to hear her tender-taken breath,
And so live ever—or else swoon to death.

Chapter 42.

AIN'T NO SUNSHINE

On the sidewalk, I hesitated, gazing up at Tom's door and remembering the first time I was here. The creamy black-lacquered paint and shiny brass fitting, so quintessentially British. It had been summer then, delicious and warm, skin-tingling breezy, our first date.

I shuddered, November cold biting straight through the cashmere of Tom's sweater to the embarrassing catsuit, my bag clutched to my chest.

It was nearly eleven. Tom taught at nine, so he wouldn't be home yet. Relief. I wasn't quite ready to face him. I could wait out the morning in a café, gather my thoughts. I was just turning to leave, when the front door burst open and Tom barreled out. He froze at the sight of me, his leather bag slung over his shoulder, and a small pink-ribboned box in his hand.

After a stunned, wordless beat, he descended to meet me on the sidewalk as birds began to talk animatedly in the trees. The harmony of his features, the broken quality of his smile had an unknown power over me, but it was the gleam of his gray-green eyes that undid me. He raked back his hair and sighed, his smile softening, and I knew I would never love anyone the way I loved him. How could this feeling possibly be wrong?

"Last night," I stammered, "after the show—"

"Please let me say something first," he broke in, clearly ill at ease having to assert himself this way. He composed himself. "You were brilliant and gorgeous last night. Truly. You soared *cloud-high,* Jane."

From *Jane Eyre.* That was when Rochester tells Jane, early on, his instinctive sense of her: a "vivid, restless, resolute captive... were it but free, it would soar cloud-high." *How precisely those words conjured the feeling on stage last night.* I felt myself crumble with love for him, for his perfect understanding, not to mention his elegance and his class and his kindness.

He absorbed me now, with that familiar broken smile of his, but this time it was weighted at the edges with real, tangible pain, and his face became blurry, because what I recognized in his eyes was resignation, about us.

"Do you have a minute?" I said, clutching my bag tighter.

"Yes. Of course," he said, his eyes unwavering.

Mrs. T was seated at the dining table, casually sipping espresso and reading the paper. Seeing us, she yanked out a pair of earbuds and grimaced a smile.

"Mrs. Taranouchtchenka was very tired this morning," Tom announced, clearly for my benefit, too. "She was up half the night caring for a friend's baby. I insisted she have some coffee before making the long trek home, and that she take the day off."

She nodded gratefully, darted a suspicious glance at the paper and then at me, and hurriedly stuffed it into her Tesco bag. The *Daily Mail,* ugh. What must she think of me? What must *Tom,* if he'd caught wind of the gossip? He'd likely jumped to his own conclusions, having last seen me running off with Jonesy.

Tom was still wavering by the door after Mrs. T left, watchful, apprehensive. For a moment I thought, *This is where I live. Nothing else is real but that I live here, with him.* But that was no longer true.

Tom shot me a tensed smile and strode brusquely to the kitchen to put the kettle on. That's what the English do in times like this. They make tea.

I sat at the edge of the sofa, observing his movements, and was struck with an acute, carnal desire for him—and *we could,* couldn't we, despite everything?

Tom brought my tea and I accepted it shakily. Unable to still my hand, I took a harried sip and set the cup and saucer on the floor. Tom sat in the wingback chair. I couldn't help noting, these were our same places as three nights ago, when I'd left this place and him.

"I didn't know you'd come to the show, until after," I said, impatient to explain what had become of me. "I looked for you at the hotel this morning, but you'd already left. I never intended to rush off last night, but Jonesy *insisted* on celebrating, and I don't know—Jonesy seems to get what he wants, *when* he wants it. And then I was there, and then I was stuck, and then it was late, and then it was—" I broke off. "And then it was morning."

He rearranged himself in the chair. "Where?" His voice was gentle and slightly rasped. "Where did you go?"

"Oh." In my exhaustion I assumed he knew. "We—we went to his house."

Now he was struggling not to react.

"I had every intention of leaving to join up with Pippa and everyone, but he had this little makeshift music room, and I felt obliged to stay after all he'd done for me...inviting me to perform with him, and I know what you must be thinking—but no, that's a line I don't cross. I've *never* done that—been with someone I work with. Not even before, with Jonesy, when we were young and he..." I broke off.

I'd pushed it away for so many years. What happened that strange night? Yet still I was shaken, stained by it. Ashamed. He'd brought me to his penthouse under false pretenses. Or maybe he hadn't? Because he hadn't crossed a definitive line. It was only his cryptic behavior that had thrown and panicked me. I'd never admitted to Pippa that *I* was the one who blew the deal, the chance to work with him—but *I had. That night.* Because as a consequence, she was summarily ghosted.

"Jane," Tom sighed. "You performed at the Royal Albert Hall last night. I was proud—I was in awe really. You don't have to apologize for anything."

Adrenaline seared through me. All that I held so tightly, my past, my secrets, my mistakes, my injured pride began to unspool.

"There's something I haven't told you," I said, breathless. "When I met you, on the plane, I'd been in this long relationship, and it had just ended, very abruptly, and very painfully, but I didn't want that to color how you saw me? I didn't want that to be 'my story.' But I feel bad now, that I've never told you. His name was Alex. He's already gotten married, a baby on the way, with the woman he left me for."

"Jane. I'm—I'm—"

"*No.* Really. It doesn't matter anymore."

Tom had paled. Yet he was looking at me with such empathy, his lovely fingers grasping the arms of the chair, and I thought: *All that matters is* you, *and* us. And I found myself zooming in to the fine details of him, the unshaven hollow of his cheek, the exquisite edge of his forearm, and I felt a desperate love, an irrepressible yearning to fuse myself into the flesh and blood of him, when I was distracted by the box with the ribbon at his feet, the words *Celebration Cakes* stamped along its badly dented side.

"You bought a cake?"

"I did," he said, flustered. "A last-minute tutorial with an anxious student—I don't know why I agreed to it? The anxious ones tend to relax when they see a cake."

Of course—he was meant to be at work.

His expression grew serious, *very,* and my stomach dropped.

"Jane—I—" He was struggling, turning the box absently in his hands. "I keep thinking, you've flown away. *Jane,* who brought the sunshine with her to this gloomy place. It was a lovely dream and this is how it ends. I keep thinking that." He gazed gently up at me. "And I don't want it to be true."

I didn't want it to be true either.

But he abruptly rose and went to the kitchen. When he returned to me, he sidled close on the sofa, our thighs touching, and he was gloriously toasty.

"Let's eat cake," he said, resting the box on our knees, his face to me, and mine to him, and he held out the spoon.

I smiled at him, our eyes still locked, when it suddenly dawned on me.

"Where is Oskar? Where is Oskar Wilde?"

Chapter 43.

WHERE IS OSKAR WILDE?

Tom's face went pale. My phone buzzed and though I didn't want to be *that* person, beholden to every ding or ping, adrenaline was searing through me, and this was an excuse to delay what I sensed was the inevitable: Surely the cat had escaped and been run over.

It was a text message from Gemma.

Gemma Chang: Omg you were brilliant last night! 💚🙌🎸 Thank you ever so much for the tickets. You and Tom must come round to dinner so we can celebrate you properly. Vik does a fantastic curry. Would Saturday next work? Let me know, rock star! 🎤 🎵 Lots of love, Gemma

P.S. In case you hadn't heard, you're free of the ex lurking about, at least for the minute. Word is Amelia Danvers is off to some depression clinic in Zurich. Very swanky, I'm told.

My heart leapt to my throat. I scooted away from Tom as an autonomic response, the way one might at the sight of a corpse or a stranger peering in a bedroom window. My pulse quickened.

"Where is Oskar?" I repeated.

Tom looked shaken. "Amelia—she came Saturday morning and collected her," he stammered. "She'd been staying with her sister in London, but now she's gone off."

She'd shown up on Saturday because she knew I wouldn't be here. They were still enmeshed. I bolted up and began to pace.

If I'd never met him, they'd still be together. She wouldn't be suffering.

Tom rose. "*Jane.* We can leave this place—we can leave Oxford."

I stopped and stared at him. "That's your solution?"

It had all only been a delusion. He'd left his fiancée virtually standing at the altar. He'd been gaslighting me all along, and yes, I admit, I'd been gaslighting myself. Out of my desperate love for him. Yet how could my joy be predicated on another's misery? How could *my* happiness override my sense of right and wrong, my empathy for another human being, for *her, Amelia?*

I felt sick, panicked, as I had when I'd put it together: Alex and Jessica.

"*Jane,*" he repeated, desperate.

I stared back. Mute. I would gather my things and get out. I snatched a large trash bag from beneath the sink and tore off for the bedroom.

"We can start anew—somewhere in Europe?" he called after me. "Anywhere you want." There was desperation in his voice, but I wasn't stopping, I was sprinting down the passage, now tearing my clothes from their hangers, pitching my things into the bag from bedside drawers by the trembling fistful.

The door to the little writing nook was ajar. I spied Alastair's guitar and Kurt Cobain slung over the chair back.

I peeled off Tom's sweater and replaced it with Kurt. The ceremony was not lost on me. Nor the fact that Tom's was cozier, warmer, lovelier, *his.* The scenario with Alex was repeating in the most wrenching of ways.

Tom was standing where I'd left him, his face wrought with pain, his eyes still luminous in the leaden gray light. I sped past him for the door.

"Jane, we could leave everything behind, we could fly down to Mexico, like in the song. We could disappear, to the south of France. Who would know? Who would care?" He grasped my arm, but all I could do was look at his fingers.

"I would," I said, gazing up at him. "I would know. I would care."

And then I was out in the cold, on the sidewalk below. I stopped short. I'd forgotten the guitar. *No.* I wouldn't go back. Pippa or Will, they would have to retrieve it. An insistent *rat-a-tat-tat* caught my ear. There was Thornbury. Sweet Old Owl Eyes, his face framed in his grimy subterranean window, flapping his wee paw for me to come in.

I wanted to cry. But I held up the bag filled with my belongings, and mouthed, *I'm taking out the trash.*

And the ancient professor shrugged, and smiled, and blew me a kiss.

It was two hours later when Pippa flung open the door to her flat, her mobile cradled to her chin.

"I'm on hold with Team Jonesy," she trilled, gesturing me excitedly in. "They're insisting you join the tour at once! They promise it will be first class all the way and quote, 'a piece of cake'!"

Tom's sofa, our thighs touching, the cake box balanced on our knees.

"An exact repeat of last night in which you simply pop out for the encore! Easy breezy lemon— *Right,*" she said eagerly, back on the line with them. I pictured myself being rolled out for the encore, night after night—popping out of a cake, like the stripper in Vegas.

"Ring you back? Yup, excellent, ta-ta!" Pippa chirped, her

optimism alien, inconceivable. I set down my things and slumped exhausted onto the sofa.

"Oh, isn't it marvelous!" Pippa said, dropping beside me. "You'll be out there again for all the world to see! They've assured me you'll have a couple days off over the holidays, possibly New Year's. The first leg of the tour goes through July, so only seven months!"

First leg. *Only* seven months. Seven months of loneliness and isolation, of hotel rooms late at night, reading snark in other languages, hitting translate so I'd know when I'd been called a slag by some diehard Jonesy fan. And seven months of Jonesy's antics. My dream of a folk singer's life...

"I don't want to," I said numbly, staring out at her garden, now barren and shrouded with rain.

"You don't want to what?"

Impersonate *"her."* The young girl in the video. *Wind her up and she flashes her crotch.*

"Go on tour." I turned to Pippa.

"Jane." She was summoning patience, her brow creased. "Finally—*finally,* some momentum."

How I disliked that word, *momentum.*

She sighed, frustrated. "You do know how very rare it is for the stars to align this way?"

"I do. I absolutely know." This kind of offer would not come again. She was right. I felt sick. There was no way out.

"And they're paying. *Well.*"

And I needed the dough. I did.

She looked at me. "Don't you understand? You can do that... *thing.* You can open your mouth, and sound"—she was gesturing—"beautiful sound pours out?"

"What? I don't..." I was lost.

She shook her head. "You can *sing,* silly. Don't you see?" she scoffed. "Not everyone can do that. *I* can't," she said, making a face.

But Pippa looked suddenly wan. "Oh *no*. What happened, with Tom?"

But all I could do was shake my head, my eyes welling.

She grasped my hand. "Chardy?"

We downed a fair bit and I told her *everything,* the hopeless truth of Tom's situation with his ex. How his guilt for breaking their engagement, and the fact of Amelia's depression, would keep them forever shackled. How it pained me to think of her suffering.

I told her about the Royal Albert Hall, about Jonesy. At last, about that night ten years ago. How it was with him, and always would be. How (almost) forty-year-old Jonesy was unchanged, he was who he was. Still a genius, still emotionally stunted. Perhaps fame had come too early and the years of entitlement were to blame.

I told her how I'd stood up to him when he'd cornered me about Tom. The crazy things he'd asked: *Who did I like better?* And about him rifling through my purse. Pippa needed no reminding of his "Kiss me" request over the phone. And finally, I told her about the "Happy Anniversary, *Baby*" card, with "Can't you see I want you" scrawled upon the back.

"Nothing *happened,*" I assured her. "And I'm not *afraid*—afraid of him. I can handle—myself—you know?"

"Jane, of course you can. But, my god—" Dear Pippa, her face was creased with anguish. "I never knew. I always wondered, of course, if *something* had happened. But I'd hate to think you've never been able to tell me. And all this time I've been blathering on about him!"

I sank back into the sofa cushion, tormented. Because the truth was—"I *love* his music," I insisted, straightening again. "And what he did for me at the Royal Albert Hall was unbelievable, and generous." And—I'd be *insane* not to do the tour. "You know what? Okay. I will. I'll do the tour. We're on the same page now, you and I, and maybe even me and him?" I blurted.

And what else was there? Especially now.

Pippa refilled my glass. We finished the bottle and started a new one. As time ticked past, we became pretty much useless, slumped side by side on the sofa staring, glazed, out at the dead garden, both of us going on no sleep and little food.

"I'm *knack*ered and I'm *drunk*," Pippa proclaimed musically.

And I'd just said yes to a seven-month tour with a lunatic. A brilliant, manipulative lunatic.

"Just so you know, performing in a catsuit night after night *commando*... well it's not a particularly sustainable environment for one's *flora*." I offered this up as a last-ditch reason to back out. A bit weak, as I was still wearing it.

"I'm sure there's a wardrobe person to see to the costumes."

Wow. *That* would be a first.

"Don't even get me started on the wig," I said, and gave my scalp a good, long-overdue scratch at the mere mention of it.

"You managed to sneak in a hair flip. Impressive," Pippa murmured, flopping her head to me.

"Yup." I flopped mine to her. "Rock and roll." I gave her my best heavy-metal hand sign, then turned it into Mr. Spock's "Live long and prosper."

When it rushed back: The anxiety dream, Jonesy and me, the crashing plane, Boo-Boo, it meant something. A bad omen. That was the night Monica Abella turned up at Tom's door. I sat bolt upright. "I just remembered! I never told you about this crazy dream I had."

She groaned and emptied what was left of the wine into her glass. "Please say you're not going to tell me your dream."

"I *know,* and I completely agree with you, but this one was different. It was an omen."

She thunked down the bottle. "Even worse. Please no."

She was right. So I told her about Monica, the wet T-shirt and mellifluous accent, the way she practically purred, caressing

Tom's face in her hands like they do in the movies. "At least *you'll* be spared ghosts of gorgeous girlfriends past showing up at all hours." Will was practically a virgin. Where was he, anyway?

Pippa took a long beat before murmuring, "He's a very quick study," with a self-satisfied smile. Before I could *shriek* some retort, she had looked at her phone and exclaimed, "Well, what do you know, an *omen,* just when you need it. You'll never guess where the next tour date is!"

Chapter 44.

SHIT FUCK PARIS FRANCE, OR
UNDER MY THUMB

We arrived by Chunnel the following day.

It was wintry outside the station, iron-skyed and vaguely melancholic—a sense of the holidays looming. Pippa, Will, and I set up in adjoining rooms in a charming Left Bank hotel overlooking the Boulevard St. Germain, with black-lacquered railings entwined with ivy and defiant pink-petaled blossoms. Pippa hunkered down to work, while Will was tasked with distracting me from my anxiety about the concert the following night at the Olympia Theater, where everyone from Edith Piaf to Jimi Hendrix had graced its iconic stage.

And then the following morning, I would depart without them for seven months.

Will did what he could for my jitters, but there was no assuaging my intractable despair over Tom. How could I *not* think of him constantly here, with book and record and flower stalls lining the avenues, couples kissing shamelessly because this was *Paris,* and that's what people did here.

There was only one cure. To gorge myself senseless on art. Will and I drank in so much beauty, I was delirious, weak with awe, hopeless and hopeful. At each museum, I bought a postcard for Tom I would not send. And when we grew tired, we drank espresso in the Tuileries, and I found my gaze drifting skyward, to the tops of the trees in their neat rows beneath the vast tumult of gray overhead.

Will snapped a selfie, and I was wondering just how many tourist selfies the cloud could hold when my phone vibrated in my lap. I prepared myself for another missive from Pippa, some query or update about the tour, but when I glanced down, I nearly toppled out of my chair.

It was from Tom. I fought to catch my breath, not wanting to let on, as Will was conveniently futzing with his phone.

> **Tom Hardy:** Darling Jane, I am so sorry for hurting you. I hope you are okay. I don't deserve to regain your trust but pray you will let me try. I miss you with every heartbeat. Ever, always, yours— love, Tom x.

And he'd attached a song link to "Something Good" from the original *Sound of Music* soundtrack. Julie Andrews and Bill Lee, the singing voice for Christopher Plummer. But how could he possibly know how deeply this song would touch me?

I couldn't help myself. I was vibrating with emotion—missing him, wanting him. I frantically stealth-typed back: I MISS YOU! OUTRAGEOUSLY IMPOSSIBLY INDECENTLY. AND THIS SONG? THIS SONG THIS SONG THIS SONG!

Shit. I'd screamed all that, in caps lock.

Will was looking at me funny, his eyes narrowed.

"What!" I barked.

He shrugged and busied himself again with his phone. Trembling, I deleted my text, planted my phone facedown in my lap, only for it to vibrate again.

Alfie Lloyd: Free at last! 🎉 Tour ended in Rome. I've wrangled a ticket for Jonesy tomorrow night! In Paris! Wot u doing right now?

Alfie was taller than I remembered, tawny and sun-kissed, his feet confidently askew on the overwrought hotel carpeting. He had on the same Patti Smith T-shirt and trousers I remembered from Vegas and they fit him just as well. A small acoustic guitar, sans case, was clutched in his hand.

"Jane Start."

"Alfie Lloyd."

He broke into a smile, pushed up a pair of white oval sunglasses, and we shared a *Wow, this is crazy, no?* moment: to have met on the eve of the start of his tour, and now this was the eve of *mine*. I envied his air of freedom, but I didn't experience the starstruck feeling I'd anticipated. Only a sneaky welling sadness I hoped wasn't apparent. *I will not admit my dread of the tour to the world's biggest Jonesy fan,* he'll think I'm pathetic. Alfie inclined his head, as if hearing my thoughts, a furrow disrupting the unvarnished breadth of his impossibly youthful forehead.

I ushered him into my room and he made himself right at home, on the sofa, and began noodling on guitar.

I thunked beside him and folded my hands in my lap. "I like the new haircut. Very Mick Jagger circa 'sixty-five," I said.

"Thanks, yeah," he murmured, ambivalent, patting the back of his neck for what used to be there.

"Now you don't match your brother."

Precisely, his pointed look affirmed. Tours, with siblings. That had to be fraught.

"Why am *I* playing?" He laughed, and extended the guitar. "I want to hear *you* play."

Nerves, shyness, sadness again. But I sang him the song I'd

written in Oxford, the one I'd played Jonesy, the one about Tom. I hadn't known then that I'd be here, and Tom would be there, miles away, the churning dark waters of the English Channel between us. Yet I'd known all along, somewhere inside me, there could only ever be yearning and longing between any two humans to bridge the unbridgeable gap that existed between us. Yearning and longing to feel connected, to *be* connected.

"Wow, great," Alfie said, beaming, when I'd finished the song. I worked up a smile despite the knot in my stomach. "What was that about? Does that mean the Oxford guy, the professor, is—"

"You don't wanna know."

"Actually, I do," he said gently, in earnest. "I very much wanna know."

So I told him my sad story.

At the end he sat, blinking, searching for some consolation. "Well," he announced, finally, "just, be kind. Take care of yourself, Jane."

"That I do," I mumbled, under my breath. But what better antidote was there, for sorrow, for stress?

Alfie began casually tinkering on the guitar.

"Well, just know, you've got a *friend* in me." He raised a brow. "Whatever kind you might need." *Oh.* Invoking the theme from *Toy Story* no less.

"Wow," I said, flustered and taken aback. "I'm flattered." I felt myself break, at just the wrong time, over his kindness. I supposed Alfie *was* a friend.

He glanced hurriedly around and, finding nothing for my tears, pressed into my hand a wool beanie from his back pocket.

"You sure?" He nodded. "But *really*. I'm much too old for you. You yourself said it."

He had, in Vegas. The last time we were in a hotel room together.

"You *are* much too old for me," he said dryly, "technically speaking. That doesn't mean I don't fancy women who are much too old for me." He gave my knee a teasing bump with his. "I figured it was obvious by now."

No drink, no drug, no anything could cure me like this. My breasts skimming lightly over his chest—now he was kissing them, our bodies moving together, swimming up and up, toward a rippling ceiling of glass—

I opened my eyes and sat bolt upright...scrambling to make sense of place and time. There were light-drenched shapes ...sun glinting off a silver-domed lid, the gleaming hip of a wine bottle askew on the room service cart ...a guitar...a bed. *Alfie.*

I stifled a gasp and covered my mouth.

He was fast asleep beside me, his cherry lips in a sleeper's relaxed pout. I clutched my breasts through my clothes. I was dressed. *Good. Okay.*

And after a sigh of relief, I risked another peek at the slumbering prince, but it only confirmed I'd been dreaming of *Tom*...and oh, *what a dream.* I sneaked my fingers past the waistband of my sweats and between my legs. Who said girls don't have wet dreams? Relief was sinking in, because I *hadn't* been unfaithful to the one person, the only person on this earth I...Alfie stirred, and I quickly removed my hand.

The adjoining door creaked open; Pippa poked her head around and registered shock at the sight of the pop star beside me.

I waved my hands to convey *Nothing happened,* slipping gingerly down from the bed and throwing on Kurt Cobain. A knock at the door made Alfie flop up like a puppet. He began scrubbing his face with his fists.

"Oh, hello?" he said to Pippa, who stared girlishly back at him.

But the knocking persisted, and no one moved.

Alfie touched his chest. "Shall I get that?"

*   *   *

Alfie proceeded to charm Pippa over the room service croissants and coffees she'd thoughtfully ordered. I had no appetite, only envy for their freedom, as panic crept icily through me. This was my ritual feeling on show day, any show day, but this day was worse.

How would Jonesy and I top the improvised dance that had spontaneously unfolded at the Royal Albert Hall? Were we expected to repeat it night after night, and make it look fresh, for seven long months?

Alfie was preparing to leave. He and Pippa were exchanging contact info on their phones.

"Well, I'm off," he said brightly, refocusing his beamy smile on me, the dimple on full display. "See you after—and break a leg." He snapped and pointed, like that was an order.

Pippa turned to him. "Text me. Any issues at the venue, with passes or, whatever," she said meaningfully. "And we've put you with one of Jane's very good friends."

Bryony was coming last minute; it thrilled me to imagine the look on her face when she found herself sitting *with Alfie Lloyd.* Her crush.

He headed for the door without the guitar, so I rushed to grab it.

"Nope—it's yours," he insisted. "I picked it up at a flea market on the way here. It was cheap. I can't get that song out of my head, the one you played me last night. Keep going." He smiled and slipped out.

"What song?" Pippa queried, intrigued, if a little miffed I hadn't played it for her. How I would miss her on the road. And though she didn't say as much, it was like she was thinking that too.

"I'll play it for you. Now, if you want." I hadn't intended to share it with Alfie before her. Something struck me, and I rushed to the window and leaned out. "Hey," I called down.

Alfie glanced up from the pavement. I'd just caught him. He looked extra cool in those oversized white sunglasses. Kurt, I realized, had worn those too. I peeled off the sweater.

"Catch," I yelled. I flung the old cardigan out the window and watched it sway on the cradle of a Parisian breeze, right into his waiting arms.

We marched down the hotel corridor in somber silence, Pippa, Will, and me. Once again, there would be no sound check in preparation for tonight's performance. All anyone in Jonesy's camp would say, as if it were a political talking point, was to "expect a repeat." But what we'd done at the Royal Albert Hall had been an improv, and improvs by definition are spontaneous, unpremeditated. I wasn't a jazz musician. Improvisation was a skill, and I did not possess it. I pictured myself on the stage tonight and felt... strangely numb.

The three of us got into the elevator, our faces stony.

"Shit—sorry," I blurted, involuntarily. "I forgot something. Meet you in the lobby. Two minutes." I darted out as the doors closed in on their confused faces.

Back in my room, I found my thoughts racing. What was I doing? I began to pace.

I pulled up Tom's text from the day before. I needed to read it again. Like a prayer. A meditation—just something *good*. A truth to believe in. That he cared for me. *Loved* me.

I miss you with every heartbeat. Ever, always, yours.

And the song link. "Something Good."

I wanted to respond, but what? I could simply add a little emoji heart to it—an acknowledgment, a receipt of sorts. But that was a pussy move.

In the midst of this, my brother texted: You ok?!!

Well, no. I was shivering. I couldn't seem to tear my eyes from the night sky, glimmering as if heaped with flung treasure.

My phone vibrated, the second text alert. I made my way, shaky, into the elevator again. Descending alone, I felt an eerie sensation at the sight of my reflection in the gold-veined doors. Back in Vegas, I'd had the very same thought: *Ding,* one opens. *Ding,* it closes. I began to picture elevator after elevator, day in and day out for seven long months, opening and closing, *ding ding ding ding ding* over and over, my face blankly reflected back to me until my features faded, until I was no one I recognized, faceless and nameless and nothing but a ghost.

And suddenly Pippa and Will were side by side, staring wide-eyed at me from the marbled lobby as I stepped out.

"I was just about to go looking for you," Will grumbled, in a bit of a snit.

"Sorry." I rubbed at my tummy. *"Nerves."*

"You're going to be brilliant," Pippa murmured gently. "Come now. Or we'll be late." And she gingerly took my arm.

Showtime!

The lights thunked onto the stage with such sudden force, it was like a fault line had shifted beneath me, vibrating upward through the wooden seat of the schoolroom chair where I sat, catsuited and stilettoed and upright, like a good girl, clutching her wireless mic and wearing her pretty pink wig.

The screen behind us flickered to life and the band fell in, and Jonesy swaggered onto the stage playing, unleashing a tidal wave of love from the crowd, his acolytes leaping to their feet. They were under his thumb and under his spell.

He glided to me, his eyes agleam as if to say: *This is my gift to you, their undying love and adoration.* As if I didn't know what he really meant: *I shall serve you up on a silver platter—feed you to them. Never again will you have to worry your pretty little head about anything.*

I began to rise, but he shot me down with a look. And suddenly, he was at my ear. "Can you feel it?" he whispered. "Can you feel them out there? That's love, Jane Start. The only love we can count on."

Jonesy was close now, so close. Conducting me, using his fingers upon the strings to play me up like a puppet—*up up up my girl, up and off your little chair.*

I let him. So much easier than resisting—*I'm yours, do with me what you will. I can be her*... yes! *I'll be* her *and everything he promised will come true.*

He played and I danced. He played and I let myself *be* played. I'm shaking my ass, *take that,* and I'm shimmying my hips, *boom boom.* This, I thought, *this* was what I was meant to do *all along.* I could feel the love now—it thrilled like a kiss, protected me like an embrace. I'd blown my chance all those years ago and I'd ended up lost on the road that was grassy and wanted wear. I'd tried, and I'd failed. This, right here, right now, was my destiny. To repeat and repeat till I was gone from this earth.

My eyes welled with tears: *Stop it—stop it this instant.* This emotion, this falling apart, did not befit a paid professional. I had to find *something* on this stage to focus on, and to pull myself together. *Woman the fuck up!*

The dark finish of Jonesy's acoustic, there beside his amp, caught the light.

It shone like the sword in the stone.

It beckoned me from its stand...

And then, somehow, I was slinging it on—a guitar, at last, in my arms—cinching the blue velvet strap when a singular whoop echoed through the vast intimidating grandeur, and the theater grew painfully, pin-droppingly hushed. Jonesy's song had ended.

I peered up and out, into the sea of wondering faces. Then I tore off the wig. It descended silently to the stage floor, like snow falling in an empty clearing.

Oh god, what was I doing? I'd hijacked Jonesy's improv. *His* show. And I had no plan. I'd acted on impulse, on sheer need.

I sensed his presence, looming, behind me, but didn't look back. Desperate now, I began strumming, knowing only that I had to play myself out of this awful mess, and knowing at least one thing Jonesy'd said couldn't be true. There *was* another love: There was this. The handheld mic was useless to me now, my hands beholden to the guitar, and I had no other option but to sing out— like a busker on a street corner, full-throated and open-voiced and for dear life, hobbling out of one stiletto and then the other to get myself swiftly to the lip of the stage, so that my unamplified voice had a prayer of being heard all the way to the back of the house...

...when a shimmering sound cascaded down and seemed to sparkle around me. Jonesy was hovering at the stage edge, a few feet to my left. Only *he* could make a guitar sound starry that way, and he knew the song, of course, he'd recorded me playing it that long night after the Albert Hall. *Show me what you can do, Jane Start,* he'd said.

He began singing in harmony and our voices braided together. Then we turned to the sea of faces and we sang to them, of yearning and of resolve, of those fleeting, fragile moments of glory and connection...and in that moment I summoned Tom, and he came rushing back to me...we were lying very close, we were skin to skin and his lips, they tasted of cinnamon—and we would always be together, in this song—

And then it was over. For a beat, there was only the perfect silence of daybreak...of barren crystalline tundras and mute ocean depths, until the faces beyond rushed back, each glowing, each beautiful; I couldn't memorize them fast enough. My eyes stung with joy-tears and my heart swelled. We were, all of us, together, in this mad moment, this mad life. I felt my hand grasped and raised high, and then Jonesy was again tugging me roughly along with him toward the wings. I steadied the guitar at my hip, as his band, his choir, his crew, came into view in a kind of ad hoc reception line, their hands clapping soundlessly, absorbed by the din of the house. Jonesy barged right past them and into the shadowy lane between velvet curtains. There he stopped abruptly, uncoupled his hand from mine, and looked down at me. His face was eerily blank.

I smiled up at him, breathless, but my smile was not returned. For a flash, I wondered if he was being cheeky, milking the suspense somehow. His musicians and crew were still within earshot when he said in a flat but decisive voice, "You're fired."

Someone gasped, and my heart stopped.

Oh. He'd hated it. Even though he'd played and sung so gorgeously. I'd crossed a line. And so he'd fired me in front of everyone—he'd made a point of it. I felt their stares on me, on us. No one breathed, dared move an inch. My throat constricted. I wouldn't break, *I wouldn't.* Scrambling for some response, I felt words forming on my lips, the only two that made any sense.

"Thank you."

Jonesy frowned down at me in disbelief.

At least I'd said it politely. And now Jonesy did something I had never seen him do. He shifted his stance just a mere fraction, his expression becoming one of confusion, and unease, a look that frankly was unimaginable on him. He stuttered, "You're...welcome."

The thunderous stomping from out in the house was becoming impossible to tune out, and I found myself clumsily untangling myself from Jonesy's guitar and holding it out to him. It was whisked away by an unseen hand and Jonesy took off, sprinting airily toward his musicians, who were clustered together, a family and a team, where the scarlet wing met the grand stage, preparing to rush out for the final bow.

I felt myself shrinking, being sucked farther and farther away, as the space before me stretched and narrowed, tunnel-like. But

Jonesy craned back and beckoned me, with the tiniest flick of his hand. I ran toward him, and into the light.

After it was over, I quickly slipped into the shadows, the cool of the wings. I felt a distinct sense of aloneness, featherlightness, I had only myself now. I'd swept up the wig from where it lay abandoned on the stage floor, and now dropped it into a trash bin as I made my way swiftly past the hardworking crew, their faces furrowed and sweating, lifting and heaving, and navigated a series of cool subterranean corridors as if I were underwater, slithering eel-like around a spangled and velvet-clad entourage, my head low, until I'd arrived at my dressing room.

Closing the door decisively behind me, I ran to the makeup counter, untethering my phone from its charger, but the door burst open and Pippa, Will, Alfie, and Bryony rushed in and suddenly there was a storm of voices. They gushed praise and wonder at the feat Jonesy and I had pulled off, the unexpectedness of us playing my song, unplugged, at the foot of the stage, until slowly their exuberance dwindled to an expectant hush.

"Thank you. Yeah. That was *crazy*." I had no idea what my face was doing. "And also I've been fired. Jonesy fired me." I shrugged.

In the deafening silence, a pleasing numbness took hold of me. I refocused on the sensation of my phone in the solid grasp of my hand and I thought, *The sun is rising somewhere on this planet we call earth, and it will again tomorrow.*

"I'm okay with it. Really and truly I am." I said this mostly to reassure them, but I meant it. I could hardly believe how calm I was. *I was free.*

Will looked stunned and mortified for me. Pippa was mostly perplexed, but I watched as she arrived at a place of understanding and of acceptance, and I was truly grateful to her for that. Meanwhile, Bryony and Alfie were simply bewildered.

That was when I was struck with a thunderbolt of an idea—a brilliant fucking genius idea. I turned to Alfie.

"*You* take my place."

It made so much sense. Alfie *was* the better candidate for the tour, a true showman, a superstar in his own right, the bigger and better story; and if Pippa could broker the deal, then Alfie could shine on his own... *independent* of his brother... a freedom I knew he'd long craved.

I turned to Pippa. "*You* can make this happen—I know you can." She did love a challenge.

She and Alfie exchanged a look. As they did, Bryony and I locked eyes, and she mouthed, *Oh my god* and *Thank you*, pantomiming a fanning gesture at her cheeks.

And as their voices swelled and plans were hatched, there in the palm of my hand was still my phone. I finally glanced down. A text message, from Tom.

Chapter 45.

YOU CAN'T ALWAYS GET WHAT YOU WANT

I did not read Tom's text. I forced myself not to.

In the few days that followed my firing from the tour, there was damage control. Will, Pippa, and I encamped at Leopard Pants's villa on the Côte d'Azur, in the south of France. He'd kindly offered it to us, as he was spending the holidays in West Sussex, with the wife, the kids, the grandkids. I was doing all in my power to move on from the mess I'd made of my so-called career, and to move on from *Tom*.

Alastair, James, and George flew down. We decided to record my new song in LP's iconic basement studio. Jonesy's team had shared the version we'd made at his rental house in London. It felt like a peace offering, a gift. Our guitars on the recording jangled seamlessly, but now that I'd honed the lyrics, I needed to record a proper vocal.

A shiver tore through me as Will unstuck the vacuum seal of the iso-booth door and handed me a mug of honey-steeped tea. I thanked him. It had been ages since I'd been in a real studio or stood before an elegant vintage microphone like this one. It seemed to stare back, skeptical. *I know. I agree.*

"Holy shit." Will gaped up from his phone. He passed it to me, wide-eyed.

Alfie Lloyd's Twitter page, his profile labeled: *Alfie Lloyd. All Lover.*

He'd tweeted: My favorite record of the year. Yeah, I know it came out seven years ago, but it's brilliant, a lost classic. NOT TO BE MISSED. The ultimate rainy-day record for lovers. I haven't stop listening for days... 🔥📷 😶 ☺

He'd attached an image of him shirtless, in bed, with the covers drawn to his waist, his hand grazing my album cover, which so happened to be a spare photograph of an unmade bed. To torment his fans, he'd draped a lacy bra across it, but at the very bottom he'd added my name and #respect.

My heart careened; a fellow musician, and a global superstar? Championing *me?* And my forgotten album? I was moved, rendered speechless.

"He's right." Will grinned when our eyes met again. "Fuck the critics. I always loved that record." I shook my head in disbelief. The truth was, I had too.

Will sidled alongside James and Alastair as they hovered over the old-school control-room board, a cockpit of dials, faders, and glowing jewel-colored lights, and played a little of the track Jonesy had sent, for me to get my bearings. They peered up at me and smiled. How lucky I was! All at once a vision of *Jonesy* materialized beside them. We locked eyes through the glass. He gave me a chiding, mischievous grin and we were swept back to his penthouse, where we stood face-to-face. Yet this time we were both smiling. This time, he was reaching out his hand. This time, I grasped it—*friends*. This bird has flown. She *has*. My eyes pricked with tears. *Please not now*. Shut up and sing.

And then I was. And then I was somewhere else. High on a hilltop overlooking an azure sea. I was driving with the top down, I was taking the curves, in my mind, the ascents, and descents, the ruts in the road, and there was only room for focus, for singing, for freeing each word, for filling each syllable with feeling—

for sharing something someone somewhere might need or want on a dark night or even a sparkling day, because they felt these things too.

"Like I always say," Pippa called out, the following afternoon, "you're only ever—"

"One good song away?" I called back.

"Precisely." Pippa was perched on a white slipcovered sofa with her laptop. The room was sprawling, of the classic Belle Époque style with wedding-cake moldings and decorative arches. A study in shades of sumptuous white, chic and minimalist, yet decadent, too. And in the middle of it, Pippa, my queen, was on fire. Not only had she succeeded in selling the idea of Alfie replacing me on the tour, but Leopard Pants had released a sassy rock 'n' roll version of "Winter Wonderland" that was storming up the charts. And a young band called Fictional Death whom she'd nurtured from their salad days in a moldering basement in Manchester was garnering brilliant reviews for their debut album. And astoundingly, *my* sophomore record had started to sell. Alfie's tweet had done the trick. The cruel snark I'd received online from diehard Jonesy fans had suddenly been replaced by YouTube clips of me hijacking the Paris performance. *Memorializing* the moment, not as an act of insanity, but as something special, even "badass."

Will strode in and presented a bottle of wine for Pippa's consideration.

"I don't think Leopard Pants would mind if we cracked open one of his Château Lafites." She peered up with a mischievous grin. "I must say"—jabbing a corkscrew in—"I never dreamed the pieces would fall together so easily."

"What's it all about…Alfie," Will melodized, doing his best rendition.

"Yes," she exhaled, twisting the opener as I got the glasses. "A simple but *ingenious* trade." And, *pop,* she unsuctioned the cork. I extended my glass and she filled it.

"Alfie Lloyd hired, and Jane Start—" I broke off, feeling their eyes on me. *"Freed."* I gulped down some wine.

Pippa was sending me to London in two days' time, for a BBC radio thing she'd insisted was crucial. I would stay in her flat. And after? My parents hoped I'd return straightaway to LA. Will and I might finally get an apartment together.

"So," Pippa cleared her throat. "I know the Silverman-Starts don't much celebrate the holidays, but since we're *here*"—she gestured to our swank surroundings—"and it's that time of year, well, I simply couldn't resist." She shrugged, and whipped a box from beneath the sofa. She extended it to me. Will watched, wide-eyed.

I hesitated. "What's this?" I accepted it reticently from her.

"Open it," Pippa demanded.

I slowly teased apart its velvet ribbon and removed the top. "Ha!" I gaped up at them. It was an ultra-chic faux fur *leopard print jacket.*

"Now you must officially stop mocking Leopard Pants. Put it on," she insisted.

"Mmm." The fit was perfect. I couldn't stop caressing the soft fabric.

"Darling, it suits you *perfectly."* Pippa crinkled her brow, beaming.

"But *I* didn't get *you* anything," I said.

She only shook her head, her eyes glossy, and looked at Will. "Oh, but you did."

There was a beat, the two of them frozen, gazing lovestruck at one another.

"I think...I'll just, go out there for a bit," I said, tipping my head toward the French doors, which spilled out onto a grand portico.

As I closed the doors gently behind me, I glimpsed Will

wrapping his arm around Pippa's waist to pull her close. I quickly averted my gaze. He would never come back to LA, not now. And I was, truly, happy for them both.

There was nothing left for me now but to focus on work. Pippa had crafted a plan. We'd release the song in the new year, and follow as soon as possible with an album. Meaning, there was much writing and recording to do. Perhaps I could write long-distance with Alfie? It might prove a good diversion for him on the road with Jonesy.

Beyond the portico and wide slope of lawn was the sea, azure and shimmering, a mirage I could have stared at until it blinded me. I thought of Tom. He was *everywhere*. In the pages of books I read, in the rustling of trees. In songs I listened to on repeat. "Darling Be Home Soon," the Lovin' Spoonful. "I Just Don't Think I'll Ever Get Over You," Colin Hay. "To Be Alone with You," Bob Dylan. That was the song he'd texted from so near, in the flat, in Oxford. *Wanna listen together in bed?* he'd said. And when I closed my eyes to "Something Good," the song he'd sent me in Paris, it was as if there was an invisible tether connecting my heart to his, and I felt its pull, so strongly. But he was still tethered to Amelia, too.

And *I* still had music.

I was aware of a muted burbling. An instant later there was a vibrating piece of metal in the palm of my hand, so suddenly alien, it might as well have been a *Star Trek* communicator.

No caller ID.

I jabbed at it, steeling myself for *his* face somehow, but Gemma's popped up. And then Bryony's, inside another little box—but why did they look so grim? Adrenaline coursed through me.

"Jane—helloo," Gemma said, plastering on a smile. Something was wrong.

"What's happened—is Tom, is he okay?"

"No, no, Tom's all right. But um . . . I'm afraid I have some rather

bad news. It's Professor Thornbury. There's no delicate way to—
He's *died,*" she said gingerly, her face pained.

"Sweet little gnome, gone forever," Bryony managed, sniffling.
Both women were waiting for me to respond, but all I could do
was shake my head in disbelief.

"His *heart?*" I murmured.

"That's what they suspect," Gemma sighed.

But it was his heart that had been broken *for so long.* A *lifetime*
of loneliness, I thought, my eyes brimming with tears.

"He went peacefully, in his sleep. A week ago," Gemma explained. "Honora found him when she woke. Tragic really, their
wee bags, readied by the door. They were meant to be off to Greece
that very morning."

No. His dream, finally, with an *inamorata.*

"And *Tom* took care of *everything.* Honora—you know she's
normally so measured? So clearheaded? She was beside herself with
grief. If not for Tom, I hardly know how she would have coped. In
the end it was just the two of them. Honora and Tom, at the gravesite.
Thornbury had no other family to speak of. And no fanfare, as
Honora decided, at least for the present. Perhaps in the new year."

I barely recognized Gemma, so gentle-voiced and composed.

"A *proper* memorial at the college," she went on. "Tom wanted
desperately to be the one to tell you, but he was rather tortured,
whether he should. He thought it best *I* let you know. I'm so sorry
to have to break the news."

His message, when Will and I were in the Tuileries. I understood now, he'd wanted to tell me Thornbury was gone, but not
over text, so instead he'd just written a note from *his* heart. He'd
sent the song.

I heard chiming in the background, the bells of Oxford.

"I can't believe it," I stuttered. "I'll send Honora a note of
condolence. And I should call him—"

"Right, yes, *well, actually,*" Gemma jumped in, clearing her throat. "Tom's buggered off. Something about visiting his parents for Christmas, in Yorkshire is it? I myself tried to get in touch, to wish him happy holidays, but it went straight to voicemail, mailbox full. And there was something else. He mentioned he'd be disappearing for a while, to work on his book. I thought, well done you—I mean, at least a good diversion, given, well—" She faltered, flustered.

"I hope you don't mind," Bryony murmured, "but I filled Gemma in. She wasn't aware that you'd *left him*. And—perhaps you haven't heard the latest goss?"

"Amelia Danvers has run off!" Gemma broke in. "To Ibiza! Eloped with a playboy earl. *I* suspect she'd been shagging him all along behind Tom's back," she scoffed, disgusted. "I'm not excusing Tom, *mind you*. He should have been forthright with you, instead of all of his behind-the-scenes drama with her. But even good men, *brilliant* men, can be utter twats—clueless about such things. God knows what goes on in Vikram's head. The strong, silent type. But what can you do?"

Oh Gemma. But she was right. How could you ever know anyone, *really?* Or trust them.

"Well, now Amelia can hobnob with *that* lot to her heart's content. But here's the best part: Apparently the earl of whatsit was in Zurich, too. Same clinic. 'Nervous exhaustion.'" She made air quotes and rolled her eyes. "The whole clinic business struck me as a ruse—Amelia's last-ditch attempt to manipulate Tom into going back to her. Not the first time she's pulled that stunt."

I thought back to what Freddy had said in the pub, about Amelia naming the cat Ophelia as a veiled threat.

"They don't fit, she and Tom. They never did. It was clear to anyone who knew them. He's loyal, and *she,* well, she took advantage of him. Now she's right where she was meant to be—on a *yacht* with a poncy *earl*. At least she had the decency to give him back *his beloved cat*."

I was speechless, their faces staring out from the small screen as they said goodbye.

I couldn't help it. I pulled up Tom's text at long last. The one he'd sent the night of the show in Paris. The one I hadn't let myself read.

Tom Hardy: Jane, please don't feel any pressure to write me back, but I wanted you to know, I have severed ties with Amelia, once and for all. I've handled things wretchedly. It wasn't fair to you, and it wasn't fair to her. I needed to tell her that there would be no making it up again as there had been in the past. It's over, whether or not you and I are ever together. You were right. Running away from the truth was not the answer. I have violated your trust. Love is as much about trust as anything else, and I've let you down. For that, I am so deeply sorry. I don't expect you to forgive me. Love, T. x

Chapter 46.

LEAVING ON A JET PLANE

"Come with me? Please? There's still time." It was two days later, curbside at the airport in Nice.

"You'll be fine," Will said. A plane roared overhead, and I felt my jaw, my whole body, tense—the old anxiety.

I was off to London for the BBC thing and had begged Will to join me. After that, I'd probably head home, on my own, to LA.

"I promised my girl I'd get the ol' rock star's place in order. The studio needs some sorting, a few updates. That should take two days max and we'll join you. But hey. We did it." He gestured around.

We had, hadn't we. We'd done Paris. We'd done France.

"And *you.*" He beamed, waving his phone. He meant the buzz online about my old record. Critics were now calling it "a lost classic." "An overlooked masterpiece." "A sonic seduction we need now more than ever." My album had even appeared on a few year-end "best of" lists despite being seven years old.

"I know. It's nuts." I shook my head.

He looked me over, uncharacteristically wistful. I was sporting the faux leopard jacket. "You've *got* it. The thing. You had it then, and you've got it now. And that's what's made being your kid brother *such a fucking bitch.*"

"What on earth are you talking about?"

"Zazz," he said, flicking his fingers.

It came rushing back. "My favorite word from when we were kids. *Sass* plus *pizazz* equals—*zazz,"* we said in unison. In the Silverman-Start family, it was the secret ingredient to all things good.

We stood there smiling, but his expression grew suddenly serious. "So, do that bullshit airplane tapping thing, for shits and giggles," Will murmured. "Do it for me."

I shot him a look. He'd always derided my silly superstition, but now that *his* life was perfect, he'd changed his tune. He was in the south of France with his Brigitte Bardot and could literally fuck her in every room of that mansion for two days straight, drunk on Leopard Pants's wine.

"I will, absolutely," I reassured him.

He sighed, relieved. "Did ya listen to it yet?"

He'd texted me a song link: "Wasn't Born to Follow," by the Byrds.

"Like a zillion times," I said to him. That song never got old.

"Perfect, right?" he said, brightening.

It was perfect. I hadn't followed Jonesy ten years earlier, and I wasn't following him now. The road that was grassy and wanted wear had been waiting for me to take another step. If not now, when?

"You know what's even more perfect?" I said to him. "That *Carole King* wrote it. Bet you didn't know *that.*"

"I did not know that." And his gaze slid suddenly to the pavement as he kicked one Converse into the other. So he had it after all, the crying gene. Small triggers—a Folgers commercial, anything involving a kid opening a college acceptance letter, Sidney Poitier tearing up at the end of *To Sir, with Love* as he says goodbye to his students. But I could make my dad cry by simply saying *bubbeh,* Yiddish for *grandma.* "Moon River" never failed to make my mom weep.

"And they call that a tree," I said. Will had heard the story of the monks a thousand times, too.

That put him over the edge. "I'd better get going." He thumbed behind him, spun on his heel, and rushed away before I could catch his face crumpling.

I stood there watching the old softy thread his way through the bustle of holiday travelers, a head taller than the rest. Just before he disappeared, his arm shot up and he gave me a quick toodle-oo over his shoulder, like he knew I was still watching him go.

There's something about airports, something about being *alone* in them—no matter how hollowed out, how depressed you might feel, when you wander around listening to music, strangers whirling silently past—and you suddenly realize, I'm *alive*. Not in a clinical sense. More of an ache, a tingling, awe-filled ache: I am alive in this world. Here, temporarily, steering my own little rowboat, as best one can.

But why after all the years steeped in loneliness did Thornbury have to die *now?* Before Honora could feed him pasta straight from a copper pot wearing only an apron? Before he could wake up in her arms atop a sun-scrubbed hill, the Aegean shimmering beyond an open door? White curtains billowing languidly in rhythm with their breaths, his head pillowed upon her breast?

Stop all the clocks. Pack up the moon and dismantle the sun.

Tom. He told me he'd given a talk on Auden. Before he'd almost missed his connection. But then he didn't.

"Passengers for London Heathrow, your flight is ready for boarding."

I fell into line, Donovan's "Colours" playing in my head for its trusty Valium effect, yet threatening to loose a tide of emotion unbefitting a woman surrounded by strangers, shuffling down a cramped jet bridge toward a plane. And when Joni's "Both Sides Now" came on, I thought of how this song had belonged to my mother, but now it belonged to me, and I found my fingertip sweeping gently back and forth over his number, across the smudged face of a phone. It would take only the barest pressure—bone, to muscle, to skin.

Like this.

Chapter 47.

BOTH SIDES NOW

This mailbox is full and cannot accept messages at this time. *Please try again.* Three lucky taps and I crossed the threshold—slogged past smug passengers already settled in their seats. I made my way swiftly to my row, staking a claim, dropping my backpack and new leopard jacket onto my seat and hoisting my rolly toward the overhead bin as bodies jostled past, struggling with the steep angle until the weight was miraculously lifted from my grasp. There was someone with manners still left in this world.

"Thank you," I said over my shoulder.

"Not at all," he said, velvet-voiced.

I whirled around. The *sight* of him. The pure geometry of his quietly towering figure, his flesh and blood and beating heart. How was he *here?* Never mind. His face was watchful and serene, his expression a disclosure of everything I'd ever need to know:

That Thornbury was *gone.* That love is the only thing that matters. That people make mistakes, but we learn from them. That when you find love, you must do everything in your power to hold on to it. I recognized it was not necessary to say these things out loud. It would be pointless, redundant; he was in receipt of my feelings too.

"Hey, buddy, you're holding everyone up." It was an exasperated

American in expensive business casual, and wearing a Guatemalan woven bracelet, no less.

"Sorry," Tom said, flattening himself awkwardly to let the man huff past. We locked eyes for an irresolute moment, and I sank into my aisle seat. The window and middle seats were occupied by an elderly couple, their sweetly weathered hands entwined. Tom stole a glance at his pass, and took *his* seat, directly across the aisle *from me!*

The world is full of wonders.

And through a blur of overbright fleece, holiday-weary travelers tramping past with bags of takeout and duty-free, we continued to gaze at one another until my phone vibrated in my lap.

I stole a downward glance.

Pippa: Make your flight ok?
Jane: Did you do this?
Pippa: No comment.

Of course. I smiled to myself. *Everyone has secrets.* I'll let her keep this one.

I found Tom's eyes but released mine to sweep over the edges and planes of his face, the line of his jaw with its sand-colored stubble. If I'd been closer, I couldn't have stopped myself from touching him there. Or resting my cheek—when I noticed gray. A few strands at his temples too, which made him even more beautiful to me.

"*Jane,*" he sighed, our eyes locked. "I'm sorry I hurt you. I— *love you…*"

There were suddenly no words. Too many words. "*I know,*" I said. "I know you do. And I—feel the *same.* I—*love you…*" And I haven't ever loved anyone—*the way I love you.*

But the pilot was making announcements over the intercom. In French, and in English. That we'd been cleared for takeoff. That he expected a little turbulence. That once we were through the clouds it should be smooth sailing.

There was so much more to say, even as the wheels began to roll. The plane aligned due south toward the Mediterranean and paused. I tore my eyes from Tom's and cued up "Shaft."

No. It had to be a different song now. "You're All I Need to Get By." That was the one.

I hit Play. Violins. A vibrato trill of anticipation swelled to meet bright silver bells. Marvin Gaye and Tammi Terrell, their voices entwined in ecstatic harmony.

Tom's lips were moving. I loosened an earbud.

"It must be good, what you're listening to," he said. Familiar words.

"Very good. Brilliant actually. Though some people might say it's a bit corny. To me it's perfectly corny. Meaning perfect *because* of its corniness. Somehow sad *and* happy. Which, if you put those words together, makes *sappy*. Which isn't quite right. Maybe you should just listen to it." I smiled and passed an earbud across the aisle.

He shook his head. "It couldn't possibly live up to that description you just gave."

At which point his face became blurry, because his face did that to me, when the chime that cut like a diamond interrupted.

The plane began to taxi slowly down the runway. Tom lowered his gaze, his long fingers wrapped tensely around the armrest, betraying some inner discipline, until he looked at me. Until his hand drifted quietly up and seemed to float over the space between us. Until our hands clasped. Until his warmth was *everywhere*. The answer to *everything*. Until we were flying down the runway.

He looked at me. "Ready?"

"Yes."

Then a sensation of weightlessness. Of the earth falling away, of sunlight, and of space, of slipping, and swooping. A wing dipped, banking into a turn. A glimpse through a window of shimmering, and the seamless—the sky and the sea. Him and me.

SOMETHING GOOD

Seven months later, on a perfect July afternoon in Honora's garden, a double wedding was taking place. Honora, who was ordained (of course she was), started in beneath a makeshift chuppah, the heart locket Thornbury had given her glinting in the sun: "We are gathered here today to celebrate the love between Ms. Phillipa More and Mr. Will Start. And the love between—"

And it suddenly hit me: I could call Pippa my sister. *I had a sister!*

"Mr. Alastair Ekwenzi and Mr. James McCloud." *At long last!*

I squeezed Tom's hand. As the couples began to make their way across the lawn, young George ran ahead, flinging petals determinedly, on the verge of aggressively, at the handful of guests arranged in rows of folding chairs.

There were Alfie and Bryony, who since Paris had been loath to spend a single night apart (she'd let me know that the now infamous bra in his tweet had been hers). Gemma and Vikram. Cy and his new friend, a goth called Olaf, and Freddy with an impromptu date—a lovely waitress he'd picked up when he'd stopped for a latte on his way from London. And of course, my beaming parents, Art and Lulu Start, her head on his shoulder, their hands tightly clasped.

At the sound of breaking glass, everyone craned back to see what all the commotion was. Leopard Pants! He'd knocked over a tray of champagnes on the patio.

"Better late than never!" he half mumbled, half laughed in his signature way, and I thought, *No one sashays onto a lawn like Ol' Leopard Pants.*

After some murmuring and harried debate, everyone returned to their starting positions.

"Let's try this again, shall we?" Honora said, faintly bitchy.

This was my cue. I sidled beside her and slung on my guitar.

Alfie was meant to accompany me but he was busy kissing Bryony. Alas, who was I to stop them? So, I started in playing my new song.

And through a blur of green, of sunlight dancing through trees, I had a sudden sense that anything was possible. I sought out Tom's face in the sea of all other faces and his eyes said: *You are my bright star.*

And I beamed back: *And you are mine.*

And that did it, and these goddamned inopportune tears were making it difficult to carry on singing, so I closed my eyes, tasting salt on my lips, and I focused on singing, *only* that, because otherwise, Reader, I was toast.

Acknowledgments

I have always loved living in other people's stories, whether in a book, a song, a film, a play. Only recently did I discover how much I loved *writing* them. Once I started, I couldn't stop. It was like I'd put on the "red shoes."

There are so many people to thank for helping and inspiring me throughout this journey.

Gratitude to my parents. My philosophic psychoanalyst father Joshua and bohemian artist mother Tamar, for bringing me up in a world filled with novels and music, art and film, and for encouraging freedom of expression and of thought in our household. They made me a student of human nature, which I learned is rarely pristine, but often beautifully messy. They also had a tantalizing library of paperback novels, which I devoured. From Updike to Flaubert, Brontë to Austen, Fitzgerald to Fowles, Baldwin to Erica Jong. These cherished dog-eared paperbacks live in my *own* library now.

Appreciation to my brothers, John and Jesse, for their camaraderie and our shared childhood and teenage obsessions with crime stories, cinema, the Beatles (cementing a love of Great Britain!), and beyond. I cherish the education in narrative and character I got watching double features at our local revival movie house with them.

To my son Jackson, who compelled me to stop blathering on about my future novel and insisted: "Tomorrow morning you're going to open your computer and stare at a blank page—*and start.*" And I did. And to my son Sam, who listened alongside his brother as I read aloud those first few pages, and said, "Mom, keep going!" And I did that too.

And later, my novelist best friend Margaret Stohl pried the manuscript from my reluctant grasp and emboldened me to share it with the brilliant literary agent Sarah Burnes. Sarah's response was immediate and passionate. We decided to meet up in New York City. I'll never forget my solitary walk to her office on that blustery January day, dressed in my suit and holding back "how did I get here?" tears. Endless thanks to Sarah for taking me on. For her commitment to the novel, her enthusiasm for the characters, her many reads, and her always incisive notes. From then on, everyone at the Gernert Company has been incredibly supportive: David Gernert, Rebecca Gardner, Sophie Pugh-Sellers, and Will Roberts.

An endless debt of gratitude to my early readers. Mary Petrie Lowen, my closest friend since we were eleven, who schlepped many miles to my house and allowed me to read aloud my first behemoth draft to her. Tori Hill and Jackson Roach gave me perceptive notes as my twenty-something readers. Helen Fielding provided excellent Britishisms and enticing locations for Jane and Tom's mini-break, as well as much-appreciated encouragement. Novelist Michelle Wildgren asked all the important questions at exactly the right time.

The day Sarah Burnes texted me that the iconic editor in chief Judy Clain at Little, Brown was reading and loving the book, I was with Margaret Stohl and her daughter May sipping coffee at a cafe. When Margaret got teary explaining to me the implications of someone like Judy enjoying the manuscript, I too teared up. From then on, Little, Brown felt like home.

Unending thanks to my brilliant, passionate, indefatigable editor Helen O'Hare, who has had as much affection and empathy for Jane Start as *I* do, and did from the start. When I discovered that Helen was as addicted to the sexy, romantic frisson between Tom and Jane as I was, I knew we were a match! And there was an immense pleasure in being able to discuss and *gossip* about my characters with Helen; my imagined cohort of characters became as real to her as they'd been to me.

I have felt so much support from my entire publishing team. Thank you to Bruce Nichols, Sabrina Callahan, Katharine Myers, Craig Young, Anna Brill, Lauren Hesse, Jayne Yaffe Kemp, Alison Kerr Miller, Liv Ryan, Michele McGonigle, and the rest of the fantastic team and sales force at Little, Brown and Company and Hachette.

To the wonderful publicist Nicole Dewey, I'm so lucky you've joined us on this journey.

Enormous gratitude to my divine film agent, Sylvie Rabineau, and our producers extraordinaire, Liza Chasin and Bruna Papandrea, and to the marvelous Erik Baiers at Universal for the thrilling movie adaptation to come. Thank you to Howard Abramson for taking such care to make it all happen.

But perhaps more than anyone, I'm grateful to my husband, Jay, who not only put up with my long hours "in the chair" writing, but who also gave me insightful notes as the brilliant storyteller that he is. Our partnership has always felt like a creative collaboration: in raising our children, in supporting one another in our work. My love, respect, and gratitude are more than I can possibly express here.

Finally, I'm forever grateful to all the writers, musicians, and artists whose stories have enchanted and inspired...moved and consoled me. You have welcomed me into your stories and reminded me of what it is to be alive, to be human, to be connected. And thank you to all those who have supported my music throughout the years, and to the readers of this novel. I cannot convey the depth of my appreciation...it would be easier to sing it, but know that I feel it in my heart.

READING GROUP GUIDE

A Conversation with Susanna Hoffs

What was it like to write a novel compared to writing songs?

For me the process was quite different. Writing a novel is a truly solitary act. Whereas with songwriting, I've almost always collaborated with other musicians. I wrote "Eternal Flame," for example, with my friends Billy Steinberg and Tom Kelly. When it comes to writing songs there are many elements to consider: rhythm, rhyme, meter, and, of course, melody! In both genres, a story is told and an emotion expressed, one that is hopefully shared by others.

One of the great things about *This Bird Has Flown* is the glimpse it gives readers into the music industry and what it's like to be a working musician. Were any of your characters or plot points inspired by your experiences in the music world?

I decided to make my protagonist, Jane Start, a musician and song-writer because it's a job I know well. I've experienced the joy of making music and the thrill of performing, but also the challenges of being in the music *business* and bouts of writer's block. I wanted to give readers a sneak peek behind the curtain what it's like to face an audience with your heart thumping so loudly you fear they can hear it too—and then, somehow, to find your voice!

I am exceedingly fortunate to have witnessed many astonishing musical performances by artists the Bangles had occasion to open for, such as Cyndi Lauper, George Michael, and Queen. *And then there was Prince*. He gave us the great gift of "Manic Monday" and graced us with his supernatural brilliance, as well as performing with us onstage on several mighty unforgettable occasions.

Are there specific books, or even specific characters, that inspired you to write *This Bird Has Flown*?

Jane Eyre by Charlotte Brontë and *Rebecca* by Daphne du Maurier are both gothic romances with themes that informed the story: Will the ghosts of relationships past threaten our chances of finding true love and happiness? Will our own personal demons doom us from succeeding in our work?

The city of Oxford, UK, itself stood in for the gothic setting I envisioned. And it was essential that Jane's love interest, Tom Hardy, Oxford professor of literature, have an intoxicating mystery and gravitas. Unlike the Rochester character in *Jane Eyre,* Jane Start's Tom is not rich or arrogant or twice her age!

What are your favorite books about music?

High Fidelity by Nick Hornby, *Swing Time* by Zadie Smith, *Norwegian Wood* by Haruki Murakami, *A Visit from the Goon Squad* by Jennifer Egan, *The Wishbones* by Tom Perrotta. Recently I've loved *Modern Lovers* by Emma Straub, *Daisy Jones & the Six* by Taylor Jenkins Reid, and *Mary Jane* by Jessica Anya Blau. Also Gil Scott-Heron's *The Last Holiday: A Memoir*. I was privileged to watch his electrifying performance at a festival in Europe in 1986, which the Bangles played as well.

Do you see a lot of yourself in Jane Start? What are some things you and she have in common?

Jane is a fictional character and all her own, but one thing we have in common is a deep and abiding love of music. For me, music is the beginning, middle, and end of each day, and Jane would agree. Love and connection are what matters most in this world.

Questions and topics for discussion

1. At the novel's beginning, Jane is struggling to write music. What do you think is holding her back? How does meeting Tom change things? Have you ever felt stalled on a project? How did you find inspiration?

2. When the novel begins, Jane feels she needs a second chance— in love, in music, in life. How does Alfie help her open the door to this possibility? In what other ways does Jane find new opportunities, and how does she address her past before she can move forward to seize that second chance?

3. Discuss the novel's many influences—from *Jane Eyre* to British rom-coms to classic rock and music of all stripes and, of course, Susanna Hoffs's own background as a performer. Did you catch other nods to pop culture as well? How do these threads come together in the larger story? Were there elements you especially enjoyed?

4. How did the inclusion of song lyrics and mentions shape your reading of *This Bird Has Flown*? Do you have a favorite song from the novel?

5. Discuss the writing style and language of the novel. Do you think Hoffs's background in songwriting influences her prose?

6. Did you agree with Jane's decision in the end? Were you surprised by her choices? What about by Tom's?

7. As Jane's journey continues, she draws together a wide range of side characters. Who were some of your favorites? Did any other couples that formed in the novel surprise you?

8. Jane has a theory "that for some reason, we feel things more deeply, or profoundly, on a plane. Something to do with the altitude. Or being captive, thirty thousand feet above the earth, untethered" (p. 45). How do you feel about traveling by plane? Have you taken a trip that has shifted your perspective?

9. Discuss Jane's relationship with Jonesy. Has his interest in her music hurt or helped her career? What does he come to represent for Jane?

10. Throughout the novel, Jane struggles with a need for love: she's quick to fall into relationships. Why do you think Jane is so ready to leap? Did you see this as a redeeming quality in Jane's character, or a weakness? What does she learn by the end of the novel, about herself and about falling in love?

11. *This Bird Has Flown* explores the many ways we can be haunted by the ghosts of our pasts. Who are some of these "ghosts" for Jane? In what ways do her past challenges help her find her way forward?

A PLAYLIST FOR
THIS BIRD HAS FLOWN

1. **Expecting to Fly**—Buffalo Springfield
2. **Friday I'm in Love**—The Cure
3. **The Tears of a Clown**—Smokey Robinson & The Miracles
4. **Danke Schoen**—Wayne Newton
5. **Alfie**—Dionne Warwick
6. **People**—Barbra Streisand
7. **Cabaret**—Liza Minnelli
8. **Sweet Jane**—The Velvet Underground
9. **Maggie May**—Rod Stewart
10. **Theme from "Shaft"**—Isaac Hayes
11. **The Only Living Boy in New York**—Simon & Garfunkel
12. **Hot for Teacher**—the bird and the bee
13. **Tiny Bubbles**—Don Ho
14. **Can't Nobody Love You**—The Zombies
15. **I'll Take You There**—The Staple Singers
16. **I Want You to Want Me**—Cheap Trick
17. **Fly Me to the Moon (In Other Words)**—Julie London
18. **The More I See You**—Chris Montez
19. **Un Homme Et Une Femme**—Francis Lai, Nicole Croisille, Pierre Barouh
20. **We Have No Secrets**—Carly Simon
21. **Wild Horses**—The Rolling Stones

22. **The Rain in Spain**—Wilfrid Hyde-White, Marni Nixon, Rex Harrison
23. **Drive My Car**—The Beatles
24. **Don't Get Me Wrong**—The Pretenders
25. **Take Me Home, Country Roads**—John Denver
26. **Dirty Mind**—Prince
27. **You Turn Me On, I'm a Radio**—Joni Mitchell
28. **Sexual Healing**—Marvin Gaye
29. **Ripple**—Grateful Dead
30. **Rebel Rebel**—David Bowie
31. **Rockit**—Herbie Hancock
32. **Pretty Ballerina**—The Left Banke
33. **Miracle of Miracles**—John Williams, Leonard Frey, *Fiddler on the Roof* Motion Picture Orchestra
34. **West Side Story: Act I: Tonight**—Leonard Bernstein, Jim Bryant, Marni Nixon, Johnny Green
35. **To Be Alone with You**—Bob Dylan
36. **Rock and Roll**—Led Zeppelin
37. **Smoke Gets in Your Eyes**—The Platters
38. **What's New Pussycat?**—Tom Jones
39. **The Things We Do for Love**—10cc
40. **There She Goes**—The La's
41. **Norwegian Wood** (This Bird Has Flown)—The Beatles
42. **Once in a Lifetime**—Talking Heads
43. **My Best Friend's Girl**—The Cars
44. **Friday on My Mind**—The Easybeats
45. **Wedding Bell Blues**—Laura Nyro
46. **O Lucky Man!**—Alan Price
47. **Who'll Stop the Rain**—Creedence Clearwater Revival
48. **How Long (Has This Been Going On)**—Ambrosia
49. **Reunited**—Peaches & Herb
50. **Jeepster**—T. Rex
51. **My Way**—Frank Sinatra

52. **I Want to Hold Your Hand**—The Beatles
53. **The Morning After**—Maureen McGovern
54. **We Can Work It Out**—The Beatles
55. **Monday, Monday**—The Mamas & The Papas
56. **Ain't No Sunshine**—Bill Withers
57. **Something Good**—Julie Andrews, Bill Lee
58. **You've Got a Friend in Me**—Randy Newman
59. **Under My Thumb**—The Rolling Stones
60. **You Can't Always Get What You Want**—The Rolling Stones
61. **Darling Be Home Soon**—The Lovin' Spoonful
62. **I Just Don't Think I'll Ever Get Over You**—Colin Hay
63. **Leaving on a Jet Plane**—Peter, Paul, and Mary
64. **Wasn't Born to Follow**—The Byrds
65. **Wasn't Born to Follow**—Carole King
66. **Colours **—Donovan
67. **Both Sides Now**—Joni Mitchell
68. **You're All I Need to Get By**—Marvin Gaye, Tammi Terrell

About the Author

Boasting one of pop's most beloved voices, **Susanna Hoffs** graduated from the University of California, Berkeley, with a degree in art. In 1981 she cofounded the Bangles, with whom she recorded and released a string of chart-topping singles, including "Manic Monday," "Walk Like an Egyptian," "Hazy Shade of Winter," and "Eternal Flame" (which she cowrote), before embarking on a critically acclaimed solo career. She also wrote and recorded music for, and appeared in, the Austin Powers movies and played herself on Season 1 of *Gilmore Girls*. She lives in Los Angeles with her husband, filmmaker Jay Roach. *This Bird Has Flown* is her first novel.